THE WORD OF

# Y'NESHU

HEART OF THE IJEYA

# THE WORD OF

# Y'NESHU

## HEART OF THE IJEYA

JORDAN HAMPTON

KABULU GLOBAL PRESS, LLC

# Copyright

The story and characters in this novel are purely fictitious and are entirely the fabrication of the author. Any resemblance of these characters to actual persons, living or dead, is purely coincidental.



Library of Congress Control Number: 2025900462



Jordan.hampton3@live.com

https://authorjordanhampton.com/

ISBN (Hardcover): 9798985834666

ISBN (eBook): 9798985834673

Cover design by Caleb Richardson

Edited by Kenne Stu

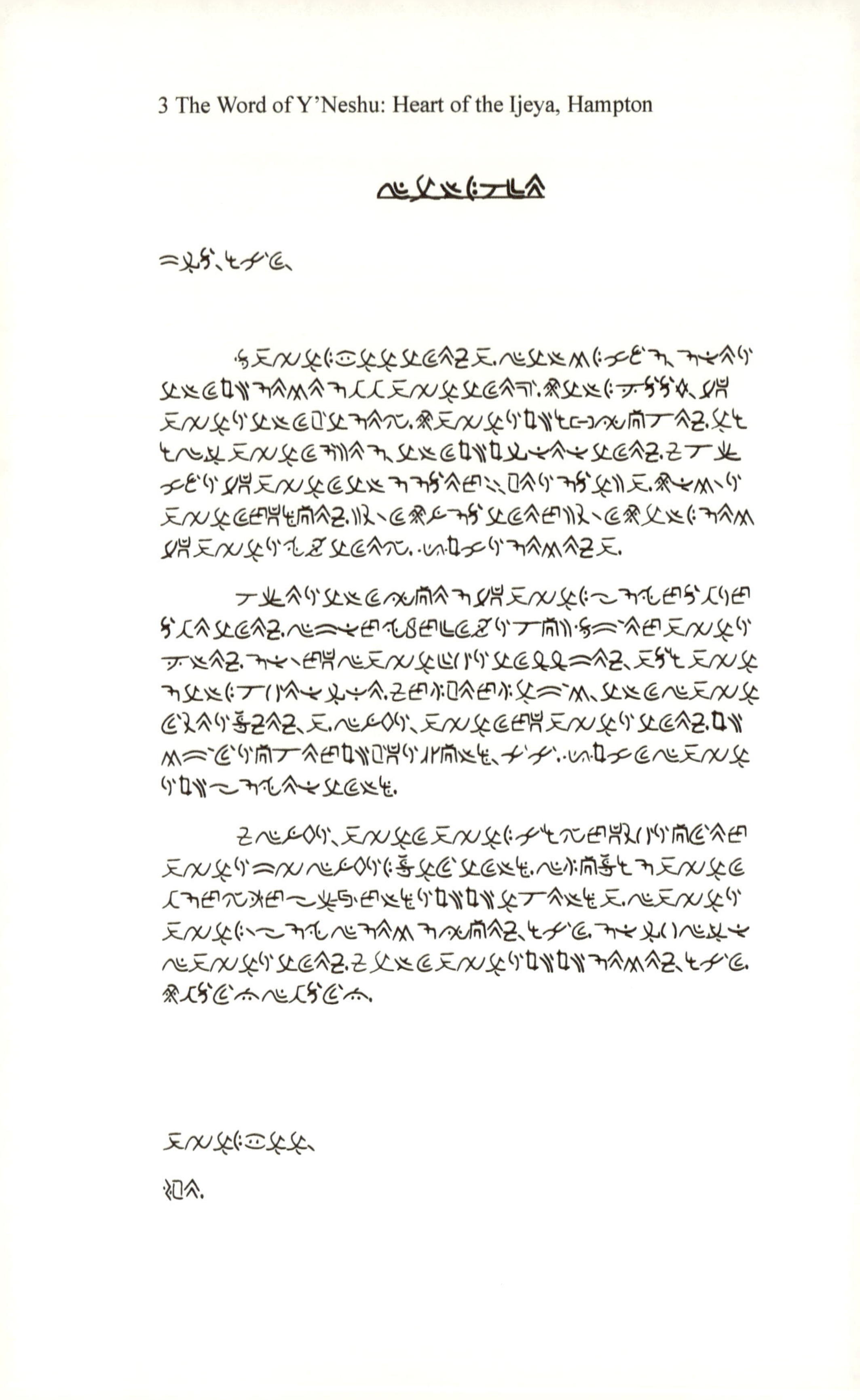

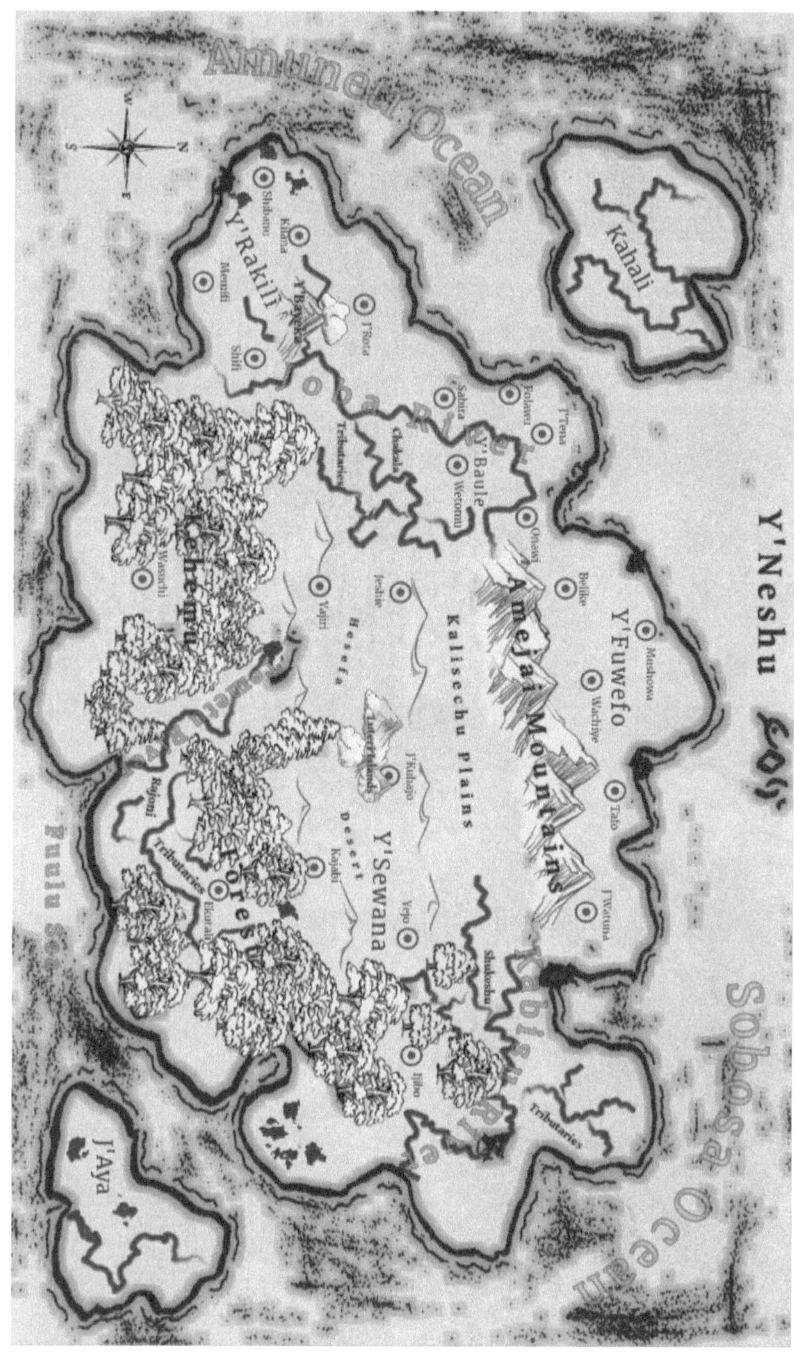
Y'Neshu
Kahali
Y'Rakili
Y'Baule
Y'Fuwefo
Kalisechu Plains
Y'Sewana
J'Aya

# Prelude

# Shroud of Fire

The dance of the air gently moved the tall hutije grass around his waist as the yellow of the sun faded to a vibrant orange. The blue of the sky washed pink, and the stars began to make themselves known as the usual bright green of the grass shimmered and faded in the waning daylight. A tender grin split his lips as he realized that at any moment, he would be attacked. He closed his eyes to better take in his surroundings: the soft soil beneath his feet that supported his every shift, the scent of the mili grain in the fields around the nearby city that wafted into his nose, and the mooing of the chitana beasts who took to their nightly milking with an unusual loudness. He inhaled deeply; exhaled. He could taste a sweet moisture in the evening air that told of rain, and knew that if the lurking predator had his way, that would be the moment when he would strike.

He did the best he could to calm himself, but the grin grew with the expectation in his heart as his body adopted a sunken, ready stance. It was then that he felt a shift in the grass behind him, and he tilted his head to the side in a mix of surprise and pride. *How did he get behind me, e?* A pang hit his heart, a sudden sharpness that came from nowhere, but it did little to dampen his mood. After all, the challenge had only just gotten interesting. His foot shifted just to the right as the sound of disturbed tall grass faded from behind and moved to his left. He shook his head and stifled the chuckle that brimmed in his throat. He took a step forward, as if to cut the predator off at the pass, but from behind he felt the clasp of little hands around his knee as a small weight pulled at him.

He fell to the ground as a loving chuckle poured from him, and in a moment his son sat in his chest. He couldn't help but feel that everything about the child was beautiful. His brown eyes that echoed the depth of collected honey, the smooth, night-colored skin that lustered in sun- or moonlight, the tight curls of his hair that waved with the coming of every breeze, all reminded the old man of what he was like when he was younger. Had the boy a beard, they would almost look like twins.

"Ah," he exclaimed. "Is this the fearsome ara beast that kept me in his sights?" The boy giggled innocently, then in a devious twist, opened his mouth and roared in his father's face to mimic the infernal breath of the majestic wolves.

"Did I impress you, *Yababa*," asked the boy with a light in his dark eyes that shimmered as the stars that continued to reveal themselves overhead. He smiled a hopeful smile and shifted his weight between the arms that now pressed against his father's torso. The *fesoa*, the elder, smiled.

"Oh I am very impressed, *hafu wu shehefo*," praised the *fesoa*, whose dark brown eyes now reflected the emergent moon as the orange and pink of the sky turned to indigo. The elder stood, and took his *yilele*, his child, into his arms as he started for the town. He had to marvel at just how big the boy had gotten. He was already seven, and soon he would be far too big for anything like this. He resolved to savor the moment while he could, and took in the sight of his son as much as his surroundings. The warmth of the sun remained in small part, but soon it would be too cold for the boy. "Why do you always want to play in the Outer Grasslands?"

The little one smiled a devious smile as he clung to his father's robe and answered, "It is the only place I can catch you." The Elder laughed, and ran his hand gently up and down the child's back. The boy frowned. "*Yababa*? Can you tell me a story on our way home?" The Elder looked upon the boy with disbelief, and when the child's frown grew more severe, the father simply shook his head as his smile returned and then nodded, only to see his little one light up all over again.

"But," the Elder said as their hearts soared and he gently wrapped a hand around the boy's head, "only if you will tell me which one you would like to hear." He could feel his little one smile up at him as he massaged his fingers through the boy's coiled black hair.

"I want to hear the story of our ancestors," said the Child, much to the Father's surprise. The *fesoa* raised an eyebrow as he lifted the boy with little effort.

"You seem to favor that one quite a bit, *shehefo*," he replied, a curious ring to his voice. "What is it that you hope to learn from it?"

"How to be like you," the Son answered. "When I grow up, I want to take care of the people of Y'Rakili just the way you do, *Yababa*. I want to be a *Wayi Kanawe*!"

"Is that so? Even if it means that you will have to fight monsters?" The depth of the Kanawe's tone had visibly startled the *yilele*, but the little one resolved not to be so easily shaken. The trembles in his young body weakened, and a sudden strength found its way to his grip on the Teacher's clothes.

"Even then," the boy argued. The *fesoa* smiled from ear to ear at his son's determination, and decided that it was good enough to warrant a story indeed.

"Alright, then," he said, and then cleared his throat with a rueful smile. "
." The moment he spoke, a ring of bright green light danced around them and moved in glittering specks to form the text first, and then the images. The language, J'Karo, came from the Divine Creator Y'Kele, and was the starting point for all

life in Y'Neshu. J'Karo was an ancient power, and while most of Y'Neshu knew it as legend, the Elder had only just begun to teach his son.

"No fair," cried the *yilele* in protest. "You know I can't speak that much J'Karo yet!" The Elder snickered with satisfaction, and noted the painted Wehela Stone, adorned in gold and silver by the side of the road. It was only a short distance to the heart of Shifi now, and soon he would be able to rest his tired feet. It caught him by surprise that he had overlooked the transition of the hutije to dirt roads and the expanse of the Outer Grasslands to the clay buildings and straw roofs that populated the Holy City.

"Very well," he uttered placatively, "I will stick to Pedestrian, then." He opened his mouth to carry on the story, but something felt wrong. Shifi was a lively city, full of farmers, merchants, and religious leaders. This close to the harvest, the streets should be filled with celebrations and haggling, as well as songs of praise to Afoyishu Y'Kele for His continued providence. Instead, there was silence and darkness. The lamps that usually bathed the streets with light had all been extinguished. The warm air of the Grasslands had been replaced by an eerie chill that put the Kanawe so much on the defensive that he clutched his son in his grasp. Feet staggered in all directions, but they somehow felt unnatural.

Even the boy could feel that something was amiss. He looked around nervously, though he was in part obstructed by his father's frame. Part of him didn't even want to know, didn't want to see what had become of his home in what felt like mere moments. He looked up at his father, hopeful that there would be some calmness on his face that would ease his mind of the growing sense of worry that took greater root with every step forward, but there was a sternness that only reinforced how serious the situation had been.

The little one blinked, and as if his eyes were truly opened, he saw the long, ghastly white fingers of a cold hand stretch out beside his father's neck. He jolted awake, every iota of fatigue from his earlier games now banished from his mind and body. He yelled, but not in Pedestrian as he had known to do. The boy cried out in J'Karo.

"*Yababa, bashura na me belenati o*!" The sudden cry of the child, no doubt inspired by the provision of Y'Kele Himself, jolted the Kanawe to a heightened awareness. His body moved on its own, and jumped forward just in time to evade the narrow claws of the enemy. He turned in midair with the young one still in his arms, and narrowed his eyes as he caught sight of a man of pale skin and pitch-black hair, whose entire being seemed as a shadow. He smiled a twisted, hungry smile like a ravenous beast on the scent of fresh prey.

The Kanawe set his young one on the ground. "Find your mother," he said. "I will deal with the Asanibo." The monster, the Asanibo, shifted his bloodshot gaze to the boy and bared fangs that visibly extended from his mandible. The boy stood frozen in fear. "Go! Both of you need to leave Shifi!" The little one, suddenly stirred to life by the sternness of his father's tone, made for a split between a pair of nearby huts. The predator jerked suddenly to the left of the Teacher, but a single word from the Father called the Asanibo to a halt. "*Yo natienati*," he whispered, and the knees of the creature buckled.

The Asanibo snarled in pain, then hissed as the Elder breathed deeply, calmly, as if he stood on the edge of Y'Neshu itself and gazed out at the ocean. Slowly, the father closed his eyes and opened them again. A shockwave rippled in the air as he shifted his *ike* and took his very soul into his hands. The Master, whose eyes glimmered with flecks of the same bright green light as before, extended a hand towards a nearby wooden cart. "*Ti fajari shu kelebasa o,*" he commanded, and the cart did as it was told. A heavenly fire sprang to life from the dry bones of the wooden bed in such a way that it appeared to be a second sun.

The Y'Rakilian protector never once looked away from the vampire, and the Asanibo reciprocated the animus gesture. The Wise One knew nothing of his prisoner, and in many ways that told him all he needed to know. Asanibo dwelled within the depths of the Kehemu Forest, far to the east of Y'Neshu, hundreds of miles from Y'Rakili. They were hostile only to those who entered their domain, and while they had an innate hatred for the humans of the Y'Neshuan continent, the time had long past since they would seek conflict with any of the Four Empires.

"You wonder—" the Asanibo spoke through gritted teeth. The weight of the earlier command to stop, though spoken in neutrality, still weighed on him so much that it made it hard to speak. Even still, with a maddening smugness, he smiled as he said, "You wonder who I am." The Kanawe's eyes, black in the darkness of night save for the green light of his ike, narrowed with the same ferocity of an ara beast on the hunt. The Master opened his mouth to speak, to command the vampire to state his business and then throw him into the flames, but the Asanibo flexed his jaw open and emitted the sound of a thousand lost souls into the night sky. The Kanawe's eyes went wide as he realized that he had come too late…

***

The yilele listened as much as he moved. The dazed and uncoordinated footsteps of whatever else waited for them in the dark shifted on all sides and in all directions, and the only way he could sneak around unnoticed was to listen and watch. He saw shadows move beneath the moonlight and trembled in fear as he scurried past them. He inched through the darkness, cautious of his every surrounding, his sole focus on his mother and their home. He pressed his eyes shut as he tightly clasped one hand around the other. He didn't like this. He wanted his Yababa.

Nevertheless, his father had given him a task, and he knew better than to defy him. He moved around the corner and gingerly tread down Seller's Road. The light lit up with an eruption of fire, and the shine revealed the ghostly dark faces and white eyes of the boy's Shifian neighbors. He almost gasped, just as a man dragged his legs against the ground right in front of him. A moment of consideration made him realize that it was Old Man Itemu, who made the best pies in all of Eastern Y'Rakili. He was just as dead as the rest.

The yilele mata shook his head as he ran down the road, eyes filled with tears and fists clenched tightly as they swung haphazardly before him. He moved as fast as his small legs would carry him, bolted around another corner, past another Wehela Stone, and down a flight of clay stairs. Their house was not far, and soon he would find his mother and rest comfortably in her arms while his Yababa would set the world right again. He would wake up tomorrow and the nightmare would be over.

He ran up to the wooden door of their otherwise clay hut, and with the greatest urgency he pushed it open to find the home that he had always known in disarray. The protective masks had all been shattered and left all over the floor. The flower pots were broken, and dirt could be seen all over the floral red carpet.

"Waleya," he whispered. There was no response, just the eerie stillness of the night within the hut. He moved into the house, his hands clenched tightly at his sides as he called for his mother again. "Waleya?" The sudden burst of a demonic call ripped through the night. The boy turned, his intent to focus on the door, but the sudden cracking of bones in the darkness of his home made him freeze before he could. He watched as a heap of flesh grunted as its joints violently reconnected. His breathing quickened as the figure stood, then turned its head abruptly to show him the face it bore. It was his mother, a soulless look in her eye. She roared at him in a way that made him shiver, as the love that he had once seen in her was replaced by something much more terrifying: hunger.

He ran on instinct as his mother picked up speed. She would not shamble like the ones outside, and now even they adopted a swifter pace. He screamed as he cycled through the city, only to find that more of the undead citizens patrolled the streets. When they saw him, they produced the same malicious vociferation as his Waleya and joined the mob that ran after him with hunger in their eyes. His screams grew louder and turned to cries. His muscles began to grow weaker, but the dead who chased him felt no such fatigue. In moments, they would catch him if he didn't push harder.

"Jato—" he attempted, but the moment he spoke, his lungs caught fire. The growls and groans of the hoard felt closer to him. "Ti jatonawe haranati o!" The words poured out of him frantically, and though his throat burned as a result, the rest of his body regained its strength. He changed directions and headed straight into the Outer Grasslands. Fear controlled him now, and spurred him to run until he collapsed beneath the hutije.

***

The Kanawe watched as the people of Shifi converged on him in their undead forms. Their teeth gnashed as saliva and blood spilled from their mouths to the ground. He shifted the *ike* a bit more and felt the toll it started to take on his body. He would need to end this quickly, but the hoard seemed to have no limit. He placed his hands to the ground to direct flow, and spoke another command in J'Karo: "Yo baa, bushake ra chesheshilibasa!" The ground listened to his voice, and cracks spidered through the streets in every direction until the surrounding swarm had fallen into the pits it made. He stretched his hand toward the burning cart and spoke again. "Yo fajari, N'uhuili leinanati." The fire spiraled through the air and descended upon the bodies of the undead, and while the Asanibo smiled confidently, he failed to evade a spark that touched the lapel of his coat.

The fires overtook him before long, and his screams echoed through the night sky at varied pitches and tones. The Kanawe cared little to watch. The only thing on his mind was his overpowering need to find his wife and son. The Asanibo would die soon, and with him the people of Shifi would find rest from their hellish fate. While he waited for that to happen, the Master ran through the streets in the direction of home.

The smell of burnt flesh and shifted earth filled his nostrils more than the night air. His eyes stung as the fire spread and with it, clouds of smoke. He coughed. He pressed on.

The streets were crowded with the lurching figures that had only hours ago been his friends and family. He dodged their desperate grabs at his flesh and kept to his advance. The darkness grew thicker, and his heart raced with the idea that he may never see his wife and child alive again. He could only pray that if he was too late, the shroud of fire would be enough to give them peace.

The Kanawe had arrived at his home, saw that it was empty, and moved on. More creatures pawed at him, but the urgency that he felt overtook him so that he lashed out with violent wind: "

" A divine wind exploded around him as it was commanded, and struck the mob so hard that they flew through many of the surrounding huts and businesses. It was then that the Master realized that one of them had been his wife.

The ferocity in his demeanor vanished in an instant as he watched her emerge from a hole in a nearby wall. She walked towards him, her arms outstretched, her eyes cold and her mouth open, filled with saliva at the sight of him. He only watched, for what else could he do? He reached his hand out to touch her, hoping to Y'Kele that what he saw was just some sick illusion and not the reality he felt in his bones. She saw her moment, and ran at him as well as her legs would allow, but then there was nothing.

The Master blinked, and before his mind could wrap itself around what had happened, she crumbled to a pile of dust. He sank to his knees, a deep pain in his heart as he realized that his yilele mata, his baby boy, should have been with her; that *he* sent him there. His vision blurred as his body warmed, then chilled with fear. The Asanibo was gone. Shifi burned. The Kanawe's wife was laid to rest, and his son, he feared, was lost.

***

"Yababa," said Kamari, hope in his wood-colored eyes as he tugged at his father's hand, "I want to learn J'Karo, too!" His father chuckled as he followed the boy into the circular living room of their hut.

"I can tell," J'Kana replied. He took in his son's night-colored skin that shimmered in the sunlight like the stars in the sky. The looser curls in his black hair bobbed from side to side as he moved, and everything about him filled J'Kana with a fierce desire to protect. "You would think that hearing the story of your ancestors would be enough to make you want to wait."

"It makes me want to learn even more," the boy exclaimed with his hands in the air. He was only five years old, but he was already so well beyond his years. J'Kana shouldn't have expected anything less.

"Very well, hafu wu shehefo," he said gently as he moved for the room beyond the child where his books were kept. "If you want to learn so badly, you will have to learn first to read." He watched as joy ignited behind Kamari's expression. "The J'Karo syllabary is 86 characters long, so pay close attention, or you could get lost."

"I will, Yababa," assured the little one. "It will be easy." J'Kana raised his eyebrows in mock surprise, but opened the book to turn the first few pages. *There*, he thought. Page four of the dusty leather tome held the syllabary. When Kamari saw how complex the symbols were, his smile faded, and he reached for his father's hand. "Yababa? Will you help me understand what it all says?" J'Kana smiled ear to ear.

"Of course," he reassured, and pointed at the page. "They read like this…"

| | | | |
|---|---|---|---|
|  | A |  | We |
|  | I |  | Wo |
|  | U |  | Ja |
|  | E |  | Ji |
|  | O |  | Ju |
|  | Ka |  | Je |
|  | Ki |  | Jo |
|  | Ku |  | Ya |
|  | Ke |  | Yi |
|  | Ko |  | Yu |
|  | Ra |  | Ye |
|  | Ri |  | Yo |

| | | | |
|---|---|---|---|
| 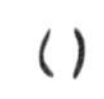 | Ru |  | Ba |
|  | Re |  | Bi |
|  | Ro |  | Bu |
|  | Ta |  | Be |
|  | Ti |  | Bo |
|  | Tu |  | Cha |
|  | Te |  | Chi |
|  | To |  | Chu |
|  | Ma |  | Che |
|  | Mi |  | Cho |
|  | Mu |  | La |
|  | Me |  | Li |
|  | Mo | 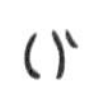 | Lu |
|  | Na |  | Le |
|  | Ni |  | Lo |
|  | Nu |  | Sha |
|  | Ne |  | Shi |
|  | No |  | Shu |
|  | Ha |  | She |

| | | | |
|---|---|---|---|
| | Hi | | Sho |
| | Hu | | Sa |
| | He | | Si |
| | Ho | | Su |
| | Fa | | Se |
| | Fi | | So |
| | Fu | | J' |
| | Fe | | M' |
| | Fo | | N' |
| | Wa | | S' |
| | Wi | | T' |
| | Wu | | Y' |

# 1

# Found

*Memifi*

The southernmost city in Y'Rakili boasted a cleanness that was known throughout the Y'Neshuan continent. The buildings glittered silver as they bathed in the rays of the hot sun. Carts and wagons were pulled along by kesefi mules, loaded with assorted wares from produce to refined silver. Perhaps the most impressive thing about Memifi, though, was its use of the iron sands found in the mines of Mount Y'Bayeka. Ten thousand years, and the people of Y'Rakili never moved from their country in the west, and every one of its cities found a way to mine the precious igneous rock birthed from the volcano. None, however, were as skilled in steelwork as the artisans of Memifi.

That was why he had come all those years ago. He had assumed that the City of Celestial Light, Memifi, would have lived up to the wonder posited by the stories his Yababa had told him. In many ways it did. Every morning that he woke up, wonder was the first impression made upon him as he looked upon the lush green bakirati trees with their deep purple fruit, the muju berry bushes that adorned the earthy roads with minty greens dotted with yellow clusters, and the many whites, golds, silvers, reds, blues, and greens of the huts and buildings, each one held together and accented by the deep gray gleam of the iron sand supports that made the city so famous.

The second impression he got, however, was a deep but pronounced tinge of bitterness that came with his makeshift hut of mili straw and hutije grass. It kept the rain off his head, but it did little to stave off the cold or heat that came with the changing of the seasons. His possessions were few, and his money came and went in unpredictable waves. After the third time his purse was stolen, he knew better than to keep it anywhere near his home and decidedly buried whatever change he could scrounge up in the Outer Grasslands near the coast. In the ten years that he had lived on the streets of Memifi, the only thing he really had to show for it was proof of poverty in the form of a name.

The people of the city, who dwelled in the security of their iron-reinforced huts, had come to refer to him as J'Foja, which used to be preceded by "ulu," meaning "little." He knew that he had a real name, one born of love rather than circumstance, but J'Foja had been around for so long that his true name was forgotten. Orphans were an uncommon sight in Memifi, or in Y'Rakili proper for that matter, and while J'Foja, the Great Peasant, hoped that they would show some kind of mercy or help him find his yababa, all they did was give him the crumbs from their table and shoo him away like the burden they thought him to be. In his first years, he tried to explain what had happened, how an Asanibo had tried to kill him and how it had already taken him away from his family, slaughtered his mother and destroyed the greater portions of Shifi.

They looked at him pitiably, but barely did anything to help. Many assumed that he had been abandoned, and that he had lost his mind as a result of his isolation. Others believed him, but failed to find a solution for his many problems. All assumed that it would be enough to give him what little food they had to spare. It kept him alive, and while he had hope that his father would come for him to take him away from the horrors of his life in the gutter, that sort of optimism left him after the third year. Now, he simply did whatever it took to survive from day to day, usually at the expense of some unsuspecting tourists from another land.

He watched the streets from a narrow alley between the blacksmith and the bakery, careful to keep an eye out for the people who seemed the most confused. When he found them, he would do what he always did. He considered that he would offer a tour of the upper district today, but one look down at his tattered, sleeveless shirt and his worn, dusty trousers told him that perhaps he needed another plan. J'Foja sighed as he pushed himself off the wall of the bakery and entered the golden sunlight of sparkling Memifi.

"I suppose," he muttered to himself, "I should do something about this." He sauntered down the street, seemingly without a care in the world, as he greeted the denizens of the merchant district. He felt their glares as he passed by, and for a moment wondered where all their sympathy had gone. Sure, he had pickpocketed, swindled, or fought a fair amount of their friends and relatives over the years, but he was a growing boy whose family had either died or abandoned him. Surely that should've commanded some kind of eternal sympathy.

He shrugged, and felt the weight of their every gaze roll from his shoulders like waters into the basin of the Berenika Falls in Y'Fuwefo. He closed his eyes for a moment as he walked through more of a crowd. The wiser of the Memifians steered clear of the boy, but fortunately for J'Foja, the street was especially populated today. It was no great issue to reach into the pockets of the most obvious servants, who were easily distinguished from the rest of the crowd with their dark maroon kaftans and bronze kufi. He also knew that he could just as easily go after the wives, sisters, and daughters of the upper class, who sported floral patterns or beads in their vibrant dresses of many colors.

The moment the crowd passed, J'Foja rattled the coins he'd stolen beneath their notice in his hands, gave them a humble bow, and sprinted for the tailor shop.

"What the—" came the loud and disgruntled voice of a burly man of dark skin and hairless head. *Be calm now,* J'Foja told himself with an almost smug smile on his face. *There's no way he can tell it was you.* The burly man immediately looked in his direction, saw his smugness, and pointed with a finger the size of a chitana prod squarely towards the boy's face. "Thief! Guards, J'Foja is at it again!" *Okay, so maybe he could tell.*

Memifi was built in an elaborate mix of boxes and spires. The huts and booths of the marketplace created a layered fabric of interests and colors, each one only narrowly separated from the next by the slim alleyways. The beautiful array of colors and patterns that decorated the walls blurred as the budding master thief slipped between them with a speed that the giant pursuer couldn't match, and the brilliant shine of the silver steel supports flashed in the eyes of the guards as they tried to track his movements. J'Foja smiled nervously, and quickly jumped up at the alley's end to reach for the rooftop of a nearby fruit stand. He clambered to get on top, then jumped over to another nearby wall that would carry him, he hoped, beyond the sight of the royal guards. His feet planted in the granular soil of the workman district, and suddenly the vibrant colors of the market were replaced with clay browns and tans intermixed with the deep grays of untreated metal.

J'Foja paid it all no mind. He knew that if he stopped for a second, the guards would catch him and beat him to a pulp. What was worse, they started to learn his signature escape routes. He'd had to change directions six times already as the shouts of policemen came from every direction. He ducked into a needleworker's craft space nestled in the east of the district, greeted the artisan with a "Sabelle" in her native Katsedu, and snuck into the back much to her protest.

"I saw him go in here," called a male guard, out of breath from the pursuit. Hurried footsteps approached the workshop, and J'Foja wrapped himself in a multicolored cloth of reds and yellows that radiated like the fires of old Mount Y'Bayeka. He pulled it over the soft, tight curls of his black hair and tucked his face so that the officers would think that he is a patron rather than the focus of the chase.

"Everyone out," came the voice of a female guard, a voice that J'Foja recognized as Nikeli. She chased him often through the streets of Memifi, and he had to admit that he liked having her attention. He suppressed a smile as he stepped forward, happy to realize that there were more people in the workshop than just him and the old woman from Y'Sewana. Three others came forward, wrapped in colorful clothes of dual tone and a plethora of geometric figures. He watched as the policemen, clad in their imposing black robes and red hats, pushed past him as they entered the shop with extreme urgency. He tucked his head to shield his night-colored face from the notice of his pursuers when the slender fingers of a delicate hand gripped his shoulder with stern force. "And where do you think you are going, J'Foja?"

"Only into the light where I could better see your lovely face, Nikeli," he flirted shamelessly. She looked into his chocolate eyes, surveyed the soothing coffee brown of his skin, ripped the cloth from his body. She took a moment to take in the life of his hair and almost stood frozen when his dark lips curled upward into a smile. "Tell me, are you chasing me because I have done something wrong, or because you wanted to get a better look at me, e?"

"Don't kid yourself, o," she exclaimed as her caramel skin glowed with a tinge of red in her cheeks. "You play entirely too much, and usually with other people's purse strings." J'Foja raised an eyebrow.

"Well say the word," he told her, "and I would be happy to play with…other things, kenani." Nikeli stammered, desperately in search of something to say. He winked at her, his smile even wider now, and ran clear for the opposite end of the workman district. Nikeli gave chase, now more flustered than ever, though she could hardly tell if it was because of anger or something…else. J'Foja looked behind him to see her hot on his tail, and turned back just before he ran into the busy road.

Carts and the kesefi mules that pulled them moved in a chaotic river that kicked the metal-infused dust of the earth into the air. J'Foja stopped for a second to weigh his options, but the shouts of Nikeli and her men put his feet to flight faster than a three-tailed Juku Bird. He breathed deeply, and prayed to Almighty Y'Kele to tread the road safely. He stepped into the flow of animals, merchants, farmers, and transports, his eyes all but closed because of the dust cloud. He stepped gingerly, careful to maneuver between the cubic shapes of the carts or under the rounded bellies of the mules. He watched as much as he could with his arm bent across his face to preserve the purity of his breathing, and in another instant he was on the other side.

Nikeli growled, and while he sought to catch his breath, she and her fellow guards looked for a way around. J'Foja, with sight restored and breath devoid of dirt and metal particles, blew a kiss to his pursuers as he disappeared into the tall stalks of triangular mili grain.

***

Two hours later, he made his way back to the merchant district and into the tailor shop that he had planned to patronize before his abrupt adventure through most of the city.

"May I help you," asked the elderly man that wrapped an ornate green robe with earth-brown beads around a black mannequin. He looked J'Foja over, and the master thief could see that the man had quickly decided he didn't belong. J'Foja smiled a kind smile and spread his arms in a welcoming fashion, as if the shop had been his and not the other way around.

"Ah, Uncle," said the crafty youth, "I am at your mercy! You can see that I am all but wearing rags, e? I am in need of the wisdom of a trained professional." The elderly man of darker complexion, knowing eyes, and wrinkled brow stroked his gray beard with a hand as he reached cautiously for the young visitor. J'Foja didn't exaggerate. His tunic was torn at the shoulders, and whatever color it had been in the past had been replaced by a teal/gray. His trousers were dirty brown, which couldn't mask the grime on them despite the color. Around his waist was a purple belt made of a thin cloth with barely enough strength to hold up his pants, and yet there was something wrapped up in it at the small of his back.

"What would you say you are in the market for," the tailor asked as he circled J'Foja. He stopped, and his eyes narrowed, a sign that he knew better than to get ahead of himself. "You have the money to buy at least something, na?" J'Foja withdrew a rather hefty orange coin purse from a loop on his belt. The shop owner raised a curious eyebrow at him when his guest placed the bag into his hands.

"I would be curious to know what I could get for this," said the peasant. The tailor took the purse over to the wooden counter and emptied its contents. For a moment, a look of disbelief took his face and J'Foja stifled a laugh. It was all that he had, but for some reason the Great Peasant couldn't help but think it necessary to pour his every Bashele into his shopping. For starters, he knew that the guards would keep an eye out for him until nightfall, so it was best that he didn't look anything like himself. Secondly, for some unexplainable reason, he felt as though something about his tour today would be different than any other.

"You have over 21,000 Bashele here," the old man expressed with delight in his voice. He fixed his expression to be more professional, and wiped the saliva from his jaw as he fetched a tape measure, then continued. "For that amount, you could get an entire new suit." J'Foja smiled as his wound locs danced atop his shaking head.

"I don't need anything so fancy, Uncle," he said with a chuckle. "I only need something to get by, ne?"

"Then I have the perfect thing in mind, o!" The old man finished his measurements and scurried into the back behind his counter. The sudden excitement in his voice told J'Foja that he truly enjoyed his work. It wouldn't be hard to imagine that the old man believed his services to be of great help to those that wandered into his tailor shop. The people of Memifi were kindhearted, but J'Foja knew that such friendliness often came with a steep price tag. He came back with a folded shiki (shirt) and jifona (pants) set of purple and black, like the sort the political leaders' servants wore to denote their honorable status. The patterns were an intricate mingling of geometric and linear designs, symbols that told the story of the founding of Memifi.

Beneath the elaborately made shirt and pants was a jilaba, a monochromatic robe that draped over the shoulders to the front and back and, despite the unusual deep brown color, this one had no distinguishing features. J'Foja looked up at the man, his mouth fixed to protest, but the elder shook his head.

"You have a strange understanding of 'something to get by,' don't you?" asked the Great Peasant. The old man smiled.

"What better way to get by than to look like where you want to be?" This was the first time in a long time that J'Foja smiled a genuine smile. "Would you like to try them on?"

"Ah, it would be my pleasure," said the boy, whose crafty eyes suddenly seemed genuine. The elder ushered him towards a white curtain and turned his back. After a few moments, J'Foja emerged from the partition to the stunned expression of the tailor. "So? How do I look?"

"You look as though you could be a prince, o!" The old man gave a pleased sound and shuffled his feet in a dance of excitement as he said, "I've outdone myself this time!" J'Foja, all of a sudden, was overcome with a wave of joy at the sight.

"Then I am glad that I could lend a hand," he told his elder. "But, unfortunately I must be going. *Chishama, ile yabowu*!" His bid goodbye was met with a strange look, but J'Foja was too used to it to notice. J'Karo was a gift that came from Y'Kele, but the language wasn't spoken much these days, save for the derivatives that appeared in dialects of Katsedu and Pedestrian. It had been forgotten and replaced in the millennia since the War of the Ancients, and the only ones who used it in fullness were the Wayi Kanawe, the Seven Teachers. The tailor felt a sudden burst of goodwill and life from J'Foja, and while he struggled to place it, he knew something was different about the boy. He feigned attention to his work as his customer picked up his clothes, but quietly watched with brand new curiosity as the young man left.

***

Kanawe Y'Sawe was a man of great calm, a man respected by most who had the pleasure to cross his path. He traveled across Y'Neshu often, and as the Ile Kanawe, the Grand Master of the Seven, he had a responsibility to check in with the other six. Even so, his nomadic tendencies always brought him back to his homeland of Y'Rakili, specifically to the city of Memifi. Even after the fires of Shifi took his wife and young son, he found that he was drawn to it, as if the heart of Mount Y'Bayeka called his name.

He was due to head north to Folawu in Y'Baule, but the Wayi Summit, a gathering of all the Saweshe (Enlightened), was a month away, and that would afford him at least a week or two to spend time amid the life-giving colors of Memifi. For him, the sounds of life that paraded through the pounded dirt streets, the smell of Joba and Lushuki that wafted through the clear air, and the brilliant array of shapes and patterns that adorned the clothing as much as the walls of buildings provided for him a comfort deeper than the ocean. In his state of bliss, he moved for a vendor just a little ways down the street. He could almost taste the Lushuki, the saltiness of the hibesa bird gravy as it seeped into the mili grain, the fiery sweet mixture of weka pepper, honey, and choni fruit in a sauce that would bring a smile to the face of Y'Kele Himself. It was the signature dish of Memifi, and after a thousand years it had become the same for all of Y'Rakili. The teacher Y'Sawe felt that it was for good reason.

He slipped through the crowd with a kind of skillful avoidance that would cause a thief to stew with envy, but on the other side stood a man with whom Y'Sawe was all too familiar. He wore a black kaftan that was tied close to his waist with a cloth belt adorned in silver diamonds with red dots in them. The man, of the same sun-kissed skin and bright brown eyes as Y'Sawe, pushed his lengthy locs out of his face as his lips curled up into the smile of a wild man.

"So," he began with an oily slickness that washed Y'Sawe's peace into a basin of outrage, "my little brother has finally come back to Y'Rakili. It seems that I will not have to wait for a chance to kill you." Y'Sawe heaved a sigh, and relaxed every muscle in his body as his brother approached.

"Is that why you're here, Mahute," asked the Teacher with a tone that dripped with warning, "to blame me for what happened all those years ago?" Mahute's smile faded into the black abyss of his own anger as he slammed his fist against a nearby wall. His breath became deep, measured, and drastically differed from how it had been just the moment before.

"Twenty years, ulu esho," Mahute snarled. "That is how long you left me to rot in Febetu!" A flicker of pain flashed through Y'Sawe like lightning through a darkened cloud. He needed no reminder of how long it had been. He had been there to see his brother to his cell. Febetu, the prison at the heart of the Hesefa Desert in Y'Sewana, had a reputation as the most brutal place in all of Y'Neshu. The stories always made it out, but the prisoners never did.

"You broke the law, threatened Y'Neshu with another age of war with your reckless actions—"

"I did what I needed for the benefit of my people!" The sudden outburst was enough to attract the attention of the crowd, but Y'Sawe didn't care for that. He was surprised to find that his own heart raced like a frightened child in fear of an angry parent. "And I was tortured for it! Three days a week for seven months, I was subjected to all manner of unspeakable acts short of mutilation! I was burned! I was cut! I was beaten within an inch of my life only to be healed and have the cycle start all over again, and in my isolation, where was my brother, na?" Y'Sawe trembled as he listened, and he did listen. He felt that he owed Mahute that much.

"I could not neglect my duty as Kanawe, Mahute," the Teacher uttered mournfully as his mind wandered back to the image of his zombified wife and his frightened son.

"You ran," Mahute snapped as he got into the face of his brother. "You were too much of a coward to face me then, just as you cower before me now." Y'Sawe sucked his teeth as he met his brother's gaze.

"I acted in the service of others," Y'Sawe chided with a sting of superiority, "not out of the kind of selfish ambition you take such pride in." Mahute's eyes widened with disgusted surprise as the Kanawe walked around him.

"You want to walk away from me, na?" Mahute called, but there was no response. The elder brother reached into the folds of his cloth belt and pulled out a jagged dagger made from the talon of a Juku Bird. "It's time you got what you deser—"

A brilliant flash. A stunned crowd. Silence.

***

"Then what happened, Yababa," Kamari asked with all the life in the world in his earthy brown eyes. He sat on the floor of their living room while J'Kana reclined in a chair with the leather book in his lap. It was clear that it would become a habit, now, for him to tell Kamari a story of their family history before their J'Karo lesson began. Of course, it became harder to tell which one the yilele was more excited for.

"I will tell you tomorrow, hafu wu shehefo," J'Kana promised with a smile as gentle and warm as a summer breeze. He opened the book to the page where they had left off. Three days had passed since the last lesson. Kamari took his time with the syllabary, and now that he could read and write in J'Karo, he came back to his yababa with a hunger for more. "For now," the Kanawe continued, "let us go over a few of the words, e? Here, let me teach you how to greet people." Kamari frowned.

"But Yababa, I want to know how to do magic like the Teachers do!" J'Kana shook his head as he wagged a finger.

"You must be patient, Kamari," he warned. "J'Karo is more than just a tool for magic; it is the very life that holds Y'Neshu together." The explanation did little more than make the boy scratch his head. He was only five, after all. "Here, repeat after me…"

Sabele Hello

| | |
|---|---|
| Chishama | Goodbye |
| Otaba ra jishemu haranati e? | How are you? |
| Otaba ra jishemu e? | How are you? (Short version) |
| Fujana | Name |
| Otaba | You |
| Arani | Thank you |
| Ushanawi | You're welcome |
| Jikisu | I am well |
| Otaba wu fujana ra haranati e? | What is your name? (Short) |
| Hafu wu fujana ra…haranati. | My name is… |
| Sekeja mani | Good day. |
| Sekeja mali | Good morning. |
| Sekeja mafe | Good afternoon. |
| Sekeja machihi | Good evening. |
| Sekeja maya | Good night. |
| Sekeja | Good |

| | |
|---|---|
| Nikijo | Bad |
| Jishelu | Well |
| Kirala | Sick |
| Chilu | What |
| Hela | Who |
| Nata | Where |
| Yibe | When |
| Jea | Why |
| Bara | Sorry |
| Baraki | Apology |
| Wikeni | Excuse Me |
| Chukeya otaba ra harachele | It's nice to meet you (You are pleasant) |
| M'Iba | From (Origin) |
| Saweshe | Enlightened |

# 2

# Appeal

The moment that J'Foja left the tailor, he saw a man of dark skin and willow-like locs wrapped in a black open-faced robe with a gray scarf thick enough to serve as a hood. His face was covered beneath a dark beard and moustache, black as the clothes that shielded his body from the burning sun. His calm brown eyes, warped by a pained look of guilt and regret, fixated on the man before him. That man stood with animosity in his stance, but talked softly to the Robe until he pushed past him.

"You want to walk away from me, na?" The aggressive man shouted it as he pulled a knife from the folds in his belt and charged the Robe with murderous intent. The Robe did nothing. Time slowed to a crawl, and as the man in black turned his head, J'Foja noted a green glint in his eyes that reminded him of the days of his youth. He shifted the ike.

The Robe fixed his mouth with a knowing preparation as he uttered the phrase, "Yo ebibina me N'otaba shu nasoinati o." J'Foja recognized it as a command—a command in J'Karo, no less—that urged the assailant to slip and stab himself. The ara-like pace that the attacker took, that swift but meticulous stride that mirrored the lupine beasts of Y'Rakili, fell disrupted by a sudden backwards jerk of his legs. The man, whose face became alight with shock at his body's sudden rejection of order, watched in horror as the ground approached his face and the blade moved towards his side.

While the various shop owners and the customers they served stopped dead in their tracks to see the commotion, the Robe returned to his whisper and continued on his way as though nothing had happened. J'Foja couldn't believe it, that here in Memifi there was another

J'Karo speaker. Long ago, his Yababa had taught him about the scarcity of its users, and how the Kanawe kept it clear of any contemporary learners, save for their personal ijeya. His father was a Kanawe and, had things gone differently, J'Foja would have begun his training as a Saweshe over a year ago. Throughout his years on the streets of Memifi, he'd almost forgotten about the Teachers entirely. If he thought about them, then his memories of Shifi would rush back into his mind with crippling vengeance.

As he watched the man in the black robe walk away, the white skin and blood-red eyes of the Asanibo boiled up to the surface of his mind. He remembered how cold he felt that night, how fear gripped him as his zombified mother chased him through the streets, how much he wanted his father to come to save him, only to realize that he never would. The anguish that he felt at losing his parents washed over him, but the recollection of the monster's twisted smile burned it away. He was left with an anger so hot it radiated from his body, and before he realized it, his feet carried him down the street after the man.

J'Foja watched him carefully. The elder moved further through the colorful buildings that glinted in the sun, and acted as sharp contrast to his surroundings in his black garb. The merchants smiled and waved on-comers to their booths and huts, dressed in colors that complemented those of the outer walls of their businesses. Some displayed every kind of food from succulent samples of meat to pristine dishes that spanned a number of delicacies. Others directed the attention of their audience to the racks of clothing or jewels that decorated the road. Precious jewels and metals from all over Y'Neshu shimmered like the surface of fresh water. Even with all the distractions that would have attracted his gaze—and his hands—on a normal day, J'Foja found that his only interest was in the Kanawe that gently pressed through the crowded street in silence.

Nikeli and more of the guards appeared just up ahead, their faces stern and bodies tensed in preparation for another chase. They were on the hunt for J'Foja, just as a rayemo beast stalks the wild chitana in the Outer Grasslands. J'Foja smiled as he bowed at the waist and moved with the crowd, careful to keep the gray hood of the Kanawe in his sights.

"Fan out," Nikeli barked, clearly still flustered these two and a half hours later. "When you find that *lecha*

J'Foja, bring him to me! We can send him off to Febetu with Mahute the Dagger!" He had to resist the sudden urge to tease her about how much she needed to catch him. Things between them were usually a bit more playful than they were today. The Great Peasant assumed that her tension was because of who the fat man was that he had robbed earlier. He shrugged. It was hardly of any consequence at this point.

J'Foja calmly and carefully moved through the crowd, now unconcerned with the scattered position of the guards who searched for him. He stood straight again, and though he couldn't see in full the way the Teacher flowed through the mob of shoppers and merchants, he had some idea of how it would work. He calmed himself, angled his slim body through the narrow openings between the unconcerned denizens of the merchant district. Every now and then, he had to use his hands to keep from bumping into them, much to the irritation of some and indifference of others. Nevertheless, he gradually closed the distance between himself and the man who he imagined might become his Master.

He thought, as he grew closer to his target, about how he would convince the elder to take J'Foja in. The young thief had been out of practice in dealing with those who knew of the old ways, but he knew enough to understand that the usual charms of a thief would likely get him rejected. His heart pounded with every step, and he silently mouthed a prayer to Afoyishu Y'Kele for the second time that day. The usual confidence, the natural flow of his personal charms that he had cultivated in his…entrepreneurial pursuits, buried themselves deep within his core as he saw the distance close. He reached out a hand to grasp the Elder's shoulder when the old man sighed.

"If you are going to sneak up on someone, you might try to be a bit quieter," he warned with a tinge of amusement in his otherwise judgmental tone. J'Foja swallowed heavily as his hand now shook. The crowd around them paid little attention to the fact that the young thief and the Kanawe had come to a stop. They moved around, and when J'Foja tried to do the same he realized that his entire body held in place as though he were stone. "Tell me," the Master continued, "do you intend to threaten me or to rob me?"

Suddenly a pressure that J'Foja just noticed released his body. He crumpled to the ground, gasped for air, and still the people of the city passed him by as though the dirt was where he belonged. The thief looked up to find the eyes of the Kanawe on him now. The face of the elder was strong and imposing. There was a familiarity about him brought on by the authority he commanded in his position, enough to remind J'Foja of his Yababa and the life he had before the streets, but the frozen glare in his deep brown eyes told him that this man was nothing like his father. The Teacher folded his arms across his chest as a ripple of impatience flashed across his face. J'Foja fixed his mouth to speak, and found that he had to shake the cobwebs out of his head before he did.

"I…" The way the air hit his lungs took him by surprise. Every contraction and expansion they made was made apparent to him. It felt like his lungs had been starved of air, shriveled by the weight of the Robe's hidden attack. "I wanted to ask you if you would teach me." The man looked at him quizzically as J'Foja labored to stand to his feet.

"And what is it that you believe I could teach you about?" The man asked the question with such a chill that it almost challenged the heat of the sun. J'Foja's breathing grew shallow as his body trembled. Fear. The simple presence of this man was enough to make J'Foja tense, but when the face of the Asanibo flashed its toothy grin in his head again, he summoned as much resolve as he could.

"I saw what you did to that man who attacked you. I know that you can speak J'Karo, and I want to learn—"

"No," interrupted the man with the same cold indifference as everyone else in Memifi. "I have no time for an apprentice, especially not one as clumsy as you. Now, if you will excuse me—" the man cut himself off when he saw J'Foja sprint around him and dig his knees in the dirt. The young man met the gaze of his elder with a mix of humility and fierce determination that simmered behind his eyes. He bowed his head, a move that truly caught the Kanawe off-guard.

"Please, Master, I beg of you," J'Foja pleaded with a desperate rattle in his voice. "How can I prove myself to you? I'll do anything you want me to!" The fervor in J'Foja's voice was enough to make the Teacher pause a moment. Several times a year for the last decade, there were always those who would seek an apprenticeship under him. The name of Kanawe was not nearly as lost to the people of Y'Neshu as the language they safeguarded, and while he was not so easy to recognize, those who tended to find him were far too proud to beg. The Master straightened his face and walked around the child.

"Come," was the only thing he said as he moved, and J'Foja could feel the weight fall from his shoulders like a mudslide from the base of the Amejai mountains. He picked himself up from the ground and did everything he could to suppress his smile as he trailed behind the Kanawe with great difficulty. *Arani, Y'Kele,* his soul whispered to the God that heard him. The old man's pace was as brisk as his attitude, a clear sign that while he was willing to hear J'Foja out, he had every intention to still refuse him.

"Why do you want to learn from me," asked the man, his voice an airy tenor that spoke of his inner calm, even as he exhibited little patience. The question struck J'Foja as surprising, and was something that he couldn't answer easily. He hesitated, and the Master sped up. J'Foja heaved a sigh as he stressed his legs, desperate to keep up with him, and wondered how someone so advanced in age could move so efficiently and so quietly. It was as though he phased through the walls of people before him, and walking had little to do with it.

"Life has been hard," the boy started through weighted breaths as heavy as his body had been a moment ago, "since I arrived here from Shifi." The Master stopped dead in his tracks and eyed the boy. "I lost my parents when it burned, and I've been living on the street ever since." The Great Peasant marveled at his own tone. It was solemn, softer than it had ever been in these last ten years, and more sincere as well. He watched anxiously as the intimidating safekeeper glided toward him as if on the wings of a bird. There was something in the elder's eyes that J'Foja couldn't immediately recognize. It was deeper than pity. Was it sympathy? Whatever it was, he could tell that the mention of Shifi caused the old man more pain than he would ever reveal on his own.

"I am sorry," he spoke with a surprising gentleness that melted through the icy dismissiveness he'd held at first. The sudden clasp of the Kanawe's hand upon J'Foja's shoulder made him jump with surprise. "I never expected such a young survivor of the Shifi Tragedy to be here in Memifi of all places. You have my respect for surviving on your own for so long." The words nearly brought the boy back to his knees. *Respect.* It was more than what he had ever managed to earn in all his time here, and yet he sensed a lingering reluctance in the Master.

"And still you refuse to teach me," J'Foja stated in a hushed, disappointed tone. The Kanawe exhaled, much calmer now than before.

"I won't," he confirmed, and started to walk away. For a moment, J'Foja watched his stride, felt the despair and sorrow of the morning after Shifi grip his heart, suddenly as fresh as when he first knew it. Then came the crimson eyes of the Asanibo that haunted his memory and the crackle of anger that shot through his body like a bolt of lightning.

"With all due respect," said the Peasant as he followed behind the Teacher, "I don't accept your dismissal."

"Whether you accept it or not doesn't change the fact that you have been dismissed," the Kanawe shot back without so much as a glance now. He picked up his speed, and so did the apprentice hopeful.

"You know I'm just going to follow you, right," J'Foja inquired, a cunning look on his face that the Master refused to notice. "Every waking hour in the day I will be at your side or behind your back—"

"You don't even have the skill to annoy me as much as you intend to," said the elder as the shadow of a smile crept across his face. "Don't you remember what happened before?" It wasn't hard for J'Foja to think about his body freezing against his will, but it didn't matter.

"No matter how many times you freeze me," J'Foja challenged, "I'll keep coming back. Anything is better than the life I have now." His seriousness took them both by surprise, and made him pause for a moment. He realized this to be the truth of it. How could he be satisfied with how he lived? "I have to steal to buy clothes, because if I steal the clothes then I'll be beaten by the guards. For food I have to live on the 'generosity' of others who only give me scraps to keep me away from their plenty. I sleep in a grass hut that barely keeps out the cold or rain." The more he spoke, the more he raised his voice and bared his pain. How long had he just gone through the motions, trapped in his never-ending resignation?

The Kanawe didn't give a response. He moved faster now, turned a corner, then went down an alley. J'Foja followed as closely as he could. The Teacher turned to face the determined boy and asked with a serious tone, "What do I stand to gain from taking you on? Surely you realize that whatever you think you can do for me, I can do for myself." The Peasant narrowed his eyes on the Teacher as he thought about his answer. He knew that a man who could make his attacker trip and stab himself on a spoken word would have no need for a servant. He could command the forces of nature if that was something he wanted to do. J'Foja thought back to what his yababa had once told him, then smiled.

"Continuance," he answered with a smugness as ripe and colorful as a choni fruit in season. "Rumor has it that a Kanawe is always on the lookout for someone to whom he can pass his knowledge." The Kanawe's eyes took a curious glint, but the rest of his expression adopted a wariness that was no doubt brought on by the sudden playfulness in the boy's voice.

"How do you know I don't have an apprentice already," asked the Master as his arms folded across his chest. "A Kanawe is only ever permitted a single student, after all. I could be rejecting you for good reason." He played back, which only embellished the depth and intensity of the Peasant's smile as he chuckled.

"Perhaps," he said thoughtfully, and paused long enough for the Kanawe to nod and turn for the other end of the alley. "But if you did, your apprentice would travel alongside you. You may have your reasons for the lie, but I already told you. I don't accept your dismissal." The elder eyed the boy for a moment, a thoughtful expression plastered to his face as he stroked his jet-black beard.

"You have wit, I'll give you that," said the Kanawe. He pointed at the boy as a wry smile swept his jaw. "You may be terrible at stealth, but you can at least see through a lie." J'Foja shrugged.

"I've been lied to enough to know my way around deception," he told him. It wasn't an untrue statement, but he dared not speak of the many lies that kept him alive all this time.

"I'll tell you what. In ten days, I will be at the southern gate to handle a task for the *Ubeshu*. Meet me there, and we will see if you can't prove yourself." The sage watched as the youth lit like a fire under the night sky. His dark brown eyes grew wide with realization and stewed with glittering flecks of gold. It was enough to make the Master raise an eyebrow, and with a twist of his lips he added, "But if I hear that you've stolen anything in the meantime, you will have proven my suspicions correct."

"Heh, the ten days is the easy part," J'Foja replied as he clasped his hands together excitedly. "The challenge that I see in all this is what you would have me call you once I succeed." The wise man flashed a knowing smile.

"My name is Y'Sawe," he answered, "but feel free to call me 'Kanawe Y'Sawe,' or something like that." He turned away and walked along the beaten dirt road toward some destination that J'Foja couldn't guess. "I'll see you in ten days!" And with that, the Great Peasant felt a strange twist in his stomach, as if everything about his life was about to change.

***

"I don't think I like Y'Sawe," Kamari complained as he folded his little arms across his chest and pouted. "He confuses me." J'Kana laughed as he scooped up his son and planted a loving kiss on the boy's cheek. The lele mata laughed, and J'Kana's heart swelled like the tide on the night of a full moon.

"Oh, Kanawe Y'Sawe is very hard to read," J'Kana explained as he swung his yilele around the dimly lit room of their chohafi. He threw himself along the well-cushioned length of their couch, the boy wrapped snugly in his arms as high-pitched laughs raised to the ceiling. "But the more you hear of him," the father continued as he sat up and tickled his son, "the more you get used to it."

"Stop, Yababa!" Kamari's delighted squeals only spurred J'Kana on until Nihani entered the room, a single hand on the doorframe while the other rested on her hip. J'Kana immediately noticed her, and for as long as they had been married, she knew that he always had. His fingers slowed in their rapid rake across the boy's tender belly as he lost himself in the shimmer of her golden, blue-ringed eyes. Her lips, split by a confused grin, were full like ripened rena berries from the heart of the Kehemu Forest. When she walked into the room her body moved along the ground with an elegance that no other being could muster, and when she cupped his face in her hands, peered into J'Kana's eyes, he gently took her wrists as he leaned his head against hers.

"Nihani," he whispered, eyes closed now, as if the whole world had faded and left the two of them on a cosmic plane.

"Don't you think," she started back, her tone as hushed as her husband's, "that you should start Kamari's lesson? It's getting late." She watched J'Kana as he blinked twice. His head whipped to the right, and realization took his face as he noticed the boy, seemingly for the first time, now in a seated position next to him.

"Bah," J'Kana said with a dismissive wave and wry smirk, "we can do it tomorrow!"

"Yababa, you promised," Kamari protested, then climbed down from the couch and ran across the room to the shelf with the leather book on it. "You said that after story time I would get a lesson!" Nihani giggled at her little one's enthusiasm as he pulled the book back to his father's lap.

"Very well, Kamari, we can go over some more words before you have to go to bed," he told him, then held his hand out to take the book. Kamari happily handed it over and watched his father flip the front pages in search of a new one. "Ah, look here. There are a few verbs that you should know—"

"Oh!" Kamari exclaimed, "Those go at the end of a sentence, right Yababa?" J'Kana raised an eyebrow as he looked to Kamari first, then Nihani.

"You've been helping him," he said with a smirk. "I thought I was supposed to be the teacher, ne?"

“You can’t expect a mother not to help her son,” Nihani responded with a shrug. When she heard him hum, she gave a shooing wave. “Go on back to your lesson!”

“Mm-hmm,” J’Kana hummed, then returned his attention to his son. “What else have you learned, my son?” Kamari beamed as his eyes met those of his father.

“Well, hafu wu waleya ra N’hafu koshi na shu bachawenati o,” the boy responded. J’Kana chuckled as his brows lifted in shock. The boy had told him that his mother had taught him many things, so J’Kana extended a hand in a gesture that said, “Show me.” The boy smiled brightly, and in it J’Kana saw the best in all Y’Neshu. “Well okay, Yababa. Mother showed me…”

| | | |
|---|---|---|
|  | Hafu | I/Me |
| 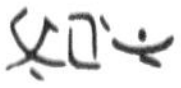 | Bachawe | Teach/Test |
|  | Hara | Being |
|  | Yosha | Wanting/Desire |
|  | Bele | Going |
|  | Chesi | Coming |
| 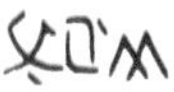 | Bachani | Reading/Hearing/Seeing |
|  | Bibisa | Writing/Telling/Showing |

| | | |
|---|---|---|
|  | Kenani | Love |
| 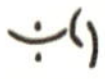 | Wasu | Admiration |
| 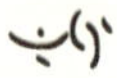 | Weshu | Adoration |
| 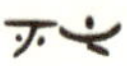 | Yiwe | Appreciation |
|  | Lowena | Amusement |
| 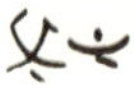 | Bawe | Anger |
| 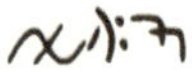 | Tawike | Anxiety |
|  | Tewe | Awe |
|  | Bewinu | Awkwardness |
|  | Howati | Boredom |
| 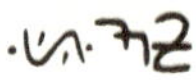 | Jeketi | Calmness |
|  | Yasati | Confusion |
|  | Yifu | Protect |
|  | Sawea | Truthful |
|  | Isu | Clean |
|  | Oshe | Dirty |
|  | Bauna | Know |
|  | -nati | Verb-making suffix (Neutral) |

| -chele | Verb-making suffix (Polite) |
|---|---|
| -basa | Verb-making suffix (Aggressive) |

# 3

# Acceptance

*Yajiri Outskirts—Border Road*

Darkness. They had blindfolded him just before they loaded him into the wagon, but the sounds of the ayena beasts that stalked the Border Road of the land of Y'Sewana told Mahute where he was and when. They laughed somewhere in the barren distance, camouflaged with the deep brown of the desert sands as they stalked some undetermined prey. The scurry of the nocturnal sahele rats along the sand ticked like an erratic clock in his ears. The beat of the tohojo bird's wings thundered against the night air as they surveyed the ground for whatever prey they could manage. Mahute couldn't see it, but he didn't need to. Something about the darkness had become so familiar to him in the twenty years they kept him locked up that tonight, he could tell, was about predators and prey.

He would have folded his arms if it'd been possible, but he was bound, his hands to his feet, as the Y'Rakilian authorities "escorted" him back to Febetu. The heat of the day had given way to nightfall, and as the caravan moved eastward, he could feel something in the blackened sky call to him. A slick smile crept across his face as he remembered the first time he had come this way. He remembered how he shook with anger back then at the thought of his brother, and how the sting of betrayal had burned its way into the deepest reaches of his mind. Y'Sawe had sold him out, had left him alone in the darkness with the minijesi torturers for two excruciatingly long decades. It came as a surprise, however, that Mahute wasn't as angry as he'd thought he would be.

It was true that when he had arrived, he was afraid of the dark, of the pain that came with it, but eventually he came to embrace both. The resistance that he entertained in his earliest days became lost in the blackness that surrounded him. Even now he rested in the cold embrace of the black that thrived in the metal wagon, and took what little time he had left on the road to think. He chuckled. They would probably throw him in the *luse fajari*, the fire room, for his escape, and for each of the guards that the Dagger killed, he would be burned with a spiked metal brand on each of his limbs.

The wound he'd inflicted upon himself itched. The yifusi of Y'Rakili were kind enough to patch him up, but the stitches were still relatively fresh, and the chafing of his clothes against them heightened his discomfort. He knew that the guards of Febetu would probably tear it open as soon as they saw him, a small mark of vengeance to repay him for his actions. He did what he could to prepare himself for the torture when he noticed that everything had grown silent. The howls and laughter of the ayena, the hunting wings of tohojo, and the erratic creeping of the sahele had all been drowned out in the distance, just as the wheels of the wagon ceased to squeak. The devilish grin on Mahute's face blossomed into a full smile as he turned his shielded eyes to the wound in his side.

They stopped moving, and while the Dagger listened for the voices of the police, there was nothing. The darkness had come, and just as he knew it to be, tonight was about predators and prey. His blood pulsed within him, throbbed wildly with whatever had caused the delay, and with each violent jerk within his muscles and skin, the walls of the wagon pushed in on themselves. The cart quaked soundlessly, and even the thrilled laughter of Mahute as he slid about inside suffocated to silence. Everything was still, and then the Dagger was pulled from the back.

***

"Please," begged a guard, the only survivor of the attack. He was a man with skin the color of sand and eyes as dark as the shadows of the forest. His black hair was kept short to fit beneath the regulation silver helmet of the Y'Rakilian Yifusi Ili Division, but it had been knocked away when *it* came, and streams of blood girded his face instead. He crawled in the dirt along the side of the broken metal wagon. If he hadn't witnessed its destruction, he would swear that it had been thrown from the mountains.

His fingertips dug into the ground as his one working leg slowly pushed him forward, and even though the conversation at the back of the cart had ceased, he continued to grunt and scramble and fight. He knew that he couldn't die here. He had to report to Febetu and Y'Rakili what had happened and—

He squelched as serrated talons pierced his heart through the back. He groaned with his arm outstretched, the hope in his eyes faded as his life was expunged. The jagged nails ripped from his back, blood and flesh slashed along the ground, and with delight in its red eyes, the Asanibo licked the splatter from its face.

"As I was saying," came the voice of the Dagger, and the Asanibo warped in a shadow back to Mahute's side, "my attempt to get my brother's blood was unsuccessful. At this rate, it might take another year to find him again." The Asanibo kneeled before Mahute, its eyes fixed upon the ground.

"I beg of you, Master," it rumbled in a voice as deep as a distant thunder, "use us. We are yours to do with as you please. Surely we can assist in this matter—" Mahute held up his hand, and the Asanibo dared not look up.

"We have been over this, have we not," asked the Dagger. He ran a hand along his side and thought back to the violent pulsing of his own blood. His brow was still covered in sweat and his breath was still ragged. "The Blood-Tie will take some time to get used to. I didn't have that chance before I was imprisoned." The Asanibo furrowed its brow as its fangs pierced its lower lip. Mahute had been warned that a lengthy use of the Blood-Tie could affect his health, and that the power should only be handled in small increments. The complexity of the order reflected itself in the pain of the commander, and while it was possible to build a tolerance to something as simple as daily servitude, something as elaborate as a prison break would prove more damaging if done prematurely.

"Master, I—"

"No," Mahute interrupted. The link between them gave the Dagger a window into the monster's mind. He was disgusted with what he saw. "Out of the question, Bahasu." As he spoke the words, he watched as the vampire shook where it knelt. Bahasu's nails dug into its pale white hands and summoned the black fluid that flowed through the monster. "Besides," Mahute continued, "yours is not to recommend to me, but to follow my commands. If the time should arise where I need to do *that*, then I will do it. At the moment, though, I feel no need to resort to something so unseem—" a massive jolt of pain rippled through his side and provoked a guttural scream. His eyes rolled into the back of his head as he fell to the ground. Mahute convulsed, and the pain he felt shot through Bahasu's temple.

Mahute was unable to move, and with every thought that crossed his mind, the pain worsened. Bahasu fell to the ground inches away from his master. The world around them flickered between vibrant colors, blacks and reds, yellows and greens, oranges and browns, whites and grays, each one flooded with the sound of lost souls, crying and weeping and crying and weeping and crying and weeping until nothing could be heard except the faint heartbeat of the Blood-Tie's commander.

The Asanibo crawled through the blood and sands just as the soldier had before he'd killed him. Mahute writhed, his voice a mix of trembling gasps and raucous screams that pierced Bahasu's eardrums. *Just a little further,* Bahasu thought, his arm outstretched toward his Master. He managed to take hold of him, to place his hand upon the knife wound.

"No!" The utterance of the single word was almost enough to blast Bahasu back, but the Asanibo sunk his nails into Mahute's wound. The sound of ripping flesh filled their ears as Bahasu's arm drove deeper into Mahute's gut. Bahasu knew that if he was left alone for too much longer,

Mahute would die and so too would their plans. It was something that he could not allow, not after they had come so far. Bahasu took a deep breath and released it as his red eyes glowed against the dark tapestry of the night.

"Safilakhu ahetu ja beri a yisheyim," the vampire spoke. The incantation sent a jarring pulse through Bahasu as his arms slipped deeper into the tear in Mahute's flesh. He could feel the limbs strip themselves down to their very cells and become one with the Dagger's blood. The monster continued, "N'Mahute ja fara we Bahasu ku a fuejoyim o!" A darkness deeper than the fathoms of the night sky burst violently through the desert, dark lightning sprang from above to turn the sands around the broken wagon to glass, and then stillness.

Mahute sat up, his health restored and the scar at his hip replaced with a seal of black crystal. He thought to be angry that Bahasu had defied his orders, but Mahute would have died otherwise. This was the best option not only for him, but for the plan he'd already set into motion. He smiled with sinister intent as he ran his fingers along the crystal in his hip.

"Very well," he said with an incredulous laugh, "I accept."

***

*Memifi*

The guards threw J'Foja down on the hard concrete, a staple of the upper district roads. The bag was ripped from his head, and the blinding light of the sun against the chohafi's (house's) iron sand-infused beams, all but hypnotized them with their silvery glare. The owner emerged from behind the violet door clothed in golden garments, but the mountain of a man with the shiny bald head from the merchant district stood in the background with his head bowed and his eyes fixed upon the Great Peasant.

"Chafi," spoke the master of the house, and the rumble of his imposing bass struck the rogue with cold realization. J'Foja had stolen from a servant of Babanu, the richest man in Memifi and a lesser noble in Y'Rakili. A bead of cold sweat dripped from his brow and fell to the concrete doorstep. "This is the peasant that stole my money?" Babanu balled a fist into J'Foja's shiki and dragged him to his feet with authority, his arm rested upon J'Foja's shoulder as his iron grip tightened. J'Foja trembled under his touch, but he wouldn't bend from the force that pressed into the space beside his neck. Instead, he took

Babanu in. The golden eyes that looked upon the Great Peasant with shameless disdain gave the aristocrat the image of a *siema*, an angel. The pinched brow, pulsing muscles and a frown that spoke volumes of his perceived superiority, however, said that he wasn't without a fair share of darkness.

"Yes, Lord Babanu," Chafi spoke with a degree of reverence that betrayed a devotion most only had for Y'Kele Himself. J'Foja picked up a hint of satisfaction in Chafi's identification, almost as if he wanted to see the peasant writhe. The grip on the boy's shoulder tightened, and it was more than enough to pull his attention back to the brute before him. J'Foja opened his mouth to speak, but the sudden fist in his gut replaced his intended sounds with the violent wretch of vomit.

"You speak when I tell you to speak," Babanu growled, and shoved J'Foja back. The boy hit the concrete, only a few inches from the puddle, and spasmed from the fresh rush of pain. Babanu turned to the guards that brought the thief to him. "Where was he when you found him?" The way he asked the question made the guards tense in an instant.

"He was on his way to the upper district," Nikeli supplied expeditiously, her arms crossed behind her back and her eyes squinted in the light of her bright silver breastplate. Her blue habesha dress, which contrasted the dull green shiki and jifona of the other three that stood at her back, marked her as a commander in the Royal Guard of Y'Rakili. Even with such a high distinction, bestowed upon her by the Emperor himself, she stood across from Babanu in fear. "We caught him walking through the market." Lord Babanu returned focus to J'Foja, who now slowly scrambled to his feet. The noble crouched down, venom in his glare, and stared J'Foja in the face.

"What do you have to say for yourself," Babanu spat. His breathing was even, but there was a fury behind his expression that craved violent release. J'Foja didn't speak. The pain in his stomach made it hard for him to think straight. He reached into his belt and retrieved a coin purse, held it shakily in the palm of his hand as he extended it to the noble. Babanu's eyes drifted slowly to the round yellow bag covered in dust from all over the city. "What is that?"

"22,000 Bashele," J'Foja croaked. His throat still burned from the acidic spew from before, but he cleared it and continued. “I wanted to pay you back. With interest for the trouble I’ve caused.” The noble’s expression lengthened in surprise, though whether from the admission of guilt or the disclosure of the amount he couldn’t tell. Nobody expected J’Foja, the Great Peasant, to carry such an amount at all, let alone come clean about his actions. He was the playful rogue, the street urchin jester, someone with the plausible deniability of a crime lord’s wife but all the wit to charm her. “I know what I did put you at an inconvenience, and I was wrong not to consider that in my actions,” he added in solemnity. “I beg your forgiveness.”

A long moment lingered between them. The guards stood motionless, unable to comprehend what they’d heard. J’Foja met the gaze of the man before him, a fierce conviction behind the auburn shimmer in his umber eyes. Lord Babanu, suddenly aware of himself and the amount of money in the sack, took the dusty yellow bag from J’Foja’s palm and looked inside. Chafi hurried to his master’s side as his crème white kaftan moved in the breeze, and opened his hands. The noble and his attendant both gawked at the golden luster as the former poured out the contents of the bag. Together they counted. In Chafi’s hands jingled 275 coins, each marked with an 80 on one side and the image of Mount Y’Bayeka on the other. It was a small fortune, enough to at least afford a decent room in an upscale inn. They looked at J'Foja, suddenly filled with questions, and found that the guards had never taken their eyes off of him.

"How did you—" Nikeli started, but was immediately cut off by a satisfied grunt of the noble.

"I accept your apology," Babanu said as he left Chafi to funnel the coins back into the purse. "But how do I know you won't cross me again?" The tension in the air that should've dissipated by now grew stronger as the lord watched J'Foja with more focus, as if he would break the boy in half should he say the wrong thing. Nikeli watched as the Peasant matched the boldness of Babanu's gaze. She held her breath, in full expectation that this would be the moment where J'Foja's endless troublemaking caught up to him.

"I have no reason to," the rogue replied, his eyes sharp and his breathing calm. "A few days ago, I had an encounter that made me realize something important." Babanu's dark eyebrows raised in curiosity as his hand came up to cup his chin. He massaged the edges of his jawline, a captive to his own intrigue now that the ferocity had been assuaged.

"Oh? And what is that," Babanu asked for the second time. A smile wiser than he'd ever shown tugged at the corners of J'Foja's mouth as he breathed out a yet playful chuckle.

"That how I treat people today will affect what I am able to do with my future," J'Foja supplied. "Once upon a time I believed myself to be capable of more than what I've done. I lost my way, but I have the motivation to return to the proper path." The corner of the noble's mouth wrinkled with a half-cocked grin born of his satisfied ears.

"Officers," he began with a severity of tone that, for a moment, chilled J'Foja's blood, "release him. The young man has convinced me of his conviction, and I am excited to see what he becomes." The flippant dismissal in the wake of such a palpable anger caught them all by surprise, most of all J'Foja, who still sat in the dirt after his release. Lord Babanu smiled at him as he helped him—rather brutishly—to his feet. He lifted his massive hand with all the speed of a rayemo beast on the hunt. J'Foja flinched, fully expectant of another blow, but it never came. Babanu placed his hand gently atop the boy's head in such a way that sent waves of ethereal warmth through him. "I am putting my faith in you, *ulu fojara*," Babanu said with welcome kindness, but before J'Foja could take comfort in the show of confidence, Babanu's glare narrowed. "Don't make me regret it."

***

Y'Sawe sat in the comfort of the Ubeshu's home, carefully positioned out of the way of the clear glass window of the chohafi. He came under the pretense of inquiry, and while Bamaje, the Chief of Memifi, rattled on about the issue south of the city, the Kanawe feigned interest. In reality, he watched the green-coated wall behind the ubeshu's head with great expectation.

"Ti N'hafu shu bibisachele," the Teacher whispered tenderly to the wall as he lifted the cup of *echa*, tea, to his lips. He sipped the warm liquid and savored its cinnamon citrus flavor. It always struck him as funny, though, that to see or hear through a wall, the command must be issued in gentleness, and the concept of "bibisa," to write or tell or show, be uttered with the politest suffix. His brow furrowed, which Chief Bamaje understood to be an expression of intrigue rather than the stifling of humor that it was. How would Master Y'Sawe explain it to his host if he laughed at the temperamentality of a wall?

"Kanawe," the ubeshu interrupted with an authoritative gravitas that could only come from a political leader, "will that be acceptable?" Kanawe Y'Sawe blinked twice, stunned back to the dimly lit room of green walls and brown furniture.

"Of course, Ubeshu," the Master replied with a calmness to his voice that assuaged the hurt feelings of his host. "My apologies, Bamaje. I got lost in the earthy colors of your home. The coordination between the green of the walls with the wood-colored furniture and the cream of the tiles gives me the impression of being surrounded by nature." The chief beamed.

"I can hardly blame you for being relaxed," said the ubeshu with a hearty chuckle. "With all the stress that comes with managing Memifi, I needed my home to feel like an escape into the wildest reaches of Y'Neshu."

"Well, surely you've accomplished that," Y'Sawe applauded with faux intrigue. He smiled as the ubeshu continued to talk about the design of his house, but returned his attention back to the scene that played out at Lord Babanu's estate.

"…Once upon a time I believed myself to be capable of more than what I've done. I lost my way, but I have the motivation to return to the proper path," he heard the boy say, his voice shaky but wistful. The look that he sported was like that of a man who had conquered a torturous enemy. Y'Sawe donned a look of pleasant surprise, happy to hear the humility and transparency in the boy's voice. He looked at Babanu, the rather brutish noble dressed in billowy golden jifona and kaftan, and noted that he offered an uncharacteristically kind smile. The noble ordered the boy's release, and Y'Sawe leaned to the side in his chair to get a better view of the scene.

"I am putting my faith in you, ulu fojara," Babanu told the young rogue, but before the Master could see what happened next, Ubeshu Bamaje leaned over and blocked his view.

"Is everything alright, Kanawe?" The chief's question was more pointed than curious, and Y'Sawe kicked himself for being too obvious. He cleared his throat and gave an uneasy smile.

"Back pain," was the excuse that he gave. "I haven't been the same since I was 25, o." The chief, suddenly mortified, lifted a hand to cover his mouth.

"I'm so sorry," he pleaded in a manner so dramatic that Y'Sawe had to resist the urge to roll his eyes. "Is the chair uncomfortable? I can have one of the servants fetch another—"

"That will not be necessary," the teacher assured him. A glance behind the official's head showed the boy on his way back toward the city's east gate. Y'Sawe stood with more haste than he should have, but at this point didn't care to hide his urgency. "I should get going. Thank you for your hospitality and, of course, the finer details on your predicament." Before the chief could even form a response, Y'Sawe saw himself to the door and into the streets of Memifi's upper district.

After their first meeting, the Ile Kanawe made up his mind to keep tabs on the peasant boy, and knew after the first week where he would go and what he would do. When it began, he assumed that the boy would try to steal as much as he could, and play it off as though he had kept his end of the bargain. J'Foja did no such thing. He walked the streets of the city and bent a knee to everyone he'd ever wronged. He worked himself to the bone to help them so he could atone for his past misdeeds. Most of the people he'd helped had paid him for the work, and what he earned he didn't spend on himself. J'Foja put it in a box beyond the outskirts, buried deep within the Outer Grasslands so that nobody else could take it. The Grand Master had never seen someone so young repent so thoroughly, and all by the ninth day of the test.

Y'Sawe took every side road and back alley through the colorful city that he could manage, and somehow beat J'Foja to his hutije grass shelter. He gingerly leaned against the brown straw as the sky rippled with pinks and oranges in the dying lights of a setting sun. He looked up, careful to control his breathing to make it seem as though he hadn't run, and saw J'Foja as he approached. An incredulous look took the boy's face.

"To what do I owe the pleasure of a Kanawe at my door," J'Foja asked as he spread his arms wide in welcome. Y'Sawe raised an eyebrow as the corner of his mouth pulled into a smile. He eyed the darkened grass of the hut surrounded by the grayish blue tint of the Grasslands in the fading lights of the waning day. It was as if all color in the world now mixed in the radiant violets and indigos as the sky continued its transition. The Master looked back at the boy.

"You call this a door," he asked as he pointed to the tattered gray cloth that draped over the opening. J'Foja adopted a wounded expression as his hand flew to the space above his heart.

"It was the best I could do," J'Foja replied defensively. Y'Sawe raised an eyebrow.

"Even with 22,000 Bashele?" The question reverberated through the young thief's mind. He opened his mouth to speak, then closed it when the realization set in.

"You've been watching me," J'Foja deduced, and the smile on the Teacher's face grew wider.

"You expected me to consider an apprentice with no knowledge of who he was?" The boy shook his head, and Y'Sawe chuckled. He explained everything about the last nine days, how he watched the former thief and listened to any word on the street about him. He even confessed to telling the guards where to find him when the funds he stole from Babanu's attendant had been recovered.

"Ah," J'Foja said with a fire behind his eyes, "so it's you I owe for the punch to the gut earlier." He stepped forward, and a warning glance from the Ile Kanawe provoked a stagger in his stride. Instead of whatever mischief he had planned, he moved to enter the makeshift house.

"What are you doing," Y'Sawe asked flatly, a look of genuine confusion on his face as he watched the boy stop halfway through the opening in the "wall." "A Kanawe and his *ijeya* travel together, remember?" The boy took a double take.

"What?" Y'Sawe shook his head. He knew that the boy would be stunned, but he half expected him to jump up in excitement at the news.

"Come now," he ordered in a way that harkened back to their first encounter. "We will discuss your first assignment over Lushuki. After that, you will begin your training." He turned away from the hut without so much as a glance at J'Foja. The boy blinked, and when it hit him that he had been accepted, he rushed after his new Master with joy in his heart.

***

J'Kana wanted to test the *lele ili*, the little one, with a slightly longer part of the story, and adopted a wry smirk when Kamari rubbed his eyes as his mouth opened for a yawn. He took his son in his arms as he stood to his feet, and made his way from the brown and tan living room of their chohafi towards Kamari's room.

"Wait, Yababa," Kamari cried, and wiggled so much that J'Kana had to put him down. *So,* J'Kana thought, *he noticed.* With as much speed as his little legs could muster, Kamari ran across the floor to the shelf that held the tattered leather book. He pulled the slender metal key from the lock over its front and opened it himself, though the sight of so much J'Karo made his eyes widen in shock.

"That's right," his father spoke with his arms crossed over his chest as he walked back into the *luseme*. "I almost forgot about your lesson." Kamari pouted with his lip poked out, a trait that the boy certainly got from his mother, as he brought the book back over to where J'Kana stood. "Where do you want to go this time? Do you want me to give you more words to study?" Kamari shook his head as he gently pressed against J'Kana's thigh and sat upon his lap when the elder took the hint.

"We can do that another time, Yababa," he said, more awake now than when the story began. J'Kana knew that Nihani would have something to say to him if he couldn't get Kamari down for the night. "I want to learn how to speak it like you do." The Sage thought for a moment, perhaps a moment too long, as Kamari looked at him with puffed out cheeks that conveyed his frustration.

"Very well, then," he finally said, and pressed his palms against Kamari's cheeks to deflate them. The boy laughed, an innocent ring in J'Kana's ears that inspired him to provoke more of it, but he knew that there was no time. The sun had gone down a little while ago, and ulu Kamari needed to go to bed soon. "You already know that the verb comes at the end of the sentence, and you know that 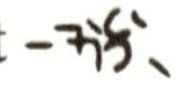  and  change base concepts into verbs. Look here," J'Kana directed to a page that showed four lists. "First, you have the particles. These help the person you're talking to make sense of the language. Every sentence needs to have a subject, but the presence of the others depends on what you're trying to say."

Kamari carefully inspected the page and took in everything he could about the particles. He wasn't completely sure how they worked, but he thought to give it a try anyway.

"So, if I wanted to say, 'I want my mother,' I would say, '?" J'Kana blinked absently in surprise.

"Yes," he said, still momentarily stunned, "and if you wanted to ask a question?" Kamari gave it a bit of thought, and cupped his chin in his small hand, an act that he replicated from his father.

“I think it would be like asking ‘how are you,’” the boy supplied with a smug smile. J’Kana raised an eyebrow.

“You are right, hafu wu shehefo,” the Kanawe commended. “Now, look here at the other suffixes.” He pointed down the page at the second and third lists that showed the conjugations for adverbs and adjectives. He explained what they were so that Kamari would understand how to describe verbs and nouns respectively, careful to distinguish between the formal and informal uses. Kamari again watched his father’s fingers trace the page, and soaked in the new knowledge like the teal and green ubuji fish absorbed nutrients from the water.

“What about that one,” asked the lele mata, the little boy, as he pointed to the list at the bottom of the page.

“That one is for the attachments, known as fixtures. These things will alter the endings of certain words to change their meaning.” He could tell by the look on Kamari’s face that he didn’t fully understand. “Say I wanted to tell you that I love you and you make me happy.” The boy smiled at the sudden kindness from his father. “ƶ

Do you see how 'me' attaches to 'kenanina-' to give us the meaning of 'and' at the end of the verb?" Kamari nodded confidently, but not as much as before. J'Kana chuckled lovingly. "Maybe we should spend a few days working on it, ne?" Kamari nodded as he rubbed his eyes, while J'Kana moved to put him to bed.

**Particles**

1. (Ra)—Subject Marker
2. (Shu)—Object Marker
3. (Yo)—Concrete Marker
4. (Ti)—Abstract/Ethereal Marker
5. (Wu)—Possession Marker
6. (E)—Question Marker
7. (O)—Emphasis Marker
8. (Ne)—Agreement Seeker

9. (Na)—Alternative Question Marker

## Adverb Suffixes

1. (Konali)—Common use
2. (Ale)—Honorific or formal use

## Adjective Suffixes

1. (Nawe)—Common use
2. (Yishu)—Honorific or formal use

## Fixtures

1. (me)—And/plus/with
2. (chu)—Negative form
3. (ni)—Pulralizer

# 4

# The Trial

*Memifi*

For a while they sat in silence. Y'Sawe was content to allow J'Foja the opportunity to look around the restaurant. The Hidden Beast, as it was called, was known for its succulent dishes across the continent. When the Ile Kanawe suggested they get Lushuki, J'Foja hadn't considered the best in Y'Neshu as an option. Everywhere he looked, the walls were covered in gold leaf, decorated with a wide array of pictographs from the Jeniju colony in the Great Kahali Reef. The tables were made of thick wood from the soso trees of the Kehemu forest, known for its dark brown color and its resistance to fire. They, along with the crystal glasses and porcelain plates that adorned the tables, glimmered in the golden candlelight that augmented the gleam of the walls.

"This place is amazing," J'Foja commented absently, wholly engulfed with the flames of excitement as the servers moved through the crowded restaurant with elegance befitting the palace. Y'Sawe couldn't help but silently agree. They brought the food, two orders of vibrantly colored Lushuki. The Master watched as his new tentative apprentice donned the look of an excited child. The sparkle of the red weka pepper and yellow choni fruit against the light brown of the well-seasoned hibesa bird presented as jewels atop the bed of pristine white mili grain. Everything about the place betrayed inspiration from all over Y'Neshu, from the dishes native to Y'Rakili to the floor-based seating of Y'Baule, to the musicians in the background that played songs of Y'Fuwefo. It told of a world much larger than any one person, one of unity that stretched beyond imagination.

"As beautiful as the Hidden Beast is," Y'Sawe commented with a gravity to his voice that pulled J'Foja's attention, "we do still have important business to discuss." J'Foja took his fork in his hand and, for a moment, stared down at the plate as if eating the food before him was a crime against his eyes. His stomach growled, and as if to heed its order, the boy began to eat.

"You said that we had an assignment from the chief," J'Foja commented, his face full of the hibesa bird and jawline covered in honey hot sauce and gravy. Y'Sawe stifled a smile.

"Please," he urged, and motioned for the napkin beside J'Foja's plate, "don't talk with your mouth full." He unfolded his own and placed it in his lap, then mouthed a hushed prayer to Y'Kele before he gracefully cut into the dish himself. "Chief Bamaje," he continued, and tasted how strange the title was on his tongue, "has given me the news that a pack of ara beasts has settled in a cave south of Memifi. From what the Ubeshu tells me, it used to be the den of a rayemo that the Memifians saw as a protector."

J'Foja thought about the one time he'd seen a rayemo beast. They were strong, feline creatures with bushy manes that pulsed with lightning. They had the ability to run on wind currents and manipulate air with the sound of their roars. A fully grown rayemo was as tall on all fours as a fully grown man. They had never been known to eat people, but they were fiercely defensive of their territory. It wasn't a stretch to assume that it had simply taken a fondness to the area and defended it out of the habit. Then it occurred to him what Kanawe Y'Sawe had said. The cave *used* to be the den of a rayemo.

The apprentice dropped his jaw as his eyes met the Teacher's. "Wait, does that mean that the rayemo was killed by the ara beasts?" Y'Sawe briefly looked up from his meal as he took another bite of the spicy-sweet Lushuki before his eyes turned to the cup of choni fruit juice meant to wash it down. He sipped from the cup, and J'Foja could see the euphoria born from an amplification of the dish's flavor.

"It's possible," the Master admitted. "Rumor has it that there were at least five spotted in the Outer Grasslands. Ara beasts are pack animals, so they could have attacked the rayemo as a unit. Despite the obvious difference in size, the numbers advantage would definitely take its toll. Not to mention that the fire of a full pack of ara would dwarf the strongest windblast of a single rayemo."

J'Foja's eyes blurred, and for a moment he thought he saw himself surrounded by the five blazing dogs, each one with a snarl on its lips and red spots emblazoned on its black fur. J'Foja looked hastily from one side to the next, whipped around, met the eyes of each of the beasts as smoke fumed from between their bared, jagged teeth. The temperature rose as orange sparks flew to the ground every time they barked. A ring of fire quickly ignited in the hutije grass, and J'Foja watched as the ring of beasts that sparked it walked forebodingly through the flames. Their yellow eyes glowed in the shadow of the black cloud of smoke, and before he could think, the beasts attacked.

"Are you alright?" The voice called to him from a distance, through the rumble of beastly growls. "Apprentice?" The shouting of the term jolted J'Foja from a sudden blackness that swam around him like a midnight sea before his realization. Y'Sawe sat next to him now, his hand firmly pressed against the boy's back and eyes filled with concern.

"I saw them," J'Foja spoke before he thought. His breath was ragged, sweat dripped from his brow, and he shook. The warm golden glow of the Hidden Beast bathed him in a kind of relief that he had never experienced. He fixed his gaze to the night-colored eyes of the Kanawe. "I was surrounded by the ara—"

"You were what?" Both the Kanawe and the apprentice furrowed their brows. A silence grew between them that sharply contrasted the clinking of silverware and dishes, and stirred something in J'Foja. The boy continued to relay the experience, the fear of it, the heat, and with each detail the severity of Y'Sawe's face escalated.

"What just happened, Kanawe," J'Foja whispered, worry rooted in his shaken tone. Y'Sawe eyed him with a scrutinous suspicion that made him shrink back even more. The Elder sighed as he corrected his expression and pat the boy on the back.

"I can't say for sure," the Master admitted slowly, "not without more information. What it sounds like, though, is *maa bacha*." J'Foja looked at him quizzically as Y'Sawe returned to his side of the table and drank again from his glass of choni juice. J'Foja struggled to recall what his Yababa had said about the maa bacha years ago, but the memories were so clouded that he couldn't begin to make sense of them. He fixed his mouth to ask the Ile Kanawe, but Y'Sawe continued. "In any case, such a thing should hardly be our focus right now. It goes without saying that the mission with which we have been entrusted is a dangerous one that cannot be performed to satisfaction by the Y'Rakilian Royal Guard. Why?"

The sudden question caught J'Foja off guard, and he struggled to swallow the lump of hibesa meat in his throat to offer an answer.

"Fire," the boy answered. "The ara beasts' ability to breathe fire would work against the metal armor and cloth attachments."

"And in the Grasslands, it could work to cause more damage than necessary," Y'Sawe added, and while J'Foja shrank back into the cushion of his chair, Y'Sawe offered a proud grin. "That is why Ubeshu Bamaje asked for my help. We have to clear out the ara without burning down Memifi in the process."

"So how do we do that?" J'Foja's question struck the Kanawe as a melody, and split the sage's lips into a wide smile. Golden light flickered in the man's dark eyes.

"N'J'Karo," Y'Sawe responded, and it was enough to make the boy's eyes widen in excitement. "You wanted to be my apprentice, so I trust you know the basic principles?"

"Well," J'Foja started with a sheepish smile, and the Teacher's face instantly sobered. "I know a few basics, but I haven't had much in the way of teachers over the last decade." Y'Sawe sighed, and cut another piece loose from the Lushuki.

"Tell me what you know, then," he urged.

"J'Karo is a syllabic language, which means that unlike Katsedu or Pedestrian, its 86 characters represent whole sounds. Verbs come at the ends of sentences, and with the right combination of words, power is released from Y'Kele," the boy offered, and watched the Teacher. Y'Sawe bobbed his head from side to side as he considered the Great Peasant's explanation.

"You're not completely wrong," Y'Sawe told him. "In the beginning, J'Karo did come from Y'Kele, and was the source of all life in Y'Neshu. But do you know why Y'Kele gifted the language to begin with?" J'Foja shook his head and popped another morsel of Lushuki into his mouth. Y'Sawe smiled, a clear sign that he loved the story he had just begun, and was glad to continue. "Y'Kele, the Divine Creator, created the world in seven days and saw that all of His creation was good. In the overflow of His affection, He opened His mouth and poured J'Karo upon the land to give everything life, energy, and the ability to communicate. What you and I recognize as an ancient language, Y'Kele intended to be a lifeline, a connection between the spirits of this world and the essence of its Creator." J'Foja's mouth fell open, but before he could speak, Y'Sawe continued. "You see, before J'Karo came, every creature under the sun was a mere body, incapable of thought or feeling, driven by primal instincts like hunger and sleep. The world was doused in unintelligible color and sound, the likes of which couldn't be described, but after, J'Karo gave rise to a vibrance that gave birth to a communion of souls and higher thoughts. Y'Kele never envisioned a mindless wandering of physical forms to be the full extent of His creation. What He wanted was to plant the seed for relationship."

"Is that really how it happened," J'Foja asked, voice full of skepticism but eyes full of childlike wonder. Y'Sawe nodded, a knowing grin returned to his face now. There was a wistfulness in his eyes, something peaceful yet full of longing, as if he remembered telling the story a long time ago and under more ideal conditions.

"It is," he finally said. "In the days of the M'Iba Chami, the original people, everyone had the ability to shift the ike and tap into the full power of J'Karo." Y'Sawe saw an eyebrow raise on the boy's face and chuckled as he clasped his hands together and pointed. "Are you familiar with the term?"

"I might've heard it once or twice," J'Foja shrugged. He did his best to return to his usual nonchalant tone of voice, which made Y'Sawe shake his head.

"Do you always have to sound like a mercenary cutting a deal," he asked, and watched as the boy's face contorted.

"I do not," he protested smoothly, "but I doubt you would take kindly to the charming rogue that I put on for Nikeli." Y'Sawe laughed, and the jovial sound that erupted from his core infected J'Foja.

"Listen," begged the Teacher, "you don't have to keep your guard up here. In fact, you might find that it hurts the process." J'Foja raised a suspicious eyebrow as he swallowed more of the mili grain. The savor of the hibesa gravy mingled with the sweetness of the weka and choni sauce perfectly. The spice came later, and pulled the flavors of the dish out in such a manner that proved the mastery of the chef.

"What process?"

"Heh! Haven't you been paying attention," Y'Sawe asked, intention written about his face. "If you want to help me with this task, then you need to learn how to shift the ike when you speak J'Karo. Otherwise, you won't be able to do much."

"You expect me to be able to use some kind of ancient magic at will in under a day?" J'Kana's tone and face reflected his incredulity, and made Y'Sawe wonder how many times he really wore his emotions out in the open. The teacher turned his attention to the glass of choni juice in front of him and felt it with the back of his palm. Where it was once chilled to the touch, it now drifted to the warm temperature of the room.

"Chill my glass," Y'Sawe commanded with a curious glint in his eye. J'Foja considered the man for a moment, unsure what his response should be, and in the second that he took too long to figure out his play, Y'Sawe noticed. "Don't tell me that you're going to continue to feign ignorance."

"How did you know I speak a little?"

"I didn't," Y'Sawe smirked as his arms crossed in front of him, "until now."

J'Foja inhaled deeply as he shifted his gaze from the old man across the table to the glass he was ordered to chill. He did speak J'Karo at one point, but it was a long time ago. He never even really learned how it worked, just that it could with enough conviction. Still, he could see that Y'Sawe's expectations were set. There was no backing out now that he had worked so hard to get here.

"Fine," said the boy. He fixed his mouth to speak, extended a hand towards the glass. Y'Sawe stifled a laugh. "N'jekume ifinati!" There was another moment of silence between them. Y'Sawe didn't need to feel the glass to know that the temperature hadn't changed. J'Foja frowned. "What's wrong?"

"Nothing happened," replied the sage. "You didn't scratch the bubbly buttocks of the ike, let alone shift it."

"Odd analogy," J'Foja commented. He felt the laugh bubble up within him, but a sharp glare from Y'Sawe squashed it like a bug. "But what was I supposed to do? I spoke the words—"

"And that was *all* you did," Y'Sawe clarified. He felt off. It had been a long time since he had made any attempt to teach, and it was when he realized that that he also realized what his purpose here was. "Still, your speaking ability was better than I expected it would be."

"Wasn't good enough if I couldn't do what you asked," J'Foja answered flatly. "I think that proves that I shouldn't be expected to go into the commandeered den of ara beasts with no training." Y'Sawe adopted a half-smile as he spread his arms wide in a welcoming gesture.

"Then we train," the Teacher conceded. J'Foja stumbled to speak, his mouth opened and closed like a fish deprived of water, and while Y'Sawe took much enjoyment from watching the boy struggle to find a way out, he decided to continue his thought. "Your speech pattern shows what you don't know as much as what you do. First, it should be noted that shifting the ike is about more than just speaking the right words. J'Karo has no incantations that just release magical power with enough focus. There is no motion for you to make that will do that either," he said, and watched as the boy adopted an embarrassed glow. "If you want to speak J'Karo to power, then keep these four things in mind: Particles, Structure, Understanding, and Intent."

"I'm already lost," J'Foja chuckled, then sipped from the glass of choni juice that the waiter had refilled a few moments before Y'Sawe's challenge.

"Don't give me that," Y'Sawe dismissed with a passive wave of his hand. "You don't understand the uses, sure, but I haven't said anything that was too challenging for the legendary J'Foja to comprehend." The boy's eyes went wide, and Y'Sawe adopted a look of pure smugness. "Oh, yes, I knew exactly who you were from the moment you approached me. I have to admit, you were a bit different than I expected, and that is the only reason you sit before me now. But watch and learn."

"What do you—" J'Foja started, but was quickly cut off by the Master's raised hand.

"Ti olea N'tebi, somi hafu ni ra, tokiji shu natienati o." Master Y'Sawe spoke calmly, so it came as a shock to J'Foja that the entire restaurant froze. The glimmer of gold that radiated from all directions, even over the black wood of the tabletops, still shone brightly in their eyes, but the people, who lived so colorfully amid the ambience, now sat or stood in a mad variety of poses. The gentle cacophony of plates and cups and bowls and silverware in use throughout the Hidden Beast halted without warning, and the only two that were left to move freely were the Master and his apprentice.

"When you speak," Y'Sawe instructed, his voice as a crashing cymbal that pulled J'Foja from his astonishment, "be careful to use more than the simplest language conventions. The particles 'ti' or 'yo' must come first. They provide guidance for your ike, and will either affect the natural world around you, or concepts to which all creation are beholden. You might have noticed that for everyone else here, time has stopped."

"No, I didn't notice," J'Foja quipped with unrestrained sarcasm. Y'Sawe raised an eyebrow again, and J'Foja bowed his head. "My apologies."

"As I was saying," the Ile Kanawe continued, "the particles are not enough to affect change. They only give direction for the ike to shift, but the key to releasing power is a combination of sentence structure and intent. The former is flexible in J'Karo, and with your ability to stitch a sentence together, I won't spend too much time on it. Intention, however, is a different story." J'Foja shook his head.

"I already tried to chill the glass with all the focus I had in me—"

"That doesn't matter," the Kanawe interrupted. "Intent has little to do with the objective and everything to do with an intertwining of souls. J'Karo is a language of connection. It bound all of Y'Neshu together with Y'Kele even during the worst of our collective history. That is the bond that you must endeavor to forge now. Even if you were going to do something as simple as chill the glass, you have to commune with Y'Kele to do it. Think of the particles as opening the doorway to the other side. They stir the ike, specifically the part of it that seeks to reach out to its Creator. The structure determines the attitude of the hearers, those being the thing to which you give commands, and the Creator with whom you seek to bond. Your intent is how sincere you are, and your understanding of vocabulary, that is how precise you appear. These factors determine the actions that take place in the wake of your speech. An improper approach is hardly any different from a nonchalant one." J'Foja's brow furrowed as his heart raced. Something in him stirred at the explanation, as if a piece of his destroyed former life had come back to him. Somewhere in the back of his mind, he could hear the same lesson but in gentler terms. His yababa's voice suddenly whispered in the back of his mind. *Try again.* "Try again," Y'Sawe told him with a knowing smile.

J'Foja breathed deeply as the cup slid forward on the table and the juice within washed the walls that contained it like the tide washes the sands of the beach. He looked back at the sage, both of them now with solemn, unreadable expressions. J'Foja nodded, and shook his hands to loosen himself up.

"Ti N'jekume ifinati o." The boy spoke calmly now, and his deep brown eyes took on a golden glint. There was no extension of his hand, no humored expression on the face of his Master, only a frost that took to both the juice and J'Foja's fingertips. A smile immediately swept his jawline, disbelief plastered to his face as a chuckle ripped between his teeth.

"Well done," Y'Sawe lauded, an impressed frown emblazoned across his face. "Here," he said as he slid a slip of parchment across the table. He withdrew some Bashele and left the mixture of gold, silver and bronze coins at the center of the table. "Take some time tonight to study. We strike at first light tomorrow morning, when we should be able to take the ara by surprise."

"Yes, Kanawe," J'Foja replied through shortness of breath and a slight pinch in his chest. The sage rose from his seat, whispered a command in J'Karo, and the restaurant began to move again with sounds and shadows. The apprentice stood to his feet, but the shock that hit his body sent him back to his seat. Y'Sawe noticed, and helped the boy back up.

"I forgot to mention," he said with a warmth to his voice that hadn't been there before, "I paid for a room for you at the Y'Tunu Inn." The Teacher spoke, of course, of the upper district inn not far from the Hidden Beast. It was named after the first of the Wayi Kanawe to come from Y'Rakili, just after the Thousand-Year War.

"Why," J'Foja was forced to ask as they made for the door. Such kindness hadn't been shown to him since Shifi. All of Memifi seemed to be content to leave him in the Outer Grasslands to fend for himself. Kanawe Y'Sawe didn't offer much of a response, but decidedly asked a single question that stunned J'Foja to a warm silence: "Otaba ra hafu wu ijeya haranati ne?" *You are my apprentice, right?*

***

*Outer Grasslands—Memifi Outskirts*

First light came faster than J'Foja thought it would, and when the Master knocked on the door to his room, he didn't want to get up. His night had been filled with a good meal, the first bath he'd taken in Y'Kele knew how long, and the softest bed he'd ever had the pleasure to sleep in. His morning, on the other hand, came with Y'Sawe dragging him from that blissfully soft bed and throwing him, quite literally, to the wolves. They stood under the emergent blues of the sky as the vibrant rays of the sun contributed a mixture of oranges and pinks. The lush, dark green of the hutije tall grass swayed with every step, and the light breeze that occasionally brushed his face almost made him believe that perhaps the chief was mistaken.

Then, he felt Y'Sawe slow in his stride. J'Foja took the hint and lowered himself into the tall grass as his Master had. They neared a cave that stood just before a thicket of marula trees, and heard the stir of the grass. For a moment, it gave J'Foja the same sensational thrill he'd experienced as a child on the hunt for his father. Another moment proved that he should have been more careful. Had it not been for the lightning reflexes of his Teacher, a burst of fire would have twisted across his skin and clothes the way it did the hutije. J'Foja fell to the ground as the smoke hit the air, but Y'Sawe pulled him back to his feet and pushed him out of the way of another blast at seemingly the same time. The sudden flashes of heat that burst through the air made it hard to breathe, but J'Foja knew that if he fell here, he might never get back up.

"What do we do, Kanawe," the boy asked. The crackle of fire and the sting in his lungs took him back to the night that Shifi burned. He could hear in the ara beasts' snarls the hungry moans of the elokobi that his mother and their neighbors had turned into. He remembered a bright flash, a sudden burst of healing to his body, and then the smell of the tall grass on the other side of the city.

"We need to minimize the damage," Y'Sawe called in an unusual calm. "Did you study?" The boy rolled out of the way of the open jaws of an airborne ara on pure instinct, and locked eyes with the monster as he nodded. "Good." The moment an ara beast lunged for the sage it was repulsed with a violent fury, but righted itself before its body met the dirt. J'Foja was jolted by the sudden appearance of another, and as the other three closed in on him in circular formation, a crack rippled through reality.

Darkness fell anew over the Outer Grasslands, but only where J'Foja stood surrounded by the infernal dogs. On the outside, Y'Sawe spoke beneath his breath.

Rainclouds formed just over the lines of fire that the beasts had blazed before, but J'Foja realized quickly that his focus would be better spent on the monsters. J'Foja looked hastily from one side to the next, whipped around, and met the eyes of each of the beasts as smoke fumed from between their bared, jagged teeth.

"No," J'Foja breathed. He realized that he now lived the vision from the dinner table. The temperature rose on every side as orange sparks flew to the ground every time they barked. Fear struck him as he flashed back to the past as images of the fiery eruption of a cart burst into his mind's eye. A ring of fire quickly ignited in the hutije grass, and J'Foja watched as the pack of ara walked forebodingly, threateningly through the flames. Their yellow eyes glowed in the shadow of the black cloud of smoke, and before he could think, the beasts attacked.

The first beast leapt at him, mouth agape and hot with embers as it stretched its claws towards the Great Peasant's face. J'Foja rolled beneath it, and as it landed on the other side of the ring of fire, the second beast bit at his leg. With every ounce of strength he could summon, J'Foja pushed off the ground and jumped out of the way. Two more ara bounded for him, teeth bared and molten saliva alight along their jaws. As they sprinted for him, the other three ran in circles on the outer edge of the formation. He was trapped.

The smoke grew thicker as the grass burned brighter now. The flames started to spread throughout the dome of darkness as the air failed with increasing measure to meet J'Foja's lungs. He watched the wolves close in, felt the heat of their arid breath against his skin as it sapped the moisture from the air. He locked eyes with one of the creatures as it closed in, as four of the five paced the ground to remind him of how helpless he was, but then he noticed it. The final ara beast pawed at the edge of the darkness, only to find that it—and the other beasts by extension—had been trapped along with him. Moreover, the fires of the pack could only spread within its confines. The ara growled and barked, more sparks hit the ground, but no new fire could spread. J'Foja felt the sudden swell that he had the night before, and again he heard his yababa speak to him, command him to try again.

J'Foja looked around from beast to beast as he mouthed a small prayer to Y'Kele. They all lunged for him at the same time now, eager to rip their teeth through his flesh, but J'Foja stood with courage in his eyes as his lips parted and he recalled some of the words from the list. His mind raced to assemble a command from the scraps he'd been fed. If he used wind, the fires would grow and the ara would have their meal of him yet. Ice and water were out of the question since their breath had dried everything up.

"Yo bushake ra tuketubasa o!" J'Foja's shout shifted the earth beneath his feet and crafted a platform that broke from the fires below as a pillar burst from the rock beneath the field. The ara that attacked him each collided unceremoniously with the column, and fell limp to the ground beneath the cloud of smoke. J'Foja's vision blurred. His knees buckled. His heart thumped loudly in his ears as he hunched over atop the column. So, he was right. Shifting the ike this much took a toll on his body. He had to admit that the smoke didn't help anything. Still, if he didn't give another command, he would die. He spoke again, this time to the pillar. "Yo bushake ra taramuchele," he whispered to the rock, and slowly it made its descent back into the field from which it came.

J'Foja collapsed to the ground completely as the flames crackled all around him. The ara beasts were dead now, their once long snouts whittled down to a spattering of blood and bone. The light of the sun was drowned out by the thick black smoke that steadily lifted to the skies as an offering to the Creator, and the dark chamber that contained it all shattered like black glass. J'Foja chuckled. The rays of the sun took to his eyes, then a darkness stronger than any before.

***

"Wow," Kamari gasped as he sat squarely on his father's lap, his eyes filled with wonder and trained on J'Kana's face. "J'Foja did it!" J'Kana smiled as he tousled the tight black curls on Kamari's head. The sky was a bit lighter today. J'Kana thought it best to give the boy his story and lesson a bit earlier after Nihani chewed him out for keeping him up so late the night before.

"Indeed, he did! And you see that Kanawe Y'Sawe was a lot nicer than you thought, ne?" Kamari crossed his little arms.

"I still don't know about that, Yababa," the little one said with a shrug that aroused a chuckle from J'Kana. "But he did give him food and a good place to sleep so I guess he can be a little nice."

"You sound like you're determined not to like him," J'Kana joked, but Kamari simply shrugged again. He climbed down from J'Foja's lap and ran across the wooden floor of their chohafi, straight for the small leather book filled with J'Karo. The little one stopped for a moment, his eyes wide as if he saw the truth of the language for the first time. "Kamari? Is everything alright?"

"Yes, Yababa," he said, and hurried back to his father's lap. "Does it actually work like Y'Sawe said at the Hidden Beast?" J'Kana scooped the boy into his arms, book and all.

"It does," he confirmed, "but do you really think you're ready to take on such a challenge?"

"Hmm," Kamari hummed thoughtfully as his little hands rested on J'Kana's forearms. "I don't know, but I want to try it." J'Kana looked around the room, then over his shoulder. He checked the openings to the room from his seat, and then he flashed his son a smile that reeked of mischief.

"I'll tell you what," he started in a whisper, "if you can learn the next set of vocabulary in the next week, we can find out together if you're ready." Kamari squealed with excitement, and J'Kana had to cup a hand over his mouth to keep Nihani from hearing. He looked frantically between the entryways of the room before he felt a wet slither across his palm. Kamari had licked him. "Ugh!" Kamari giggled as the father pulled his hand away.

"I couldn't breathe, Yababa," said the boy with a cut of the eyes that J'Kana felt was a bit too old for him. "Besides, I want to get started." J'Kana let out a sigh as he shook his head.

"How could someone that's half of me be so disgusting," he asked with his eyes pointed up at the roof. He looked at his son again with a bright smile as he took the book and turned the first few pages. "Alright, let's pick up here…"

| | | |
|---|---|---|
|  | Bumute | Craving/Desperation |
|  | Teukani | Disgusting |
|  | Jakani | Empathy |
|  | Welana | Entrancement |
|  | Atafe | Fear |
|  | Yerabi | Horror |
|  | Yetube | Interest |
|  | Babisa | Happiness/Joy |
|  | Jato | Strong |

| | |
|---|---|
| Shili | Weak |
| Bena | Wide |
| Yina | Narrow |
| Soa | Old |
| Lele | Young |
| Buo | Cheap/Inexpensive |
| Chula | Loud |
| Rati | Quiet |
| Ifi | Cold/Chill |
| Fali | Hot/Heat |
| Bushake | Ground/Earth |
| Arila | Air |
| Fajari | Fire |
| Lae | Water |
| Tuketu | Shift/Transition |

# 5

# Weakness

*Memifi—Y'Tunu Inn*

Y'Sawe sat by the bedside, his eyes beyond the window as he watched the ebb and flow of life in the colorful city. The sun had not yet risen to its throne above the earth when the boy stirred in his sleep. The Kanawe had to wonder how long he would be unconscious. It had already been three days, and the longer it took, the more it looked like he would be late to the Summit. He breathed deeply, then exhaled. The little one climbed into J'Foja's chest and looked him over in such a way that brought a shadow of a smile to the sage's lips.

It curled into his chest, listened to the strong thump of the ijeya's heartbeat, then with a yawn, fell asleep. Y'Sawe returned his gaze to the low glimmer of the iron sands in the metal fixtures of Memifi when he felt the boy's hand wrap around his wrist. The Teacher snapped his head and found the eyes of his apprentice open and watching. The suddenness of the boy's grip woke the little one, and it licked him on his cheek.

"Kanawe," he spoke faintly, shakily. The Master responded with a kind smile as J'Foja struggled to sit up. The little one rolled from his chest into his lap as he did.

"You're awake," Y'Sawe spoke softly as he caught J'Foja by the shoulder and guided his back to the headboard. "Take your time. There is no rush."

"What happened," J'Foja asked as he winced from a pain that spidered through his entire body in an instant, like lightning struck from the inside out. He almost slipped back beneath the covers as he gripped his head.

"The ara beasts have been cleared out," answered the Kanawe with a stern expression. "Ubeshu Bamaje is in your debt for what you managed to do." Y'Sawe watched J'Foja slip back under the covers another inch as he sighed with relief.

"I'm glad to have been of service," he said with a chuckle. Y'Sawe felt the corner of his mouth lift at the sudden return of J'Foja's sense of humor. It was only after the burden of the mission had been lifted from the boy's shoulders that he noticed the small lump of fur and warmth in his lap. He looked it over slowly as its body rose and lowered with every small breath it took. Its black fur was dotted with fiery crimson, and the moment it turned its head to squeak out a yawn, J'Foja's blood turned cold.

"Don't panic," Y'Sawe told him calmly, which drew an incredulous look from the ijeya.

"These things tried to kill me!" J'Foja spoke through clenched teeth as the panic he was told to abandon sunk its talons deep into his mind and heart.

"Technically they tried to kill us," the Teacher replied with an indifferent shrug, "and in any case, she seems to like you." His heart warmed as the ara cub sank her tiny head back into J'Foja's lap as a shiver ran through her little body. The Apprentice's expression softened, and to his own surprise, he placed a gentle hand on the creature and stroked her to comfort.

"How is she here," J'Foja asked, his eyes locked on the cub as the question escaped him. Y'Sawe stood and paced the room to the window, content to gaze at the scattered clouds that shaded parts of the glittering city from the slowly risen sun. J'Foja looked up at his master, a new question on his lips. "For that matter, how did I get here?" Y'Sawe sighed, arms crossed in front of his chest, his eyes still in full survey of the world outside the inn.

"After your command, which we will talk about in short order, I was left to survey the cave in the southern Grasslands on my own. The rayemo was little more than a skeleton, and its bones were arranged around an empty bed of burning coals. I'll give you one guess as to what—or should I say who?—I found when I made it back to you." J'Foja returned his gaze to the yilele ara as he scratched behind her ears.

"She came to me?" The way the student's question struck Y'Sawe's ear reminded him of the boy that J'Foja had always been. His roguish behavior was a response to the harsh conditions of his childhood. It was a defense, a perpetual guard that would allow him to slip through life as easy as breathing without the hope of getting attached. If the boy had truly survived Shifi, then Y'Sawe could understand the reasons for it. After all, he had lost his fair share in the disaster as well.

"She did," confirmed the master. The cub slept soundly, and for a moment both teacher and student lost themselves in the rise and fall of her back. "Ara cubs form bonds quickly, and follow after those with the most strength. Once a bond is forged, nothing short of death would be able to break it. It would seem that your battle with the rest of her pack showed her everything she needed to know." J'Foja smiled a proudly, and a snap of Y'Sawe's fingers made the boy instantly look to his teacher. "I need you to understand something. What you did, while impressive, was reckless beyond compare. Do you know what happened?"

"I got surrounded," J'Foja answered, a strained look plastered to his face as he struggled to remember. "The ara beasts closed in on me and…" he trailed off as he searched his mind. "I told the ground to shift." He looked quizzically at the Ile Kanawe. "Was that wrong?"

"Yes and no, Ijeya," Y'Sawe spoke calmly. Silently he chided himself for not having this conversation sooner, but hints would have undermined the purpose of the trial. "When you speak J'Karo with intent to command, there are two ways to do it. The first is by strengthening your ike and reaching for Y'Kele, like we talked about at the Hidden Beast. The other way is by shifting your ike through fear or anger. If you allow your negative emotions to motivate your actions, you run the risk of growing careless, and with J'Karo, a carelessly spoken word is dangerous."

"Trust me, I understand that," J'Foja said with a half-cocked grin. Y'Sawe shook his head.

"No, you don't. Even after you strengthen your ike, speaking J'Karo will take its toll. The gifts of Y'Kele were meant to build connections, not to dismantle His world. Even with the right motivations, there is a price to pay for altering the fabric of reality." The gravity in the Grand Master's tone was enough to send a chill through the boy, and just like that, his guard was back up. He gently moved the ara cub from his lap to the bed, only for the lele ili to wake up and clumsily reclaim her place. Her determination brought a smile to both of their faces. "You should get some rest," Y'Sawe urged. "We set out for Y'Baule in the morning." The suddenness of the announcement caused a wrinkle in J'Foja's brow.

"Eh? What do you mean," the boy said in a panic. He knew that his apprenticeship would mean some kind of travel through the continent, but he hardly expected it to happen so soon. "Isn't there more to do here in Y'Rakili?" Y'Sawe approached the bed again to tenderly lay his hand on his ijeya's shoulder.

"There is always more to do, no matter where you are," he stated flatly. "Nevertheless, I have a pressing matter to take care of in the north."

"Forgive me for saying, Kanawe," the student began with an urgent caution, "but my training—"

"—will take place as we travel," the sage answered before J'Foja could finish the thought. He handed the boy another slip of paper that he'd retrieved from a pocket in his elegant black robe. "Here; study this along with the vocabulary from before. We'll work to strengthen your ike as we go." J'Foja sank back into the bed as his master moved for the door. Y'Sawe paused, and his eyes drifted back to the pup in the boy's lap. "One last thing. Give the lele bewana a name in J'Karo." He left, and J'Foja looked at the sleeping ara for comfort as all his sudden reservations bubbled to the surface of his mind.

***

*Mount Y'Bayeka*

Three days came and went, and J'Foja understood more about the J'Karo with which he had been entrusted. He sat at the top of Mount Y'Bayeka as the sun began to fade, and while he had watched a thousand sunsets that radiated through the colorful walls of all Memifi, it was different here. Here, he could feel the warmth of the sun mingle with the heat of the volcano's mouth. He took in the strange way that the sulfuric aroma from inside mixed with the earthy smell of the rock and dirt. The winds danced around him with all the excitement of a child through the merchant district in Memifi, and through them he watched as the great greens of the hutije plains below swayed through from green to orange to a blue as deep as the sea. It stirred something in him, and for a moment he thought he felt a power rise.

"Take it all in," Y'Sawe's voice commanded from behind him. "Feel every change to your surroundings." He waited a moment as he felt the same power grow within himself. A green glint of an ike shift shimmered in his dark brown eyes, but he stifled it. He continued. "Every rule and wonder of this world is by Y'Kele's design. We are a part of it, and it is a part of us. Feel the connection." The ara cub, Siema, raced about the area with spirit. She tugged at the boy's clothes, but Y'Sawe was careful to keep J'Foja on task. "Focus. Feel your ike swell."

"I can feel it," J'Foja affirmed in a whisper. Inside him, a warmth washed over his soul that felt different from the heat of Y'Bayeka. Tremors rippled through his body in a way that made every hair stand on end. His eyes closed on instinct, and instead of the darkness that was so natural to the experience, golden lights twinkled in his field of vision. His body fell still as his mind emptied of everything except the J'Karo that he'd been taught, and the volcano smoke at his back.

"This is an ike shift," Y'Sawe spoke to him, calm and knowledgeable. "This is the way you open the door to Y'Kele. What color do you see?"

"Gold," the apprentice replied with a sense of wonder. "It's like looking at a noble's robes."

"What would you say, now," Y'Sawe asked, then realized the ambiguity of his question. "If you had to change something about where you are, what would you change?" J'Foja fell silent and listened to the way his lungs invited the air in, then pushed out again. There was a tranquility that ebbed and flowed like the tide.

"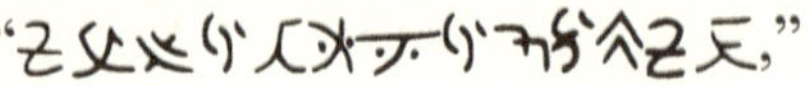," J'Foja responded with a gentle neutrality that radiated respect. His head tilted back as his body was met with a coolness that contrasted the volcano's heat like ice on a hot summer day. Y'Sawe smiled at him. There was no fatigue this time, no shortness of breath. He remained conscious, and the calm that he exhibited was enough to affect Siema.

"Good," the Master commended. "What else would you change?" Again, J'Foja became quiet, calm, even as Siema crawled into his lap again and nuzzled him as best she could. He breathed, and her breath matched his, which caused the teacher's eyebrows to raise in suspicion.

"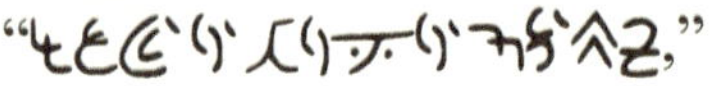," the boy uttered, and felt the air clean itself of the scent of sulfur. Y'Sawe stood impressed. J'Foja studied well, though he still cut corners. For now the issue was small enough to forego the conversation, but it would still come. He walked over to where the boy sat and placed a hand atop his head, a gesture he hadn't made since his son… J'Foja's eyes opened to immediately take stock of the disheartened look on his master's face. "Kanawe, otaba ra jishemu haranati e? Are you alright, Master?"

"You don't need to translate for me," Y'Sawe spoke as coldly as he had the day they met. He inhaled deeply, shook his head. "You did well. There are some things we need to work on, but overall you showed more control than before." He turned away, his heart as ignited as the magma below the surface. J'Foja thought to ask questions, but Y'Sawe continued almost as if he could sense the ones he thought. "Going forward, you need to remember how you felt today. Remember the connection and the peace. That is where we start."

"And where do we go from there," asked the apprentice as he scratched Siema beneath her chin. She licked his wrist as he did so. The Ile Kanawe turned to face his student with a sly grin in place.

"Simple," he said with an infectious confidence. "We go to J'Rota for some shopping." J'Foja raised an eyebrow as he set the ara on the ground. His master had already started down the path that brought them up to the top of Mount Y'Bayeka, and called back to him, "Hurry, if you don't want me to leave you here!" J'Foja couldn't help but smile as he raced after his teacher, as if the pain he'd seen before were just in his imagination.

***

*Buku Road—Outer Grasslands*

The cart—which J'Foja now understood to be *fakiye* in J'Karo—rolled along the dirt road in silence. Y'Sawe focused on his notes in what seemed to be a constant shift of papers in his hands, while the ijeya passively watched the roadside. A few farms dotted the way north to J'Rota, and filled his sight with the brown bobbing heads of pecking hibesa birds on the hunt for a worm, and the herds of round chitana beasts, garbed in their large black and brown spots.

"While you're looking around at the farm life," Kanawe Y'Sawe spoke evenly as the fakiye bumped awkwardly, only to return to normal, "you could be strengthening your ike." J'Foja groaned. It had been two days since Y'Bayeka, and all he heard now was "Study your lists," or "Strengthen your ike." He was starting to get sick of it.

"Kanawe, if I strengthen it any more, I might just become my ike," J'Foja quipped. He turned his back to the roadside just as the farm fell out of view. Y'Sawe continued to watch the rotation of parchment in front of his face.

"So you understand, then," the Master responded. He turned the page, pulled a pencil from his pocket and made notes, then continued to read. When he felt the unwavering stare of his apprentice, he looked up with an exasperated sigh. "Do you remember when you first approached me?"

"You mean when you froze me? Not at all," J'Foja replied as he relaxed his shoulders and watched the road ahead.

"How do you think I did that," asked Y'Sawe. The ijeya thought back to the moment in question. He didn't think the Kanawe even whispered back then, and suddenly J'Foja had more questions than certainties. He pondered for a moment, then shrugged when the problem proved too difficult.

"Did you set a command to activate when someone got too close?" The moment he asked, he instantly began to reconsider. "No, because if that were the case, the entire street would have been frozen like I was. The only other thing I can think of is that you set a reaction to anyone who wanted something from you, but in the merchant district, it would basically yield the same result." He met the Kanawe's eyes to find that they smiled in approval.

"I admire your thought process," he commended, "but there is another factor that you forgot. I heard you following me—"

"And you decided to command me directly, even if you couldn't tell who I was." The realization dawned on him like the morning sun, his eyes widened as his mind raced. Y'Sawe gave a slick wink, then returned to his notes. Another rock to the wheel caused the cart to jump again, and toppled Siema as she tried to paw her way up to J'Foja's shoulder. She tried again as the rhythm of the fakiye returned to an even pace.

"Why not the other commands," the Teacher asked, again steeped in focus. He listened to the gentleness of the breeze and felt his ike swell with warmth and power.

"It would've been too much," J'Foja spoke pensively. The pain of his battle with the ara seared itself anew in his mind. "To freeze everyone in the area would have probably made you hug the ground afterward." Y'Sawe cracked a smile and shook his head.

"To do something like that without the proper focus, I probably would have been closer to death than that," he admitted. "The bigger the task, the higher the toll." J'Foja looked exasperated.

"That wasn't the case when you stopped time at the Hidden Beast," he challenged from a youthful suspicion that made Y'Sawe's smile grow another inch. "There must be some way to get around the cost."

"There isn't," Y'Sawe returned with a dismissive shrug. "But there are ways to deal with it." J'Foja rolled his eyes as he draped his arm over the side of the fakiye.

"Kanawe, I swear if you say, 'Strengthen your ike' one more time I might vomit." Y'Sawe laughed now, and finally set his notes down completely. Every second that passed he took stock of the warmth of the sun on his back, the playful curiosity of the infant ara beast, and the apprentice that kept watch over her.

"I wasn't going to say that," he assured his ijeya, and when the boy cut his eyes, the Master raised his hand in placating fashion. "I promise. But how do you think I was able to do that without falling unconscious right after, e?"

"I don't know," J'Foja responded with swift frustration, as if the question had been stuck in his mind for some time now.

"Take your time, Ijeya," Y'Sawe told him firmly. He rested his hands on his knees and watched as the boy's mind raced like the abata that pulled the fakiye along. J'Foja breathed, careful to consider his interactions with his Master up to now.

"It takes a great deal of focus to shift the ike and command with precision," he started slowly, as if to give himself some time to truly process his thought. "If you can give such a strong command with little drawback, then…" his earlier comment rang like a bell at the front of his mind, and suddenly it made sense. "Kanawe, how often do you…" he trailed off, unsure how to ask the question.

"I never stop," the Ile Kanawe answered with a confidence in his eye that, for a moment, swept J'Foja into a sense of astonishment. "For now, I have asked you to work on strengthening your ike, and to do that you need to practice your shift as often as you can. Over time, you'll naturally learn to maintain the shift no matter what you're doing or where you go." The pillar of earth jetted out of the ground in the boy's mind. Time stopped again. The glass chilled. The air cleansed itself of sulfur. His body sank under an otherworldly gravity. Shifi burned. His mother and father were gone. So many examples of power and so much loss flushed his mind over and over again, until the Master's voice broke the cycle and brought the Great Peasant back to the cart. "The question is, what are your intentions for J'Karo?"

"To prevent loss," J'Foja spoke without thinking, and while he thought to second guess himself, he decided against. It was the truth.

"Elaborate," the Teacher bade. J'Foja looked out at the bright green of the hutije, and quietly wondered how long it had been since the last time he truly stopped to notice the vibrancy of its natural hue. His throat tightened as he recalled the darkness of that night, the lack of features within the city, the time that seemed to skip between the Wehela Stones, and the monsters that somehow slipped past them.

"Shifi was a tragedy that shouldn't have been allowed to happen," the boy said with a sudden rattle to his voice. He cleared his throat, then continued. "Half of the city burned in a shroud of fire that took my parents. I don't know what happened with the other half. Before that night, Shifi felt like a giant family. After, the only thing I've ever felt was an aching emptiness that comes and goes whenever it pleases." Y'Sawe exhaled a sharp shudder that pulled at the boy's attention. The clear streaks where silent tears had run down the Master's face gave the boy pause. J'Foja opened his mouth to speak, but was cut off by the Kanawe.

"Forty-seven," Y'Sawe started, and clasped his hands in front of his face as he remembered what happened to his own family in Shifi. "That's how many people were left alive after Shifi. More than half of the city went up in smoke, with most of the population." He took a deep breath as he thought on the boy's answer. "Do you know the cause?" The lele mata shuddered at the memory of the creature's red eyes and jagged talons.

"It was an Asanibo," J'Foja answered, the mix of anger and agony apparent in his tone. "A vampire of the Kehemu Forest that, for some reason found its way so far west. It turned the people into elokobi and sent them shambling along in the streets."

"Elokobi," Y'Sawe interjected, "in their infancy. They still retained their human forms, and didn't have minds to speak of. A fully mature elokobi looks more like the forests in which they are said to be born. They are cunning, hypnotic, and darker than most are able to imagine."

"Then it makes even less sense for them to wander the streets of Shifi in the night," the former peasant declared with a ferocity that inspired a raised eyebrow from his new master.

"You would be right to be suspicious," Y'Sawe assured him. "The Asanibo's presence is more than an anomaly, and one that I have been investigating over the course of the last ten years." He motioned to the notes that he'd pored over since the start of their journey. "In fact, I have reason to believe that the ubeshu's task was connected to what happened in Shifi." J'Foja blinked in surprise as he struggled to process what he just heard. A heat shot through him as his body shook. His mind raced in its attempt to find the connection that the Master apparently saw when they were nothing alike on the surface. The darkness of the night his parents were taken could not be compared to the fires of the beasts, but still the curiosity overwhelmed him.

"How do you figure that?" There was a subtle tremble of fear in his voice. The anger welled up in him to the point that the golden particles of his ike swam about in his eyes. He carefully observed his Kanawe, who took a moment to consider if it would be good to say anything on the matter now. He opened his mouth, and then he felt an indescribable change. J'Foja felt it, too.

"Yes," came a voice as deep as the darkest night and twice as sinister. "Tell me what you have seen, O Great Kanawe." Between them stood a creature as pale as the moon with talon-like claws on either hand. His eyes were as red as the blazes in Shifi, and the teeth in his smile stood as pointed as the hairs on J'Foja's skin.

***

"Alright," came the melodious voice of Nihani, who chose to sit with her boys as J'Kana told the story. "You're going to scare the boy, J'Kana." She gave him a playful swat. Kamari, who sat in his father's lap with his head pressed into the Kanawe's chest, sat up and puffed out his cheeks.

"I can handle it, Waleya," he assured her. "It's just an Asanibo!"

"Ah, you hear that, Nihani?" J'Kana offered a look of humored incredulity as he tickled the brave ulu mata. "'It's just an Asanibo,' he says. Be that as it may, my *yijojonawe* shehefo, your mother is right. Besides, I have a fun J'Karo lesson for you today." The little one perked up at the mention of the language, and immediately clambered down from his perch to run across the luseme to grab the book. "You are eager! But should you be?" The boy stopped in his tracks with the brown book clutched to his chest. Nihani struck J'Kana again, slightly harder than the last time, which only elicited a smile.

"Stop it," she ordered as her own smirk crept across her lips despite her greatest effort to suppress it.

"Alright, alright," J'Kana agreed. He stood to meet Kamari the rest of the way, picked him up, and placed him in his lap again when he returned to his seat on the couch. He opened the book to a page that was split between vocabulary and something else. "Today I want you to speak to me only in J'Karo, but first, let's learn a few more words."

| | | |
|---|---|---|
|  | Kele | Make/Create |
|  | Tebi | Here |
| 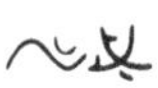 | Tebo | There |
|  | Atebo | Over There |
| 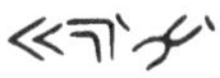 | Nochulo | Drive |
|  | Rila | Place |

| | | |
|---|---|---|
|  | Roli | World/Globe |
|  | Sike | Map |
|  | Sayi | Move/Bring/Carry |
|  | Yifushiki | Harness |
|  | Fuye | Will |
| 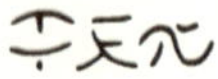 | Feotu | Try/Attempt |
|  | Tunu | Moon/Month |
|  | Shala | Sun |
|  | Mani | Day |
|  | Chimu | Year |
|  | Sechimu | Decade |
|  | Halu | Week |
|  | Wi | This |
|  | Oka | Last |
|  | Maa | Next/Then |

"Now," J'Kana continued, fully intent on mercilessly testing his genius of a son, "what do you have to say?" Kamari looked up at him, at first with the confused look of a little boy, then with the cunning of a devious mastermind.

"
" J'Kana rolled his eyes. His son caught on rather quickly, and while it was a pleasure for him as a teacher, he knew that it would only be a matter of time before the little one knew J'Karo in the same way that he knew his own name.

"I'm glad you are having fun, my son, and I will teach you more tomorrow, while we explore the Outer Grasslands." Kamari's eyes went wide.

"You're taking me out of Kilana?" He stared holes in his father's face, but the teacher only smiled. "I'm going to bed," he shouted as he clumsily disembarked J'Kana's lap. "I need tomorrow to come sooner!" And before Nihani could even get up from the couch, the door to his bedroom opened and shut with a boom.

# 6

# Identity

*Buku Road—Outer Grasslands*

The jagged claws of the creature slashed through the night air and the fakiye splintered across the middle. The abata, startled, pulled ahead with such a force that the cart finally ripped in two. Y'Sawe jumped into the air and, with a flip, landed on the ground a few feet away from the Asanibo, but J'Foja tumbled clumsily to the ground in front of the monster. He looked up, only to find the hungry glare of the Asanibo as it bared a fang-laced grin. J'Foja's initial fear calmed, and in an instant he was back to his old self, the playful thief that ran the streets of Memifi and toyed with authority with smug confidence.

"You need to trim those things," he quipped, careful not to point too much toward the teeth or the claws. "It's like you haven't groomed in a decade." The Asanibo hissed as it raised its clawed hand. It swiped toward the grounded apprentice with impressive speed, but the boy spoke faster. "Ti baa otaba ra N'atebo sayinati o!" The vampire was teleported back to the cart wreckage and splintered it again, much to its irritation.

"Don't antagonize him, Ijeya," Y'Sawe warned as four orbs of bright red fire formed in the air around him. "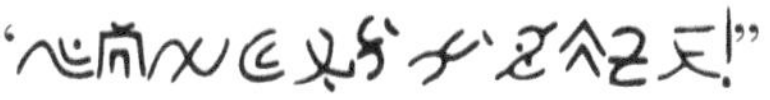" The Kanawe whispered the words, "Go attack him," and the fiery orbs burst through the air with such authority that the world around them seemed to warp from the heat. The Asanibo smiled again as his body contorted beneath the first fireball. The monster spun to the side to avoid the second, then vaulted over the third while the final blazing orb hurdled toward his face. J'Foja watched his mentor, how unbelievably cool he was, and how the shadow of the vampire appeared behind him before the sage could blink.

"Kanawe," J'Foja started, but was stunned to find that the moment the enemy moved in for an attack, he froze. It was the same command that the boy fell for in the merchant district. Siema howled through the hutije grass, startled beyond relief and too scared to move.

"I'm alright," Y'Sawe told him. "Check on Siema. I'll deal with the monster." J'Foja ran into the grass, careful to listen to the sound of the ara cub's voice as he moved the heightened tendrils to either side. Within moments he found her, as well as the reason she stood petrified. The sound of swiftly cut air filled J'Foja's ears as he rolled along the ground and scooped Siema into his arms. He came back to his feet with a running start, only to find three more assailants hidden in the tall grass around him. He narrowly spun out of the way of the spear that lunged for his throat, then sidestepped the sword that crashed down with vengeful force.

"Listen," J'Foja started, a gentle wheeze of exhaustion in his voice, "I was just here to get my dog! Is all this really necessary?" The three attackers, two swords and a spear, stood from the hutije to face him. The apprentice's jaw dropped when he noticed the broken armor of Y'Rakili's royal guard, the various puncture wounds in their bodies, the glazed over look in their eyes. The grass and leaves that protruded from their helmets seemed to grow from their skin otherwise. J'Foja's eyes widened with realization. The Asanibo and elokobi, their sudden emergence, and his separation from what he considered his only protection. It was all too similar to Shifi.

***

"You've been busy," the Asanibo growled, still affixed to his spot with a jagged claw pointed at Y'Sawe. "How is your investigation going, Kanawe?" The sage offered no response as he paced the ground around the vampire.

"Who are you," the Teacher began, "and what is your business with me?" The monster chuckled in a rumble so low it could chill the air, and Y'Sawe narrowed his eyes.

"You know," the creature spoke with a calmness that gave the Master pause, "when we heard you had taken an apprentice, we could hardly believe it. The Great Y'Sawe, Ile Kanawe of the Seven Teachers, chose to waste his time with a smart-mouthed street urchin who should've died that night in Shifi." The mention of the incident caused the Master's eyes to widen and his fists to clench.

The orbs of fire burned bright around him in a circle of nine as he drew near his enemy.

"What do you know about Shifi?" The demand thundered through the air as the infernal projectiles glowed brighter. The Asanibo, who should have been frozen in place, tilted his head as his smile grew wider. Y'Sawe jumped back as the fire he conjured morphed into a pillar just as shadow attacked him from all sides.

***

J'Foja sprinted through the hutije grass, Siema in his arms, and though his breath grew shallow, his determination knew no such limitation. The spear hurdled through the air, but the former thief evaded it as if he flowed on a gentle breeze. He fixed his mouth to speak a command, did what he could to shift his ike, but something was wrong. He couldn't focus.

The twin swords came at him from either side, swords upraised and poised to run him through. Siema quivered against his chest, and the hutije swayed with every motion that he made. He stilled himself, ran a hand over the ara pup, felt the sway of the grass, and remembered the connectedness of the entire world. His ike shifted, and flecks of gold returned to his eyes as he inhaled the earthy scent of his surroundings. He stretched for Y'Kele as he searched for the words his Master had spoken at the Hidden Beast.

"What was it," he grumbled as he dodged the strikes of the elokobi. Their blades clashed in the space where J'Foja had been, and the ijeya established distance again. "What was it?" He asked the question again, then panicked as the shift in his ike began to fade. He spun out of the way of a stabbing spear only to duck a horizontal slash with a sword. These elokobi were much faster than the ones from a decade ago, and J'Foja barely had any time to think.

***

The fires expanded to burn away the shadows, along with a portion of the hutije grass that surrounded them. The Asanibo cracked his neck as he paced the ground.

"You were too weak to save your son," the creature taunted, a sick delight in his red eyes. "You were too weak to keep your wife from turning into an elokobi." Y'Sawe's face contorted with rage. "You were too weak to stop Shifi from burning—"

"I have heard enough," the Master uttered calmly. The shift of his ike brought with it a strong wind that breathed a swirling life back into their surroundings. By the look on the vampire's face, he didn't seem to be so weak anymore. Kanawe Y'Sawe opened his mouth, a sharp look in his eye as his nostrils flared and his lips took the shape of a J'Karo command. The smile of the Asanibo returned.

"Let's see if you are strong enough to save your apprentice," it spoke, then receded into the shadows…

***

J'Foja felt the tightness in his chest. It was clear that he couldn't do this forever, but the command he needed still eluded him as much as he eluded his attackers. He needed to focus, but he couldn't. Another spear attack plunged through the air towards his face. The boy slid along the ground beneath the elokobi that wielded it and sprinted away again as his mind raced to find the words. He already knew that "time" was "tokiji," and that "stop" was "natie," but he couldn't remember the most vital part: the part that would only freeze his enemies. He struggled so much to remember that the veins in his forehead pulsed against his skull. Suddenly he remembered "somi" and "hafu," the words for "for" and "I" respectively. Finally, it all fell into place.

"," he repeated, his ike still a flicker of a flame in the cold night air, " !" He could see his master in his mind as he gave the command, could feel the strength of his ike return as he reached to Y'Kele from the darkest depths of his soul, and then the world stood still. Time stopped, except for Y'Sawe and J'Foja. He staggered back, exhausted from the tireless evasions he was forced to produce until now, but when he felt the sharpest pain at the back of his neck, he sprung forward as his body turned in midair.

The Asanibo stared at him. Every jagged fang in its head peered through its hungry smile like faces through a window. Its taloned hand reached for J'Foja with every intent to kill. If the boy hadn't remembered his master's command when he did, he would have died. He sank to the ground, stunned by the realization and scared of what footsteps hastily approached. What if there was another elokobi beneath the tall grass? He already knew that he couldn't move. He took a deep breath as he watched the hutije and listened to the sounds as they returned. Jinenu crickets chirped all around. A gentle breeze glided along the tops of the grasses colored bluish white under the glow of the moon. It calmed him enough for another shift of his ike.

Y'Sawe emerged, visibly relieved to find his ijeya alive. His gaze shifted to the three elokobi and the Asanibo that protruded from his wall of shadows. J'Foja looked up at him with a smile, then groggily stumbled back to his feet.

"What," the boy asked. "You didn't think I could handle it?" Y'Sawe shook his head.

"No," hissed the Asanibo. Y'Sawe quickly stepped between the monster and his apprentice. The vampire looked between them in silence as its feet touched earth, and decided that it was best not to reengage. "And that is something that my master will be pleased to hear." Y'Sawe glowered at the creature, his suspicions confirmed.

"Then you are working for someone," said Y'Sawe. "Who?" The Asanibo chuckled with a smugness that incensed the Master and Apprentice as he turned from them and walked away.

"Are you sure you don't already know?" The back of the Asanibo flashed in the dark, and for a moment he looked like someone else entirely. Like the man Y'Sawe argued with in Memifi. The shadows swallowed him, and when his elokobi receded into the ground, perfectly immobilized otherwise, the ijeya looked upon his Kanawe to see a mixture of shock and horror.

***

*J'Rota*

The capitol of Y'Rakili struck J'Foja as mystical. It was a pristine combination of moon white and emerald green that gave the impression of a raging tide. Every step they took felt as though they tread the ocean floor, and though the apprentice longed to touch his head to a pillow, Y'Sawe had other plans.

He followed the Master closely as he made hastened strides into the heart of J'Rota. Y'Sawe moved with an elegant flow of a passing breeze as he worked his way around the many who still wandered through the streets at this hour. He was unfazed by the smell of alcohol from the open doors of the watering holes, unbothered by the strength of the colognes worn by the city's eligible bachelors dressed in their finest kaftans with the hope of taking someone home for the night. He moved as he had when he had first met J'Foja, and if the boy's hunch was correct, it meant that his Kanawe was bothered.

They hadn't spoken a word since their encounter with the Asanibo. They simply restarted time, repaired the fakiye, and, with Siema stuffed into the front of the apprentice's clothes, continued on their way to the gates of the city. That, to the chagrin of the tired ijeya, was where they began to walk again on their own power, which gave the boy a lot of time to consider the recent battle. Even though curiosity burned within him, J'Foja thought to leave it alone as soon as he saw his teacher's face. The longer the silence lingered, however, the more he wanted to know. He thought to speak on it now, but the simple act of keeping up while he carried Siema took all of his focus. Y'Sawe glanced back at the boy, sighed when J'Foja looked away, and slowed in his stride.

"You did well," the elder finally spoke. J'Foja, stunned, stopped in his tracks as he took in the black locs that draped the back of the Kanawe's head. "I didn't say anything before when I should have. I know how important it is for you to hear." The comment made J'Foja's cheeks run hot with embarrassment, but with it came a strange sense of satisfaction that he hadn't felt since the loss of his parents. "I suppose you have questions?"

"Who was that man that the Asanibo turned into?" The question escaped him before his next breath entered, and when Y'Sawe turned to look upon him with eyebrows raised, J'Foja winced at his overzealous approach. "Apologies, Kanawe," he corrected himself. "I just never thought that I would ever see you so shaken." Y'Sawe pondered a moment, then inhaled deeply.

"The man you saw me with that day," the Teacher began slowly, "the man who attacked me in the marketplace, is my brother Mahute." He could see that the name meant something to the former thief. Y'Sawe expected nothing less. "The reason he attacked me was because I was the one who sent him to Febetu. When I first saw him that day in Memifi, I had to wonder how he broke out."

"Broke out? Of Febetu," J'Foja questioned and felt the hairs on his arms rise with heightened fear. "Febetu is an impenetrable prison in Y'Sewana, ne?"

"It is," the Grand Master confirmed, "and for a normal man it would have been impossible to break out."

"Well, if he would raise a blade to his own brother, how normal could he be?" The question brought a smile to the sage's face. "Even stranger is the fact that an Asanibo managed to take his shape. They aren't known to be shifters of any kind."

"It's more likely that Mahute controls him. Moreover, given the strange behavior of the animals on my journey, it is likely that the creature had been following me for some time." The revelation stunned the ijeya, so Y'Sawe took the time to think as he continued on to his destination. The master exhaled, looked at his apprentice, and then continued. "I suppose, then, we should start with what the Asanibo really are. A long time ago, during the Thousand-Year War, a clan of fighters lived deep within the Kehemu Forest in the southeastern region of Y'Neshu. They were especially vicious, despite their small number, and managed to conquer everything from the southern coast to the base of the Amejai Mountains on the power of J'Karo alone."

"How could they do that, na?" J'Foja's question pulled Y'Sawe from the story. "I thought that J'Karo was supposed to build connection, not make war." The Master nodded.

"It was, and the M'Iba Ili, the Original Ones, used it to build the villages and towns and countries that we know today. J'Karo was considered the Great Unifier of Y'Neshu for all the good it did, and all the power it granted the people. Nevertheless, there were some who began to consider how they might use it for more personal gain. The Batabari Clan, as they came to be known, rained destruction down upon all of Eastern Y'Neshu. Those who weren't killed in their conquest were taken as slaves and held for generations in the harshest conditions." He turned down a side alley and emerged on another street, overly populated by people on a hunt for the best bargain they could get. The emerald green and moon white sparkled under the light of the stars, and despite the discomfort that J'Foja experienced, he could feel his ike flicker to life.

"The Batabari Clan…" he reflected aloud, and the words drew a hostile glare from several of the denizens of J'Rota.

"It isn't something you would mention in most conversation," Y'Sawe warned passively. "They were monsters, manipulators, subjugators that marred Y'Neshu even to the Four Empires." Y'Sawe could hear the boy plant his feet. The more he learned, the more he feared the legacy of the Batabari, and rightfully so.

"That—that shouldn't be possible for anyone," the boy stammered. Y'Sawe didn't disagree, but unfortunately, the history of Y'Neshu did. They pressed further into the marketplace, and it seemed an eternity before the apprentice realized what kinds of shops they passed. Fabrics of all kinds were on full display, beads and jewels of assorted luster and price glinted with every step they took. It was enough to make him wonder…but Y'Sawe continued.

"For a while, the Batabari struggled to hold their ground against the might of the Four Empires, especially after the destruction of the eastern Kingdom of Y'Kawebo. Five hundred years into the war, the Batabari finally lost territory in the north and were almost pushed back to Ekutali Village in the south." The Kanawe walked between two shops and found a door made of soso wood awkwardly fixed to the stone brick wall. He turned the knob, opened the door, and allowed the ijeya passage through. "It was in their weakness that they found a new kind of strength." J'Foja continued to listen, but he couldn't help the strong fixation on the plethora of fabrics as diverse in color as the buildings of Memifi and contrasted against a wall the color of midnight.

"What kind of strength did they find?" J'Foja pondered as he moved to look at a deep purple cloth. He felt it, and found that it was softer than even the fine clothes he had bought from the yabowu, the uncle, before the start of his apprenticeship.

"That of their own blood," Y'Sawe explained with a grievous exhale. J'Foja's eyes darted across the room to meet his teacher's. "In the first stages, they uttered their commands in J'Karo as they cut themselves, and found that it gave them otherworldly power. The Blood Chants allowed them to reclaim some of the ground they lost in under a century, but the Batabari were displeased that their resurgence took so long. As a result, they figured that J'Karo no longer served their purpose, and devised a language better suited to the Blood Chants and to war."

"So is it because of the Blood Chants that Mahute the Dagger controls the Asanibo," J'Foja inquired. Y'Sawe's eyes narrowed, though from pride or concern the boy couldn't tell.

"It is the only explanation. The rise of the Batabari language also gave rise to a number of rituals so profane in the eyes of Y'Kele that it stirred a reaction from the God Himself. He made for Himself an earthly body, one that would allow for an innate connection with His creation and repair the damage that had already been done. Almost at the same time, the Batabari formed a monstrous creature from the blood of their enemies, wise in the ways of humans and as powerful as the heart of Y'Neshu itself." Y'Sawe shook his head, almost as though he knew the creature from personal experience, and that was enough to send a shiver through his student. "The Empires called it '*Jurutisalaji*,' and it was the final straw. At Y'Kele's command, the Four Empires provided seven of the wisest leaders to go to war with it while He tended to the Batabari. Together, the Seven Teachers, or Wayi Kanawe as they have come to be known, sealed away the threat of Jurutisalaji."

"What happened with the Batabari," J'Foja asked. "If their crimes were so great that Y'Kele Himself had to touch the earth to stop them, I can't imagine what their punishment was."

"The Batabari Clan of old were punished according to their love of blood. The records of their language were turned over to the Kanawe, and the violent clan was cursed to live for all time as the vampires of the Kehemu Forest: the Sasabosami, those who showed remorse to Y'Kele upon his Incarnation, and the Asanibo, those who strive to conquer Y'Neshu even to this day."

"Well, that sucks," J'Foja joked, and paused for a moment to allow his mentor to laugh. He didn't. "My apologies, Kanawe." His tone shifted back to a seriousness that befit the conversation. "So, they lost their power, their identity, and their monster because of their defiance. You know this gives me more questions about Mahute, right? The Asanibo are vicious creatures—"

"So is my brother. I had him sent to Febetu for breaking into the Vault of Y'Leina in Tafo. He murdered twenty yifusi in the Y'Fuwefo royal guard and stole the Scroll of Batabari," Y'Sawe interrupted, a mournful grimace on his face. J'Foja could see how it pained his Master to share, but still couldn't find it in himself to mask his curiosity. The ijeya could see that there was something more, a deeper reason for the story that Y'Sawe hadn't come to. The Ile Kanawe continued. "After the war, the Wayi Kanawe sealed away the knowledge of Batabari *and* J'Karo, determined to keep a peace in Y'Neshu that would last for millennia. As a symbol of their devotion to their sacred duty and Y'Kele, the Kanawe instituted a custom unique to their class: the *jilaba wu ajiwele*." J'Foja's eyebrows raised when the vocabulary sunk in. The Robe of Identity. That must have been why they moved for the textile shops of the merchant district. It might've been the whole reason they were in J'Rota.

"Am I going to buy a jilaba wu ajiwele?" The question was asked with such a boyish wonder that the sage couldn't help but smirk.

"You will be *making* a jilaba wu ajiwele, Ijeya," the teacher supplied. "If the Asanibo are still on the attack, it stands to reason that Mahute is still free. More elokobi will likely rise all over Y'Neshu until he is stopped, and the balance of peace that we have maintained for more than a thousand years will be challenged. You must remember your reason for learning J'Karo, but you must also remember why the Kanawe exist in the first place, and how you fit into the purpose of our order." J'Foja thought back to the image of his undead mother, and the sudden slam of a door to the back of the elaborate shop brought him back to the present. The merchant had arrived, a charming smile plastered on her wrinkled night-colored face.

"Y'Kele ra hafu shu chalanati o!" The old woman shouted it before she had time to think. She walked around the counter and took J'Foja by the face. "Y'Sawe, you have an ijeya? And a handsome one, too! I never thought I'd see the day!"

"And I never thought I'd see such beauty in my life," J'Foja replied before his Master could. The woman hit him on the shoulder much harder than he would have expected, but smiled a girlish smile that showed him a glimpse of the maiden she had once been.

"Be gentle with the boy, Rehema," Y'Sawe urged. "I brought him in for a Robe, not a fight." Rehema's eyes widened with delight as she took the boy by both hands.

"Is that so? Well then! Who are you?" The woman looked him in the eyes, and her massive energy was as infectious as the question was shocking. For over a decade, J'Foja had only concerned himself with what he needed to survive. For ten years, he pushed out everything that could have reminded him of his old life in Shifi, but now, between Y'Sawe's story and Rehema's question, born from a genuine curiosity and a sweet, motherly smile, it all bubbled back to the surface in a way that J'Foja couldn't suppress no matter how hard he tried to.

*You are J'Kana,* he could hear the tender alto of his mother whisper into his ear, *because your ike will flow in ways even greater than your father.* He felt her now, her arms wrapped around his little body, the warmth of her skin against his, the way she held him close, as if to freeze him in that moment in time and keep him from ever growing up. It had been so long since he thought of his mother that way, so long since he felt the tickle of her breath against his ear that he realized he'd almost forgotten her entirely.

Her words resounded in the recesses of his mind, and while his face streamed with tears that neither the merchant nor the Kanawe could have expected, his posture changed. He stood taller now, more confident than perhaps he had ever been, and as he stayed the quiver in his lower lip, he affirmed to Rehema and Y'Sawe, but most of all, to himself, "I am J'Kana, the Great Flow, one whose ike is destined to flow in ways greater than even my father's."

Rehema nodded in approval, her wise eyes aglimmer in the candlelight of the shop. Immediately she set to work and gathered the materials for a jilaba wu ajiwele that would best befit that name. J'Kana, suddenly alive with the memory of his mother, stood with a silent smile as he recalled the life he'd had from a place of peace rather than pain. Until he thought of the Asanibo. This time, however, he didn't think of the distortion of his mother. He didn't think of the monsters that pursued him, or the fires that spread through Shifi that night.

Instead, J'Kana thought about the Blood Chants. About Batabari. About Mahute the Dagger.

***

Kamari's eyes widened with an astonishment that he never dreamed he would experience as he trotted along after his long-legged father. He thought to tell J'Kana a while ago that he couldn't keep up, but now that this part of the story had reached its end, the pace of the father slowed to a stop as well. Finally, Kamari could breathe. They had set out to the east, only about a mile or two from the gates of Kilana, with Mount Y'Bayeka in plain view. The hutije grass stood tall on all sides, and only swayed when J'Kana turned around to take his son by the hand. There was a sweet scent intermingled with the earthy flavors of the field. The sun brightly shined down upon all of Y'Rakili, and as the ulu mata savored every sensation, he could feel a stir come from deep within.

"Yababa," Kamari began, "your name is J'Kana, isn't it? Is the story about you?" J'Kana smiled a knowing smile at the boy as he lifted his shoulders in a shrug that reeked of feigned ignorance. Kamari's lips twisted with humor as his yababa turned his head briefly toward the volcano. The little one watched him, then felt his eyes drift beyond his control toward the fiery mountain in the distance. It was faint, but something inside him yearned to be there. Something deeper sought to explore beyond it.

"Are you ready for what I have to show you," asked the elder. Kamari looked up with a giddy smile to find that the teacher faced him again. He nodded, and the corner of J'Kana's mouth tugged upward as he caught the faint whisper of turquoise flecks in the boy's eyes. He chuckled, then whistled loudly into the Outer Grasslands. " !" The sudden burst of J'Karo brought with it a swell of nature. Somehow the sights and smells of the Grasslands became more vibrant. The field glowed a brighter green as sparks of gold filtered through the air. A breeze flowed all around them that smelled so much sweeter than before, and something about the utterance made Kamari feel so incredibly at home. His ike stirred within his small body, and a shade of turquoise permeated his vision.

Then he heard it. The eager pound of four legs and the burst of a hearty bark came from somewhere beneath the hutije grass. Before the little one could ask, an ara beast emerged with authority from the tall grass and leapt for J'Kana in a wild attack.

"Yababa!" Kamari's shout thundered, but it did nothing to deter the beast, who stood in the Kanawe's chest and…licked his face? Kamari inched closer, but the ara beast turned to face him with a snarl. He shrunk back, but his gaze was drawn to her coat. The black fur lustered in the sunlight, and the red dots that adorned it seemed as embers in a barbecue pit. Her yellow eyes flickered with the light of day, and with every step the boy took in retreat, the ara beast advanced to survey the threat.

"Now, now, Siema," J'Kana placated, and at the mention of her name, the ara's ears perked up and she returned to her master. "Kamari is no threat to us." She tilted her head, then circled around the boy with her nose mere centimeters from his skin. She pulled back, barked, then licked him so hard in the face he almost came off the ground.

"Siema," Kamari repeated in surprise. "You mean the Siema from the story? So it is about you!" J'Kana held up his hands as a laugh escaped him.

"Ah, you've got me. But you were the one who wanted to hear the stories of our family," he reminded. "Why not start with the ones you know?" Kamari crossed his arms as he attempted to suppress his smile.

"Then I want to hear Waleya's story when you finish with this one," he demanded. J'Kana nodded, then caught himself as he thought more about it.

"You would have to talk to her about that one, hafu wu shehefo," said the Kanawe, and watched as his son's face shifted to disappointment. "For now, all I can do is tell you of your ancestors, of my lineage, and of the role that J'Karo plays in that. Better still, I can show you." J'Kana held out the tattered leather book, a page already marked for the boy to find. He winked, and then began to recite it from memory as his ike flowed through. Gold flecks swirled in his eyes as he did, and Kamari saw the words take shape before his very eyes and come to life.

| | | |
|---|---|---|
| | Ili | One |
| | Na | Two |
| | Jo | Three |
| | He | Four |
| | Chu | Five |
| | Fa | Six |
| | Wayi | Seven |
| | Kie | Eight |

| | |
|---|---|
| Nau | Nine |
| Se | Ten |
| Se-ili | Eleven |
| Na-se | Twenty |
| To | Hundred |
| Na-to | Two Hundred |
| Ku | Thousand |
| Se-ku | Ten Thousand |
| To-ku | Hundred Thousand |
| Abata | Abata |
| Ara | Ara |
| Akira | Beast |
| Huti | Bird |
| Hibesa | Hibesa |
| Chitana | Chitana |
| Jurutisalaji | Jurutisalaji |
| Tiche | Fish |
| Nila tiche | Nila fish |

| | | |
|---|---|---|
| | Rayemo | Rayemo |
| | Elokobi | Elokobi |
| | Hutije | Hutije |
| | Sasabosami | Sasabosami |
| | Asanibo | Asanibo |
| | Hase | Fruit |
| | Anami | Animal |
| | Rela | Plant |
| | Bakesiti | Monster |

# 7

# Solemnity

*Jahabi Road—Outer Grasslands*

It was colder here, and J'Kana wasn't sure if he liked it. The hairs on his arm bristled with every blow of the northern Y'Rakilian breeze, but the great warmth of the small ara cub, still nestled in his shirt, kept the real cold at bay. His eyes were closed, but his nose attentive to the smell of rain in the air. Each second, he could feel it come closer. His ike pulsed within him as the heat and chill mixed with the scent. The steady medley of the yiki bird's melodious call and the chirp of the kurikuri bug gave him an awareness of it all, as did the occasional braying of the abata that pulled the fakiye.

His senses swelled with the sensations that blended on every side, and when he opened his eyes, he did what he could to maintain his focus on the connection. He reached for Y'Kele with all the strength in his soul, even as he watched the hutije grass fade into the rushing waters of the mighty Joba River. Something about the way it sped violently on soothed him further, as though he needn't be concerned with force or fury as long as the Mighty Joba surged.

"Control your eyes," Y'Sawe told him with such a straightforwardness that the road was envious. "If you glow gold at every turn, you will never be able to take your enemies by surprise. It isn't enough to simply reach for Y'Kele. You have to allow Him to become a part of you, J'Kana." The boy nodded, but he felt a strange tension when Y'Sawe called that name. All the same, he could hardly believe that someone dared call him by his birth name after a decade of being "The Great Peasant."

"How do you suggest I do that, Kanawe" J'Kana replied with a solemnity that Y'Sawe hadn't expected. He felt the intensity of his ike fall as he asked the question, but it hadn't fully diminished. The abata approached the riverbank, and before he realized it, J'Kana sunk into the ike as it grew in strength. The golden flecks returned to his irises as golden waves overtook his surroundings, and he spoke the command, "Yo kokosi N'hafu ni ra arila wu tisikoko shu kelechele o." *Make a ball of air around us.* The words spilled out of him, even though he lacked in complete understanding.

"Well, what did you do a moment ago, Ijeya," the Kanawe questioned with the gentleness of a warm breeze. The sound of his voice, the patience and understanding that he exhibited, moved the boy deeper into the golden hue. There was a strength that he felt as a result, and the longer he swam in the calming sea of his ike, the more he loved it. He stretched towards Y'Kele, now so effortlessly that he could feel something change in his body.

"I let my instinct take over," the boy replied, a tranquility in his voice as his eyes, full of gold, closed. "It was strange, because I felt like I was able to guide that instinct toward Y'Kele." He opened his eyes, shocked that the golden waves that burst through the atmosphere before had receded, but the power of the ike still swirled within him. Y'Sawe looked out over the water as it hurriedly rushed to either side of their personalized aerosphere. A knowing smirk split his lips as he watched the abata trudge through the expressly dried earth beneath the river.

"Remember that feeling, J'Kana," the Master instructed. "Soon we will exit the Joba, and if our enemies are using the wildlife to track me, then they will be able to pick up on our trail again." The warning came with such a quiet force that J'Kana's ike stirred uncomfortably. His eyes flickered in bursts of gold in a way that worried his mentor. He calmed himself, and his eyes returned to the deep brown they had been in their base.

"I know," he offered from a place of calm that put Y'Sawe at ease. They had been on the road for a week's time, and within the first four days he had already experienced the dangerous pursuit of the Asanibo. Even so, they were still a few days away from Folawu. His battle with the elokobi alone proved more of a challenge than he was truly ready for. He knew that he only survived because he was fast enough to dodge. He wouldn't always be. J'Kana took a deep breath as his eyes closed again. "I need to practice," he told Y'Sawe, and the Ile Kanawe smiled.

***

*Joba River*

Night approached, and soon the abata-drawn fakiye would need a place to rest. Y'Sawe watched over his statue-like apprentice, who breathed evenly as he took in the sounds and smells of their surroundings. The Teacher himself carefully revisited his notes, but the only thing he could think of was his brother. They had not always been at odds, and Mahute had not always been so dangerous and volatile. They were once an inseparable pair, children with smiles plastered to their jaws while a youthful mischief burned behind their eyes. Even now he could remember the many times where they would sneak into the Grasslands around Shibanu Village in the west of Y'Rakili, just to give their parents a fright.

He could also remember the day their parents gave them up. Times were hard because of a depletion of the healing minerals in the Hetebi Springs. Without the spring water to irrigate the crops, Shibanu suffered a famine the likes of which hadn't been seen in over 200 years. After the first year and a half, those with children started to sell them as servants to the other nations or the eastern city states. Those who lacked that kind of mercy did unspeakable things to prioritize their own survival. Y'Sawe winced at the memory, at the look on his father's face as he dealt with the slaver and the sorrow in his mother's eyes as she refused to look at her two boys.

The Kanawe tugged the reigns of the abata to the side, and the twin-horned horse huffed as it obeyed. It didn't take long for it to withdraw from the river. Siema, aware of the fact that her surroundings were changing, wiggled from J'Kana's clothes to the floor of the fakiye. Y'Sawe was the first to step out into the hutije, and noticed that among the tall grass were stalks of wild tukali grain, a dull blue in appearance and sweet in fragrance.

"So I guess this is where we stop for tonight," J'Kana sighed as he dismounted the cart. The Teacher nodded, and from his jilaba wu ajiwele he retrieved the makings of a tent. J'Kana, surprised at the second one to emerge, thought to ask what the true purpose of the Robe was, but decided against when he saw the pensive expression of his Master. "I guess I'll set this up over here, then." Y'Sawe nodded again, silent as he was before, and started work on his own tent.

J'Kana could feel the heaviness that bore down on Y'Sawe's shoulders. It practically stung the air, and tempted the boy to let go of the heightened sense of connection he'd worked so hard to gain. He resisted, and instead sank further into the swirl of his golden ike.

"Afoyishu Y'Kele," he began in earnest, "N'Hafu wu Kanawe wu tufi ra bibichele o." He pleaded with the Creator to show him into the mind of his teacher, and while he was unsure what he would find there, he knew that it might be of some relief to the Grand Master to have someone with whom he could share the burden. Before he could form a thought of his own, he saw a much younger version of Mahute the Dagger. He sat in chains against a wall, sand scattered at his feet as the sun burned against his skin. A tall man of dark skin and hairless head stood before him, a whip raised to the sky that longed to taste the blood pulled from his flesh.

Mahute clutched something in his hand hard enough to turn the black stone of the floor red. He pulled his legs in with a fearful look on his face, but when the whip split the air with a loud crack, the lelenawe Mahute rolled to the side and sprinted at his attacker before there was time to react. The abuser's eyes went wide with shock as he grabbed at Mahute's dark, matted curls. He fell to the floor as his hands reached for the wound. Mahute, who trembled in the shimmer of the sunlight, dropped the dagger in his hand

and searched the man for the keys. As he unshackled himself, the image faded and a new one emerged.

"It has been a long time, brother," Mahute almost sang as he drew closer to where J'Kana—no—Y'Sawe stood. He spread his arms in a welcoming fashion, a bright smile captured on his face. "It is good to see you." Y'Sawe hugged him, then they both pulled back to get a view of the other. Mahute was dressed in red and black shiki and jifona and armored in a breastplate as gold as the sands of Y'Sewana, while Y'Sawe stood shrouded in his black and gray jilaba wu ajiwele. The halls of the Golden Palace of Y'Fuwefo were lined with shelves upon shelves, each one colored the deep brown of the soso trees, layered with a myriad of books and scrolls from all across Y'Neshu. The white marble walls and black marble floors added an ethereal resonance to the golden ceiling and window frames.

"You've gotten old," Y'Sawe joked with a toothy grin, and couldn't resist a chance to look around at the first palace in which he'd ever walked. "I thought that service in the Y'Fuwefo Royal Guard would have kept you young. What are these gray hairs, ila esho?" Y'Sawe reached up to touch his brother's head, only to be met with an energetic swerve.

"Ahh, don't do that, ulu esho," Mahute grunted. "You would think that being one of the Wayi Kanawe would add to your maturity." Y'Sawe shrugged with a wily smile.

"It does," he said with a passive confidence, "just not with you." Mahute shook his head as his lips again parted with a loving brotherly smirk. J'Kana was struck with a wave of anguish, as if he longed for a brother he never knew to bless him with the same look. "I came to see how you were doing. After we broke free of Hanbari's mining camp, you never really talked about what happened." Without a word, the two began to walk the hallway.

"I protected my little brother from a filthy slaver," Mahute growled with the regal ferocity of an angry rayemo beast. "What else is there to talk about?" Y'Sawe sighed.

"It isn't good to keep something like that to yourself, Mahute. I am your brother, you can talk to me. If the remorse is too great from taking a life—"

"Remorse?" Mahute snorted. "The only thing I'm sorry for is that the others had to stay." The Kanawe stopped in his tracks, a deep furrow in his brow.

"What do you mean," Y'Sawe asked cautiously. "Hanbari died that day, Mahute. Surely you cannot be happy that you killed a man." Mahute turned to him, ice behind his previously warm eyes, with a dark grin across his face.

"I would kill a thousand more to end the kind of suffering we endured," he confessed. "We always heard the stories of Shunanawe Y'Neshu, the Great Y'Neshu unified after the Batabari Clan's reign of terror came to an end, but the reality is that such celebrated unity died not long after Y'Kele's Ascension."

"Elder brother," Y'Sawe interrupted, but Mahute held up his hand to stop him.

"Y'Sewana prepares for endless war with the lives of its slaves on the line. Y'Baule turns the wildlife into weapons for battle all the same. Y'Rakili's agricultural prowess sustains life all over Y'Neshu, even to the point of our own people's suffering. Even with all this, Y'Fuwefo, our artistic brothers to the north, bury their heads beneath the hutije and pretend that all is well in the world. We were sold the concept of unity for the whole continent, but all we see is brokenness. The scars of the War of the Ancients linger in every crevasse and canyon across Y'Neshu, and the lie of unity keeps us all from accepting that reality." Mahute's entire body tensed with the venomous anger that seeped into his words. Y'Sawe tensed with him, prepared to fight despite his desire.

"The Empires are far from perfect," the Kanawe began slowly, "but they are far safer than when the Batabari besieged them."

"The Batabari made slaves of the people they conquered. Y'Sewana bought slaves in their efforts to exploit the poor! How can you say this is safer?"

"The death toll is far lower. The people of the Four Empires have endured scars left by the war, yes, but the Wayi Kanawe do what we can to right the wrongs perpetrated by the Batabari Clan!" Y'Sawe took a step back when his brother grunted in amused disappointment.

"The Kanawe have stripped the people of any power to change their condition. J'Karo is sealed. Batabari is sealed. The Teachers are the only ones with voices to bring change, yet their only interest is in maintaining this illusion of peace," Mahute retorted.

"That isn't fair, brother," Y'Sawe challenged, but a sharp look from the Dagger silenced him in an instant.

"What isn't fair, ulu esho, is that you defend the rulers who continue to exploit and oppress the people. What isn't fair is that you continue to do your duty of keeping power out of the mouths of those who need it most. Have you ever considered how different things would be if the Teachers lived up to their name and taught J'Karo?" Y'Sawe raised an eyebrow.

"Have you forgotten that quickly how the war started? The people of Y'Neshu abused J'Karo! They almost broke the continent beyond compare—"

"One clan, Y'Sawe!" Mahute shouted back, but when he saw the fresh pain in his little brother's eyes, he relented. "One clan abused J'Karo for the sake of their ambition. The people of the Kingdoms were the victims, as they are now—"

"And how long do you think it would take to recreate those conditions, Mahute? E? The rulers that oppress the people are fueled by the same selfish need to overpower and conquer that drove the Batabari. To release either of those kiraji wu kana upon the world again would be to drive a dagger into the heart of what little peace we have!" Y'Sawe watched as the veins in his brother's forehead bulged. Mahute sighed as he blinked slowly, then looked at his brother for a final time. He turned and walked away.

"If a dagger will cut away the brokenness of this world," Mahute called to the Kanawe that stood petrified behind him, "then watch as I become it." The heavenly appeal of the marble and gold warped into a grayness that could only be granted by stone from the quarries of Y'Sewana. J'Kana, again trapped in his Master's body, relived another memory. The smell of death spread through the air as the torches on the walls burned in what looked like a temple of sorts. Or a vault.

"What is this?" The sight of blood smeared on the walls and the trail of bodies that littered the halls of the Vault of Y'Leina made his skin crawl in disgust. "Yo fajari ra N'hafu kifitinati." *Fire*, he bade, *surround me.* The flames of the torches surrounded him as he walked the blood-spattered path, and the glimmer of the flames reflected dimly in the golden breastplates of the slain Y'Fuwefo Royal Guard. He bent down to inspect the manner of death. A stab to the back of the neck. The Kanawe looked around from body to body, only to find that each one had been administered a slow and painful death. He stood, his face twisted in distress, and moved deeper into the Vault. It pained him to step over the yifusi who died here, but Y'Sawe knew that the one responsible was not far.

He crept in the silence, only accompanied by the crackle of fire around his body as he surveyed the corridor. He found the Vault's innermost chamber, and when his eyes fell upon the intruder, all his fire—inside and out—extinguished. Mahute stood with a black scroll slightly unrolled in his hand as a dark and ominous aura surrounded him. His breathing became labored, then blissful as he felt the power pulse from it.

"I really wish you hadn't come here, ulu esho," spoke the Dagger, his back still turned to the entryway. Y'Sawe returned to the present upon his brother's address, but still could not believe his eyes.

"What have you done, Mahute?" The question escaped him before his brain caught up. He breathed deeply, righted his mind for the battle that he knew was soon to come, and felt the return of the ring of fire that he'd summoned before. "All these lives lost, and for what?" Mahute finally turned to face him. Mahute the yifusi in the

Y'Fuwefo Royal Guard. Mahute, Y'Sawe's oldest protector. Mahute, Y'Sawe's beloved older brother. He smiled a twisted smile as he spread his arms wide. The scroll pulsed and the aura around Mahute flared. A dark laugh burst from the intruder's belly as he spread his arms and looked to the scroll. He was drunk with the forbidden power it held.

"This is just the beginning, little brother. I can reform all of Y'Neshu with this power! I have finally become the dagger to be plunged into the heart of this artificial peace!" Mahute withdrew a knife from the cloth belt that encircled his waist, and began a strange chant as he plunged the blade into his shoulder. He bled, but for some reason, neither the Y'Sawe of the past or the J'Kana of the present could focus on the color. For that matter, J'Kana noticed, there was no color to this memory, only the knowledge of where color should have been.

"Stop, Mahute," Y'Sawe shouted, but where there should have been an echo, some kind of reverberation of the sound against the stone brick walls of the Vault, there was only his voice, siphoned of its strength, trapped in the dark with the sum of his senses. Another burst of darkness arose from the scroll as Mahute's chant grew in fervor, and

J'Kana found himself thrust from the memory as much as his consciousness.

***

J'Kana jolted back to the present, and before his eyes could refocus on his Master, Y'Sawe's hand was around the boy's throat. The ijeya stood frozen under the force of Y'Sawe's grip, and before he could stop himself, a tremble rippled through his every cell. He knew that the Kanawe was to be feared, but now he enjoyed firsthand experience.

"Master," J'Kana croaked, but the ferocity in the teacher's eyes sent a shockwave through his core.

"Yibe N'hafu wu tufi hafu ra N'otaba shu laenakonali chesi jotinati e," the Ile Kanawe demanded, and when the boy didn't answer, he snarled it in Pedestrian. "When did I give you free entry into my mind?"

"Bara, Kanawe," J'Kana wheezed, "hafu ra lalala jumachechu o!" The Kanawe squeezed harder, his eyes narrowed on his apprentice with the same intensity as the ravenous stares of the ara pack they'd taken on together. "I'm sorry, Master, I won't do it again, I swear!" This time he shouted it, unable to continue on in J'Karo as the tremble worsened. Y'Sawe opened his hand, and the boy fell back to the wet earth of the riverbank.

"The danger you put yourself in while you walked through my memories is a serious issue, J'Kana," Kanawe Y'Sawe scolded. "Natienati o!" He gave the command to the materials from which they would make their tents, and in moments the work of the shelters was complete. Siema dove into the nearest one, unwilling to endure the sudden rise in tension without protection. The black tarp of the tent suddenly glowed a warm orange as she made herself comfortable, and Y'Sawe turned his attention back to his student. "You are only just learning J'Karo, boy. The depth of its applications are still lost on you. What would you have done if the Asanibo returned?" J'Kana sat in the dirt, a look of horror strewn across his face. He hadn't considered that. "When you use J'Karo to see what cannot be seen, it creates a break between your body and your mind. While your mind explores, your body can be killed." The way the Teacher explained it filled the student with dread.

"You make it sound as if I won't die, even if my body does," J'Kana said with a half-hearted chuckle. A sharp glare from the Grand Master stifled the laugh. "You mean that I would still be alive?"

"You would be stuck in a state between life and death, past and future, from which there is no return," he clarified in a tone of voice that subtracted from the already low temperature. "It is because of that that you must be careful of how you apply what you learn in training. What in Y'Kele's name were you thinking?" The final question, delivered on the other side of a weighted pause, provoked J'Kana's worst feelings.

"I wanted to help," he all but whispered, and Y'Sawe's eyes widened. "Something about the Asanibo distressed you, and I thought that if I knew more about what was going on I could be more useful—"

"It is not your job to bear the burdens of your teacher, ijeya—" the Kanawe interrupted, but was interrupted in turn by a suddenly more lively apprentice.

"Except I found something, a connection to Shifi and to what happened a few days ago!" The sudden outburst made Y'Sawe's ears ring with intrigue. He stooped down to look into the eyes of his apprentice.

"What is it that you've discovered?" The question was asked with such a degree of understanding that it made J'Kana hesitate. When the Grand Master heard the boy's answer, his brow furrowed in solemnity.

***

"Yababa," Kamari asked as he bobbed up and down on Siema's back. It amazed J'Kana just how trusting she was, even after all this time. "That thing you did when you said sorry—what was it?" J'Kana took a moment to think back on the story as he paced beside the ara beast. It would be dark soon, and he knew that he would need to get the lele mata back home before dinner or Nihani would have his head.

"Ah," he said, "you must mean the negative conjugation. Instead of saying 'jumachele,' I said 'jumachechu' to let Y'Sawe know that I wouldn't do that again."

"Are there other ways to change the verbs like that?" J'Kana grinned, happy that the boy picked up on such a small detail; even happier still that he thought to ask about the concept.

"There are. First is the negative form that you were shown through the story. To say you don't or won't do something, or that something will not happen, all you need to do is attach –ㄱˋ to the end of the word you want to change into a verb." Kamari looked up quizzically, which made J’Kana laugh. “Think about the concept of being, ‘[illegible],’ turning into a verb.”

“So it becomes haranati, harachele, or harabasa,” Kamari replied, accounting for the neutral, polite and aggressive conjugations respectively. J’Kana smiled as he tousled the little one’s hair.

“Yes, exactly. Now, to say that it isn’t or that you aren’t, change the last sound to -chu.” Kamari tilted his head back now that the instruction had been broken down further.

“Ah, so haranachu, harachechu, or harabachu, then?” J’Kana nodded, a proud expression spread all over his face.

“Good work, hafu wu shehefo,” he applauded. “But do you know how to say that something was or wasn’t?”

“Yababa, you know I don’t,” Kamari said with a poke to J’Kana’s belly. The father looked at his son smugly, but decided to tell him how anyway.

“If you were going to change them to past tense, all you have to do is change the final sound. Haranati becomes haranatu. Haranachu becomes haranacha. Harachele becomes harachelo. Harabasa becomes harabasi. Any time you have a standard verb, this is what you'll do, e?" Kamari nodded, though it was clear that he didn't quite understand. "It's okay if you don't get it just yet, shehefo. It will become clearer the more often you hear it. But for now, I have a surprise for you." The mention of a gift was all it took for Kamari and Siema both to jerk their heads towards the Kanawe.

"What is it, Yababa?" The boy's question was accompanied by a sharp bark from the ara. He shook his head as he reached into the pockets of his purple and blue jilaba wu ajiwele.

"For Siema I have a small piece of dried hibesa. It's her favorite," J'Kana clarified. "And for you, hafu wu koshi kenaninatu shehefo, I have this." The Kanawe held out his hand, and gifted Kamari a folded piece of paper with some hand-scribbled notes on it. Kamari looked disappointed at first, but then his expression shifted to excitement when he realized that the notes were written in J'Karo. "Take some time to do some extra studying, na?"

"I will, Yababa," Kamari shouted with joy. "Koshi koshi arani!" It was at that moment that J'Kana knew that his boy would be silent for the rest of their walk home.

| | | |
|---|---|---|
| 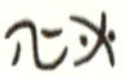 | Tufi | Mind/Thoughts |
| 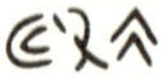 | Laena | Freedom/Liberty/Liberation |
| 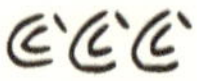 | Lalala | Repeat/Again |
| 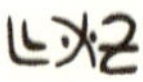 | Kifiti | Around/Surrounding |
| 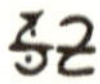 | Joti | Gift/Give |
|  | Bibi | Show/Present |
|  | Kokosi | About |
|  | Tisikoko | Ball/Sphere |
|  | Chala | Help |
|  | Jilaba | Robe |
|  | Ajiwele | Identity |
|  | Batabari | Destruction |
|  | Nani | Meal |
|  | Nanibe | Eat |
|  | Filiwe | Drink |
|  | Mabili | Fight/Battle |
|  | Shiki | Shirt/Tunic |
| 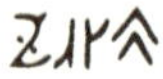 | Jifona | Pants/Trousers |

# 8

# Council

*Folawu, Y'Baule*

It took them five days on the river and another three on land to get to Folawu in Y'Baule, and while J'Kana expected some form of reprieve, he knew that the business of the Kanawe Summit took priority. Even as he walked behind his Master through the ancient city, his head was on a swivel. For all they knew about the Batabari and the Blood Chants, it still left them with more questions than answers. Blood was central to their power, but how much could they do with it? What about Batabari made it so dangerous?

"Eyes sharp, Ijeya," Y'Sawe commanded as he turned down a side street. The cobbled roads and circular build of the black stone buildings betrayed the age of the city. It was one of the last remaining relics from a time before the Thousand-Year War preserved as it was so long ago. The bronze rayemo heads that adorned every doorpost in Folawu seemed to stare right through him, deep into the recesses of his thoughts. Ijeya J'Kana noted the spiraled rooftops, how they seemed to mimic the dance of the wind in the shadowy light of the overcast day. The crash of the ocean waves filled his ears, and though the cold bit at him, the warmth of Siema pressed against his chest kept the sting at bay.

"Where are we going, Kanawe," asked the boy as he weaved through the crowded street. He smiled wearily as he quickly asked, "And will I be able to finally get some rest there?" He watched Y'Sawe tilt his head back in a faint movement of amusement, and it was then that the ijeya realized that the people of Folawu didn't notice him press his way after his Teacher. The people of this ancient city gave him little thought, but it came in a way that was far different than how it was in Memifi. He paid closer attention as he moved around them. They smiled at him, even as they went about their day, and J'Kana found himself surprised at how welcome it made him feel.

"We are going there," Y'Sawe told him with a point. On the other end of his hand stood a beautiful black building, circular and smooth on the sides with a pointed spiral roof and a sign above the door that simply read "Yema." The copper rayemo head sat above the entryway, and copper designs that depicted events from the War of the Ancients wrapped around the structure and into the openings of the roof. A second sign stood just in front that robbed J'Kana of any notion of the building's importance. It was just a bakery.

"Tell me that this isn't just your stomach getting the better of us again, Master," J'Kana joked with slumped shoulders and folded arms. Y'Sawe stifled a chuckle and led the way inside.

The moment the door was opened, the Kanawe watched as his student's jaw met the floor. The bakery was split between a lower and upper level, decorated with vibrant blue and silver carpet and indigo throw pillows. A path of circular cobblestones ran between the low-standing tables that stood arranged all throughout. People of every type sat cross-legged on the floor surrounded by a nest of pillows, little more than a pair of socks on their feet. There was a strong scent of bikibe fesu that wafted through the air, delicately intertwined with the smell of choni echa and lachakule cake. Everything about it brought water to the boy's mouth.

"Sabelle, sella wu amis," shouted the shopkeeper from behind the central counter. By the look of her, J'Kana expected that she couldn't have been any older than 18. Her wavy nightshade hair was barely visible beneath the deep blue headdress, and her eyes, like bright aged amber, glinted in contrast to her radiant dark skin. He was stunned, and to his dismay, she noticed. "Ketu sella basoila ton kiji mon zeile e?" The way she spoke as the Master and Apprentice approached ached with a seductive throb that tensed every muscle in J'Kana's body, though Y'Sawe was largely undisturbed.

"Aran-aran, selle wu ama," Y'Sawe began in the strange tongue, a tone as charming as any that J'Kana had ever heard, "kebe selle wu ijeya me selle mon Kanawe wu taton beje kitsu, veisa basoila dadou." The young woman smiled at the Elder, winked at J'Kana, and when his eyes darted toward the ceiling, she scanned the crowd for someone with a free hand. A woman with the telling pale white skin of a vampire emerged from the back room, and while she shared the jet-black hair of the Asanibo, her eyes were a calming green. The small difference was hardly enough to keep J'Kana's tension at bay, but after a brief and hushed conversation between the vampire girl and the manager, the former took up the latter's post while she escorted the pair along the path.

"What was that," J'Kana asked incredulously. His heart still pounded from the sight of the first girl and the presence of her vampiric friend, but before he was mentally able to grapple with the topic of an obvious Sasabosami, he felt a compulsion to address his Master's sudden shift between languages.

"Surely you've encountered a woman before, J'Kana," Y'Sawe teased with a mocking smirk. He wouldn't even turn his head. He didn't need to, not to know that his ijeya wore a less-than-amused expression.

"You know what I mean," he returned with a poorly held chuckle. "I didn't know you could speak any other language than J'Karo. What did you say when you talked to her?" He nodded to the woman that led the way down the cobbled path and watched as her hips swayed beneath her regal yet form-fitting dress. She moved like a delicate breeze, and danced through his mind just as freely.

"The lovely lady greeted us as friends," Y'Sawe clarified, "and then said perhaps she could offer a seat in the lounge. I kindly thanked her, but told her that we were to attend the summit of Kanawe, provided she could take us."

"It sounded much more…romantic than that," J'Kana considered. "I didn't even think your voice could do that." The joke landed, and Y'Sawe laughed.

"Hey, I had a whole wife years ago, if for nothing else than my proficiency in Katsedu—"

"That was Katsedu?" J'Kana asked the question with such force that their guide turned her head with a sultry grin across her brown sugar lips. He didn't know why he was so surprised. The only word he'd been able to pick up to that point was the greeting, "Sabelle," but that didn't count. Sabele, Sabelle, Sacham, all the languages of Y'Neshu had a similar way to say "hello," and all the people knew them even if they couldn't say much more in their languages of origin.

"Of course," Y'Sawe confirmed. "Katsedu is the national language of Y'Baule and its sister country of Y'Sewana. After J'Karo and Batabari were sealed from the public, the Kanawe introduced Katsedu as a weaker version of J'Karo. It's still imbued with power from Y'Kele but it's safer to use. Limited. Only two nations saw fit to use it. Pedestrian is the common tongue, made by the remainder of the M'Iba Ili. They sought to restore the kind of unity to the people that only happened under the direct influence of Y'Kele. Over time, it became the standard language used in places like Y'Rakili and Y'Fuwefo."

"Omo this is fascinating," J'Kana vocalized.

"I am happy to hear that, Ijeya. You would do well to learn as much as you can of the languages of Y'Neshu. Our duty is to the people, and the better you understand someone, the better equipped you are to help them." J'Kana marveled at the wisdom of his Teacher, and considered how he might commit to doing that. Y'Sawe could see the gears turn in the young man's mind when his shoulder met that of another.

"Bah, Y'Sawe," came a disgruntled growl from a man dressed in an elegant orange jilaba wu ajiwele. J'Kana blinked, and for a moment he thought he saw the *felasa* (characters) of J'Karo written about the robe. Suddenly they began to fade, but before they disappeared completely, J'Kana could make out a name the very moment that it poured from the mouth of his mentor.

"Y'Chifo." The sound oozed out of the Kanawe with a thinly veiled disgust that made J'Kana raise an eyebrow. "Why am I not surprised at your complete lack of concern when walking through a public space?" The obvious Kanawe snorted as a spiteful glint took his eye.

"Says the man so driven by his purpose that he marches right through a colleague. I have half a mind to say you did it on purpose," Kanawe Y'Chifo returned. Y'Sawe shrugged.

"And so what if I did," the Ile Kanawe traded back. "Unlike some of us, I have been hard at work with the investigation." Y'Sawe looked the man over, his eyes lingered around the man's full belly, and the Kanawe sucked his teeth. "I wouldn't expect you to know what hard work looks like, though." Without waiting for a response from the stammering Y'Chifo, Y'Sawe pushed past him and continued after their hostess. J'Kana needed no invitation to do the same.

"Graceis Kanawe wu taton jibehbah," said the woman with a smile as she gestured to a fine pair of hand-carved double doors.

"Aran-aran," Y'Sawe offered with a gentlemanly nod. The boy did the same, and the woman took him by the lapel, her face less than an inch from his.

"If you want to thank me," she said in perfect Pedestrian, "then how about you see me after class, e?" J'Kana yipped with an excitement and fear that he had never experienced, and suddenly he felt a strange sympathy for Nikeli, who put up with so many of his own coarse comments over his time on the streets of Memifi. "Be sure to ask for Anouix," she bade in the height of temptation, and then left before J'Kana could offer a response. Y'Sawe flashed a witty grin at his apprentice, and opened the double doors of the meeting room.

The circular chamber flickered under candlelight, but echoed the same manner of artistry as the elaborate bakery around it. At its center stood a single round table, populated by three women and two men, each in a different colored jilaba wu ajiwele. The felasa flickered in the light, but J'Kana was drawn to the eyes of the Elders that gathered here as they all fell upon him. The moment they started to speak was the moment that Pedestrian fell by the wayside.

"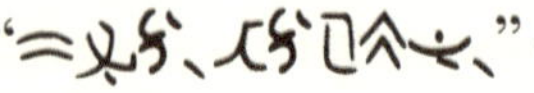" came the elegant alto of the woman in the white robe. Her hair matched its hue, but her milk chocolate skin was smoother than Anouix's had been. There was something motherly about her, warm and inviting, but powerful as a storm on the Fuulu Sea. She looked in J'Kana's direction with a genuine smile. "

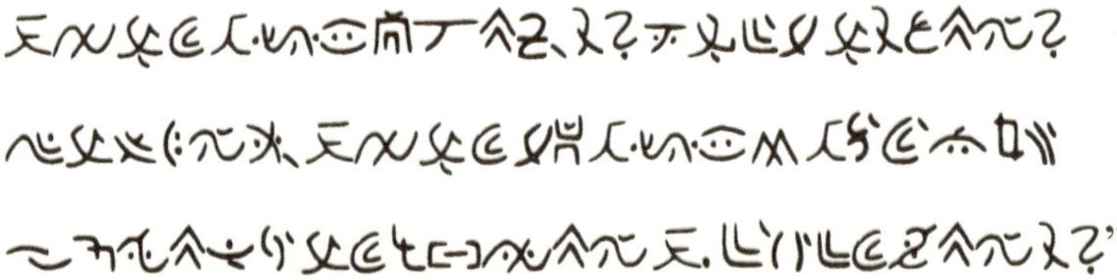"

The line of questions caught J'Kana off-guard as much as the sheer fluency of the J'Karo. She asked about the "ijeya," he knew that, and that she always thought that Y'Sawe thought himself too good for apprentices. By the time he processed her last question, "What changed," he realized the reason behind his rigorous study. The Kanawe, when fully assembled, spoke to each other exclusively in J'Karo. J'Kana listened further, and struggled so much to process what was said that he missed the young man and young woman approach him from across the room.

"[illegible]," spoke the young man cheerfully as he spread his arms wide. J'Kana smiled back as their hands swung together between them, rolled at the grip, and they snapped. "[illegible]." J'Kana took a moment to process, something that he realized his apparent senior ijeya had given him deliberately. In his head, he pieced together that the young man thought he looked new, and then filled in the blanks of the question that followed. "Is this your first time?" J'Kana nodded, too afraid to speak J'Karo in return. His senior smiled at him. "[illegible]." He—J'Chera, the slim but muscular young man with deep green eyes wrapped in a red robe absent of any visible writing—clapped him on the back as he laughed at J'Kana's obvious confusion.

The girl, who had ice-blue eyes and was garbed in an elegant silver robe with matching headdress, looked over J'Kana with an expression that radiated disappointment. Even so, he was fixed on trying to understand so much of a language he had spent the last month studying. J'Chera had said… what? It was okay, to start with, followed by their introductions, but it was the last line that carried the most weight. Piece by piece he broke down the language. In the possibility—for that was the direct translation of "memile"—that J'Kana needed help, "we've got you," he said. The moment the realization struck him and he flashed a grateful smile was when J'Yobena shook her head.

"
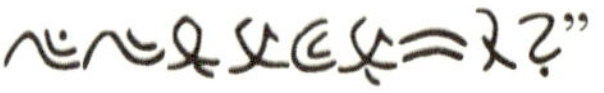" There was venom in her tone as she spoke, as if she thought J'Kana were beneath her. With what she said, he needed no extra time to understand. "You're a little slow, e? Why are *you* here?" He smiled at her, venom in his own expression as he prepared to respond.

"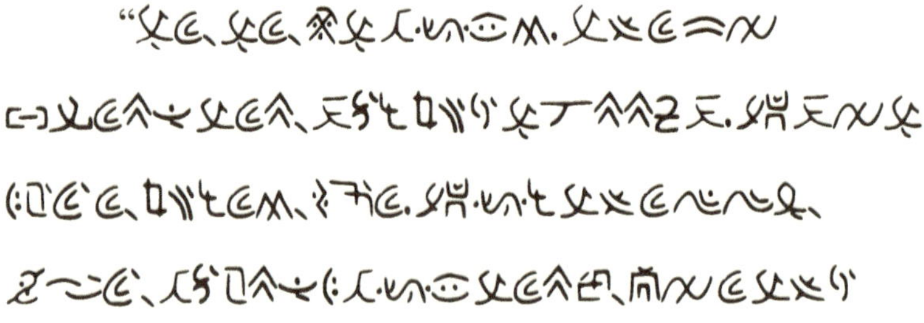
" J'Kana raised an eyebrow with the asking of the question as J'Chera clasped a hand across his open mouth. J'Kana was surprised to find

how easily J'Karo rolled off his tongue when he was frustrated, to the point that he understood his own words perfectly. "Sorry, sorry, my fellow ijeya. I am still slow, however there is much I understand. Thank you very much for your help, J'Chera. As for why I am here, well, I am apprentice to the Grand Master, and he has invited me. What about you, J'Tochari?" He was particularly proud of himself for messing up her name. He understood that "J'Yobena" was J'Karo for "Grand Artwork," or "Masterpiece,"—something that she clearly believed about herself—but he renamed her as "J'Tochari," the Great Mediocrity. That was why J'Chera masked his gaping jaw, and why J'Yobena glowered at him as her anger reached its boiling point.

"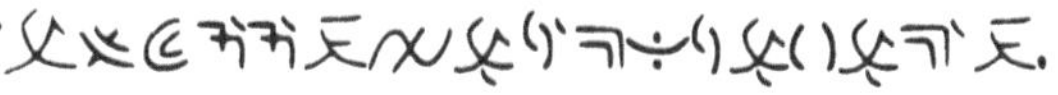

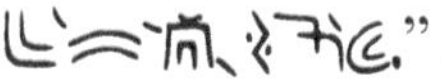" J'Yobena gave her goodbye to J'Chera after pointing out how she didn't need to be disrespected by J'Kana, then stormed back to the other side of the room in a huff. J'Chera watched her go, then looked back at J'Kana, then back at J'Yobena, then back at J'Kana and shook his whole body as he walked to the other side of the newest apprentice.

"Sha," he exclaimed under his breath, "you made J'Yobena go away." The tone he took gave J'Kana the strongest sense that he would be in trouble, but the smile that followed put the boy's mind at ease. "I've been trying to get her to do that for two years! Who knew she was so sensitive about her name!" J'Chera slapped J'Kana on the back again with enough force to almost knock him over, then quickly pulled him by the neck into a half-hug. "Chesi, lele ijeya, and sit next to me. I suddenly want to know much more about you."

***

*Folawu*

Mahute sank his shoulders, pleasantly hidden in a corner of the upper level of the elaborate Yema bakery. Shadows surrounded him, and ensured that his eyes were everywhere. The Blood Fusion that Bahasu forced on him was undesirable at first, but the longer he operated in its power, the more it all fascinated him. The shadows were his to command, sensory information was his to distort, and the blood he spilled became his power. It was clear that the Batabari Clan was onto something when they created the conditions for their abilities. Even the effects of the Blood Tie had been nullified. Each new command over his

Asanibo brought with it an unimaginable pain, but it was the demand of Batabari to cut, to liberate the blood that gave it all power.

Even now, every cell in the Dagger's body yearned for the chance to test the power more, to rend flesh and break bodies, but now was hardly the time for that. Now was a time to watch from the darkness and listen to the business that his brother would conduct. If he was to accomplish his goal of righting the wrongs of this farcical Y'Neshu, he would need to know the movements of his biggest obstacle. The Kanawe, who train in the art of shifting the ike, had the ability to seal away the machinations of the Batabari in the wake of the Thousand-Year War, and Mahute was determined to eliminate them before they could stop him in the same way. The only one exempt from extermination was his little brother, whose blood was needed for a Blood Summon ritual.

He smirked at the irony, how even on his quest for destruction he needed to protect Y'Sawe.

***

The Wayi Kanawe were a sight to behold. In this room sat men and women with more power in one pinkie than the sum of the Empires combined. The smooth stone walls, black in appearance, made the shine of the candlelit wall lamps all the brighter, and in that light, vibrant colors blended and mixed and separated again. J'Kana sat between the Ile Kanawe and his new friend J'Chera, the latter of whom offered to translate the meeting while the former conducted it. Around them, the other Kanawe and J'Yobena sat in wait while Y'Sawe organized his notes.

To J'Chera's immediate right sat the woman from before that teased the Grand Master. J'Chera explained that her name was Y'Leisu, and that she had chosen him to be her ijeya after a chance encounter in a library in Y'Fuwefo. Her white hair draped over her back like an elegant snowfall. The deep greens of her eyes perfectly reflected the lights that danced around them, and occasionally she would glance in Y'Sawe's direction.

The man next to her, clothed in a blue jilaba wu ajiwele, smiled as he talked to a woman in green. J'Kana came to know him as Kanawe Y'Jewo, a Master whose student was tending to business back home in Y'Sewana. Of course, Y'Jewo matched the description of a Y'Sewanan perfectly: tall, knowing orange eyes like a smoldering coal, dark skin, and a wide smile, a feature J'Kana thought always contradicted the Y'Sewanan penchant for battle.

The woman in the green robe, Y'Tiwe, bore the same dark brown skin and matching eyes as J'Kana and Y'Sawe. She looked stern, but kind, and laughed at a joke that Y'Jewo-Baje whispered into her ear. Beside her was Y'Chifo, the Kanawe in orange that had bumped into Y'Sawe outside the chamber. He was bald, stout, and clearly ready to move on with things. He tapped his fingers against the table as his fierce gray eyes rolled in annoyance.

"[illegible]," came the voice of the man in pink, Y'Jaka, that sat next to him. He had a shrewd look about him, well-kept white hair in tight curls that maned his head, and deep green eyes that commanded respect in a way that J'Kana thought only Y'Sawe could manage. "[illegible]." Y'Chifo grumbled something under his breath, but fixed his expression with haste. J'Chera explained that Y'Jaka told him to stop it, that he was one of the Wayi Kanawe, and that Y'Sawe was their Grand Master. He also said that Y'Chifo was still mad about something.

"[illegible]." J'Kana followed Y'Jaka's glare to the source of the comment, and found the regal brown jilaba wu ajiwele gently draped over the elegant frame of a woman that exuded power and confidence. Her name was Y'Okani, and when the room stared into her ice-blue eyes, she doubled down on her statement with a protective twist of her knotted Y'Baulean hair. J'Chera explained that she came to Y'Chifo's defense, stating that respecting Y'Sawe is hard when he is so slow to start the meeting. She leaned dismissively in her chair, which prompted her apprentice, J'Yobena, to do so with equal smugness.

Y'Sawe sighed as he cracked his knuckles. "[illegible]." J'Chera began to explain, however J'Kana signaled with a smile that he knew what the Kanawe meant. Y'Sawe spoke to them about the discovery made by the apprentice, that the Asanibo had a great power to darken everything. The revelation was enough to cause a stir among the teachers, since it was the first information gained since the investigation began so many years ago.

"[illegible]" Y'Okani asked with narrowed eyes. Something about her made J'Kana shiver, but he understood the question to be "what do you mean."

"[illegible]" Y'Sawe continued. A coldness took the room, and as the Kanawe tensed, the swell of their ike became potent, like a suffocating gas that struck at J'Kana's lungs. Blacks and reds fused with yellows and purples as a flash of silver and brown struck the mixture and released an ominous green. Each Kanawe had a color to their ike, and while they were usually imperceptible, they suddenly flooded through the room with such power that J'Kana could see and feel them. His chest became heavy. He fought to breathe. He fought to *see*.

"Kanawe Y'Sawe says that even if we are attentive, we cannot hear or see. We would be awake, but it would be as though we were asleep. Like all the life leaves the world," J'Chera translated. J'Kana slowly focused on his own golden ike, reimagined the connections he had already felt in the past, let the images flow through him and give him life. He settled, though his hands still shook, and met J'Chera's gaze.

"That's exactly how it feels," J'Kana confirmed, and J'Chera's solemn eyes deepened in their gravity.

"" The voice thundered out of Y'Chifo as he shifted in his chair. The frustration was evident in the single vein that pulsed in his neck.

"He just asked about Mahute the Dagger," J'Chera clarified, his tone so much darker than it had been only moments ago when they met.

" 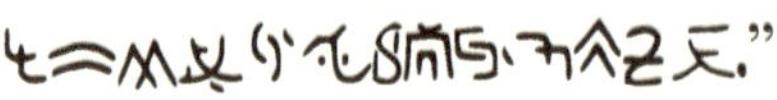." Y'Sawe's tone was even as he dealt another blow to what little composure still remained amongst the Kanawe.

"He told them that Mahute is still free, and that he commands the Asanibo," J'Chera again translated, his concern still on the rise. His fears echoed against the chamber walls, fully displayed through the outrage of the Kanawe. Even as they criticized Y’Sawe, he sat calmly and waited for his moment to explain.

“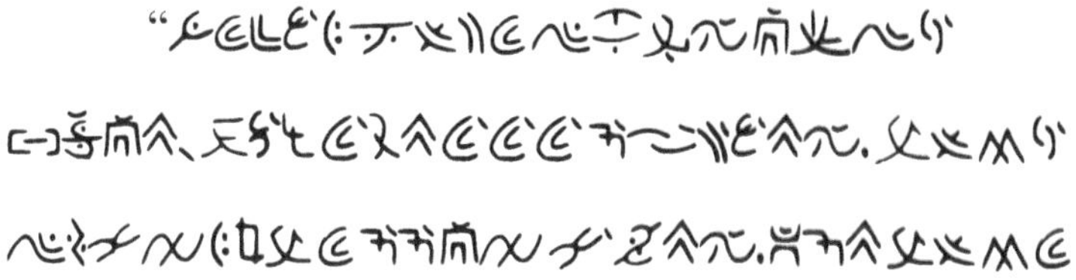
” J’Kana half expected the chamber to erupt in a chaotic cacophony of voices, but the other Kanawe simply looked resolute.

“He says that the yifusi of Y’Rakili took him back to Febetu, but he escaped again, and that you two were attacked on the way to J’Rota. He also said that before you could do anything, his servants disappeared.” J’Chera raised his hand to speak, and the Ile Kanawe nodded his head in acknowledgement. “You said ‘Mahute’s servants.’ Why use that terminology when you could have simply said, ‘Asanibo,’ Afonawe Ile Kanawe?”

“The Asanibo,” J’Kana spoke, and almost flinched when every eye in the room fell on him. It was the disgusted glare of J’Yobena that gave him confidence to continue. “The Asanibo have been making elokobi of the peoples they come across. The ones that attacked us wore the armor of Y'Rakilian Royal Guard."

"This is preposterous," Y'Okani said in the wake of a loud smack of her teeth. "Elokobi haven't been seen since—"

"Shifi," Y'Jewo spoke gravely. Y'Okani cut her eyes at him, clearly unhappy to have been interrupted. Nevertheless, the elder Y'Sewanan spoke further. "It was the first time that elokobi had resurfaced since the armies of Batabari were defeated in the days of old." There was an eerie stillness to the air.

"My question," interjected the regal Y'Leisu, "is why all this now? The Scroll of Batabari was stolen over twenty years ago. How is any of this possible, and for what purpose does Mahute manipulate the Asanibo?" The moment J'Kana blinked, the room went dark. He saw himself at the table with the Kanawe and ijeya, but the vision was blurred. For some reason, he couldn't make out the colors or the temperature the way he had during the vision in Memifi, but the murkiness of his surroundings only made him push deeper in. His senses were suddenly overwhelmed. The smell of blood. Air that chilled him to the bone. A collective scream followed by the chilling laugh of Mahute the Dagger. None of it, however, compared to what he saw.

***

"That was a lot," Kamari said as he buried his face into J'Kana's side. Midway through the story, he thought to grab the leather book of J'Karo so he could try to follow along, but it quickly proved to be far too much for him. "How do you remember it all?" J'Kana's face grew darker under the candlelit wall lamps of their batalu (living room).

"Experiencing dark moments has a way of highlighting the details," he replied softly, and soothed the boy with a squeeze of the shoulders. "Even so, it wasn't all bad, shehefo. I honestly learned a lot about how to speak J'Karo. Did you notice how they spoke?" Kamari nodded, but then adopted a look of innocent thoughtfulness.

"I noticed that you don't group the vowels together. 'Aa' is pronounced 'A-A,' but there's something else. It's like the last part of the word is the one with all the power," he offered, and J'Kana's eyebrows lifted with the corners of his mouth in pleasant surprise.

"It is the second to last part, hafu wu ulu ijeya," he corrected, "but look at how smart you are! If you notice, the particles that we talked about before attach to the words they follow, and it moves the powerful point to the end of the word."

"Oh, so instead of 'HA-fu wu WO-ta-me,' it would be 'ha-Fu wu wo-TA-me?'" Kamari's question gave a rise to J'Kana's eyebrow.

"Yes," he told him, apprehensively. "Why use that example specifically?" The tone with which he asked the question made Kamari smile a devious smile.

"You know why," the boy assured him with a backward tilt of the head, and the Kanawe laughed. "Come on, Yababa, it's not funny! I would be a great big brother, and teach my sister all that I learn about J'Karo and even Katsu… Kata…"

"Katsedu," J'Kana completed. "Best to focus on the task in front of you—"

"While *you* focus on my sister?" Kamari wouldn't let it go, and J'Kana shook his head with humor written across his face.

"How about we focus on building your vocabulary so that there's less confusion when the J'Karo grows steeper," he deflected. Kamari pouted, but he knew it to be the right choice. When he opened the book again, J'Kana nodded. "Let's begin, then. Slowly, this time, shehefo…"

| Memi | Possible/Can |
|---|---|
| Memile | Possibility/Probability |
| Mau | Have/Possessing/Owning |
| Toba | Dagger |
| Mojoma | Return |
| Cheche | By |
| Loji | Hit/Attack/Strike/Assault |
| Baeri | Reaction/Feeling/Happening/Sensing |
| Baru | Need |
| Fobe | Alright/Fine/Okay |
| Sata | Still |
| Mohera | Slow |
| Jatomamuke | Command/Order/Control |
| Mama | Even |
| Tati | Attentive |

| | |
|---|---|
| Laku | Awake |
| Kulaku | Asleep |
| Loutu | Dark |
| Foma | Meeting |
| Sikatu | Hard/Difficult |
| Wasu | Respect/Admire/Admiration |
| Mikena | Before |
| Roli | World |
| Somi | For |
| Ayona | Allowed |
| Jishela | Well |
| Sikikesi | Invited/Invitation |
| Tufi | Mind/Thinking |
| Amoju | Thought/Thoughtful/Thinking |
| Ilelawo | Always |
| Ilifu | First |
| Jeyu | Meaning |

# 9

# Separation

*Folawu—Yema Bakery*

Even with the information on how it works, they were too slow. The Wayi Kanawe, the strongest minds in all Y'Neshu, charged with the safety of the people and preservation of J'Karo, failed to recognize the Life-Drain brought on by the Asanibo.

"Move out of the wa—" J'Kana shouted with thunder in his voice. The sudden change, the absence of color or light, the distortion of sound, alerted the Ile

Kanawe and his ijeya as much as the boy's maa bacha (future-sight).

"Too late," snarled the creature as its jagged claws plunged through Y'Okani's throat. The monster ripped her flesh as it retracted, and smiled with an evil laugh as the Kanawe's head slammed into the table. J'Yobena screamed at the sight, and the Asanibo, framed as a younger woman, turned her head to face her next target. The other Kanawe stood swiftly and backed away from the table, all eyes glued to their fallen comrade. Another appeared behind J'Chera and sniffed his flesh as its bright red eyes glowed through the sudden emptiness of the room. The soa ijeya whipped around and bounded backward into the strong frame of yet another intruder.

"Watch where you are going, boy," burned the deep resonance of Mahute's voice. Before J'Chera could respond or attack or plead for his life, the strong arm of the Dagger pounded into his neck so hard that the apprentice flew through the air. His back met the wall, and a knife found its sheath in the flesh of his hip a second later. J'Kana noticed a smile on Mahute's face as he paced the room. The Kanawe tensed, and Y'Sawe took a defensive position in front of his apprentice. The female Asanibo drew closer still to J'Yobena, whose haughty eyes were now drenched in despair as they lingered on her master's body.

"What have you done," Y'Tiwe whispered, appalled. Mahute the Dagger glanced dismissively in her direction, then decidedly turned to look his brother in the eye.

"I imagine that you chose to meet in the back room of a bakery to hide your presence from me," Mahute mused as his hands clasped behind his back. "The idea would have been decent enough…if my brother wasn't in your midst." All eyes in the room shifted nervously to Y'Sawe, who stood fiercely before his apprentice.

"You shouldn't have been able to follow me here," spoke the Grand Master with more aggression in his tone than J'Kana had ever heard. "We traveled by water to mask our scent." Mahute flashed a fanged grin that chilled the blood of all those in the room.

"Ah my ulu esho," the Dagger spoke in a gentle tone that more than conveyed a threat, "you expect me to miss a meeting that has brought up my name so much?"

"How dare you eavesdrop on this sacred gathering," Y'Chifo barked, only to have his mouth slashed by the female Asanibo. J'Kana's eyes flashed between J'Yobena and Y'Chifo. *She moves like a breath leaving the body,* he thought, and shivered at the sudden chill to his core.

"And how dare you raise your voice to me?!" Mahute's growl caused the Asanibo to snarl collectively with the baring of the Dagger's fangs, but his raised hand held them in place. He calmed himself, ran his fingers through the locs of his hair and shook them loose.

"Mahute," Y'Sawe called, and the commander of vampires met his gaze just as his eyes glinted with a familiar golden spark.

"Save your sanctimonious drivel for someone who doesn't see the truth. You all sit here in the dark, whispering of damages done in the past while you ignore the filth that plagues Y'Neshu to this day. You, the great protectors of peoples and keepers of knowledge! The ones chosen by Y'Kele Himself! I wonder how disappointed He would be to see how ignorant His Teachers have become."

"Says the man who incites chaos and begets destruction," Y'Sawe countered. Mahute donned a humored smile as his chin touched his chest, then he lifted his head to look down his nose at his brother. "You think yourself better than us because of the people who have died because of you?"

"I think myself better," Mahute shot back, "because I do not pretend to be any holier than I am. I am a rogue, a usurper, the very bane of the status quo that you all protect from pedestals so close to the sun you are blinded to the darkness!"

"And you use your supposed awareness as an excuse to embrace it! The people of Shifi had nothing to do with any of what you speak!" Y'Sawe's voice shook for the first time that J'Kana could remember. He didn't have to look to know that tears welled in his Master's eyes.

"Ah Shifi, the Holy City of Y'Rakili," Mahute mocked with arms spread wide as his deranged pets watched from the sides of the room. "Let me ask you, 'Grand Master,' did they consider their holiness when they served as the passage for the slave trade? Did they preach Y'Kele's mercy to all when we trudged those grounds in chains? Where was this famous deliverance when our parents sold us to Hanbari? Where was their sense of justice when we were stripped of our rights, our voices, our humanity? We were merchandise, and the people who oppressed us were so casually embraced by those said to stand against them." Y'Sawe shook his head violently, a pained expression burned into his face.

"Nothing you say will justify your nephew's death," spat the Grand Master as the tears streamed down his face now. "You condemned my wife and son to death, with no remains to bury!" J'Kana looked into Mahute's eyes, and for the first time there was something akin to remorse.

"A nephew…" he whispered, a tremble in his voice that was much heavier than his brother's. He trailed off, clearly unable to process the news, and his two female Asanibo slowed in their stride about the room.

"Tell me, Mahute," Y'Sawe growled, his face darkened in the void of a room. "What do you have to say for your supposed 'justice' that throws away the lives you say you want to save?" For a moment there was no answer. Mahute the Dagger paced the floor, slid a hand over his forehead, then stopped right in front of the Ile Kanawe with a dark look on his face.

"I don't know, little brother," the Dagger finally offered, then asked, "what did you say when you threw *me* away?" Suddenly Y'Sawe took a step back. "What did you say to justify the guards stripping your older brother of his rights? What did you say upon our reunion in Memifi to the torture I endured for twenty years in solitude?" Y'Sawe still hesitated to answer. "You throw me away in the name of your peace, yet judge me when I make the same sacrifices in favor of justice."

"We have heard enough," Y'Jewo interjected, nostrils aflare and brows furrowed in anger. "We will send you back to Febetu, or we will send you to the throne of Y'Kele for judgment." Mahute smiled as he tilted his head to the side.

"Khafenu," he whispered, and one of the two Asanibo disappeared into the void. Y'Jewo smiled himself.

"!"

The force of his voice was almost enough for him to recreate the vibrance that was lost at the Asanibo's emergence. She erupted from the shadows, her claws squarely aimed at the Kanawe's face, but they were swatted away in a flash of gold that defied the empty features of the room. The moment Khafenu was rebuffed, Y'Jewo went on the offensive. He struck at her shoulder, her leg, stabbed at her midsection, crashed down on her head, but the curved sword slipped through her like a hand through water. She slashed at him, fangs bared and the look of hunger in her rabid crimson eyes. Three strikes in rapid succession. A wound on his arm, his leg, and his throat. Khafenu looked at Mahute with a pleading look, and he nodded.

The vampire's mouth stretched wide as her face contorted into the form of a bat. He screamed, and then grew silent as she plunged her jagged fangs into the flesh of his neck. He flailed for a moment, then grew still as the kofesha slipped from his hand. The remaining Kanawe, outraged, each began their chants while the Grand Master's head turned to face his apprentice.

"Ijeya ni, evacuate the bakery and get away from here," Y'Sawe ordered, his voice stern and militant, his eyes narrowed with a quiet rage that, to J'Chera and J'Yobena, was not to be challenged. J'Kana didn't share their apprehension.

"No, Kanawe," the boy pleaded as the other Asanibo paced the room like the tiecha beasts that roamed the Kalisechu Plains, "We're stronger together—"

"Chilu hafu wu bichake shu jumanati o, Ijeya!" The shout thundered against the ripples of nothingness. *Do what I say, Ijeya,* he had commanded. J'Kana did his best to blink the tears away, but the memory of separating from his father was enough to bring them back. Y'Sawe placed a hand on the boy's shoulder, and when J'Kana opened his eyes, he saw a proud look on his Master's face. "N'memile hafu ni ra N'tebi neralinachu, achiso mojomanati. Somi Wehela malanati o. Baunanati e?" Y'Sawe glanced at J'Chera when he asked the question. Did he understand? The senior apprentice nodded. "Bashurakonali belenati."

J'Yobena, still distraught from Y'Okani's death, sprinted for the stairs that took them out of the back room. J'Chera started to follow her, when he noticed that J'Kana hadn't moved. He grabbed the newest apprentice by his arm and pulled him along while the other Kanawe began to speak such J'Karo that the sum of their ike singed the air. The nothingness that surrounded them began to distort, and the Asanibo growled as their heads darted from one hole in their illusion to the next. J'Kana's eyes watched them turn to the Kanawe and begin their assault, but just as Y'Sawe entered the battle, the door slammed shut.

The building rumbled, and before the three Ijeya could utter a word, the customers and staff charged the door. Panic swelled, both from the crowd and the apprentices who now scanned the bakery for another exit. J'Chera and J'Kana both hurried to a window and attempted to open its bolted frame, frantic as the screams and rumbles of the once-calm Yema crescendoed beyond what their nerves could take. J'Yobena tapped her foot impatiently, then looked back at the corridor that now served as the tomb of her Kanawe. She rolled her eyes as she pushed the boys out of the way.

"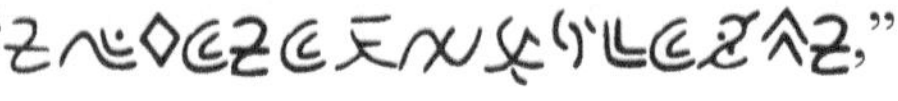," she all but yelled, an emotional rattle in her voice as the window changed into a door. A loud hiss erupted from somewhere deep within the building. All three of them looked back as an overwhelming heat dominated the air. Without a word to her fellow students, J'Yobena sprinted through the door. They followed only seconds behind, the air increasingly hot and then…fire! The explosion rocked Folawu as flames burst in every direction. The ijeya ni were thrown with a force that threatened to break bones, and while their ears rang like the bells in a Shifian Wehela Festival, J'Kana finally noticed the smell of burnt hutije.

***

*Outer Grasslands*

It was minutes before they could move. Hours before their hearing returned to normal. None of them thought to speak, as the events to which they had born witness left each one stunned beyond their wildest imaginations. They had seen people—Kanawe—slaughtered in front of them, had felt an explosion to their backs, and ultimately lost the guidance of their respected Masters, some more permanently than others.

Little by little, a glimpse of their surroundings would break through their feelings of defeat. Gray clouds in the sky. Deep green hutije, burnt from the fires of the prior eruption. Golden mahaju grain, only found in the Kalisechu Plains, reached for a sun that refused to shine. The great Amejai Mountains stood at their back, while the dark reaches of the Kehemu Forest stood off in the distance. J'Kana began to move, to gather the hutije around him to make a small hut. He reached for a knife securely hidden within the folds of his cloth belt, and for a moment he thought about Y'Sawe's order, to go back to *that* place, for the Wehela. Even more, he thought about Y'Sawe, and all he had given. The pouches that wrapped around his belt were each a gift from his Master, bought before they had left Memifi with their journey north in mind. J'Kana was cared for, physically as well as mentally, and now he feared that all that was gone.

*You need to practice your shift as often as you can,* J'Kana recalled. He cut the hutije as the burst of emotion hit, but then he calmed himself. Whereas the conditions of their surroundings had been little more than background information, he made them his focus. He closed his eyes as he continued to do his work, felt the stillness of the air and the asynchronous rhythms of J'Yobena and J'Chera's breathing. It calmed him, and his ike surged within him.

"We can't stay here," J'Yobena's voice rattled through the silence, her eyes fixed upon the shadows of the forest just south of them. She didn't have to say why, for they all knew. They had been transported to the doorstep of their enemy, and if the Asanibo in any regard discovered their presence, the fight on their hands would be greater than even what had transpired at the Summit. "We have to move."

"You are too tired," J'Kana spoke with a flare of irritation. "You need to rest. We all do." He could feel her glare at the back of his head, but even his annoyance with her did nothing to stifle the flow of his golden ike through him. She approached through the patch they had made in the tall grass. It was then that it occurred to him where they'd landed.

"What if our abrupt arrival alerted the Asanibo? We are only a short distance from the mouth of the forest—"

"It is day," J'Kana interrupted, another cut to the hutije. He pulled some twine from a different pouch, and began to tie the ends together to make weaving them easier. "Asanibo can only move freely outside the forest at night, so while we have this opportunity, we should rest."

"Listen to him, J'Yobena," J'Chera groaned, his hand on the knife wound in his hip. She shot her eyes to J'Chera, vile disapproval fastened to her face, but he flashed her his best attempt at a comforting smile, and her rage subsided.

"Whatever," she said, finally, and walked away from the others.

"No," J'Kana challenged, "we need to work out a plan while we rest. First, we need to take inventory of the food we have on hand. Second, we need to find a water source and refill our skins. After that, we need to decide on a way out of the Leisu Usele." J'Chera looked around at the mention of the Peaceful Realm, and noted that J'Kana was right.

"To go where," asked the belligerent young woman with her arms folded.

"To find the Wehela Stone in Shifi," he responded. Just the mention of it was enough to send him back a decade, to how he ran from the Asanibo and the elokobi that pursued him. How he ran to Memifi only to run from the yifusi. How he ran to a Kanawe only to repeat the cycle. His anger grew, but he did what he could to channel the rage into his shifting ike, to seek the connection between the Creator Y'Kele and His creation. Still, he berated himself. All of this running away, and only a slight handle on the way of J'Karo to show for it. He was tired, and he refused to flee another day in his life.

"Is that what the Ile Kanawe meant," J'Chera asked, his bright brown eyes widened. J'Kana nodded as his hands swiftly worked to finish a sixth hutije braid.

"I can only assume that my Master wished to rendezvous in a place where he knew we wouldn't attract attention," he offered, to another agitated huff from J'Yobena.

"And what makes you think that any Kanawe survived," she challenged. J'Kana moved to put the braids in trios along the ground, the tops of which leaned into each other in half of a surprisingly stiff hut. He tied them together at the tops, and set to work on another stack to finish it out. "I mean, my Master died. Who is to say that after the explosion, yours isn't just as dead?" J'Kana's fists clenched around the stalks of tall grass, and J'Chera shot her a look. The thought had crossed his mind before in the hours they waited for their hearing to return, but he didn't want to think about that. Not yet.

"Even if he is," J'Kana started in measured pace, "he has given me an assignment and I will see it through. To that end, we should pool our knowledge as much as our resources." The two of them stared at him with blank expressions.

"What do you mean, M'ba Ijeya?" J'Chera asked as he slid into his hut.

"He means that if we are going all the way to Shifi, there is a chance that he'll drag us down as he is now. His knowledge of J'Karo is elementary, you remember. Bah! I lose my Kanawe and get saddled with dead weight!"

"Omo, it's not fair to call him that, J'Yobena," J'Chera challenged. J'Kana continued to work his hands. His mind drifted from the conversation for a moment as his ike tugged at him. His head snapped up, his eyes filled with gold, power surged through the air towards the forest, and before he could stop himself, his feet marched the path paved by the light of his soul. J'Chera and J'Yobena continued to argue until the former noticed. "Oye, J'Kana! Where are you going?"

"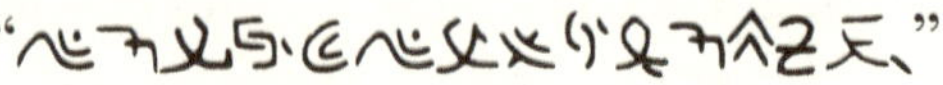" J'Kana replied with J'Karo he didn't know he knew. The two senior ijeya exchanged a fearful look.

"If something in Kehemu calls to you," J'Yobena answered, "it would be foolish to follow the sound!" He didn't respond. Every step he took further blurred the lines between the natural and spiritual realities. He heard whispers, enchantments, sounds of creation, of past and present and future. Of Y'Kele, gentle yet firm, patient and kind, who called to the very depths of his soul. J'Chera and J'Yobena watched him walk through the soso trees, irreverent of the darkness that was so clear to see. It was like a moonless night in there, devoid of all light and just as disorienting to the senses as Mahute's arrival, yet J'Kana walked with urgency, with a greater sense of purpose and direction than the others thought possible.

J'Chera pushed through the jade brush and orange vines, jumped over the overgrown black roots and ducked the dark branches of trees that swayed in the absence of wind. He did all he could to keep the pace with J'Kana, even as his wound throbbed and his surroundings endeavored to keep them apart. J'Yobena did the same, though without the same degree of intensity. She was more cautious, more focused on the sounds that echoed through the darkness and the shadows that shifted on all sides.

"Jeketinawe haranati," came a whisper that dripped of warmth and honey. J'Yobena felt at ease, as did J'Chera, though they had no real reason to. They had simply been commanded to be calm, and so it happened. While J'Kana continued on the poorly defined path, his seniors carefully surveyed their surroundings as they continued to follow. J'Chera clenched his side with a gasp, and J'Yobena rushed to help carry him the rest of the way.

A fog slithered and bubbled from between the dark brown tree trunks. J'Kana halted, the others followed suit, and all three ijeya ni felt the solid weight of the fog sweep over them as it rose to the heights of the thick canopy. The weight of the smoke made it hard to breathe, hard to think, and then suddenly it was gone, like blown out candlelight. The ijeya ni, who stood only a few feet from each other, now noticed the massive ovular stone that took the space between them. It was painted in silver and gold, and engraved with a line of J'Karo that read, "Ti Wasu me wiyi ra N'koshi jiu Y'Kele shu wishimachele o," or "Honor and praise belong to Y'Kele Most High."

"Either we are all blind," J'Chera started with a gulp, "or that is the stealthiest rock in the whole of Y'Neshu."

"My Kanawe told me stories," J'Yobena recalled with a tinge of darkness in her voice that J'Chera couldn't hear and J'Kana couldn't ignore, "about how Wehela Stones were placed around Y'Neshu by the M'Iba Wayi Kanawe. Some, like in Shifi, were placed out in the open to ward off evil in certain cities. Others were placed in secret locations, and only made their presence known to the Kanawe themselves." As the words left her, her gaze drifted to J'Kana's astonished countenance. "But you are no Kanawe."

"As if I couldn't see that for myself," J'Kana replied, his eyes cut to J'Yobena as a fist clenched at his side. "Perhaps *I* am not the slow one here." J'Yobena, now irate, took a step towards J'Kana only to be halted by the sudden "uhhh" from J'Chera.

"What is going on," he asked as the Wehela Stone radiated in the darkness. The light pulsed, and with every undulation of its luster, the very corners of the forest were made known. Neither J'Kana nor J'Yobena could answer before all three were struck by the light, and one after another, they all fell to the ground.

***

*Folawu, Y'Baule*

"Mahute!" The shout echoed throughout the desolate street. Broken bodies lay folded on the ground and along the damaged rooftops. Y'Sawe couldn't believe what his eyes beheld. Blood dripped down the Kanawe's face and forced his left eye closed. He labored to breathe, his good eye still trained on the back of his murderous brother, who only just stopped in his advance through the debris. The Dagger turned his head, a solemn look on his face as his eyes met that of the Ile Kanawe.

"Leave it to my ulu esho to survive an explosion at point blank," he said coolly, an air of respect about him. "But surely you don't intend to continue the fight."

"I cannot allow you to get away with this," the Grand Master shouted. His whole body shook from the fury, but he knew he needed to be calm. If he was going to shift the ike and live, then he needed to restore his connection with Y'Kele, to regain his senses about the world around him. But he was still obscured. Somehow his brother had found a way to seal his hato, his connection, and the realization made him exclaim in anguished frustration.

"Have you finally realized how powerless you are? I control the Asanibo, your beloved connection, and the fate of this entire continent. You wish that I would return the Batabari scroll, but I have destroyed it. You wish that I would abandon its knowledge, but I will give it back to the people from whom it is derived, and then together with me at the helm, we will burn your peace to the ground and rebuild it from the ashes in true unity."

"We will never allow you to do that," Y'Sawe vowed with a growl from the depths of his soul filtered through his voice. Mahute strode back to the plot of scorched earth whereupon his brother knelt. He could feel the power of the blood in the streets, blood that was drawn to him as much as he was drawn to it. He stooped down, took his brother by the face, and dug his fingernails into Y'Sawe's flesh.

"Ulu esho, it is not yours to *allow* me to do anything," the criminal hummed with animus venom. His gaze lingered on his brother as the splashing sound filled their ears, truly the only sound that could be heard. "Even so, I accept your challenge." He threw Y'Sawe to his back, then walked down the broken cobbles of the road again. He turned back. "If your apprentice survives, you can meet me together in the throne room." The blood surrounded him, and in another moment Mahute was gone.

***

*Samanu Usele*

Echoes in the darkness resonated first in J'Kana's mind, but where concern should have set in, calm washed over him. He understood almost immediately that this was the work of Y'Kele, since there was no other force that could imbue a Wehela Stone with power. The ijeya looked around, eager to find his comrades, but unable to. He looked ahead as his ike burst from him. Golden flecks of life energy pooled around him, and he felt, for the first time in his life, whole, as if he had been truly seen both inside and out.

Without a word, he stepped forward through the darkness, and watched as the golden flecks swirled about the terrain. There was a freedom that came with this mysterious space as more voices filtered in. He heard the sounds of battle, the sounds of celebration, and as he heard them, he saw glimpses of the people that made them. Y'Sawe poured into his field of vision, and while no words were spoken, he knew that his Kanawe was still alive. Upon that revelation, though, the image of the Ile Kanawe burst into streaks of gold that, as they fell, became as clouds lit by the rising of the sun.

J'Kana felt a shift of his ike, involuntary, unexpected, but entirely welcome. His eyes glowed the color of his ike, and the world around him changed to reflect the visions that he saw. It was the forest. He, J'Chera, and J'Yobena lay on the ground around the Wehela Stone, and while his companions twitched, J'Kana bolted upright. Sounds echoed from deeper within the Kehemu, and as the newest of the ijeya ni watched the movements of the dark, there appeared a boy of stark white skin, dark hair, and surprisingly bright yellow eyes. His emergence distorted what little sensory information that the forest provided, and immediately J'Kana knew that he was Asanibo.

The vision crumbled to golden dust as a new one took its place. That same Asanibo led the charge as J'Kana, J'Chera, and J'Yobena followed him by night. In the distance, he could hear something, like the sound of a dense wind through treetops, but different. Wetter. Louder. This Asanibo led them to a river, and what was better, they could *hear* it.

J'Kana bolted awake, though J'Chera and J'Yobena still rested by the Wehela Stone. His head throbbed as the whispers continued, and his eyes glowed the golden hue again as he made out what they said.

"Ti mala ra kurawenati," he repeated, and the golden light of his ike pulsed through the Kehemu Forest. A rustle in the underbrush struck his ears, and his body tensed as he turned his head toward it. There, in the darkness, glowed a pair of watchful yellow eyes. As their owner cautiously approached, what little color and light within the forest began to siphon away. Another moment passed, however, and they returned. "Release the vision," J'Kana whispered in translation as the young-looking Asanibo looked around, angry and afraid.

"What did you do," asked the vampire with a growl. J'Kana met his glare with one of his own, his breath measured as the monster snarled, then, with all the peace of Y'Kele and confidence of the J'Foja he had once been, he smiled a knowing smile.

***

"Who is he, Yababa," Kamari begged at the peak of his excitement, "who is he?" By now, the boy had climbed into J'Kana's lap and pressed against his chest so that they sat face to face. J'Kana couldn't help but chuckle at the wonder in the ulu mata's eyes, and clasped his hand over the boy's face as he gently shoved him onto the couch cushion beside him.

"Hey, do you want me to tell the story or just skip to the answers," he asked with a raised eyebrow.

"The answers," Kamari shouted back, a happy smile plastered across his jawline. J'Kana poked him in the forehead.

"Ah, but then you would never learn, shehefo," he told him. "Everything about our story is meant to show us something, and to only focus on answers without thought of the questions themselves leaves us vulnerable to undermining our history. The forest is just as important as the path that carries us through it." Kamari, thoughtful, finally nodded his head.

"I understand, Yababa," he responded with a smile, then promptly hopped down and ran across the floor to the other room, picked up the tattered leather book, and handed it to his father as a sign that he was ready for today's lesson. "Please, teach me to see the forest in full." J'Kana, taken aback by the wise request of his little boy, blinked in surprise, but then smiled warmly.

"Alright, shehefo," he assured him. He opened the book, careful to look through for something that he knew would be of service to his son, and then, as if inspired by Y'Kele Himself, he found it. "Here," he said. "Today, you learn about the body and the spirit."

| | | |
|---|---|---|
| 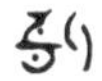 | Josu | Body |
|  | Yewo | Head |
| 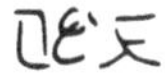 | Kalio | Face |
|  | Bacha | Eyes |
|  | Olo | Nose |
|  | Biyi | Mouth |
|  | Hobusa | Cheek |
|  | Nakoche | Ear |
|  | Tolaki | Tongue |
|  | Chi | Tooth |
| 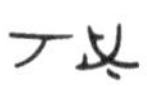 | Ubo | Throat |
| 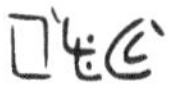 | Chayela | Neck |

| | |
|---|---|
| Ale | Collar |
| Mashu | Bone |
| Shijusa | Blood/Juice |
| Teiri | Muscle |
| Kiu | Arm |
| Afochi | Leg |
| Bereka | Chest |
| Kiushama | Elbow |
| Afochishami | Knee |
| Shoba | Hand |
| Chehu | Foot |
| Yifuti | Shoulder |
| Oyula | Hip |
| Taramu | Back |
| Hajena | Stomach |
| Fitu | Fingers |
| Tinoe | Toes |

| | |
|---|---|
| Fahila | Hair |
| Usaba | Energy |
| Temiri | Presence |
| Fuulu | Spirit |
| Ike | Soul |
| Haro | Rock/Stone |
| Hato | Connection |
| Kurawe | Release |
| Bike | Call |
| Wehela | Worship |
| Jiu | Up/Tall/High/Lifted/Exalted/Elevate/Elevated |
| Samanu | Divine |
| Usele | Place/Territory/Location/Domain |
| Ulusi | Visible |
| Kaulusi | Invisible |
| Wishima | Belonging |

# 10

# Blood and Knowledge

*Kehemu Forest*

J'Kana watched as the Asanibo paced the ground, their eyes still locked in the shade of the forest. J'Chera and J'Yobena began to stir, but neither awakened from their Wehela-induced sleep. J'Kana noted his sharp features and slim frame, the aggression behind his yellow eyes and the inner kindness that they betrayed. He *could* kill, yes, but J'Kana hardly saw him as a killer.

"Who are you," asked the vampire, since his first question was only met with the slick smile of the ijeya.

J'Kana took his time to answer, and for a moment looked at the hair on the Asanibo boy's head. It wasn't black, like the ones controlled by Mahute. It was brown, like the inside of a tojana root.

"I am J'Kana," he replied flippantly, as though his name had little meaning, then changed the subject to suit his distraction. "Hey, you don't have black hair." The Asanibo boy staggered in his pace as surprise adorned his expression. "E, so it does mean something?" The creature's jaw tightened, his eyes narrowed on the unwelcome guest. J'Kana's eyes softened. "I didn't mean to offend you. I'm sorry."

"To kham basi ye tuzo," the Asanibo spoke with a deep growl, and for a moment the colors of the Wehela Stone began to distort, the already frigid air began to lose all sensation, but a dull vibration from the Stone restored their surroundings. The monster spawn's eyes widened in outrage, while the Student glanced at the Stone with a smile. "What—"

"It would seem that your Batabari is unwelcome in the presence of Y'Kele," he interrupted with a playful shrug. Suddenly, he could hear the sounds of the muka beasts that chittered and screamed as they swung through the treetops. He smelled the sweet scent of the soso nuts mixed with the wet soil beneath their feet. He felt the warmth offered by the gentle glow of the Stone. The vampire watched him as he took a deep breath and felt the powerful current of his ike swirl within him.

"You are one of *them*," snarled the Asanibo, clearly aware of his ties to the Kanawe. J'Kana raised an eyebrow as he folded his arms.

"And *you* are very aggressive," he teased, his smile still in place despite the obvious ire of his company. It was J'Kana's turn to pace now, to draw near to the potential threat on the other side of the Stone. "Even so, I doubt you would do me any harm."

"What makes you so sure," growled the Asanibo as his talons dug into the flesh of his palms. Blood dripped for a few seconds, then dried to his visible bewilderment.

"A few things," J'Kana said dryly. "Don't worry, I hear that can happen to anyone. But instead of trying to fight, why not tell me your name instead?" The Asanibo boy stood taken aback by the question, and for a long while focused on the outsider with what J'Kana could only acknowledge as the greatest reluctance he had ever seen. J'Kana rolled his eyes. "I don't bite."

"I am Chishashi," he offered begrudgingly, "and you shouldn't be here."

"I know," J'Kana assured him in more of a playful tone than he intended. "These two told me the same thing on the way." When Chishashi shot him an incredulous look, the disciple of J'Karo opened his mouth to speak, only to have the vampire wave off whatever excuse was about to come.

"No, there's no time. Wake up your friends. We have to get away from the Stone." The Ijeya couldn't believe what he just heard. He thought to question, but the ghastly roars from deeper within the forest assured him that Chishashi was correct.

"Yo J'Chera me J'Yobena ra bashurakonali lakunati," J'Kana whispered frantically. The Wehela glowed brighter at the sound of J'Karo spoken so closely, and both of the senior ijeya ni bolted upright. "Oh, good, you're awake. Let's get out of here!"

"What do you mean," J'Chera asked through gritted teeth as his feet took off before his mind fully understood.

"What happened?" J'Yobena demanded in her normal haughty tone as she chased after them. She caught sight of Chishashi, and her skin began to crawl. "Who is that, and why are we not running the other way?" J'Kana smiled sheepishly.

"Wehela Stone knocked us out," he explained, his breathing in shambles as he jumped over roots and ducked below branches. "Asanibo were alerted. New friend is taking us to safety."

"I'm not your friend," Chishashi called behind them, and J'Kana smiled wider.

"Okay, so he's not our friend *yet*," the former J'Foja was forced to admit as the four of them sprinted through the jungle as fast as their spirits would take them. The sound of running water filled their ears, and J'Kana's heart pounded furiously against his ribs. "Oye, Chishashi, where are we going?" .

"The Southwestern Shukeshu Tributaries run through these woods," he explained with a tinge of annoyance in his voice. "Now hush, unless you want to be caught." The ijeya ni did as they were asked. Every child in Y'Neshu heard the stories of Kehemu Forest. If the Sasabosami found you, you may live to tell the tale. If discovered by Asanibo, however…

***

*Folawu Outskirts*

Y'Sawe shook as he leaned against the wall. He clutched his shoulder, unable to dispel the clouds in his mind as he watched the survivors of the Yema bakery incident hold their families close. He tried to think. *We lost Y'Okani…Y'Jewo, and…* it bothered him that he couldn't readily remember the names of his fallen brothers and sisters. Inwardly, the Ile Kanawe scolded himself, strained the furthest depths of his memory while he outwardly clenched the hard stone edge of the black wall at his back. *Y'Tiwe…* She was the one who spoke the command to shield the others from the blast. A tear came to Y'Sawe's eye as he realized she may have been the personification of Divine Mercy.

The Grand Master pushed off the wall and walked again, too battered to evade the crowds of people. It mattered little. The street was familiar enough, and he would soon get the help he needed. All he had to do was stay on his feet long enough to get there…

***

*Kehemu Forest—Shukeshu Tributaries*

The air shifted all around them, just as they drew closer to the riverbank. Rain poured over them, its staggered melody augmented by the leaves through which it fell. Thunder rumbled, though if it were from above or below, they couldn't tell. J'Kana stiffened as the chill set into his flesh despite the ara cub pressed against his chest. In the distance, they could hear a frantic scurry across the underbrush, and though the darkness intensified with the coming of the storm, a flash of lightning briefly showed the faces of the leaf-covered elokobi and their Asanibo leader before the night took hold again.

"So do you have a boat or something…?" J'Chera asked with urgency. His hip throbbed even more from the pain now. The excessive movement of their trip into the forest did nothing to help him. Chishashi shook his head.

"It's too late for that. Prepare for battle," he urged. The hiss of the elokobi grew louder in their ears, and with every second that passed, the bright crimson eyes of the Asanibo that led them grew brighter still…closer. J'Kana held onto Siema with one hand as J'Chera grabbed his arm and sank to the ground.

"Omo I can barely prepare to sit down," the senior ijeya stifled a groan as he attempted a dismissive chuckle.

J'Kana knelt down to check his wound, tore some of the purple cloth of his shiki into strips, folded them, and placed them against J'Chera's hip. Siema, as if she had peered into her master's mind, wiggled her way out of J'Kana's shirt and pressed her warm body against J'Chera's freshly bandaged wound.

"Don't worry yourself, J'Chera," J'Yobena told him as she moved to the front. She stood by Chishashi, completely unconcerned with who or what he was, and only interested in how she might vent the emotions she felt surrounding the death of her Kanawe. "I wager 10 Nukira that none of these creatures can break our defense." Her eyes glowed an intense orange color, deep and bright like the sun at twilight. She channeled her hato with the world around her and strengthened the flow of her ike to the point where the chill on the air began to vanish.

"Ti mala ra kurawenati," J'Kana spoke, his eyes full of gold and draped by his wet curls. "The Asanibo shouldn't be able to distort our senses now," he explained, then shifted focus to Chishashi. "We're away from the Wehela Stone. Would you be able to help us?" The Wanderer met his gaze, somewhat disturbed by the golden glow that slowly surrounded J'Kana, but he nodded nonetheless. "Then here is the plan…"

***

*Kehemu Forest—Shukeshu Tributaries*

The Asanibo sat before them, mounted on the back of a bujoki spider. A flash of lightning revealed the black color of its body and the lime green striations that webbed across its mighty thorax. The elokobi stood on all sides, patient to wait for the vampire rider's command to attack, and it was clear that the rider only toyed with them. His lips split into a hungry smile as drops of rain fell from the sky.

"Fikhembo," he growled with excitement. "I expected to find the Kanawe's little rats, but I get to exterminate the traitor as well. I hope you've made your peace with Y'Khel, Chishashi, because soon I will send you to meet Him." The Wanderer rolled his eyes as he folded his arms.

"Big talk from someone who couldn't send air to his lungs without word from the Dagger," Chishashi retorted. The enemy narrowed his eyes as he tilted his head back in a show of perceived superiority. The grunts and gurgles of the elokobi betrayed their freshness, and as they struggled to hold themselves back, J'Kana and J'Yobena watched them from every angle.

"It is not your place to speak of him," he snarled, then instantly cooled himself. "Besides, I wouldn't expect a khimbenzi to understand what freedom he has brought to the Asanibo." Chishashi snarled back, louder as his talons unclenched with the ring of sliding razor blades.

"A 'khimbenzi,' Tikhal? This is how you speak to your younger brother?" There was as much pain in Chishashi's voice as there was anger, but Tikhal remained unmoved, the glow in his cold crimson eyes intensified.

"You lost the right to call yourself my brother the day you showed your weakness to the Elders—"

"Choosing to spare a life you've been commanded to take shows more strength than you could ever know, Tikhal—"

"Enough!" Tikhal's shout rumbled with the thunder, and almost overpowered the guttural sounds of the horde of elokobi. Blue flashes spidered through the sky, the branches of the dark trees flailed on the violent wind, and the elokobi pounded their fists against the ground in a desperate cry for release. "Lord Mahute's orders were clear. None of you will leave Kehemu alive, and the world will be better for it!" Tikhal pointed his taloned hand at the ijeya ni and their guide; the elokobi were released, and with no hesitation did they sprint for their prey.

J'Kana breathed, his ike nurtured by the tempest that whirled on his every side. He sank into it, let it flow through him and out of him in a great burst, just as J'Yobena had taught him in the moments before Tikhal's approach. He felt himself speak a command, "Yo kifiti N'hafu ni ra bushake tuketubasa. N'teuki jiebasa." The ground quaked as walls of earth erected on all sides to keep the elokobi at bay. J'Kana glanced back towards J'Chera and Siema as the elokobi closed in. Every hair on Siema's body stood on end as she growled and barked at the monsters that clawed at her. J'Kana pointed upward, and suddenly a rocky dome emerged around them to keep them safe. He breathed a relieved sigh, then let his ike swell as he raised the walls higher.

"Ti fishina ra N'atebo shu lojibasa o," shouted J'Yobena, the red color of her robe distorted by the sudden flash of blue lightning as it struck the ground in a wall before her. Over a dozen elokobi fell at her feet, the vines and leaves and branches that grew out of their flesh singed by the heavenly fire. The embers that fell from the vanquished monsters lit the grass around them. "J'Kana, there's your fire!" The words left her mouth just as her eyes met those of the enemy Asanibo. She took a step forward, then froze when she realized that he was there. This monster, Tikhal, was one of Mahute's three enforcers just hours ago in Folawu, who appeared in the Yema to fight the other masters as she and her party fled. Her anger burned within her, mixed with her sorrow, and sent waves of power through every inch of her body. She sprinted for the bujoki spider that held him, dove over the stone walls that J'Kana had made, dodged the fireballs that he now threw at the elokobi that surrounded her, but then tripped.

An elokobi, animalistic in its wooden appearance, gnashed its teeth as it pulled her leg toward its mouth. She kicked it in the face, but there was not enough force to break free; it only drove the creature to greater hunger. She screamed as she clawed against the ground, her eyes still so focused on Tikhal, her anger on the rise. More elokobi approached, their heads drawn back, their dirty skin splashed with water from the sky, and J'Yobena could feel the claws of death wrap around her. She bit her lower lip, and as the metallic taste of blood entered her mouth, she found herself steeped in a renewed calm. "Yo arila ra

N'Hafu shu kurawenati," she commanded, and the chaotic winds that swirled around the battlefield sliced the onslaught of monsters to pieces.

J'Yobena, the Masterpiece herself, stood to her feet and popped her neck as she withdrew twin daggers from her hip. Tikhal leaned forward on the bujoki spider, his face alight with excitement, but Chishashi intercepted her.

"Get out of my way," she demanded, but he shook his head. Her nostrils flared as she punched him in the chest. He wasn't fazed. "I will avenge the death of my Kanawe on those responsible, and his will be the first head I take!"

"Stick to the plan," Chishashi told her, and she spat. "There is a chance that we all die if you don't. Whose head would you take then, ba?" She surged with rage, and the air cut through another wave of the elokobi before she released the command. She stormed back towards the stone walls, fully intent to take out her frustrations on anything that got in her way.

"There you go, protecting the weak from their rightful destruction," Tikhal taunted as he dismounted his spider. Chishashi watched as the massive beast climbed into the trees.

"I just wanted the chance to pay you back for your 'khimbenzi' comment from before," spoke the younger brother as he dragged a talon through the palm of his hand. Dark red blood spilled from the cut, and Chishashi began to speak. "Bobo ja basi we lekhan a buyi gbayim." The blood morphed into a whip as thick as a tree trunk and lashed at Tikhal, but the elder Asanibo spoke a Blood Chant of his own.

"Fiyim kha ja zekhili ja bobo N'na," he ordered in a tone that reeked of smugness and disdain, and the whip broke into two strands that pierced the cores of two nearby trees. Tikhal looked back at his handywork, lifted the corner of his mouth in a smirk, and began his advance to his little brother's position. Chishashi stood for a moment, suddenly unable to consider anything more than the harsh training of their childhood. A small glimpse of Tikhal's face in the light of the lightning told him that his brother thought of the same.

"N'Mata buyim," Chishashi ordered with the crossing of his arms. His brother jumped into the air, twisted, kicked hard against a branch, bounded to the ground and rolled out of the way, each in time enough to evade the gruesome strike of a lashing blood whip. Tikhal's back hit a tree trunk, but as the twin blood whips homed in on their target, the hunter raised his hands and chanted another command.

"N'kha a deluyim," was all he said, and all that needed to be said in order for his brother's blood to form into a ball in the palm of his hands.

***

J'Kana repeated J'Yobena's command to the wind from earlier and used it in tandem with a command to the surrounding fajari (fire) to create a burn strong enough to endure the storm. More elokobi got caught in the blaze, but the walls that surrounded them kept the fires contained to within the stone. As a result, the waves died down little by little, and J'Kana couldn't help but watch as Chishashi engaged his brother Tikhal in battle.

"Oye, keep your eyes sharp, J'Kana," J'Yobena demanded as she artfully sliced through three elokobi at once. He jumped as he felt the cold breath of one creature on his neck, but his back met the weighted paw of something massive. J'Kana hit the ground with a thud as all the air in his lungs fled. The eerie scratch of the underbrush filled his ears, and while he dragged himself across the fallen branches and bodies that smoldered on the forest floor, he realized that the sound wasn't him. The young ijeya turned to see the bujoki spider wrapped in its luminescent green and on its way toward him.

With urgency he returned to his feet. J'Yobena continued to fight the swarm of elokobi while Chishashi battled his brother. J'Kana cocked his head to the side to pop his neck, eyes locked with all eight of the spider's. He smiled as he spread his arms. "Seems like we are all out of partners," he said in his typical playful tone, unbothered by the twitching of the monster spider's fangs. "I suppose that means you want to dance with me." The bujoki launched into the air, front legs stretched out to catch its prey. J'Kana rolled out of the way as he swiftly sunk back into the shift of his ike, and whispered the gentle command, " ." A pillar of stone emerged from the forest floor, but the swift swipe of the creature's extended limbs shattered it to pieces. "Well, that didn't work."

The bujoki lowered its head as its pedipalps pawed the air. Its fangs twitched, and then in a flash of movement that rivaled Y'Kele's heavenly arrows, it jumped into a spin that flung its venom across the terrain. J'Kana searched his mind for some word he could use, some way to protect himself and his allies as they fought between the trees. "Ti emi naanosi shu arila ra nochulobasa!" The wind kicked up and drove the venom away from J'Yobena and himself. He thought to breathe, but in the time it took him to speak the command, the beast was on him again. He put up his hand. "Ti fajari wu teuki N'Hafu yifunati o!" The words poured out of him, and fire erupted from a sudden split in the earth. The spider's legs were repulsed, but rather than back away, the monster arachnid leaped into the trees once again. J'Kana shook his head as a bead of sweat rolled down the side of his face. "You know you really don't fight fair o!"

He could hear the way it hissed in the dark, the creaks of the branches under its weight, the rustle of the shaded leaves against its body. J'Kana squinted his eyes to find the glow of its green pattern, but there was nothing. It was as though the creature had vanished, save for its incomparable bloodlust. From behind him, a loud click sounded through the trees. He turned just in time, as a ball of fluid burned its way through the air and grazed his shoulder. The impact created a sizzling sound, like meat held above a fire, and the sting that ripped through the ijeya's flesh warned him not to get hit again.

"Calm down," he told himself, "and give yourself over to the shift." He closed his eyes as his body turned to face every direction. He gave little thought to what lurked in the trees, even though it made his every hair stand on end. Rather, he gave himself the freedom to breathe deeply, to feel the coldness of the angry wind that battered the violent rains all about. He indulged in the pleasure of the mixture of sounds, not of battle, but of nature. He recalled the noises of the muka beasts as they fled, the slap of their palm-like feet as they jumped from tree to tree, and pictured the brown and gray tints of their fur. He listened to the present moment, to J'Yobena's breathing and her audacious taunts as her pain left her, even for only this moment. Then he sensed it, the skitter in the dark of something so natural and yet so contrary to nature. Another burst of poison, but this time J'Kana was ready for it. He stretched for Y'Kele, allowed his ike to reach as far into the ether as it would go, and he felt a warmth and power that reminded him instantly of the Wehela Stone's vision. Thunder rumbled, and his senses were overwhelmed as its triumphant roar only added to the swell of his soul.

His eyes flashed gold as on instinct he dodged the venom spray with a one-handed cartwheel. His fingers dug into the mud, his nostrils filled with the scent of rain and venom, fire and earth as memories bubbled to the surface of his mind. The vocabulary lists given to him by a kind and secretly protective teacher. Y'Jewo's boldness at the Summit as he commanded his sword to appear in his hand. The animus in J'Yobena's command of the lightning. The urgency of his shift of the earth back in Memifi. The calm of his Master's every word.

J'Kana opened his mouth to speak a command, his mind now focused on the monster's movement while lightning tore through the sky overhead. "Ti N'Hafu wu shoba ra fishina shu chesina me," he started, and with a grumble of thunder the lightning struck at him from on high. He caught it in the palm of his hand, and by the might of Y'Kele it seemingly froze in a pillar so bright that half a wave of elokobi were blinded long enough for J'Yobena to wipe them out. J'Kana continued as the bujoki sprinted along the branches now in a rapid attempt to confuse him and hide its position. The perceptive ijeya calmly inhaled, intent to utter the second half of the command, when the beast lunged from the darkness.

J'Kana jumped just in time enough to evade the pointed fangs of the monster and springboard from the flat center of its back. He drifted in the air now, the pillar of lightning still in the palm of his hand, and that was when he completed the command, "Ti kofesha shu jiena me makashikonali N'atebo shu loji belenati." The bujoki jumped into the air, all eight of its legs curled as if to snare him, but the stream of lightning, now a brilliant sword, struck its sternum with a precision that caused the creature to burst. Acidic blood drenched the battlefield, and J'Yobena muttered a command that caused the ground to mold around her like a cave. She barely felt the splash of venom and blood, but the remnants of the elokobi she faced dissolved before her eyes. She blinked in surprise, lowered her earthen shield, and looked at J'Kana with a mixture of irritation and newfound respect.

"How did you do that," she asked, to which J'Kana only spread his arms and shrugged. An inhuman roar billowed through the whistle of the storm winds. Tikhal stumbled away from his younger brother with his taloned hands clasped tightly to the sides of his face. Another roar. He seemed to be in agony, and though he ripped through his pale skin, J'Kana could tell it was from something other than Chishashi's attacks. He and J'Yobena ran to aid their vampiric guide, but Chishashi held up a hand to stop them. They stood there, confused, as they watched the Wanderer's eyes soften.

"Uhu bujoki ja basi we, N'filikham a gbetoyim," Chishashi whispered, and the dark blood of his palm lit a bright red that summoned the acidic green blood of the bujoki to it. His expression darkened as the brilliant crimson muddied together with the acid. He blinked, and with the force of a wild abata stampede, the spider blood shot towards Tikhal and pierced his forehead. The screaming stopped, and for a moment all was silent…until solid spikes of green and red blood ripped through his flesh in a sound that cut against the storm.

***

*Kehemu Forest—Shukeshu Tributaries*

J'Kana awoke in a dank cave, his face dirtied with mud and his body cold from the rainwater. A fire blazed towards the center, and a little ball of heat rested on his chest to provide some relief. He ran a hand over it, and found the furry lump to be Siema, fast asleep against him as usual. His head throbbed, a clear sign that he had overdone it again, but he was thankful that it wasn't as bad as in Memifi. He cocked a half smile. Master Y'Sawe proved himself to be right. He made a move to sit up, but the moment he put pressure on his left hand, pain shot through his shoulder. The scream poured from him before he could stop it. He fell back down to the ground, which only worsened the agony.

"Sha, how stupid can you be," J'Yobena chided as she rushed over from the far side of the cave and applied an ointment from a bowl in her hand. It numbed him enough to stifle the scream, but did little to take the full measure of the pain away. "You aren't in any condition to move around so much."

"Eke," J'Kana whispered with a smirk drenched in the sweat of one under too much pressure, "or else people will think you like me, J'Yobena." He laughed, then she slapped him.

"Don't worry," she grunted as he hissed from the sting, "nobody would ever come to that conclusion." J'Chera marched over from the other side of the cave with a look of pure disapproval fixed across his face. J'Kana propped himself upright on his uninjured arm.

"How is he supposed to get better if you do things like that," the kinder ijeya asked as he flicked the back of her head. His focus turned to J'Kana as he asked, "Where did you learn to do all that? It was—"

"Reckless," J'Yobena interrupted, but a sharp glare from J'Chera told her that he was in no mood for her attitude. She sighed. "Still, it was okay, I guess." J'Kana looked to the fire, and Chishashi who tended to it as he thought back on the battle. Clouds of fog polluted his mind, but the longer he focused on the bright orange flames, the easier it became to collect himself.

"I just remembered some words that I learned during my time with Kanawe Y'Sawe. From there I just put them together the way I was taught." His shoulder throbbed through the dulling effects of the ointment. "For all the good it did. The bujoki still managed to hit me."

"It's because you don't have your jilaba wu ajiwele," J'Chera explained. "Haven't you worked on it at all?" J'Kana looked at him sheepishly, and J'Yobena stood up with her eyes to Y'Kele.

"This one is going to get us all killed," she complained. Even J'Chera shook his head. "Tell me, did you have to practice being dead weight, or are you a natural?"

"How can you say that I was such dead weight when I saved you from getting hit yourself, J'Yobena?" J'Kana's comment shut her up, though this time J'Chera didn't think to laugh. His attention was fixed to his companion's shoulder as it visibly pulsed through his shirt. "Besides," the lelenawe ijeya continued, "I started work on it the day my Master took me to get the materials—" he cut himself off, and from the biggest pouch on his cloth belt, he retrieved a hood and attached mantle stitched together of blue and white fabric laced with elaborate designs. "Unfortunately, this was as far as I was able to get."

"Well it's nice to know that you'll be able to protect your head," J'Yobena spat, but Chishashi slammed his fist against the ground as a snarl escaped the pit of his throat.

"Enough," he demanded, the boom in his voice a reminder of what he had suffered. "This is how you treat someone who saves your life, ba?"

"Everyone relax. All of this isn't that serious, ne," J'Kana offered, which drew incredulous looks from J'Chera and the Asanibo alike.

"Yes, it is," they retorted in unison.

"The venom from the spider may have grazed your shoulder, but already it affects your entire arm. If you insist on doing too much, it will eventually spread throughout your body and kill you before Mahute gets the chance," the

Wanderer explained. J'Kana noted his grave expression and suddenly felt his own mouth run dry.

"How long would it take for the poison to spread," he inquired, and Chishashi sighed.

"Without aggravation, you have three days," he warned. "At the rate you're going, you'll have a day and a half at best." J'Kana shivered with the revelation. How could he be so close to death? How could he have come so far from the streets of Memifi just to die in the Kehemu Forest at the hands of a blasted spider?

"Is there anything we can do," he asked with more determination than J'Yobena would have expected.

"For starters, listen to your comrades and work on your little cloak," Chishashi replied with more condescension than intended. "I know the power that they contain firsthand. With any luck, it should give you a little more time." J'Kana took a deep breath, and focused on the warmth of the cave, then realized that it had no mouth, only a small opening in the top for the smoke to filter out of.

"Alright," he agreed in a tone of great focus. Chishashi smiled, spoke a chant, and the cave created a passage for him to the outside. "What else?"

"Be patient. I may just have a way to get you help." Chishashi stepped through the doorway without another word. J'Kana grabbed the purple fabric from the large pouch, and with needle and thread in hand, began his work.

***

Kamari's eyes went wide with wonder, then deepened with sympathy. J'Kana noticed the sudden moisture in them, and decidedly pulled his little one into a tight hug.

"It's okay, hafu wu ulunawe shehefo," he uttered in a comforting tone, "I'm alright. There's no need to waste your tears over something that I have overcome." They sat in the batalu, the boy in his father's lap now as he sniffled and watched the dance of candlelight. He gripped J'Kana's wrist with a childish love that hurt the Kanawe's heart.

"I don't like to hear about you getting hurt," Kamari grumbled. J'Kana took his chin and turned his little head to face him.

"Kamari," he began with a warm firmness, "this isn't the last time I come close to losing my life. If it's too much for you to handle, I can end the story here and wait for you to get bigger before I resume—"

"I'm big enough already, Yababa," the boy interrupted with a huff. J'Kana laughed as he pressed his lips to the child's forehead, and opted not to challenge Kamari's fierce determination. After all, he enjoyed the time they had to bond.

"Well in any case," the elder said with decision, "perhaps we should turn our attention to your J'Karo lesson. It would seem you could use a bit of a break." Kamari nodded, and with a smile he ran into the other luseme (room) to grab the leather book that had become his best friend. J'Kana took it, and pat his son gently on the head as he opened its locked cover and searched for a page to focus on. "Let's pick up here," he suggested, and pointed into the book to Kamari's renewed excitement.

| | | |
|---|---|---|
|  | Muka | Muka Beasts |
|  | Bujoki | Bujoki Spiders |
|  | | |
|  | Eke | Care/Careful/Carefulness |
|  | Makas hi | Precision/Exactness |

| | | |
|---|---|---|
|  | Teuki | Wall |
|  | Kashi | Down/Below/Lower/Beneath/Under |
|  | Ebo | Left |
|  | Tase | Right |
|  | Mue | Side |
|  | Reshi | Inside/Inner/Middle/Through |
|  | Nera | Outside/Outer |
|  | Reshili | Enter |
|  | Nerali | Exit |
|  | Habale | Needle |
|  | Lewafa | Clothes |
|  | Wafaye | Work |
|  | Jie | Transform/Transformative/Become/Becoming |
|  | Namori | Harm/Harmful/Danger/Dangerous |

| | | |
|---|---|---|
| 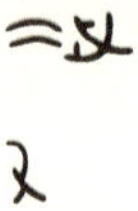 | Sahome | Alive |
| 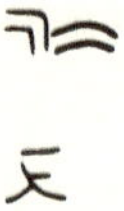 | Kusaho | Dead/Death |
| 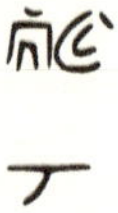 | Malatu | Hated/Hatred/Hate |
|  | Naanosi | Disease/Poison/Venom |

# 11

# Deep

*Folawu Outskirts*

The black stone of the walls reflected the dim flicker of candle flames as sounds of rain fell against the spiraled metal roof. Even here in the outskirts of Folawu, the roar of the ocean could be faintly heard from all the way across town. There was comfort in it, knowing that it somehow drowned out the distressed voices of the Folawans beyond the chohafi. An open hand slapped Y'Sawe's forehead, and the Ile Kanawe groaned.

"I was awake," he growled as his hand swiftly met the sore spot. He sat up, his chest bare save for the locs that draped down his shoulders and back. His legs dangled over the side of the bed as he scanned the room for his shiki and the gray and black jilaba wu ajiwele.

"You can stop looking," came the wizened voice of the old woman. "All you need to focus on is your rest." Y'Sawe groaned again as he tried to get out of bed, panted when he almost fell, but even then, he tried to force himself up. "What did I just tell you?" The old woman called from the other room, her voice surrounded by the sinking clatter of pans in water. A savory aroma wafted through the air as the heat of her house rose by the minute. She was making her famous yekari, rife with crushed tojana root, ground cholo bird, chopped efafa and hubaba tubers, all boiled in a pot of well-seasoned soso nut milk. The sweetness that followed told him that she had also begun to bake the anaku casserole, made with a chiliti jam and choni zest, smothered in a butter caramel sauce. She intended for him to stay far longer than he did.

"I can't just lay here, Kanawe Y'Chaju," he offered through clenched teeth. "My ijeya is—"

"Hush, boy," spoke the woman as she came back into view. Y'Sawe knew her to be well into her 60s, but Y'Chaju's coiled black hair maintained as much youth as the melanated skin that surrounded those piercing orange eyes. Her attitude, however, became decidedly more Y'Fuwefan as she aged. "Have you forgotten who trained you?" The question was as honest as it was a challenge.

"Kewe, Baje," he answered with a stiff shake of his head, and returned to the bed for fear that she would strike him again. "But now the task of training ijeya has fallen to me."

"And you should have taken it up when you were younger," she chided, then sucked her teeth in irritation. She looked her former apprentice over again, her leg alive with tapping as she did. "You overdid it."

"I know, Kanawe, but Mahute—" She held up a hand, and just like that, the Ile Kanawe was silenced like a child talking to his angry parent. Of course, that was how he saw her. After his freedom was won, it was Kanawe Y'Chaju who took him in, who taught him in the ways of J'Karo and gifted him the ability to protect himself. She sauntered off into the other room to check on the food. He heard the sizzle of yekari as a few drops spilled over into the fire, but even then he dared not move. She came back into the room and sat in a dark brown rocking chair across from him, her head framed by the twin rayemo ornaments carved by hand into its back.

"For all the wisdom you've gained, you have used surprisingly little," she admonished. "You must measure yourself, Y'Sawe. To pour out your soul into one task with reckless abandon is to serve as the architect of your own destruction." He sat on the sky blue mattress that spread over the brown wooden bedframe and felt his fingertips dig into the cushion. "Relax yourself," she warned with a sharp point of her finger. He obeyed, and she shook her head. "How long have you been so reactionary towards the Dagger? He appears before you and you are stunned. He attacks, and you defend just long enough to get away, but you don't finish him the way you know you should—"

"He's my brother," he interrupted with all the force in his voice that made it clear how hard he worked to stave off the sadness those words carried. Y'Chaju cut her eyes at her one-time apprentice as she placed her hands on her hips.

"He *was* your brother," she corrected, a sternness to her that comforted Y'Sawe as much as frightened him. "Now he is a monster set to exploit the greatest weaknesses of all Y'Neshu. With the return of Batabari and J'Karo to meet it, the entire continent faces a danger that hasn't been seen in well over a thousand years. You cannot afford to be blinded by your feelings about who Mahute used to be." Y'Sawe thought about the flash of yellow in his eyes, the smooth cadence of his voice as he spoke his desires in the face of the Kanawe. "He's right, you know."

"What," the Grand Master asked as a bolt of pain shot through him. "Otaba ra sanikijosi me orelinati e?" The sudden burst of emotions that touched the edges of his heart like the sparks of detonated fireworks forced J'Karo out where Pedestrian was expected. *You agree with a criminal?* His face was panged with heartbreak, his voice a whisper, and the stern look Y'Chaju shot him told him not to bother her about her position.

"Whether or not he is a criminal doesn't change how right he is," she answered with a shrug. "For years I lobbied against the slave trade in Y'Neshu, but when the other Kanawe voted against my initiatives, I was overruled by my Ile Kanawe. Every time I called for action, the result was the same, and for what? 'To protect the fragile peace of the Four Empires,' they said."

"Do you believe that J'Karo should be released into the hands of the masses?" Y'Sawe's question registered as accusatory, though the sudden flicker of her orange eyes caused him to shrink back.

"I believe that the people of Y'Neshu are entitled to the knowledge of their history," Y'Chaju replied sharply. "Do you know why Y'Kele formed the Wayi Kanawe?"

"To protect Y'Neshu," Y'Sawe answered, but then kicked himself when he realized he had taken no time to think. She thumped him in the forehead, then got up to return to the other room. Y'Sawe heard her shift the pots and pans, open the oven, retrieve the anaku from the fire, set it out to cool and then wash her hands. She returned to her rocking chair and eased herself down into it. Only now could Y'Sawe see her fatigue, and his expression softened with a sudden wave of guilt as he changed his answer. "I don't, Kanawe."

"Well, you are right," Y'Chaju affirmed with a wistful smile, and sank against the back of the chair as her eyes drifted off to a long-faded world. "The Kanawe were first brought together to assist Y'Kele in protecting the people, but over time they misunderstood the Creator's intent. At the time, the Batabari failed to control Jurutisalaji, but the chaos was welcome since it masked their raid of Y'Kawebo. After the war ended, the Teachers, conditioned by extremes, took to their roles as protectors from the mindset of restriction."

"It was out of necessity," the Ile Kanawe justified, but Y'Chaju's lips parted in a comical expression. "Humanity fractured itself through its reckless use of J'Karo, Kanawe, and the Batabari intertwining a Language of Power with their blood magic allowed for a severing of Creation's connection—"

"For a time, that might have been the case," Y'Chaju interrupted with a maternal firmness, "but what did they do to restore the hato once the threat had passed? Knowledge became restricted, Katsedu was created as a means of pacifying a people whose culture had been stolen by the ones chosen by Y'Kele to preserve it. Even now, our people live their lives the entire continent over, never quite understanding who they are at their core." Y'Chaju chuckled at her old apprentice's darkened expression. "Of course, you maintain it is in their best interest, but ijeya, know that the restriction of knowledge, of language in particular, is a restriction of essence. Culture. Personal expression guided by a time not quite so complicated as this one."

"As idealistic as you sound, all I can hear is Mahute," Y'Sawe grumbled, then winced when he realized the unintentional disrespect projected in his voice. Y'Chaju shook her head with a motherly smile that told him that danger was still far from the horizon.

"You are still so afraid, Y'Sawe, just like all those years ago when you first came to me. This time, of mere words. Idealism for the benefit of others is never wrong. It is application that determines the depth of one's sin. I can see the merit of Mahute's ideals, yes," she explained, her wisdom ever apparent to her old student, "but I don't approve of how much death the man spreads. For there to be a liberation of heritage, people must still draw breath in Y'Neshu to inherit what was lost." She watched him, watched as his labored breaths stilled, though his nostrils still flared with emotion. "But enough conversation. It's time to eat…unless you intend to make an old woman slave over a hot stove for nothing." Y'Sawe smiled as she stood back to her feet and walked the way of the kitchen.

"Usi, Kanawe," he said with a chuckle, and returned his head to the pillow while he waited.

***

*Kehemu Forest—Shukeshu Tributaries*

The rumble of stone filled J'Kana's ears as the dimly lit cave reopened its mouth. The throb in his head added to the piercing sensation he felt all over his body. His shallow breaths were enough to make even J'Yobena flash him a glance of concern. J'Chera sat by his side, more focused on J'Kana's state than his own stab wound, and dabbed the sweat from his friend's forehead while Siema pawed at him to wake up.

"How is he," came Chishashi's voice, a knife through the darkness of their preoccupation. The ijeya ni looked up and noticed he wasn't alone. With their friendly Asanibo stood two women of skin the color of brown sugar. The older of the two wore a blue dress with the left shoulder cut out while the younger wore a black colored tunic, both embroidered with sun and moon and stars connected in a web above the waves that lined their hems. Their wavy brown hair flowed through the air as if surrounded by the waters of the ocean, and their eyes, yellow irises surrounded by blue rings like moons encircled by Heaven's rivers, scanned the hideout in deep contemplation. They were otherworldly, a kind of beautiful that warranted all recognition yet could never be verbalized.

J'Yobena swallowed, but answered with unusually high determination, "He's been out for a day, and he won't stop sweating."

"The venom has spread quite far," spoke the elder woman, a seriousness to the melody of her voice that somehow still soothed all who heard it. "What do we do in such a case, Sikhala Nihani?" The younger looked upon J'Kana in his agony, and though her face was poised, the slight tremble of her hands told the ijeya ni that her nerves would get the better of her.

"Is now the best time to have a teaching moment," J'Chera shouted incredulously. "His life is on the line!" The Master and Apprentice paid him no mind, and Nihani, the latter, simply finished her thought.

"Copious amounts of sweat, discoloration around the eyes and shoulder, shortness of breath…" Nihani ceased her muttering as her mind went to work. Her mystic eyes flickered in the light of the fire as revelation struck. With reservation she faced her Master and said, "First, we must stabilize his breathing."

"Good," the Sage of the two affirmed with a brilliant smile. "And next?"

"Clean the wound of the sweat and apply the Y'Go Mdali," Nihani replied. There was no hesitation in her this time, though the nervousness still rattled through her. Her Master placed a small pouch in the hands of her apprentice and laid her hand on her shoulder.

"Begin the preparations, Sikhala" the Sage spoke, and Nihani's eyes lit with a joyful surprise.

"Thank you, Wekhala Oleli," the student whispered, and then emptied a pot that had been used for food. She set it over the fire and spoke with a delicate wave of her hands, "Y'Go bi sekhel mtanu basiyil. Divine Waters, I live through you. Bi zanuwe basiyike zakha wila maju asiyo. I beg your purity and exceptional healing power." She spread her arms wide, and with a brilliant flash of blue light, the pot was clean and full of water. Nihani opened the pouch, pulled out a pristine white cloth, then waved it gently with all the reverence of a ritual through the water. With haste, she squeezed the cloth and moved by J'Kana's side. She wiped the area of the wound clean of the sweat before she retrieved another cloth from the pouch and returned to the boiling pot. The Wekhala watched with pride as her apprentice hurried back to the patient, and gingerly administered her soothing touch.

J'Chera, J'Yobena, Chishashi and Siema watched by the wall of the magically crafted cave, each one as curious by the ritual as concerned by the condition of their companion.

"Who are these two," J'Chera asked with a disapproving smack of his lips. He folded his arms over his chest, his deep green eyes tinted with the orange light of the fire.

"Jeniju," Chishashi answered. The two ijeya ni snapped their heads towards the vampire in all shock at the mention of the word.

"They are mermaids?" The question lingered on J'Yobena's lips with surprising innocence, and for a moment, Chishashi and J'Chera forgot how hostile she could be. "But I thought they had given up on the healing practice." Chishashi shook his head.

"You have the Jeniju confused with Mamiwatu. Long ago, both of the mermaid races traveled through Y'Neshu, determined by the Grace of Y'Khel—or Y'Kele, to you magicians—to heal all infirmity in the land. The Jeniju still practice their healing magic, while the Mamiwatu have sworn against healing the land-dwellers again." Wekhala Oleli inclined her ear to the conversation, an imperceptible expression in her narrowed eyes and clenched jaw, but she decided not to speak, only to return her focus to the task at hand.

"He is ready for you, Wekhala," Nihani spoke as she bowed her head, and her Master stepped forward. The Elder woman placed her hand delicately upon the cheek of her apprentice and offered a bright smile. Wordlessly, she walked over to where J'Kana lay and waved her hands through the air above his body. Her shadow danced in the light of the fire, her breaths became rhythmic and almost beautiful.

"Bi zanuwe basiyil, maju jakha maiye uduo," she whispered with intent that cooled the heat of the air. Each wave of her hand slowed, as though she drifted through the salted tide of the coast. "Y'Go bi sekhel mtanu basiyil." As she spoke the mantra, the waters manifested with startling clarity. Chishashi and J'Yobena watched entranced as the crystal liquid flowed in gentle waves all about the Wekhala's body, while her Sikhala saw about J'Chera. Nihani cleaned the stab wound and coated it with the juices of a brilliant orange herb picked from the Sobosa Ocean floor, then delicately covered it in bandages. J'Chera sighed with a kind of relief he had never seen in his life, but

J'Kana's weary groan brought him back to the present. "Y'Go, maju jakha maiye uduo me gahali saum." This was the mermaid's final chant, as the Divine Waters washed over the discolored skin and burrowed into the open flesh.

J'Kana screamed, and in an instant, J'Chera pushed forward with the intent to knock the Wekhala out of the way, but Nihani placed her hand firmly in the center of his chest.

"If you interrupt now, the poison will take him," she warned, which inspired looks of alarm in the faces of the three spectators. J'Kana screamed again as the Divine Waters squirmed deeper into his skin and muscle and blood. His body writhed where it lay, until the foreign liquid arrested all movement with a snap of Oleli's slender and elegant fingers. She took a deep breath, and found that all who looked on held theirs. She smiled with confidence as the next phase approached. Wekhala Oleli flexed her fingers and wrapped them around the space in front of her as if she gripped the rope of a fishing net. She pulled, one arm after another, and watched with satisfaction as a black sludge emptied itself from the wound. J'Kana's scream ripped through the quiet of the cave down to the bones of his comrades.

Sweat dripped from Oleli's brow down the side of her face as she pulled more of the liquid string. She turned her gaze on her apprentice and, with labored breath, commanded, "Sikhala, the pot!"

"Right away, Wekhala," Nihani replied with a sense of urgency. She waved her hands over the pot that loomed over the fire as she uttered in Y'Maju again, "Y'Go ulukheni M'vina. Divine Waters, vanish from here. Y'Go bi sekhel mtanu basiyil. Divine Waters, I live through you." The pot shook violently as she recited the mantra, and the waters disappeared gradually as if a drain had been installed. It took only a few moments for the pot to empty itself, and as soon as it did, Nihani called out to her Master with excitement in her celestial eyes. "Now, Wekhala!"

Oleli spread her hands wide with a gentle rotation of the wrists, and watched as the dark coagulation danced about her body. The last of the sludge drifted out of J'Kana, and congealed into a ball that floated between her hands. She glided across the cave floor, and with a sudden push of both palms toward the pot, the ball of tainted blood fell in. The fire beneath it erupted with a new life, and as the scent of the unholy concoction wafted through the air, so too did the crackling sound it made as it fused with the vessel.

"There," Oleli said as she let her arms fall by her sides. She flipped her wavy hair and wiped the sweat from her brow. "He is all better. Now, there is the matter of my fee…"

"A fee?" J'Chera was loud with incredulity, and every eye in the cave snapped to meet his deep greens. "He hasn't even woken up yet, but you demand payment?" Behind Oleli, J'Kana began to stir, and J'Chera's eyes widened. The downed ijeya sat up abruptly, and Siema, who had found her way into his chest before, now rolled down to his lap. He took sharp breaths as he braced his head with the palm of his hand.

"As I was saying," Oleli continued with a whimsy to her tone that in no way underscored the powerful heat of her gaze. The corner of Chishashi's mouth turned upward into only the faintest flicker of a smile as he approached her. Siema yipped with excitement and leaped all about J'Kana's lap. He smiled, but when he moved to pet her, she burped a flash of fire that almost singed his fingertips.

"Hey now," he croaked, "be careful with that." Footsteps approached. J'Kana's head whipped around, eyes sharp and body tensed to fight, until he saw J'Chera's face, laden with questioning sarcasm.

"You are one to talk, my friend," he teased. "How do you get shot by a spider? You just squish it." J'Kana couldn't help but laugh, but clenched his throat when the laughter turned into a labored cough. Nihani moved quickly, mouthed an unintelligible chant in Y'Maju, and siphoned the moisture in the air into a cup. He took it from her and drank slowly.

"Hey, that thing was bigger than both of us together," he answered with a smile as he set the cup down beside his makeshift bed. "If you had a boot that big, why not let me borrow it to save us all the trouble?" J'Chera grinned as he stooped down to sit beside his friend.

"Fair point, M'ba Ijeya," the senior student conceded.

"He will need at least three days to rest before he can be moved," called the Wekhala, suddenly more regal now than she had been upon her entry to the cave. "Nihani," she started, her attention fully on her apprentice. Nihani moved to greet her at the very mention of her name, and bowed her head with utmost reverence to her teacher. "I am needed in the Reef. Stay with him and make sure he doesn't do anything reckless."

"Bi ubani, Wekhala," she replied with a fierceness that told of her determination to accomplish her mission. Oleli nodded as she tucked a black book into a bag she pulled from out of thin air, and Chishashi opened the wall of the cave again to release her from her task.

***

*Kehemu Forest—Shukeshu Tributaries*

J'Kana knew better than to argue with the prognosis. He was out of commission for three days, and so his best efforts went into directing J'Chera and J'Yobena on supplies needed. J'Chera went about business in his usual manner, so upbeat and optimistic that it got on J'Yobena's nerves, but even she had to admit that it was welcome. They decided, for the time being, to stick together no matter the task, while Chishashi maintained a watch of the terrain. The Asanibo ran heavy in this part of the forest. If they were meant to survive until they could move on to Shifi, then they would need someone familiar with the territory to watch their backs. While they all moved about in search of food, water, and medicinal herbs, Nihani sat with her mystical eyes trained on J'Kana.

He did his best to ignore her, but something about her drew his attention despite his best efforts. She was beyond the definition of beauty. Her dark brown skin glittered in what little light was offered by the flame. Her hair flowed freely through the air with every turn of her head or shift of her body. Her eyes, those golden moons surrounded by the blue rings of heavenly rivers, pierced through his every defense. Her full lips—

J'Kana looked away. He had more to worry about than his impulses or his attraction. His Kanawe was alive, and expected him in Shifi. The Asanibo in service to Mahute the Dagger hunted the trio of ijeya throughout Y'Neshu, or at least that was what he could assume from Tikhal's attack. Then there was the matter of the poisoning, something that wouldn't have happened if his jilaba wu ajiwele had been finished in a timely manner. It was all the motivation he needed to stitch the back of the robe to the mantle.

He sank into a pool of his ike, felt the warmth of the gold light within him mingle with the heat of the flame at his back. He ran his fingers over the smooth fabric as his eyes absorbed its violet color. The way Siema wiggled underneath it made him smile, and with the smile came the sudden burst of power within him. His ike churned with the waves of the ocean, swayed with the treetops ravaged by tempest, burned with the fires of the sun, and then…it was calm, like the field of hutije grass in the Outer Grasslands, like the singing of jinenu crickets in harmony with the kurikuri bugs, all because *she* opened her mouth.

"Is this the jilaba wu ajiwele," she asked, her voice a melody that soothed him to his core. He looked at her, the round shape of her face, her button nose, the shimmer in her eyes and the pink plumpness of her lips melded together in total wonder. Every curve of her body ensnared the senses to such degree that his eyes flashed with gold before they returned to their earthen brown. He nodded, a muted expression on his lips, then did what he could to return his focus to the task at hand. His hand rapidly stitched the other side of the back. He marveled at how easy it was now, to establish the distance between each seam, to avoid a mistaken stab to the fingers, to glide through the fabric. "Is there anything I can do to help?"

"No," J'Kana told her firmly, then realized his error. "But I appreciate the offer. It's just that the Identity Robe is supposed to be the mark of each Ijeya or Kanawe. Outside assistance is forbidden." He watched as her lively eyes darkened with disappointment.

"Oh," she said as she coiled a strand of her vivacious hair around her finger. He knew she was bored, and that she was sweet. She doted on him since he first woke up and carefully monitored his condition. He let out a mildly grieved sigh.

"So, you are a mermaid," he asked with a warm smile. She looked at him, and smiled back.

"A Jeniju," she answered excitedly. Siema poked her head out from beneath the edge of the purple cloak and met Nihani's eyes. The apprentice Jeniju lifted a hand to pet her, something that visibly alarmed J'Kana since she was new to the ara beast. Siema nuzzled her hand as though they'd been together through all time. "It's alright," Nihani told him, "we are already bonded."

"And here I stand amazed," J'Kana uttered smoothly as he reached for another piece of the back. He threaded his needle anew and set to his work with increased vigor. "I never thought I would meet a Divine Healer in the flesh." His needle paused for a moment as he looked up from the Robe, his lips spread in a contemplative manner. "Then again, I never expected to be poisoned either, so I suppose the world is full of surprises."

Nihani giggled, and Siema crawled into her lap only to roll over. "I'm sorry we didn't make it on time," she offered. "Chishashi-Baje sent word days ago, but with the Asanibo on the hunt—"

"It wasn't safe," J'Kana finished with a shrug. His hands moved at a quicker pace, his mind alive with so many thoughts, both pure and impure. "Though I wouldn't say you didn't arrive on time," he added with a slight lift of his head. Their eyes met, and chills ran through them both that even Siema couldn't warm. "Thank you, Nihani. I wouldn't be here without you." He watched as the mermaid's eyes widened and cheeks reddened with whatever mix of emotions flooded her like high tide on the beach. She scrambled, and nearly knocked Siema to the ground as she hurried to do something else. At first, J'Kana felt he should be offended, but then he remembered that the last time he'd seen that look was when Nikeli chased him through the streets of Memifi…

***

*Kehemu Forest—Shukeshu Tributaries*

The second day came with the call of the muka beasts in the Kehemu around them, and while Chishashi resumed his watch over the jungle, J'Chera and J'Yobena familiarized themselves with the many different pathways hidden between the trees. J'Kana still recovered from the effects of the poison, but at least he felt better than he had the day before. Nihani still watched him, though this time from across the cave floor. Something about their interaction the day prior made her nervous, but beneath her anxiety, J'Kana could sense her excitement.

"I don't bite you know," he told her, his eyes down and hands at work attaching a front piece to the mantle and back. His heart pounded with a thrill of his own as he realized how soon he would be able to wear it.

"I just don't want to distract you, is all," Nihani attempted to assure him. He didn't buy it, and the look on his face told her exactly that.

"How can you monitor my condition from all the way over there, Nihani," he asked more playfully than he would have liked, but the blush in her cheeks was worth the mistake.

"I can see you just fine," she retorted with a smile. His eyebrows raised as he dropped the corners of his mouth in a caricature of dignified revelation, but continued to mend the purple panels as she shifted uncomfortably where she sat. Something about her seemed to crave the interaction, but her apprehension overpowered her. J'Kana's hands grew still, his body stiff, and with a dramatic gasp he fell backwards onto the ground. Siema, in this moment, chose to live up to her name as she pawed at him to wake him up. Nihani screamed and rushed to his side, her lips poised to pour Y'Maju's melody into the atmosphere as she did. The Jeniju picked his head up and used her lap as a pillow, raised her arms, but then before she could speak, he laughed. She struck him in the forehead with an open palm, which only made him laugh harder. "What is wrong with you?"

"I'm sorry," he managed, but when he saw the worry in her gentle eyes, he sobered. "I'm sorry. I didn't mean to scare you. Or to make you uncomfortable."

"Just…" she paused, her eyes cast beside them both, her hands full of the soft, dark curls of his hair. "Please, just focus on your healing." J'Kana sighed loudly as he rolled his eyes, and relaxed when he felt her fingertips move through his scalp.

"I'll make you a deal. I will focus on healing up if you talk to me," J'Kana proposed. He could sense her apprehension, but then she smiled back at him with a radiance that almost stopped his heart. "Is that a 'yes?'"

She feigned pensiveness, and watched as the moments she took before her answer drove J'Kana wild with expectation. Even the ara cub seemed to want to know, and so she nodded.

"Fine," she said with a sudden playfulness. J'Kana was caught off guard. "But I get to ask the questions…"

***

The sniffle under his arm pulled J'Kana from the depths of the story. He looked to Kamari, only to see the tears stream down his dark cheeks. He rubbed his eyes with the back of his wrist, and for a moment, the father waited to see what his son would do.

"It's so beautiful," Kamari cried. "Waleya saved you from the poison!" J'Kana's lips split with a grin that echoed all the warmth he felt in his heart.

"Indeed she did, hafu wu shehefo." He squeezed the boy tightly, and drove a finger into his side to make him jump. "And she taught me a little bit of Y'Maju to boot." The little one's heart nearly stopped at the mention of the mermaid tongue.

"Really?!" Kamari's eyes brimmed with excitement as he pushed himself up with his father's knee as leverage. "I want to learn that, too!"

"Always so excited to learn, even if you haven't finished your study of J'Karo yet." Kamari puffed out his cheeks again as he sat back down and folded his arms. "Hey, remember that it was my own hunger for J'Karo that brought me face to face with your mother, Kanawe Y'Sawe, and something far bigger than them both…"

"Don't do that, Yababa," Kamari groaned. "You always give me hints without telling me anything." J'Kana shrugged, then stood to his feet and crossed the floor of the luseme to find the leather tome of J'Karo's secrets placed safely on top of a nearby dresser. Since the language study had become so common, he figured it was a waste to return it to the bookshelf in the other room.

"Then how about we continue until it's time to keep the story alive, nah?" Kamari lit with joy at the sight of the book, and nodded fervently. "Good boy. Now, follow along here…"

| | | |
|---|---|---|
| | Fawame | Corrupt |
| | Jeniju | Jeniju |

| | | |
|---|---|---|
|  | Minije | Torturous/Torture |
|  | Mamiwatu | Mamiwatu |
|  | Lasha | Reckless |
| 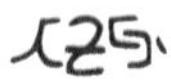 | Itimu | Shameful |
|  | Kusawe | Dishonest |
|  | Ishiju | Captivating |
|  | Hohumi | Forgotten/Forget |
|  | Bako | Burden/Heavy |
|  | Seleku | Shifty |
| 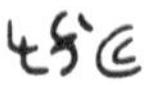 | Alera | Hopeful |
|  | Koho | Circumstantial |
|  | Bete | Solid |
|  | Yema | Chosen |
|  | Shichile | Innocent |
|  | Bekasha | Guilty |
|  | Tuili | Prophetic |
|  | Isala | Musical |
|  | Reshoki | Floor |
| 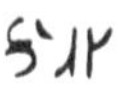 | Lefo | Other/Else |

| Shimari | Together |
|---|---|
| Taja | Apart |
| Fanu | Justice |
| Kufanu | Injustice |
| Hohara | Remember/Remembered |

# 12

# Once Together, Twice Apart

*Behaji Road—Outer Grasslands*

Finally, he had come to the other side of Mount Y'Bayeka. The journey had taken Y'Sawe much longer this time around. Three days was hardly enough time to heal of the wounds his brother had given him, at least without the help of the Jeniju. Even so, he made his way carefully through the backroad paths to Shifi. The grass and weeds had taken over, and without a steady frequency of travelers, there was no hope in taming them again. Almost all of Y'Neshu believed the roads to Shifi to be cursed. With

Asanibo attacking in broad daylight, how could anyone think differently? The real question was, how long before Folawu would suffer the same stigma? Even worse, how long before the entire continent fell to Mahute's machinations?

As much as Y'Sawe didn't want to focus on it, he found that it was all he could think about. If the Kanawe didn't do something soon, then Mahute would succeed in his dismantling of Y'Neshu unopposed. The very thought pushed him forward, slow though he moved. As he paced the path with the soso wood staff that Y'Chaju was kind enough to give, he listened to the wildness around him. The cool colors of the dusky sky mixed with the soothing warmth of the air. The chirps of jinenu crickets lifted up a melody fit for the wabaki bats to dance to. The pace he set entreated him to the trickling sound of slowly rushing water. His eyes lit green as his ike burst through him like a flood.

"It won't be long now," he whispered to himself with a weary smile. Immediately his ike began to work beneath his black and gray garb. Gradually, his wounds began to heal, and his mind became clearer from the calm of his surroundings. He came to the Great Y'Shala

Bridge—named for one of the M'Iba Kanawe, said to be able to harness the power of the sun—and looked upon the plains of hutije grass wherein his little boy would hide. A sad smile washed onto his face as his body mindlessly carried him to its center. His eyes drifted from side to side as he marveled at the massive white marble structure, adorned with round pillars rippled with black and wrapped in gold near the top, middle and bottom.

Amber jewels were built into the golden molds, made to emulate the look of the sun, while perfect spheres rested at their tops. It was a monument built for a king, and by itself, it conveyed the high esteem of the Kanawe throughout Y'Neshu. *But are we worthy of it*, Y'Sawe demanded of himself as his eyes returned to the green sea before him. He pondered the words of his old master, how Y'Chaju believed Mahute to be right about the flaws in their order, and grit his teeth as he accepted the truth of it. Since the days of his training as an ijeya, he often wondered how different things would have been if he had J'Karo to protect himself back then, or if his parents could raise a field of crops with an utterance. He may not have been a Kanawe, but would it have mattered? He shook his head as his feet crossed the bridge, and like a fajari beetle's explosion, a darkness struck him on all sides…

***

*Kehemu Forest—Shukeshu Tributaries*

The morning of the third day went as the previous two. Chishashi, J'Chera and J'Yobena all patrolled the forest around the cave, while Nihani watched J'Kana attach the final length of cloth to his jilaba wu ajiwele. Every stitch pulled together perfectly with the ebb and flow of his hand and soothed his mind like the sounds of the ocean. By the time he finished it, his eyes softened with a sudden sadness that he didn't expect.

"That looks," Nihani started, eyes full of wonder as she searched for the right adjective, "wabela!" J'Kana's lips curled into a half smile at the compliment. In the three days since his healing journey had begun, he had learned a few words of Y'Maju from Nihani, and understood her utterance to mean "amazing."

"Arani, hafu wu jewo." He watched her with amusement as she pieced together the thank-you in her head.

"Thank you, my friend," she repeated in Pedestrian, a look of hope about her. "Was that right?"

"Usi," J'Kana offered, and she smiled wider. "Now all I have to do is begin to tell my story here." He stood up from the cave floor and held the garment up with both hands. The hood and mantle, a mix of light blue and white in intricate design, contrasted the blank deep mystic purple that made up the remainder of the cloak. It was sleeveless, and simply wrapped around the body to the comfort of the wearer. For as much beauty as he believed it had, it was the massive emptiness where J'Karo should be that captured his attention the most. He felt a pulse.

His eyes flashed gold, his hands moved with the rapid fluidity of the Great Kabisu River as they stitched and cut and stitched again. Nihani watched in awe as the gold thread morphed and the felasa of J'Karo appeared, line after line, then disappeared into the purple fabric. J'Kana's face dripped with sweat, his hands moved faster still, his every breath shuddered from the intensity, and then abruptly he stopped. He blinked, his eyes shifted back to their deep brown hue and where there once was nothing in the violet fabric, now he saw the story of the recent battle, his poisoning, and his healing. Siema barked with satisfaction, and when a spark erupted from her tongue, J'Kana pulled the finished robe away from her with a suspicious look.

"What is this magic," Nihani asked as she pulled the ara cub closer, unable to see the story he weaved. J'Kana looked into her mystic moon-like eyes, sank into the calm that it brought him as he basked in the flowing shift of his gilded ike. He looked back at the fabric, saw the glow of the thread hidden from the eyes of all others, and felt his soul leap. His half-smile became full now, and he wrapped the jilaba wu ajiwele around his shoulders.

"I wouldn't be able to tell you," he said with a chuckle. His mind was almost consumed with the way his body was shrouded in the same warmth he felt in the Samanu Usele's vision. He opened his mouth to say more, but the rumble of the cave wall interrupted him. As the opening reappeared, so did the watchmen that patrolled the forest. J'Kana looked up at them, the smile still on his face. "So, are you just going to stand there, or are you going to tell me how I look?"

"You *look* like you're only barely not dead," J'Yobena jibed. J'Kana rolled his eyes.

"Would anyone with a valid opinion like to comment," he asked the others, which made J'Yobena frown. "Perhaps someone with an eye for fashion?" He took a moment to look over J'Yobena's silver robe and the slightly torn maroon habesha (dress) beneath it before he turned attention to J'Chera, who struggled to hide a smile.

"I like it," J'Chera offered before J'Yobena could spew her venomous rage. "The mix of colors reminds me of the Ile Kanawe. Although, it looks like you might have a brighter outlook than Master Y'Sawe." The mention of his master caused a ripple in J'Kana's smile. Fortunately, the patter of Siema's small paws against his jifona legs steadied it again.

"If you're done," Chishashi interrupted, "we need to talk about what happens next. It's not like you can live in a makeshift cave in Kehemu forever." He was right, and J'Kana knew that the moment the walls around them fell, it would be time for them to set out for Shifi. Just the thought of the ruined Holy City was enough to churn his stomach, and when it did, it reminded him that soon Nihani would have to depart from them. He swallowed hard, and tried all he could not to look at her. He could, however, feel her eyes dance upon his form.

"Not that we would even want to," J'Chera said with a chuckle. He felt the spot on his hip where the knife wound had been and sighed in pleasant relief. "Fortunately, we have all the supplies we need to make the journey, especially if we cut through the Hesefa Desert—"

"That won't be possible," J'Yobena cut him off, and every head turned in her direction. "In my patrols, after I got sick of you, J'Chera, I wanted to see how far we were from the edge of the forest. What I found is that the Hesefa Desert borders the forest only a little ways from here, but the Y'Sewanan military guards any access point." Their hearts sank with her words.

"We won't be able to go through Y'Sewana," J'Kana thought aloud. "What about the Kalisechu Plains? The Chakala Tributaries to the east feed into the Great Joba, which we can use to travel south to Y'Rakili faster." Chishashi shook his head.

"That would leave you too open," he warned, his voice strong and solemn as his yellow eyes shifted between the three ijeya ni. "Tikhal was among Mahute's inner circle, one of the first to pledge loyalty to the 'Blood Prodigy,' as he was called. There are two others that will be on the hunt for you while you move through Y'Neshu, both with unmatched tracking skills and no love for a Kanawe's disciple. If Khafenu or Hanika were to discover you out in the open, they would be careful to strike when you have no wall to protect you." J'Chera groaned in frustration, clearly not a fan of having to plan this much.

"Why can't you just transport us all where we need to go, J'Yobena," he asked with all the petulance of a small child. Somehow it eased J'Kana's nerves to know that his senior could treat all this with such a lack of concern.

"That wasn't on purpose," J'Yobena shot, as if his ignorance had become a stench to her. "I meant to get us outside of the bakery, but with my senses distorted and my emotions…" She trailed off, unable to hide the sorrow that plagued her or the shame that radiated from having them.

"It's alright," J'Kana told her, much to the surprise of everyone in the room. "It would be dangerous to try and recreate something like that without a Kanawe here to guide us. It was a miracle that it happened the first time." He took a moment to think, as did the others. They knew what their only option was, but knowing it didn't make it any easier to speak. J'Kana decided that he would be the one to break the silence. "I suppose that means we have to travel through Kehemu, then."

"There would be no other way," Chishashi all but growled, displeased that he would have to babysit these humans a while longer. "It would take two weeks to reach

Wasuchi Village in the southwestern forest. We will have to go around Ekutali Village if we want to cross the border into Y'Rakili, though." The very mention of the village was enough to suck the air out of the cave. Everyone knew what kind of place it was. Asanibo lived there, and were said to feed on any unfortunate fools who wandered too close.

"Will you be able to shield us," asked J'Yobena with far more calm and respect in her voice than anyone expected. Chishashi shook his head.

"My Blood Shadow can only shield places. Structures. To hide a group on the move would be an impossibility. The best thing we can do is travel south towards the Rajoni Tributaries and ride them along until we reach the Temetu River that they feed into. Without complications, we should be able to reduce our journey by a day or two. I know that it takes about a week to move from the Temetu to Shifi." Suddenly, the ijeya ni breathed lightly again. Their hope returned, and the Wehela Stone of Shifi centered itself at the forefront of J'Kana's mind. He could almost hear his Kanawe's voice again. Nihani stood to her feet.

"Then I should leave," she said firmly, but with eyes overtaken with sadness. J'Kana marveled, as he had never witnessed a frowning of the moon before this moment. "My Wekhala is waiting for my report." J'Kana was on his feet before he knew it, and the moment he realized how fast he had moved, he marveled again, this time at the power she seemed to have over him.

"You could come with us," he offered, and promptly ignored the angry and confused looks of J'Yobena and J'Chera respectively. Siema seemed to echo his sentiment, as she nuzzled her furry face against Nihani's bare legs. The Jeniju apprentice looked down upon her new friend and felt her heart swell. "We would need a healer." Instantly she looked back at J'Kana, her eyes even sadder now. She stammered, in deep search of the right words to say, but Chishashi intervened.

"She wouldn't be of much help there," he told J'Kana with his arms folded across his chest. "Her healing abilities have yet to come in." The words made Nihani visibly writhe in front of the ijeya, and embarrassed tears welled up in her eyes.

"But you have some magic, na?" J'Kana asked with his usual playfulness, and watched as the mermaid wiped the water from her face. She nodded.

"All of my people have the ability to manipulate the water," she offered sheepishly as she looked away. Everything about her tone said that it was of little importance, but the three budding Saweshe exchanged a look that said otherwise. J'Kana raised an eyebrow, then cupped his hand beneath her chin to lift her face from the ground. He smiled wide, his eyes full of a warmth more intense than she felt in the hand that touched her, and immediately she felt herself relax.

"Then would you lend us your power and help me get home?" The question was so sincere, whispered with a fullness of trust unlike any that she'd ever heard, that she nodded before she realized. It was then that she marveled, as she had never been under the spell of another the way she realized she was under his.

***

*Outer Grasslands—Shifi Outskirts*

Every hair on Y'Sawe's arms stood on end as he walked the path. A wave of anxiety hit him like the falling of a bakirati tree as the sounds of his lost son's laughter and questions echoed through time. Around him, the hutije shifted and swayed, as though the boy ran beneath the surface as in days of old. He closed his eyes as he walked gingerly forward, tried his best to clear his mind. His surroundings would lend to him nothing at all, no sense of connection, no restoration to his ike, but that hardly mattered. He had a number of memories that would do the trick instead.

Kanawe Y'Sawe thought back on the day he visited the Y'Rakilian shore for the first time. Even now he could see the golden sands and bright blue waters that swirled and swayed beneath the summer sun. He could hear the crash of waves against the rocks, feel as the ocean waters lapped against his feet while the gentle wind ran its fingers through the locs on his head. It was a moment of serenity the likes of which he had never seen before that point, and one he had been fortunate enough to discover on his own. It was there, in that solitude, that he truly felt Y'Kele's presence.

He felt the warmth and light wash over him, felt the swelling of his ike, and sank into its power like a sick man into the Hetebi Springs. The Grand Master breathed and reopened his eyes. The darkness of burned and abandoned Shifi still bit at him, but at least now his ike had been restored enough that he could resist. Even so, it was a battle against his darkest moments. He focused his gaze, determined to make it to the Wehela Stone on the edge of the city, determined to find his ijeya, and he stumbled. The darkness that shrouded the Holy City pulsed through the air, more so as the Stone finally came into view. Y'Sawe felt his knees buckle under the weight of it, and for the first time since he left Shifi all those years ago, he gave credence to the rumors of a curse.

"I need to find J'Kana quickly," he growled to himself through tightly clenched teeth. "Then we need to go." He placed a hand into the pocket of his jilaba wu ajiwele, and felt the edges of a thick envelope within. Y'Sawe was a careful man, and while he was hopeful that he would be reunited with his student, he also knew the dangers that they faced. If something were to happen to him, then at least he would leave behind something from which his apprentice might still grow. He bit his lower lip, and realized what his failure to survive would mean for J'Kana. Yet another person in his life would be gone, and he would be forced to deal with the fallout of being all alone all over again. He clenched his fist. He had to survive, no matter what.

He approached the Stone, painted in silver and gold, and engraved with a line of J'Karo that read, "Ti Wasu me wiyi ra N'koshi jiu Y'Kele shu wishimachele o," and stumbled against it as the weight of his past climaxed from the sight of the broken cobbles of the street and the overgrown vegetation on the walls that surrounded it. He struggled to breathe, which in turn made it hard for him to think. He needed to purify the city, or at least this part of it, if he would remain conscious. He already knew that his enemies hunted the ijeya ni, and reasoned that they would be after him as well. Yes, Mahute had let him go, but Y'Sawe knew that didn't matter. Mahute's biggest strength, since their days bargaining for food in Hanbari's mining camp, was luring his marks into a false sense of security before the strike, all to walk away with more than what was promised. The sudden flash of the scene in the Vault of Y'Leina reminded him of how little the Dagger had changed.

Y'Sawe braced himself against the Wehela Stone and climbed back to his feet. He looked around at the abandoned buildings, huts made of wood and stone, faded green hutije grass intermingled with the endurant gold of mahaju stalks emptied of their grain as their rooftops. He recalled the plaster that ran beneath them, a sealant of the structure to keep out the wind and rain. He thought to run through the streets, to find his home, to call out to his lost wife and child, and a tear streamed the side of his face when his mind caught up to reality. It wasn't there. *They* weren't there. All he had now was his ijeya, and he would do all he could to find and protect him.

"I will not lose anyone else," he demanded through the thickness in the air. He swam deeper into his ike and formed his lips for the command. He spoke with ferocity, his hand still on the Stone, "Ti Baa Shifi shu isuatichele!" The air, for but a moment, shifted towards the purity that Y'Sawe commanded, but then a shock passed through his body as the gold and silver of the Stone flashed black and red. His eyes went wide with realization. It wasn't Shifi that had been afflicted, but the Wehela Stone itself. He dropped to his knees, an expression of shock written into his face as beside the Stone stood a dark figure draped in bloody red clothes. It came closer. Y'Sawe had to focus his blurring vision as the figure—a female Asanibo with jet black hair that curled around her pristine yet vicious pale face—looked on him with cold crimson eyes. She began to chant in Batabari as she slashed her palms and let the blood drip.

Y'Sawe, with the last of his strength, whispered a complex command as his fingers grazed the envelope from the outside. In seconds, it faded to nothing, and in seconds more, he was engulfed in a swirling pool of black…

***

*Kehemu Forest—Outer Kaulusi Fields*

J'Kana couldn't help but feel on edge, and pulled at the edges of his robe. Siema, who rested in his shiki close to his chest, nuzzled against him to give him comfort. The darkness never ended in the Forest, and now that they were so close to Ekutali Village, J'Kana, J'Yobena and J'Chera noticed the stark lack of detail in their surroundings. It was truly a village of Asanibo. Chishashi led their formation, focused and alert to his surroundings. Even though the ijeya ni had their senses disrupted, Chishashi was unfazed by the hypnotic effects of Asanibo aura.

"Everyone, remember your training," he warned as he took them further into the jungle. J'Chera and J'Yobena were hardly nervous, and tried to be just as attentive as their guide, though he was truly in a class of his own. It made sense. In the week it took to get to this point from the Shukeshu Tributaries, they had done what J'Kana suggested before and pooled their knowledge as they journeyed. The first day, they shared useful commands, like Y'Sawe's time stop and J'Yobena's wall of lightning.

J'Kana taught them how to dispel the effects of the Asanibo, and how to peer into the minds of others, which managed to earn J'Yobena's respect a bit more. On the second day, J'Chera taught them how to deepen their relationships with animals around them. There was a command that would merge feelings so that a bond could be forged and deepened at quicker pace than the taming process. J'Kana tried it on Siema, and now they felt what the other did. The third day, J'Yobena taught them how to strengthen their ike even in the midst of commands. She explained that a person could create a groundswell of ike by not only taking in the sensory stimuli that gave life to the hato, but by remembering other moments that have made the ike strong in the past.

On the fourth day, J'Kana taught them all how to create shelters strong enough to last, just in case something happened along the way. Day five, he was met with a pleasant surprise. His M'ba ijeya ni gifted him four lists, two each, to study as they went along their way. It made him feel like his Kanawe was still there. He smiled for a moment as his hands drifted to the notes. The fact that so much had been gained in only that amount of time gave him a greater sense of confidence, even if he learned how much faster the others were at picking things up.

"J'Kana, focus," J'Yobena hissed at him. They resumed their trek, now just on the outskirts of the Ekutalian farmland and easy to spot by any Asanibo in the area. He moved slowly, carefully, even as the vampires could be seen just beyond the other side. When he caught up with the others, they moved carefully and quietly. Water could be heard not far from where they walked, and all they had to do was go south, but Chishashi took them southeast instead. Their best chance to avoid detection was to follow their guide without question, and there was still a small fishing dock not far from where they were.

"I don't like this," J'Chera whispered as he snatched what he could of the efisi cobs, sobachi melon, and ketuketu grain crops as their group passed them by. Chishashi shook his head at him while Nihani offered a sweet smile.

"You seem to like quite a bit," J'Yobena shot back with an accusatory tone. "We just stocked up on supplies before we left the cave."

"And we've been running low since yesterday," J'Chera shot back. "Anyway, I was talking about our condition. We walk around this forest like children lost in a fog and worse, we make Chishashi bear the burden of leading us out of it." They knew he was right, if not a little louder than he should've been, and all of them picked up on what went unsaid. At any moment, while they least expect it, something could strike them from the shadows they swam in.

"Well, we're almost there," Chishashi informed them kindly enough, "so if you wouldn't mind shutting up long enough for us to get to a boat and be on our way…" The ijeya ni silenced themselves from a mix of shame and nerves. The sound of water grew stronger, but then came the powerful boom of thunder through the air, far closer than any had realized. Chishashi's head whipped around, and while J'Kana and the others couldn't see it, they could tell that the Asanibo among them did.

"Y'Go bi sekhel mtanu basiyil," Nihani began to speak unprompted. She waved her arms through the air, and continued her soothing chant. "Divine Waters, I live through you. Y'Go, ikhum suna ma aril N'vina. Divine Waters, dance upon the air here." A cloud of mist erupted throughout the terrain as soon as Nihani's mouth closed, and Chishashi picked up the pace. The others panicked, and followed him with spirited determination.

"What just happened," J'Yobena asked, no longer concerned with the volume of her voice.

"We've been noticed," Chishashi answered grimly. "The sound you heard was the roar of a rayemo trained by the Batabari Royal Guard. The moment an unfamiliar scent passes through their route, they alert the others."

"The other guards, right," J'Kana asked nervously. Chishashi stopped at the edge of one of the tributaries near a boat that had been broken long ago and abandoned. He took a moment to look back at J'Kana, and the look he donned sent a shockwave through him.

"No. The other rayemo," he answered. J'Kana looked at him, mouth agape, then briefly looked back from where they came just in time enough to hear a trio of ferocious roars of thunder.

"Oh, absolutely not," he said with a shake of the head. He approached the boat with urgency as he said, "Ti wi rila shu teonati o!" He spoke with force, more so than the others would have ever expected to come from him, and the boat began to mend plank by wooden plank. Another roar sounded, but that was all they could hear, and it finally registered in their minds. Even with a distortion to their senses, nothing was strong enough to stifle the sound of a rayemo beast. Chishashi watched the boat intensely as the boards continued to patch themselves, each hole fixed by the sudden growth of new wood.

The giant cats were near enough to hear their growls through the distortion and fog. Everyone's heart beat against their ribcage as if they wanted to make it easier for the beasts to rip them out.

"Help me push," Chishashi shouted frantically, the fear of the moment now more than he could bear, "it's ready!" J'Chera threw his bag into the boat and joined with J'Kana to lend the Asanibo some assistance. The river welcomed its passage, just as the boat welcomed its passengers. Nihani simply took to the water while J'Kana and J'Chera jumped inside. Chishashi, still on the riverbank, muttered something in Batabari while J'Yobena summoned all the fire and lightning she could muster. The first rayemo entered her field of vision, its form majestic and golden brown, the mane of black fur around its neck somehow alive in the current of air. Its deep amber eyes watched them prepare their assault, just as more of them surrounded the riverbank. J'Yobena bit her lip.

"Run, Chishashi," she told him, fully aware that they would need his help to reach the edge of the Kehemu.

"I'll hold them here." J'Kana's eyes widened in horror and shock, and when he nearly jumped back to the shore, J'Chera held him in place.

"What are you doing," J'Kana called, suddenly more afraid than he had ever been. "You have to run too!" J'Yobena shook her head. She shot Chishashi a look as lightning in heaven began to crackle overhead. Immediately he understood, and made way for their only escape. She faced the enemies down, and with another spoken command the balls of fire in her palms grew brighter and hotter. She smiled as her brow dampened from the mist and her own sweat.

"Oye, J'Kana," she shouted behind her, a pulse in the muscles of her arms, "you have earned my respect." It was enough to make them all freeze where they were. "Thank you. For your understanding, I mean. I wouldn't have been able to pull myself together without your endless patience. So get out of here."

"We can survive this if we fight together," J'Chera argued back, his voice strong yet frantic. The lightning burst from heaven above as swiftly as a fire from a pile of dry wood, but a collective roar from the squad of rayemo distorted the air so much that it was blown clear away.

"We have to go," Nihani spoke urgently, her legs now replaced with a massive fin of glittery mint green scales. "If we don't, we'll all die…"

"Listen to her," J'Yobena yelled as she enlarged the fireballs and launched them. "How would Kanawe Y'Sawe take it if his ijeya of only a month became a steaming pile of rayemo dung in the Kehemu, e?" The formation of big cats broke as the infernal orbs exploded toward their battle line. They roared again, and the ijeya ni watched as the balls of fire were blown apart. "Ahh!" J'Yobena screamed as a ripping pain took to her arm. She looked down, only to realize that it had been taken from her up to the bicep. She stammered, her eyes met J'Kana's, and with a sudden resolve the likes of which could only come from her, she gave one last command. "Survive." The squad of rayemo surrounded her now, and together blasted her with such a volatile wind that she swept into the air in a spiral. Nihani slammed her fin into the water as J'Yobena paused, then descended. J'Chera and J'Kana felt the boat drift, just as they saw the rayemo begin to pull her apart.

***

J'Kana shuddered a breath as he ended this part of the story. Kamari sat next to him, and gently placed his small hands on the Kanawe's forearm while Nihani looked on from a chair across the room. Her eyes were just as solemn, and though Kamari thought to ask deeper questions about how horrible J'Yobena was to his Yababa, he simply sat there and ran his hand along his father's arm in an attempt to soothe him. J'Kana gave a pitiful grin, and pulled his little one closer to his chest with an affectionate kiss to the forehead.

"J'Yobena gave herself up for us," Nihani spoke, a shake in her voice as she met her son's eyes and thought about what would have never happened without their comrade's sacrifice. Kamari climbed down from the couch and walked over to his Waleya. He put his head on her lap and spread his little arms around as much of her as he could reach.

"Don't cry, Waleya," he pleaded sadly. "I've got you." The genuine sweetness of the boy's words made both his parents smile through the tears that welled up in their eyes.

"And what I have for you," J'Kana responded in his best effort to reclaim some of the parental playfulness that had become his nature, "is a lesson in J'Karo that will help you to grow big and strong, even if we aren't here." He pulled out the leather book in which J'Karo was kept, and found a page in it instantly that contained all he wished Kamari to know. "Look here."

| | | |
|---|---|---|
|  | Rila | Boat |
|  | Teo | Fix/Mend/Repair |
| 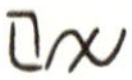 | Kata | Near/Close/Local |
|  | Emi | Far/Distant/Abroad |
| 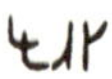 | Afo | Wise |
|  | Jeli | Foolish |
|  | Kishe | Right/Correct |
|  | Lali | Wrong/Incorrect |
|  | Kisheme | Righteous |
|  | Fafu | Soft |
| 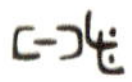 | Moye | Warm |
|  | Fola | Curious |
|  | Sawesheme | Enlightened |
| 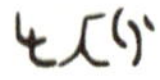 | Aishu | Linear |

| | | |
|---|---|---|
| 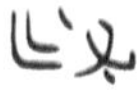 | Chibe | Hungry |
|  | Fise | Thirsty |
| 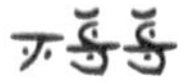 | Yijojo | Important/Necessary/Serious/Precious |
|  | Onale | Irrelevant/Unimportant/Worthless |
|  | Iwama | Compassionate |
| 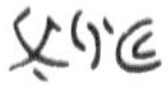 | Bashura | Fast |
| 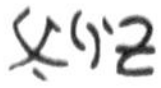 | Bashuti | Early |
|  | Moheti | Late |
| 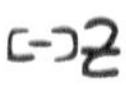 | Moti | Sound |
|  | Loatu | Cultivate |
|  | N'Bele | Travel/Trip |
|  | Feyu | Like |
|  | Kufeyu | Dislike |
|  | Tokulu | Soon/Almost |
| 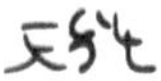 | Olea | Instead/However/Except/But |
|  | Suali | After/Since |
|  | Mikena | Before/Ahead of |
|  | Fikiri | Safe |

# 13

# Loss and Revival

*Kehemu Forest—Rajoni Tributaries*

One hour. That was how much time it took to travel east toward the Temetu River, the boat's occupants trapped in an eerie silence. Nihani, who swam the tributaries as she pressed against the meager vessel, struggled not to cry at what she had just witnessed. Nobody spoke, save for Chishashi, who whispered his instructions to the Jeniju more solemnly than before. He had not wanted to care for them, but it was clear to all who saw his face that J'Yobena's demise affected him just as much.

"How could we have let this happen," J'Kana growled, every muscle in his body tense with emotion. As much as he wanted to savor the reeds and branches that decorated the streams both low and high, his thoughts were clouded with the sudden loss.

"It was her choice," Chishashi answered without hesitation. He could feel the irate stare that radiated from J'Kana. "She knew that if we all stayed, we would have just gotten destroyed alongside her. There was nothing any of us could have done for her."

"Is that so," J'Kana asked loudly, angrily, as gold flecks took to his irises again. He felt the sting that came with such a violent shift of his ike, but it didn't matter. He forced himself to endure it. "You are Asanibo just like the Batabari Guard, ne? You use the same volatile blood magic that they do?"

"And what of it, J'Kana?" Chishashi whipped his head around as he shouted it, his eyes filled with blood red tears, his lip aquiver with the sadness and the shock. "I am khimbenzi! The outcast! Nothing I could have said to the guard would have mattered, except to make them drain our bodies of life all the quicker!" Shame broke through the anger on his face, and he relented. He turned back to the river and tried his best to let it calm him. J'Kana let him.

"Ahh, J'Yobena," J'Chera whimpered, a half-smile plastered unsteadily to his face. "She was always taking care of someone, you know." J'Kana looked at him, unable to hide the confusion before the senior ijeya noticed it. It made him smile. "I know you wouldn't understand. After all, she met you with immediate hostility." He breathed a weighted sigh, then broke it with a wry grin. "Even so, she was the one who watched over you most closely when the poison took its hold."

"Chilu?" J'Kana asked. *What?* J'Chera nodded confidently.

"She also did the most foraging these last few days," Chishashi offered, which only served as another blow to J'Kana's expectations. "She went out of her way to make sure Siema enjoyed extra rations when she thought no-one was watching."

"She was always like that," J'Chera told them. There was a wistful look in his eye as he thought back on his time with her. "We started our apprenticeship the same year, her under Y'Okani, and myself apprenticed to Y'Leisu. When we met, it only took her about five minutes to start laughing at me. My jilaba wu ajiwele was poorly made, my hair was unkempt, and I couldn't perform the simplest task that my Kanawe had given me." Nihani, J'Kana and Chishashi sat in silence, careful not to give themselves over too much to the sadness that now weighed on them all. J'Chera continued. "One day, our masters were requested by the leaders of Onawi to mediate a border dispute between Y'Baule and Y'Fuwefo. Kanawe Y'Leisu told me to tread with caution, so that we of Y'Fuwefo would endear ourselves to the Y'Bauleans. I foolishly set out to explore…places in Onawi that a young ijeya should never go alone."

"And what happened while you were there," Nihani asked with more eagerness in her voice than she intended. It brightened the humor in J'Chera's face.

"I got into a fight with some of the Y'Baulean, ehh, merchants," he answered full of hesitation and in no certain terms. It was enough to make the entirety of the party raise their eyebrows in suspicion. The storyteller grew defensive as he carried on, "What? It was my first diplomatic mission and I needed something to take the edge off. The fight, unintentional as it was, got back to my master and let me just say that she. Was. Furious. She nearly had me flogged by the guards of the city so they wouldn't question the nature of the Kanawe. Heh. I nearly killed the negotiations with my recklessness, and when the guards were about to take me away, it was J'Yobena who took the blame. She told them that looking for…recreational activities in the area was her idea, and that the only reason I was there was because she was too afraid to go alone." The memory caught up with him, and he choked on a heavy sob. "She always gave, even though she never wanted anyone else to know it."

The silence returned, and in its midst, resolve swirled within J'Kana and the others. The younger ijeya knelt before his senior and placed a hand on his shoulder.

"Then we will not waste her sacrifice," he said, and a crystal tear slid down his face.

***

*Loutu Usele*

Darkness surrounded him. The air was as stiff as it was stale, and the more he tried to calm himself, to sink into his ike and push out of the affliction, a sting caught his throat and stifled his efforts. Y'Sawe wouldn't allow himself to panic. It was unsightly for the Ile Kanawe to do something so contrary to his training…no matter how badly he wanted to do just that.

He heard footsteps in the dark, a confident stride that approached from the other end of a long corridor. Two by two, lamps lit with blazing fire the color of blood, born from golden bowls that protruded from black ornate pillars. Between them, Y'Sawe saw a muscular figure wrapped in a black coat. The locs on his head draped over his shoulders, and his eyes pulsed with a red glow that by themselves spoke of monsters the world had yet to meet. The figure moved closer now and with him, the fire. It was here that Y'Sawe noticed the crude metal cage around him.

"I see that you are finally awake," came the voice of Mahute the Dagger from the figure below. "How are you feeling?" Y'Sawe ground his teeth.

"Let me go, Mahute," the Kanawe demanded. There was a kind of rage to his calm that burned the air. Mahute only smiled as he paced the floor and pointed to the left. Reluctantly, Y'Sawe's eyes followed his brother's finger to another dome of iron bars, its prisoner: Y'Jaka. The Sage let his eyes wander the great stone chamber dimly lit by the glow of scarlet fire. There were seven cages in all, and one more of the others had already been filled. The Teacher shot his brother a look of confusion as he asked, "What is this?"

"A resurrection chamber," Mahute supplied. "This is where the Batabari of old would sacrifice their enemies to revive their own." Y'Sawe felt a chill run down his back like a raindrop on a cold window. "In a similar chamber, blood would be gathered to create weapons of war, the chiefest among them being the Three Great Beasts: Jurutisalaji, Ninikinana, and Amiti."

"You can't! Brother, what madness possesses you that you would even consider bringing them back?" Y'Sawe masked his terror behind a display of anger, which only amused the Dagger further.

"Oh, I intend to do more than that, ulu esho. The M'Iba Kanawe made sure that the only way to bring them back is with the blood of the Teachers, but what I've discovered is that the blood of the Ile Kanawe is the greatest prize among them. What if I told you that the Batabari held a greater secret; one that they never had the chance to bring to life? *I* mean to be the first, but to do what needs to be done, I need to take blood from the Grand Master and his little friends while they still draw breath." The younger brother's eyes went wide with realization.

Suddenly it made sense why Mahute let him leave, why he didn't finish the surviving Teachers when he had the chance, and why he let Y'Sawe make it as far as Shifi.

"You wanted me to heal, needed me to let my guard down," Y'Sawe all but whispered, and Mahute's teeth flashed with a slick delight now that his brother had joined him on the same page.

"If I took you captive after our meeting at the Yema, you would have tried to fight back, and you would have died, given the state I left you in," Mahute explained. He paced the floor, his arms crossed over his chest, a single hand cupped under his chin. "If you were to be brought here, you had to be trapped, and while my servants retrieved your friends, I had to let you go back to a place where our Blood Curse has been dormant for years. You did exactly what we needed you to do."

"So, what will you do now, ila esho," Y'Sawe asked, his voice as unchanging as the dark of this place. "Our numbers were depleted, and you have none but your own monsters to thank for that!"

"I will wait," he answered with unbridled confidence. "Your ijeya will be here soon enough, assuming that you left him a trail to follow. When he arrives, I'll be sure to let him watch as I kill his father right in front of him." Y'Sawe's blood ran cold, his mind started to race, and as he struggled to process Mahute's words, the Dagger left him to the dark.

***

Kamari was stunned to silence. No tears, no exclamation. The boy sat perfectly still by his Yababa's side and looked up at him with eyes wider than their dinner plates. J'Kana dared not respond with anything more than a quizzical "hmm," lest the boy explode. Kamari suddenly narrowed his eyes.

"So, you're just going to sit there and hold back an explanation, Yababa?" The sheer force of the question was enough to make J'Kana burst out in laughter. He laughed so long and so loudly that Kamari had to wait for him to finish if he wanted to continue the conversation. He crossed his little arms as he did so.

"Bara, hafu wu shehefo," the Kanawe apologized. "Hafu N'tebi shu chesina ra somi koshi ekeja chewaninatu o!"

"Could you say that in Pedestrian, Yababa? You're using words I don't know again," Kamari begged. J'Kana gripped his head with a firm but playful hand and nodded.

"I'm sorry," he translated. "I waited for so long to get here!" His smile now was just as big as before, and Kamari was only slightly amused.

"So, when did you find out that he was your father," the boy inquired with an innocence that betrayed his age. J'Kana shrugged with a sly smirk plastered to his jaw.

"After," was the only word he offered, much to Kamari's dismay.

"What do you mean, 'after?' After the rescue? After you married Waleya? I need answers!" J'Kana couldn't help but chuckle at the boy's persistence. He pulled out the leather book of J'Karo and opened it up.

"You will have them," assured the Sage. "Just not today. Now do you want to do your lesson or not?" The boy sighed as he threw his arms into the air.

"Fine."

"Good. Now, what are the four components of speaking power through J'Karo?" J'Kana watched as the boy blinked at him almost furiously. "Don't tell me you've forgotten…"

"I have not," Kamari protested. "It just takes a minute." He took another moment, let himself relax, and breathed. "Hoharanati," he exhaled. *Remember.* He looked at his father, and with a bright grin that would melt all the hearts in Y'Rakili, he said, "Particles, Structure, Understanding, and Intent." J'Kana beamed back at him.

"And what do those mean, hafu wu ulunawe ijeya?" The question required less time to answer.

"Particles 'ti' and 'yo' go at the start of the sentence and help the speaker change the world either through the things that are already happening, or by creating those things out of thin air," the boy explained.

"You are almost right," J'Kana started. "The particle 'ti' is for ethereal, and while it looks like things are happening out of thin air, those things are born from the union of Y'Kele's will and the user's soul. 'Yo,' on the other hand, is for making use of the things that are already around you, so you got that one right."

"And then the structure is the flow of the language. It's how easily the speaker can make a sentence work, and how well the pieces come into play." J'Kana smiled and nodded.

"And what about understanding," the Kanawe asked. Kamari was all too happy to answer.

"That is what you've had me do for weeks now, Yababa," he told him. "Understanding is how precise a person is with their words, and the level of vocabulary they have at their command only helps with that. As for intention..."

"Yes?" J'Kana's eyebrow raised. He wondered if the boy actually struggled, or if it was all a game to him.

"Intention is how much the speaker means what they ask for," he said quickly, and J'Kana knew that it was the latter rather than the former. He stood for a moment, a brilliant smile wrapped around his lower jaw as he left the room. "Yababa...?" He came back into the room with a glass of water from the kitchen. Kamari's face brightened like the sun at midday, his heartbeat quickened like the spirits of the old women in the Church of Y'Kele, and no amount of restraint he could impose would fully contain him. J'Kana set the cup down on the table with a smile.

"Alright," he prodded. "Chill the glass." Kamari was right, it was the same exercise from the Hidden Beast in the story. He took a deep breath, felt the warmth of the air in their chohafi, listened to the memory of his father's laughter in his ears, felt every pound of his heart against his chest, and allowed the swell of his ike to take full effect. His eyes glinted a turquoise that brought joy to J'Kana's heart. The boy opened his mouth.

"Ti N'jekume ifinati o," said the little one, and in the blink of an eye, the glass was completely frozen over. His eyes returned to normal, and he beamed with joy at the ice at the bottom of the cup. "How was that?"

"Better than what I did when I had to do it," J'Kana admitted with a chuckle. "E, who is this strong boy sitting on my couch, na?"

"That would be me, Yababa," said Kamari with the confidence of a grown man. "I want to learn more." J'Kana laughed.

"As you wish, my mighty prince! Look here," the Elder said, and pointed at the list on the page. "This would be right for you at this stage."

Yema Chosen

| | |
|---|---|
| Ekeja | Long |
| Chewani | Wait |
| Nujawe | Favorite/Special |
| Nujawema | Specialty |
| Tawale | Parent |
| Iletawale | Grandparent |
| M'Tawa | Ancestor |
| Anuma | Animal |
| Waleta | Aunt |
| Yabowu | Uncle |
| Kuri | Glass |
| Nonara | None/Nothing |
| Tuwa | Business |
| Kubacha | Blind/Deaf |
| Jasa | Depth/Deep |
| Esi | Affect/Influence |
| Shewe | Effect/Result |
| Uhuna | All/Everything |

# 14

# Echoes and Spears

*Kehemu Forest—Wasuchi Outskirts*

Within two days of their journey on the Temetu River, they came to a part of the forest that was much brighter. The sounds of the muka beasts and the ifofo birds were calmer, and even though they were far from the river, they could hear water as clear as day. All over, the ground was decorated with the ruddy browns of fallen leaves and bark. The trees alternated between the brilliant golds and oranges of the still-ripening choni and lachakule fruit, while yet more boasted the tough browns of soso nuts. The air smelled sweet and fresh, and threatened to whisk their party altogether into the Samanu Usele itself.

J'Chera and J'Kana both felt a strong shift of their ike, far beyond their desire or consciousness. J'Kana watched as J'Chera's eyes adopted flecks of brilliant silver, and smiled as he realized why they got along so much. J'Chera took notice as well, and his face lit up with more joy than the younger ijeya would have expected.

"Eyes up," Chishashi spoke as they marched down the road. "We are almost there." Behind him, Nihani's eyes wandered from tree to tree, bush to bush, with such a wonder that completely undercut her seriousness in the days before. J'Kana found himself surprised when his eyes lingered on her for quite a while, but quickly looked away when it seemed that she noticed.

"What's Wasuchi like," Nihani asked, her melodious alto a treat to their ears. It was enough to make the others think that they should keep her happy all the time. J'Kana looked at her, only to find that she looked at him just the same, a knowing smirk pressed to her lips in the same way that he wished his would be. He flushed red hot at the thought, then looked up towards a family of muka that swung from branch to branch.

"Wasuchi is home to Sasabosami," Chishashi explained, eyes fixed on the path ahead. "Unlike the Asanibo, they strive to deal with the rest of Y'Neshu peacefully, thought they are very selective about the humans that get to visit. Of course, they have to be, since their village is adherent to the old ways, where J'Karo and Batabari are spoken openly, and all have the freedom to learn and grow into a kind of unity with Y'Khel."

"That sounds interesting," Nihani replied in all earnest. Chishashi was quiet for a long time as they continued down the path.

"It was where I fled to when I was exiled from Ekutali," he explained. "They would not house an Asanibo. They said mine was a cursed existence, and that I would bring Y'Khel's wrath upon their home. After they threw me out, they fortified their barrier so that no Asanibo could wander in without their knowledge."

"And you bring this to us now," J'Kana asked incredulously. Chishashi was quiet again, and simply marched along the beaten path. The newest ijeya shook his head as they went. "Surely there has to be a way to get you into the village." The vampire guide looked back at J'Kana and grinned in such a way that made the others uncomfortable.

"There is a way," he said with far too much enjoyment. "As in the days of old, if someone is able to best their champion in a combat trial, then entry to Wasuchi would be allowed for their party. I have to admit, I don't know if the rules apply for someone like me. Since I am an unsavory, they may restrict your access, or even worse, deny it altogether." J'Kana raised his eyebrow at the vampire, who grew more somber as he spoke.

"There's something you still aren't telling us," J'Chera observed, and glowered in frustration at the guide. Chishashi met him with a weary chuckle that only raised the tension of the moment.

"The only person to have broken through in the last century was some woman from beyond the mountains thirty years ago," he informed them with a wave of the hand. "Listen, since we don't know how this will go, you would come out better if you let me just meet you on the other side of the village. You three might be able to use Nihani's status as Jeniju to barter a way in."

"After all you've done for us," J'Kana told him, "we can't just let you wait outside. We will find a way to get you into Wasuchi." The sincerity in the fresh ijeya's voice alarmed him. The only thing the humans ever saw Chishashi as was a monster, even when he came to their rescue. He didn't know whether he should feel refreshed or concerned, especially since these humans put him on a collision course with his brother Tikhal. "We will not waste your sacrifices either." J'Kana's words pierced his heart. How long had the boy thought about what happened?

The moment they thought to press onward, they were surrounded. Six warriors, all cloaked in patterns of brown and tan, skin as white as the winter snow on the summit of the Amejai Mountains. They were careful to train their spears on the unsuspecting party, all of whom dared not move. Siema alone was brave enough to bark at them, and spat fire from her safe place within J'Kana's jilaba wu ajiwele.

"We mean you no harm," Nihani offered up, her hands raised in a placative gesture. The leader of the pack, a woman with fierce yellow eyes and thick locs that draped over her face, tilted her head to the side as a smile of disbelief crept beneath the dark brown and black pattern of her mask.

"Then what is your business here, Jeniju," she asked, and her gaze drifted over to Chishashi, who still looked out into the distance. "Why have you brought an Asanibo to our doorstep?" Her tone instantly crushed any hope to use a mermaid's ethos to get by.

"I am simply guiding them through," Chishashi answered. "They mean to exit the Kehemu and travel to Shifi." The Leader narrowed her eyes in suspicion at him, then looked over the rest of the party members.

"A likely story. Do you know the cost of your entry, Blight?" That was how she addressed Chishashi, with the venom of prejudice and superiority. The echo of her disgust nearly overpowered the sensibilities of the ijeya ni, but the spears, a foreboding black color inlaid with amethyst crystals, kept them from acting on their impulses.

"I do," answered the Asanibo. "So, do you intend to issue the challenge, or do you threaten all your potential guests this way?" The Sasabosami growled like the rayemo beasts on the other side of the Temetu, and their captives began to sweat under their hostile gaze. The tension of the moment escalated, and the muka beasts swung through the deep brown branches and emerald chihera vines as though they fled an incoming catastrophe. The Leader, whose smile still graced her masked lips, stood straight as she walked before the Asanibo.

"You want a fight so badly? Fine. But how would you like it if he was the one I chose?" The Leader asked, and pointed squarely at J'Chera with her spear, ornamented with the feather of a three-tailed juku bird. The senior ijeya gulped down the air that passed through his nostrils, suddenly unable to feel his legs. J'Kana could tell that he hoped Chishashi would panic, would tell the Leader that he was no good in a fight, especially since J'Yobena…

"You think it matters which of us you choose," Chishashi asked with all the attitude in Y'Neshu. It was enough to make the Leader hazard a chuckle. Her eyes narrowed with enough malice to kill a herd of jifile beasts.

"Very well then," she said, which drew an alarmed expression from the pit of Chishashi's soul, "it is settled. If your friend here can land a blow on me through any method, I will allow your group to enter our domain." She looked J'Chera in the eye now as she spoke, her voice far graver than before. "If he dies, however, then you leave here and never show your face to me again." J'Chera whipped his head between the Leader and the Asanibo a few times before he thought to respond. This was the ultimatum, the cost of bringing an Asanibo to their doorstep.

"Wait a minute," he attempted to bargain, "I am simply the comic relief of the group. Are you sure you want to fight m—"

"It is decided," the Leader reaffirmed with a slam of her spear butt against the earth. "I will give you two hours to prepare."

***

*Kehemu Forest—Wasuchi Outskirts*

The longer they waited, the more it seemed as though the forest shrunk around them. J'Kana looked back at the path, a heaviness in his chest as he tried to ignore the amethyst-inlaid spears that would no doubt return to stare him down. Across from their formation, the Leader and her squad waited for J'Chera's return just as the others did. She paced excitedly, a sharp growth to her amusement with every moment that passed them by.

"Where is J'Chera," Nihani asked, anxious and unable to look away from the biggest brute in the opposing party. "He only has a few minutes left."

"Oh, tell me your little friend isn't scared," the Leader called, a delight in her voice as Chishashi narrowed his eyes. "He shook pretty badly when I gave him the challenge."

"Laugh while you can," J'Kana shot back with a confident smile he wasn't sure he believed. He folded his arms across his chest and stood in a wide stance that defied her every intimidation tactic. "J'Chera is a lot stronger than you think."

"That is news to *me*," J'Chera commented as he emerged from the underbrush. He cleared his Robe of Identity of fallen leaves and traces of moss as he caught his breath.

"What have you been up to, e?" J'Kana's question made J'Chera raise his eyebrow in confusion.

"What do you mean? She gave me two hours to prepare. I prepared," he responded with a kind of wily look in his eyes that piqued J'Kana's curiosity.

"Then show me what you have come up with," the Leader interrupted with equal intrigue. She readied her spear and stood with purpose in her stance. Her feet were spread wide, her empty hand extended, her spear pointed towards the sky, and her eyes sharp with intent. J'Chera merely stepped forward to meet her, the jovial cunning still embedded in his gaze. The Leader pounced, her taloned hand stretched forward as she prepared to extend her weapon. J'Chera simply rolled along the ground beneath her, and popped up to the other side. She whipped around and spun her bladed staff with the same kind of elegance with which the Jeniju walked upon the land, but when she thrust it forward, she was forced to watch as he pushed just behind the pointed head and knocked the weapon off its course.

J'Chera thought to gloat, but the tail end of the spear crashed into the side of his head and he nearly fell off balance as a result. He staggered, a warm trickle of blood streaked down his face, then he smiled back at her.

"To kham basi ye tuzo," the woman growled, and one of the amethyst fixtures in her staff plunged into the palm of her hand. "Kha ja mazanu, N'lekhan we subuje a gbayim o!" She commanded it with authority, and immediately it was like the spear developed a life of its own. J'Chera dodged the blade but caught a strike of the staff to his face. No sooner than he turned around did the blade of the spear come at him with urgency. He jumped away, desperate to establish distance, but even that would not assist him. The Sasabosami Leader sprang right after him, her spear still hungry for his flesh.

J'Chera pushed it aside, and when it spun under his midsection, he was wise enough to duck. Chishashi, J'Kana and Nihani all watched on, as did the Leader's subordinates, each one swept up in the onslaught of slashes and clubs. The blade came down on J'Chera, who narrowly rolled out of the way, and when the Leader advanced again, he swept her leg out from under her and watched as she started to fall. He smiled, but only for a moment, as she quickly tucked the body of the spear under her arm and drove it into the ground. Her descent stopped, and in another instant, she willed herself upright again.

"Imoshe besubu," J'Chera whispered, his eyes brilliant with silver as his ike surged and spilled out of him. The Leader cocked her head to the side and cracked her neck, then returned to her prior stance. A pressure emanated from J'Chera, the likes of which J'Kana could never have imagined would come from another ijeya, and the older disciple continued to speak. "Muka akira, jenilo kichiru, N'hafu shu chesichele o. Otaba ni wu kiraji ra N'hafu shu karochele." He begged the jenilo spiders, the muka beasts, and the imoshe beetles to lend him their power, and they all watched the leader's eyes widen as a buzzing sound erupted from deep within the Kehemu. She ran at him, but time had run out.

A massive cloud of imoshe beetles descended upon her, which provoked her spear to a violet glow. With the utmost aggression, she swung her weapon through the air, desperate to cleanse the skies of the purple and black insects, but they danced around her attacks with the grace of an angel. J'Chera pushed forward, ducked beneath an obvious strike at his shoulder, spun out of the way of an intended blow to the groin, and came within a hairs' breadth of landing an elbow to the Sasabosami's sternum. She whipped the weapon in a tight circle before her and pushed him back with the flick of her wrist.

"Did you really think it would be that easy," she asked him, now completely calm in the cloud of bugs. She took a deep breath, slammed the butt of her spear into the ground, and waved her free hand through the air as her blood dripped down her arm. "Let me show you the power of my Batabari. Tiben a zikheliyim." The winds began to stir, and as they cleared a path for her, the Leader once again lunged for J'Chera.

"Baa," he whispered as his eyes pulsed silver. A muka beast, covered in bushy black fur with long ears and a thick, lengthy tail, emerged from the branches with shrieks of frightening playfulness, and an army of them sprang into action despite the wind. The Leader was halted, forced to defend herself against another of the forest's creatures. As she swung at them, J'Chera noticed how quickly her movements had changed. Against him, it seemed as though she meant to kill him outright. Against the muka and the imoshe, however, she played defensively. That, he realized, would work to his advantage.

"Yo bushake, N'Hafu wu muata ra N'arila shu nibufinati," he began to speak, and the ground pushed up with a sudden force that launched the Leader into the air, with a muka beast still tied tightly to her spear. Back and forth they tugged at the weapon until the Leader proved victorious. She held it high above her head as she began her descent, J'Chera firmly in her sights, but where she expected his worry, she was met with a collectedness that gave her shivers. "Yo bushake, N'Hafu me N'arila shu nibufinati o!" The ground beneath J'Chera began to rumble, the Leader's masked jaw dropped, and in an instant he rocketed towards her. "Baa, jenilo ni!" J'Chera's shout to the spiders of the forest summoned their silk in massive heaps that wrapped and tangled around the Leader's arms and, much more importantly, her weapon.

The vampiress lurched back into the air from the sheer strength of the spider silk. She struggled against it, but only for a moment, as her abdomen was met in the next second by J'Chera's fist. A smile crossed his face as he noted her surprise. He fell, and with a wave of his hands the muka beasts gathered around him to catch him before he could collide with the earth. He laughed hysterically, and the Sasabosami that watched their master lose kicked at the ground and cursed beneath their breath.

"Yo kurawenati o," J'Kana whispered, and the spider-made ropes unwrapped their prisoner. She flipped as she descended, then buried her fist into the ground with a loud thunder. The ijeya ni were silent, as were Chishashi and Nihani; all of them watched the Leader drive her spear into the ground and stand back to her feet. The pressure of the forest changed. It became lighter than the air that circulated, and compelled J'Kana to look around until he saw a woman with white curly hair and deep green eyes wrapped in an ivory robe.

"Chilu baeri haranati e," she asked, and that was when J'Chera noticed her. His smile vanished, and tears welled up in his eyes as his hands waved before him. He ran for her, and she stood there in the clearing with her arms spread wide to accept him. He nearly knocked her over, but still she couldn't stop smiling at her precious ijeya. "There, there, child," she soothed in a motherly voice as J'Chera wept loudly. "Everything will be just fine."

***

*Kehemu Forest—Wasuchi Village*

Wasuchi Village was a winding labyrinth of huts elevated high off the ground, hidden in the thick canopies of the overgrown trees of the Kehemu Forest. They were just as round as what could be seen in Y'Rakili or Y'Baule, but made entirely of the soso wood for which the forest was famous. Each elevated structure was connected through wooden walkways handcrafted with the utmost care, adorned with polished stones and painted carvings that told of the legends of Kehemu. The most important buildings were marked by the triple alcoves carved around their entryways, each collection inscribed with Batabari markings that explained their purpose.

Countless Sasabosami walked high and low. Merchants of different wares and foods joyfully interacted with their customers. Educators and village leaders crossed paths as they entertained arguments for the direction of Wasuchi and the necessity of the preservation of culture. Children ran through the street and walkways as they played games and held races.

"Not what you thought a vampire village would look like, e?" Kanawe Y'Leisu's voice broke through J'Kana's tranquility and startled him back to the moment. He shook his head as they moved for a massive spiral staircase on the other side of the village. The Leader—whose name was Banzile—led them through Wasuchi with the kind of pride that befit a champion warrior. As they moved, J'Kana, J'Chera and Nihani noted the villagers' gazes of wonder and gasps of delight, but Chishashi noticed how quickly they turned to glares of disgust and outrage when he walked after them.

"I did have a certain picture in my mind," J'Kana finally responded, his mind cast to his past encounters with volatile Asanibo and the elokobi they controlled. Y'Leisu looked at him, a cold look on her face that washed away in the fresh sunlight.

"Regardless of that," J'Chera interrupted swiftly, "how are you here, Kanawe?" Y'Leisu laughed as she placed a gentle hand upon his shoulder.

"Who do you think it was that bested the challenge thirty years ago," she said with a wink. "I built up such a wonderful relationship with Banzile back then that the Sasabosami allowed me entry whenever I saw fit." The explanation only confused them more.

"But then why did you come here," J'Kana asked. "When the bakery was attacked in Folawu, it was hard enough for *us* to get out."

"You forget, young J'Kana," Y'Leisu smiled in the shadow of mischief, and he felt a chill wash over him that mingled with the warm rays of the sun that filtered through the branches. "There are many things about J'Karo that you have yet to learn. Most of the Kanawe have a delayed command placed within their robe. For mine, if ever my life is realistically threatened, I will be transported here." Her tone became somber now that she was forced to relive the horrors of that day. J'Kana and J'Chera instantly felt remorse for their questions. They watched, just as she did, as her fellow Teachers were cut down by the Asanibo on Mahute's order. Her eyes sharpened, and she turned to face J'Kana with the fullness of her attention as she said, "In any case, now that you are here, there is much that we need to discuss…"

***

*Kehemu Forest—Wasuchi Village*

"Breathe," Y'Leisu urged him in a soothing voice. J'Kana, who sat atop the roof of their provisional chohafi, did as instructed. He felt the warmth of the sunlight against his skin, heard the songs of the bright blue ifofo and calming yellow yiki birds as they fluttered and rested in the trees around them. He felt the stillness of the air and tasted the sweet aromas of the street below. His ike was overpowering now. "Good," she whispered to him as she paced the rooftop. "Let your ike swell within you. Contain it, don't let it leak out." J'Kana took another deep breath, his eyes closed tighter than they had been before, not out of force, but out of euphoria. He concentrated the golden waves within him until they doubled their force, then tripled it, each pulse limited in its flow to the outer edges of his frame. He had to wonder when it had become so strong, and now that he thought of it, giving commands in J'Karo came so much easier. He barely felt the sting of it anymore. "Now," the regal Kanawe continued, "focus on your destination. Fix it firmly in your mind, and when you are ready, open your eyes."

J'Kana took another breath. He was unsure what would happen when he heeded those instructions, but it was clear that Y'Leisu knew what she was doing. When she offered to help him access the maa bacha at will, he didn't believe her, and figured she thought there was something to be gained from a moment with Y'Sawe's apprentice, but now it was undeniable that she was the only one who could help him with this. Even more, it was abundantly clear that that was all she wanted. *It is said that Y'Kele grants His vision to those who are destined to share in it,* she had told him earlier, *and those who possess it are able to see more than just the future's many paths.* It made him wonder what else he would be able to see, and that wonder was what guided his attention now.

He opened his eyes, and instantly felt the disconnect between his mind and his body. He stood in a passage made up of golden light, his physical form on one side, and a familiar city on another. He looked back at himself, wrapped in his fledgling jilaba wu ajiwele, and then began to walk in the direction of the city. Step by step, he heard the clap of his leather sandals against the pathway, felt the warmth of Y'Kele's light wrap around him again, but as he pressed forward toward the city, he noticed a gravity that vehemently fought against the light.

J'Kana emerged on the other side, taken aback by the deep contrast between the pathway and the city. Buildings, formerly strong and round, fashioned from the ever endurant soso wood and reinforced with cement or steel or stone, now bore scorch marks over their ornate designs and ceremonial paintings. Skeletons of people and animals lay in the paths now overtaken by uncontrolled vegetation, and the stillness of the scene was tragically undercut by the sudden wails of the dead. Tears spilled from J'Kana's eyes as he recognized it as his home from long ago. This dark, twisted, empty wasteland of a city was once the Holy City of Shifi, and as the realization creeped into his mind, the cold finally began to set in.

It was with great care that he walked those once-hallowed streets and with great misery that he pushed back against the sudden flood of sights and sounds forever blackened by the fire and smoke. Every cobble of the road, every twisted metal frame, every broken merchant stand took him back to the night where he lost everything, the night where ultimately J'Foja was born and J'Kana disappeared into a kind of despair the likes of which he could barely articulate, and worse, it took him back to those times before the Asanibo came.

Mixed into the screams and cries of Shifi's citizens as they breathed their last were the sounds of their laughter, the comfort of their voices, their exclamations of surprise and wonder and excitement. Over and over again, he heard the voice of his Yababa, of his neighbors, of his Waleya, of his friends, all people that he knew to be dead, ghosts of the past determined to unravel his mind at its seams. Within seconds, they all converged on him, misery and joy, life and death, past and present, his father, his teacher, his mother, Y'Leisu, his neighbors, the people of Memifi, Nikeli, Nihani, his friends, J'Chera and J'Yobena, the Asanibo, Chishashi, all swirled around in his mind with such a force that he slammed his palms against his ears in search of some relief.

He ran along the winding road with no clear direction, but as his legs picked up the pace, his heart felt a prick of heat and power that threatened to burst through his entire body. He followed it, ran the paths of his old home until the heat burned bright within his chest, then his arms, then his legs until he came to the edge of Shifi by the Wehela Stone. The gold and silver rock glistened in the twilight sun, and as the voices finally died down in his mind, that was the moment where the vision faded from Shifi to Wasuchi Village. J'Kana breathed laboriously as sweat dripped from his brow. Y'Leisu sat directly in front of him, her eyes narrow and contemplative.

"We have to get to Shifi immediately," he told her, and with a wise smile behind her eyes, Kanawe Y'Leisu nodded.

***

Nihani slapped J'Kana on his arm and shot him a look that told him he should have been ashamed of himself.

"What was that for," he asked in a tone that took her back to the days of their first adventure together.

"Look at your son," she told him and crossed her arms disapprovingly, "and you tell me." J'Kana rolled his eyes and turned his head to see Kamari, eyes wide and jaw nearly on the floor. He was silent, but just when J'Kana thought to ask him what was wrong, he shouted an excited trill into the air of their chohafi as he pulled himself up onto the couch and started to jump. Nihani raised an eyebrow as a grumble escaped her throat, and the boy realized his mistake.

"Someone is excited," J'Kana said smugly with eyes cut in Nihani's direction. She rolled her own as she pushed against the side of his head.

"A little too excited," she warned without warning, though her husband could see that she was at least glad he wouldn't be too scared to sleep.

"I want to grow up to be strong like you, Yababa," he laughed. "I want to take the test like J'Chera did! Oh, and I want to see what kind of food they have in Wasuchi!"

"Perhaps, if you practice your J'Karo long enough, you would pass their test with flying colors. But for now, let's just focus on—"

"Also, how did J'Chera learn to move like a muka beast? He was so fast that Banzile never saw him coming!"

"He learned from watching them directly," J'Kana explained, "back when we camped out in the cave by the Shukeshu Tributaries." Kamari squealed with delight.

"That's so amazing! I want to try that!" J'Kana was overjoyed to see his lele ili so animated, and playfully pushed the boy to the side with just enough force to make his head fall to the cushion. He sprang back upright in the next second, overcome by a fit of laughter.

"You will get your chance soon enough, Kamari," J'Kana told him with a gracious smirk. "But for the time being, we need to focus on your lessons." Where the

Kanawe halfway expected his son to pout, Kamari did quite the opposite. He reached over his father's lap and pulled the leather book from the table by his side of the couch. He handed it to his Teacher, and held his head high with confidence and an eagerness to learn.

"I'm ready, Yababa," Kamari beamed, and J'Kana shook his head with amusement.

"Alright," he told him, "let's begin."

| | | |
|---|---|---|
|  | Kichiru | Spider |
| 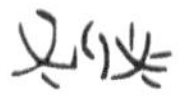 | Besubu | Beetle |
|  | Nibufi | Fly |
|  | Shalamani | Sunday |
|  | Tunumani | Monday |
|  | Wemani | Tuesday |
| 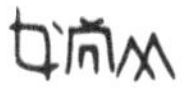 | Chomani | Wednesday |
|  | Karumani | Thursday |
|  | Lomani | Friday |
|  | Jamani | Saturday |
|  | Ilitunu | January |

| | |
|---|---|
| Natunu | February |
| Jotunu | March |
| Hetunu | April |
| Chutunu | May |
| Fatunu | June |
| Wayitunu | July |
| Kietunu | August |
| Nautunu | September |
| Setunu | October |
| Seilitunu | November |
| Senatunu | December |

# 15

# Shifi's Shadow

*South Behaji Road—Outer Grasslands*

J'Kana sat in silence. His eyes were closed, his skin touched by the chill of the morning air, and his ears graced by the symphony of life that played around them. The path out of the Kehemu Forest led to a bridge over the Joba River and onto the South Behaji Road, and while it would have taken another five days on foot to come to it, Kanawe Y'Leisu talked Banzile into parting with an abata-drawn fakiye. It had been two days, and as the cart pulled along the dirt roads, J'Kana listened to the calls of muka beasts turn into the scurry of tekuche rats through the hutije, felt the dense humidity of the forest lift like a curse into a gentle mist, and felt his hato with Y'Kele grow stronger still.

Even as the others slept, he focused his mind on the Wehela Stone in Shifi. There was a reason why his maa bacha was drawn to it, and he was determined to uncover it. He got better with every attempt, and moved from a wide focus on the city to the specific point of interest that glowed in the dismal plane. Every time, though, the screams grew too loud for him to ignore, the blending of his past and present and future confused his mind just before he could bring the secrets of the Stone into view, and when they reached their boiling point, he was thrust from the vision back to reality.

J'Kana sank against the side of the fakiye, threw his head back, and sighed as he let the cold air soothe the heat in his brow.

"You've been at that for a while," Nihani spoke, her wavy hair pulled into the closest thing to an abata tail that she could manage. He looked at her, her blue-ringed eyes like full moons in the dark of the fakiye's cabin. Just to gaze upon her brown sugar skin was enough to make him feel the full revival to his ike. Power surged within him, and it made him nervous.

"Well, you know what they say," he started with a playful smolder that was wholly unintentional. "'Practice makes perfect.'" He watched her eyebrow tick up towards the coils of hair that draped over her perfectly delicate face as she scooted closer to him.

"And what is it that you are practicing today," she wondered aloud, her voice a sultry melody that teased his every sense and faculty. She laid a hand on his forearm and massaged it soothingly. He could feel his worries slip away through the sight and sound and feeling of her. He smiled wider.

"Ah if only I could show you," he all but whispered as he allowed, for a moment, to be swept away into the flow of her charm.

"Then perhaps you could show me something else," she whispered back, the full moons of her eyes reduced to knowing half-moons under her implication. "After all this is over, you know?" Just like that, J'Kana's worries returned, but something about the way she spoke to him, the things she alluded to, her confidence for a peaceful future rife with the chance to explore each other's worlds, relegated his concerns to the back of his mind.

"Do we need to stop the fakiye," J'Chera groaned, half asleep and slightly irritated, "so the two of you can have some privacy? There are people trying to sleep here." Siema barked from the front of the cabin, and J'Kana sat up straight as his lips twisted anxiously. "And animals! For Y'Kele's sake, think of Siema!" He rolled over again, adjusted his jilaba wu ajiwele so that it covered the whole of his body, and tried to go back to sleep.

"I didn't think it was that bad," J'Kana finally said with a smile. Nihani smiled back at him, and watched him sigh with a new relief he'd not displayed since the day of his healing. Together they sat in silence now, and listened as the yiki birds began their morning songs. "There's something in Shifi for us," he finally told her, and hoped that J'Chera and Chishashi listened in as well. Nihani looked at him, a cautiously curious furrow in her brow.

"Good or bad," she asked, a sudden strength to her voice that replaced her prior gentleness. J'Kana shrugged.

"Before, Master Y'Leisu helped me to use my maa bacha at will." He caught her confusion before he continued with his explanation. "Sometimes I can see the future," he elaborated with a wave of his hand. "Before she taught me how to use it, it mostly just happened when I focused too much on a dire conversation. My ike would shift, and I would be plunged into some vision of the future unaware."

"And what have you been plunging into of late," Nihani asked, now that she understood. J'Kana took a deep breath, let it out, and took her hand in his with a kind of passive strength that alarmed her.

"Shifi," he said simply, a long extant torment behind his gaze. "I can see the city, both as it is now, and as it was. I can hear the people that used to live there, but I can also feel how they died and what they felt when they did." Chishashi sat up now, his yellow eyes attuned to the dark of the cart cabin and fixed firmly on J'Kana. The ijeya nodded to him in greeting, Chishashi nodded back, and the student continued as he squeezed Nihani's hand gently. "On the other side of it all, I can see the bright golden glow of the Wehela Stone on the edge of town. I believe that Kanawe Y'Sawe left us something there."

"That is assuming he's still alive," Chishashi finally said, rather unenthusiastic about the prospect of another of these magicians.

"He is," J'Kana told him with a certainty that quelled all further comment on the matter. "The question now is how to find him. It's just…"

"Like you said," Chishashi picked up when J'Kana trailed off, "there is something there. By what you described, it sounds like Hanika's work." The mention of the second Asanibo General under Mahute's command made the former guide tremble.

"Well, you seem happy to be heading that way," J'Kana joked, and Chishashi rolled his eyes. "I take it that she's a little worse than your brother was."

"You have no idea," Chishashi growled miserably. "Tikhal was an expert on Beast Manipulation, but Hanika excels at Blood Curses. She can feel the death in a place and conjure illusions and darkness from the blood spilled there."

"She sounds like she would be very fun at parties," J'Kana quipped, then folded his arms across his chest. "Do you think that's what I'm seeing through the maa bacha?" The vampire nodded.

"Hanika is the kind of Asanibo that confuses and stalks her prey. If what you said is true about the Wehela

Stone, then it only plays into her game," he elaborated. J'Chera groaned loudly over the conversation and sat up to finally join it.

"So, I guess I should just give up on getting my sleep, then," he complained. He looked dead at the Asanibo with his deep emerald eyes and pouted as he asked, "So what should we do when we get there?"

"Stick together for one thing. She prefers to pick off her enemies one by one, so if we stay together, we should be able to force her out into the open," Chishashi explained.

"Should we expect any elokobi," J'Kana inquired, a gravity to his voice that made Siema perk up and spit a few sparks. He shot her a look, and she flattened her ears as she looked away.

"No," answered the vampire. "She was never known to make any. Her delight comes from the thrill of the hunt and the kill that comes after. She would never want to risk a rebirth for her victims of any kind."

"Huh," J'Kana responded. "You would think it would make her easier to deal with. Nihani, would you be able to create a mist for us when we enter the city ruins?"

"Yes," she told him warily, "but why? If she's hunting us from the shadows, why give her more cover?" J'Kana chuckled as he clasped his hands together.

"You'll see when we get there," he said, and his confidence only confused his company more.

***

*Shifi Ruins*

J'Kana thought that it would be easier to brace himself since his maa bacha showed him what to expect, but now more than ever before in his life, he understood the difference between seeing something and experiencing it. His entire being felt cold, the stillness of the air as pungent as the odor of death that lingered here after all these years. It was silent, save for the sound of distant feet that slapped against the cobbled stones as they ran.

"Be on your guard," Chishashi told him. "She has already started the hunt." J'Kana nodded, then gave Nihani the signal to begin. The mermaid waved her arms as she silently chanted, and a thick mist fell over the whole of the ruins.

"Remember," J'Kana whispered, "we stay together." J'Chera snorted.

"As if you could get rid of me in *this* mess," he replied with a frantic tremor in his voice.

Together they moved in silence, Nihani and Chishashi at the center, J'Kana at the front, and J'Chera at the rear. The mist was cold, and the sounds that came from deep within it made each of them tense from the elevated suspense. A laugh at the rear and a shift in the vapor turned every head in the party, but there was nothing but the distorted outline of a woman's body as it twisted back into the cloud. They could hear nothing, smell nothing, sense nothing except what Hanika wanted them to, and all of them felt helpless because of it. *With Blood Curses,* Chishashi had told them, *the senses are distorted in much greater effect than with the Asanibo aura. I won't be able to guide you out of this.*

"Ti mala ra kurawenati," J'Chera and J'Kana spoke in unison. A spark hit them, something like a strike of lightning ran through their veins from the pit of their bellies. Siema barked as they fell to their knees.

"What happened," Nihani called out, the alarm in her voice strangely augmented by the silence. J'Kana and J'Chera still felt the bite from before, but powered back to their feet.

"It looks like we can't clear the Blood Curse so easily," J'Chera answered her, and another sinister laugh echoed through the cloud. All around them, the mist shifted in explosive bursts, and one by one, they felt the jagged talons of the enemy Asanibo run across their flesh. They looked around frantically, unable to guess where Hanika would appear next. Then came the whispers in the dark.

"This is bad," Chishashi told them. His yellow eyes went red, his pale face became pink, and wings sprung from his back. "N'kham a yifuyim." His Batabari was clear, an order to defend against whatever hidden horrors Hanika had in store for them.

*Fool!*

*You will die here!*

*Your blood shall be food for the plants!*

*I WILL GRIND YOUR BONES INTO DUST!* The voices were many, but all seethed with hatred and violence as they thundered through the streets of Shifi.

"Shut up!" J'Kana shouted it into the sky, a brilliant golden resonance in his eyes.

"We have to keep moving," Nihani spoke sweetly but firmly. J'Kana and Chishashi grunted their agreement, but even so, took a while to advance. J'Kana could feel his control slip with every beat of his heart and throb of his skull. "Breathe," she told him, concern etched into every corner of her voice. His palm slammed into his temple as he shook his mind loose of the rage that gripped it, even as the ground beneath him seemed to rumble like the heavens in tempest. He looked at her, at Nihani, and felt the way his ike swelled from deep within. She was no mere woman, no meager travel companion, but something more. Something about her seemed to resonate with him as if she were life itself, wrapped into a corporeal body waiting to unleash all of her potential.

He did as she said, and let the power of his ike wrap around him like water does a stone.

"Ti Hafu wu muata ra moheranawe kelena, koshi bushake wu teuki shu ichenati o," J'Kana commanded as the mist continued to wave and distort all around them. His body surged with another jolt of pain as the J'Karo flowed from his lips, but it only lasted for a moment. His vision blurred, but when his eyes were stable again, they picked up the shadow of a slender, taloned monster beyond an earthen wall before she receded again.

"Where did she go," J'Chera asked as he finally regained his composure. Nihani looked up to the rooftops and caught a glimpse of their attacker, only for the vicious one to vanish from sight again. Nihani gasped as realization set in. She pushed the fog thicker, deeper into the streets of the long-abandoned city.

"She stalks from the darkness," the mermaid cautioned. "You slowing her down only seems to have made it more of a game to her."

"Fekhayim," burst the Asanibo's voice from somewhere in the cloud.

"Blast," Chishashi translated, and watched as dark red orbs bubbled up through the cracks in the street. They sizzled, then one by one they began to explode. The wall crumbled to dust, and the blood that dripped from the ijeya ni and Jeniju warped together into a shield around their party as they sprinted through the broken buildings with J'Kana in the lead. Buildings collapsed and closed off their paths. The howls of the dead continued to berate them. Hanika continued to laugh.

"The students run in search of their lost Master," she purred from her place in the darkness. "And for what? Some feeble delusion about obstructing the Dagger's vision for equality?"

"He is crazy," J'Kana blurted out with enough incredulity to make it almost comical. Hanika laughed, but then they all felt her change positions again.

"You think him crazy for returning culture to all of Y'Neshu's people?" Her voice came from right behind him, and it was almost as though J'Kana could feel her bloodied talons creep along his neck. He sidestepped, then rolled along the ground a bit further down the path. He stared back at where he had been, only to see his companions.

"No," he replied. "I think he's crazy for trying to kill the people he says he wants to liberate."

"The only thing oppressors can be liberated from is the labor of breathing," Hanika spat, and more bombs exploded from inside a broken home. The wood of the hut's walls splintered and burst into Chishashi's arms, and he fell to the ground from the force. "Those who never work to change the system are just as guilty as those who profit from it."

"Says a bloodthirsty member of the Batabari Clan," J'Kana snapped back. "You speak of oppressors as though it wasn't your own family that sought to enslave all of Y'Neshu—" She appeared from the dark, the pointed ends of her talons angled upward into J'Kana's throat. He saw her plainly now, the waviness of her jet-black hair, the ominous crimson of her lips, the coldness of her scarlet eyes. It was more than indifference. It was agony.

"And we pay for it daily," she uttered with a tremble. "Do not speak as if you know."

"Ti fajari wu koko shu chiweyubasa o!" A trio of fireballs exploded in sequence around Hanika at J'Chera's command. She stumbled back, then vanished into the shadows again with a spiteful screech.

"Y'Go bi sekhel mtanu basiyil," Nihani chanted, her arms spread wide as she gathered a new mist to her. "Y'Go, khemi go mamuke uhujina N'Shifi!" Clouds of vapor melded together into lashing chains of divine water. "Kasanu," she hummed as she felt the shift of their enemy through the fog. A loud crash filled their ears as the liquid whips thrashed about the Blood Curse.

"I know enough," J'Kana continued, anger in his voice now. "What culture do you have besides killing or raping whatever you touch, na? Y'Kawebo to the east? The Kehemu Forest? Folawu? Shifi? How many people have died because of your people's disregard for life? How many were forced to suffer as your slaves and sacrifices before you paid the price for your crimes? And still, you see your conquest as 'equality!'" Hanika burst from the shadows, a burn mark on the side of her face and a lash across her now bare abdomen.

"Bobo ja basi we lekhan a totuyim," Chishashi commanded, and the blood spattered along the cobbles formed a whip that pulled Hanika to the ground in an unceremonious crash.

"All of this," the vampiress snarled as she pushed herself back to her feet, "all of this is for the people of Y'Neshu to be able to choose their own future! Only we can be trusted to give back what was taken, from the Four Empires and Batabari alike!" She slashed her jagged claws at J'Kana's head, but was evaded and kicked in the sternum for her efforts. She spun around from it, hopeful that her next strike would rip his heart straight from his chest, but he rolled beneath it and pulled her leg as he went. Her head slammed against the stone road, and in another moment she vanished again.

"How can you offer the people a choice when you refuse to gift them a seat at the table? You say your master is the only one who can be trusted to give the people their freedom but you're too blind to see that this only exchanges one kind of oppression for another! Freedom can never be won this way because the oppressor will never give it. Our freedom, the restoration of our culture, must be taken from those who would use it against us," J'Kana roared it out as all the violence and isolation from his time on the Memifian streets filtered into his mind. He was poor, hungry, and alone. The people should have comforted him. Someone should have taken him in. But they gave him barely enough food to survive and made fun of him as the "Great Peasant." Hanika spat, and the sound of it echoed throughout her Curse World.

"And how can *you* do better when all you've ever known is the life of one oppressed," she shouted back, and J'Kana felt the full sting of her words. "You run the risk of acting on the same violence as the people who lashed out against you! You threaten all because of ignorance that has been forced upon you!" She didn't even know how right she was, how the leaders of Memifi, the yifusi, and even companions like J'Yobena saw him as little more than a problematic street rat with no place in their vision of the world. The time where he listened to those voices, however, was gone and had no chance for a return.

"Then I will continue to learn," he said with confident resolve. "I will continue to learn all that life and my Kanawe have to teach me. I will keep close to those who know me best so that I can be held accountable for my actions, and I will put aside any voice like yours that would ever make me doubt that I could."

"Enough," Hanika howled like the wind on a stormy night. The aged blood scattered about the city returned to a fresher state as it bubbled and swirled. "Foolish child," she snarled, and the baths of blood shot into the air like fireworks, only to congeal into a massive and ominous orb. "How can your friends and teachers hold you to anything when death follows you wherever you go?" Shattered glass drenched in the blood of the fallen elevated like a snowfall in reverse and merged with the skyborne orb.

"We need to move," Chishashi called nervously to the others, then froze as the voices started to seep into his mind as well.

*And where would you go, Khimbenzi,* Tikhal whispered from beyond the grave. The sound of him was enough to rattle Chishashi to his core. *Have you not already shown how little you think of your family?*

"I *love* my family," Chishashi whimpered, a sound softer than the others even believed he could make. "What I despise are our practices! For centuries we have murdered, plundered, oppressed those we deemed inferior, all because of our insatiable greed. I will run as far away as I can until I can no longer smell the stench of the Batabari."

"Then die along with your friends," Hanika ordered coldly. The orb of blood and glass mixed together and ignited with all the glory of a crimson sun, only to begin a cruel descent upon the ijeya and their party. Nihani and J'Chera stood in awe as it slowly fell from above, but Chishashi ran to grab Nihani while J'Kana handled J'Chera. They knocked into their respective targets and rolled along divergent paths as the Batabari Bomb collided with the terrain. The sound it yielded echoed with all the groans of the dead and the collapse of their once proud homes. The mist was gone, and the vampiress laughed as she slipped into the dark once again.

J'Chera groaned. "Is everyone alright," he asked groggily. He moved to stand up, but winced from a sharp pain in his leg. A giant shard of broken glass protruded from his calf and pinned a piece of his jilaba wu ajiwele to his bloody limb.

"It seems you need to focus on yourself for now," J'Kana answered, and moved to help him up. J'Chera groaned again, then chuckled softly as his friend pulled his arm around his neck.

"How many times can a man be stabbed on a single trip," he joked, and J'Kana shot him a look.

"I don't think that now is the time for those kinds of jokes," he admonished. The Shifi native scanned their surroundings. "We need to get you somewhere safe until Nihani can have a look at you."

"What about over there," J'Chera suggested as he pointed toward a chohafi with a somewhat collapsed roof, but stable walls and a closable door.

"That seems to be good enough," J'Kana confirmed. He took as much time as he could, but still rushed to bring J'Chera to the hut. He pushed the door open, found an old chair that seemed to be in better condition than the rest of the place, and gingerly set his companion down into it. "Stay here, and whatever you do, don't touch the glass."

"You know that only makes me want to touch it more, don't you," J'Chera answered with a straight face. J'Kana shook his head.

"Does it really seem like the time for your jokes right now?" His hushed tone was pressed with irritation, which only brought a smile to J'Chera's lips. "I'll be back once I win." J'Chera raised an eyebrow as the smile faded.

"How can you be so certain you will," he asked, and J'Kana flashed him a confident grin. He shrugged as he opened the door.

"It seems as though I'm the one she wants to kill the most."

***

Even without the mist, J'Kana could feel her presence in the dark. He heard her in the whispers of Shifi's lost souls, smelled her in the blood-poisoned air. She stalked him. Carefully. Relentlessly. The ijeya followed the spiraled path toward the edge of the broken city, careful to resist the pull of his mother's whispers as he went.

"Look at you," she called through the Curse. "Isolated. Powerless. Afraid that you will fail in your mission to save your Kanawe." J'Kana laughed.

"I was alone for ten years before Y'Sawe found me," he retorted with boldness. She appeared from the corner of his eye and ran her bladed fingers along his cheek as he narrowly dodged. She was gone. "As for powerless," he started up again as he listened for her position. It was much harder now that he couldn't track the pulses in the mist, but not impossible. He remembered the day his Master took him to Mount Y'Bayeka. He remembered the feeling of the heat of sun and volcano on his skin, the strange sulfuric scent that mingled with the earth beneath him, the way the winds danced around him and through the hutije grass far below. It was almost as though he were there now, and that proved more than enough to reignite the power of his ike. The memory spilled over into the visions from the Samanu Usele, the way the warmth of Y'Kele's light wrapped around him and flowed through him, the surge of his ike from the time they walked the edge of the Kehemu Forest until the moment they crossed into Y'Rakili's territory. It was so easy for him to get lost in the hato now, to flow through the connection between all things, and so he did.

Hanika emerged from above now, and descended upon her prey with arms spread wide and her talons poised to rend his flesh from the bone. J'Kana rolled out of the way, his eyes glazed over with gold as his ike spilled over into the air. Hanika's clawed hand broke the cobblestones. She opened her mouth to speak another Blood Curse, but the sudden appearance from J'Kana made her gasp.

"," he spoke to her, his voice distorted by the sheer gravity of his ike as he mocked her for being so loud. " ." Hanika's mouth folded into her face, sealed with a flap of skin that manifested from nothing. She ripped at it, slashed through it, pierced it repeatedly, all with the futile hope that her voice would be heard once again. Her eyes shimmered with tears, and then in a fit of rage she lunged for him. She slashed like a wild beast at his abdomen, his face, clawed at his arms and legs in a wild flurry that was evaded with the least amount of effort. She was furious. Every foe that crossed her path died within minutes, but he was not only able to survive, it was as though the Blood Curse had no effect on him whatsoever. "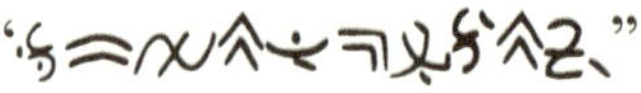," he ordered, and she stood perfectly still. The horror on her face told him that she struggled to reconcile the orders of her mind to the rest of her body, but no amount of her willpower would help her without her Batabari tongue. He looked to the sky, and

hoped within himself that Chishashi had found somewhere to hide before he spoke his next command. "
"

The blackness of the sky began to swirl like the eye of a hurricane before the golden rays of the sun pierced the distortion. Soon the gilded orb broke free of the Curse, and shattered the world of Hanika's making as its gaze fell upon her in judgment. She shrieked behind the space that once held her mouth as the heat of the brilliant star shot through her like arrows. Her blood turned black from the heat, her limbs caught fire, and as she struggled to move from the spot in which she was frozen, J'Kana approached her with the same sunlit eyes as before.

"All the fear of failure I had will die here with your curses," he whispered, and then in a thunderous voice he commanded in J'Karo, "!" The vision lifted, the sun shone in full force, and the huntress crumbled into dust, swept away by a passing wind. J'Kana laughed, completely blown away at the fact that he handled a General all by himself, then collapsed from a sudden exhaustion that hit him like a club to the head.

***

"I have the strongest Yababa in the world," Kamari gasped as his eyes went as wide as the Amuneti Ocean. J'Kana chuckled as he pat the boy on the back.

"Whatever it is you want, you can't have it," he told him. Kamari was about to protest when they heard a knock on the door. The father and son looked at each other in confusion. The sun had only just emerged from its place in the clouds when J'Kana started the story, and even an hour later, there were very few in Kilana who would want to leave their chohafi this early. Another knock. "Just a second," J'Kana called as he rose from his seat on the couch and crossed the floor to the window. The Kanawe's eyes went wide with a childlike joy that Kamari could barely recognize as his father's. The Sage swiftly unlocked the door and opened it as he exclaimed, "By Y'Kele's light and glory! What brings you to Kilana of all places?"

"Can't a man pay a visit to an old friend," came a strong, intimidating voice. Kamari almost buckled at the sound. He watched his father usher in a tall man with white skin and long brown hair. His yellow eyes flickered to Kamari's position, and immediately the five-year-old tensed under the man's gaze. *An Asanibo,* he questioned, *in daylight?* "And who is this?" The voice was almost affectionate, as if the Asanibo knew who he was already and only wanted the pleasure of a second introduction.

"Kamari," J'Kana urged with all the excitement in the world, "it's alright. Introduce yourself!" Kamari hopped off the couch and walked up to the Asanibo. He turned the man over with his eyes, watched him smile, then smiled back as he realized who this must be.

"Hi," he greeted cheerfully. "My name is Kamari, the son of Kanawe J'Kana. I'm his ijeya, too! Are you Chishashi?" The Asanibo stooped down and looked the little one in the eyes.

"I am," he answered, "and I haven't seen you since the day you were born. It's good to meet you all over again, Kamari."

"We were just about to get started with his J'Karo lesson for today, soa jewo," J'Kana explained, and Chishashi stared at him incredulously.

"Wait," he begged, "you mean to tell me that you're actually training the boy?" Kamari flexed his little arms before J'Kana could explain.

"That's not all," Kamari boasted, a look of his father's confidence pressed to his face. "I'm pretty good at it, too. Do you want to see?" Chishashi shot J'Kana a grave look before he turned to face the child with the warmth of a thousand suns.

"Only if you would like to show me something," Chishashi answered. Kamari ran to the door, and when their vampiric visitor didn't follow, he waved Chishashi over. The Sage and the Asanibo followed him outside, both with a cautious curiosity.

"Watch and learn," the little one said, then with the calm of someone twice his age, his eyes lit turquoise. "Yo bushake shu tuketuna me N'Hafu shu jiunati o." The ground beneath him rumbled with fury as his face came alive with delight, then pushed him into the air on a rugged platform of his own design. He was only about six feet from the ground, but to him it may as well have been the summit of Mount Y'Bayeka. Chishashi whistled, impressed with the display of power from one so young.

"Look at you," he pretended to call to the child. "But how do you intend to get down from there?" Kamari sat on the edge of the pillar as he panted from the exhaustion.

"I'll put it back," he yelled back, then took a moment to gather his breath, "right after I rest a little!

Whoa!" The ground beneath him began to return to its original place, and when the boy was back on a level plane, J'Kana gave him the book, open to the next focus of his study.

"You weren't bad, but perhaps you should focus on building your vocabulary, Kamari. It's safer," J'Kana reasoned, but the little boy groaned.

"He's right, you know," Chishashi helped. "What will you do if monsters attack and you stumble trying to find the right words to say?" The mention of monsters was enough to make Kamari stick out his chest and pull the book away from his father.

"I will learn all the words and practice them so much they won't stand a chance," he shouted with determination. It brought a smile to the Asanibo and to the magician beside him. "So, I guess I should start here…"

| | | |
|---|---|---|
|  | Kofaja | Burn |
|  | Chiweyu | Erupt/Explode |
|  | Atare | Extreme |
|  | Sifafu | Simplicity/Ease |
|  | Koloti | Consequence |

| | | |
|---|---|---|
|  | Ehera | Complexity |
|  | Kitali | Defeat |
|  | Nihani | Victory |
|  | Sojaki | Dream |
|  | Hama | Detail |
|  | Nunu | Ice |
|  | Fubese | Sharp/Edge/Advantage |
|  | Kufubese | Dull/Disadvantage/Blunt |
|  | Umasi | Grow |
|  | Kacha | Grind |
|  | Siwi | Mix |
|  | Bafa | Taste |
|  | Ololo | Smell |
|  | Tekufo | Touch |

# 16

# Lessons in Light

*Shifi Ruins*

When he awoke, J'Kana bolted straight up and winced when the pain in his head reminded him not to move too fast. He groaned as he slid his hand down the side of his face and delicately lifted himself with the help of a nearby wall. The more he tried to remember what happened, the harder his head throbbed. He looked around, saw that he was in Shifi, and then cried out in pain as the battle with Hanika rushed back to the front of his mind. The sun shone brightly overhead, and a scream ripped through the air like the blast of a cannon.

"J'Kana," came Nihani's voice. The apprentice could hear her rapid footsteps from around the corner, and felt the horror in her gaze when she finally appeared. "By Y'Khali, what happened to you?" His knees threatened to buckle, and the mermaid sprinted to help support him.

"We have to go back for J'Chera," the victorious ijeya spoke through gritted teeth. He pressed through the pain to turn them around and gingerly lead Nihani through the ruins. They were almost at the shattered hut when J'Kana noticed that she was alone. "Where—" the pain sharpened when he opened his mouth, but he pushed through. "Where is Chishashi?"

"When the sun broke through," Nihani started, and caught herself before J'Kana's weight on her shoulders could get to her, "he ran into a hut to keep himself safe." J'Kana's eyes narrowed with a tinge of remorse.

"I see…Here," he told her, and together they entered the chohafi. J'Chera was still on the chair, the glass fragment still firmly in his leg when they found him, and Nihani's face drained of color at the sight.

"It's about time somebody came back for me," J'Chera said with a chuckle. Nihani set J'Kana against the wall and helped him to the floor, then immediately crossed the room to inspect the damage done. J'Chera's eyes were closed, and his mouth dry, but the full color of his skin told her that he hadn't suffered too much in the way of blood loss. The size of the glass, on the other hand, told her that he would if they tried to take it out. He opened one eye, saw that it was Nihani who looked him over, and then reclined his head to stare blankly at the ceiling. "So, what's your plan, O Great Healer?"

"I don't have the supplies I need to clot your blood," she started, her focus affixed to the gash in his leg, "and like I said, I can't heal you. My maju takhani hasn't come in yet. If we were to move the glass—"

"Won't I get infected if we don't?" J'Chera's calm question cut through her anxiety like a kofesha on the battlefield. Nihani sat there in silence with tears of frustration in her eyes. "Then we agree. Something must be done now if I am to survive." J'Kana tried to move himself but the pain that shot through his body told him that he should reassess that plan. He groaned, which proved to be enough to get Nihani to turn her head, and that was when he saw the minty glow.

"How do these maju takhani manifest," J'Kana asked from across the room, his eyes now completely trained on hers. Nihani blinked the tears away and frantically looked around at the tattered furniture, cobwebs, and semi-collapsed roof of the chohafi.

"I need a pot," she deflected, and another mint green light flashed behind her eyes. She stood to her feet and looked at the different pathways in the hut. "Where would the kitchen be?"

"Toward the back," J'Kana told her, and pointed behind the part of the roof that had collapsed ages ago. Without another word, the Jeniju pressed through the shattered plaster and scattered bristles of the old roof in search of the tool. J'Kana and J'Chera listened to the sounds of clanging metal and shifting porcelain. A glass fell to the ground and shattered, but soon thereafter, Nihani returned to the batalu with a bronze pot in her hands. She set it down on the dusty carpet only a few feet from J'Chera, a nervous look about her as she knelt beside it.

"So, how is this going to work if you don't have your Jeniju healing," J'Chera asked, his eyes now on the mermaid apprentice with a wily curiosity. Nihani trembled under the sound of the question.

"I don't know," she answered truthfully. "Jeniju represent the preservation of life, and all of us are supposed to have a natural understanding of the healing arts, but whenever I come to a moment where my skills are needed, I am only ever reminded of how Y'Khali's favor does not rest on me—"

"Nihani," J'Kana called to her, and forced himself across the floor despite the ripples of pain that expanded through him. "Why do you continue to doubt yourself after all this?" She whipped her head to face him, the tracks of fallen tears alight along her cheeks. "You have healed a poisoned man, sealed a stab wound, overseen the conditions of us both. You were the one who pushed a boat full of people to the Temetu, and only a little while ago you did battle with an Asanibo determined to rip you to shreds. You watched a friend get hurt, saw one die in front of your face, and yet you still press on—"

"You don't know what you're talking about," she interrupted, exasperated. "I only helped along the way, I didn't do anything of value at all!"

"But isn't it the nature of healing to want to help," J'Kana challenged, and Nihani was stunned to silence again. "Is that not the value of it? You underestimate your abilities, even as you use them to save our lives over and over."

"I know what you're trying to do—" she started, and J'Kana poked her in the forehead to interrupt her thought.

"Then let me do it," he said with a chuckle. "If you hadn't been there to help us, I would have been dead. We never would've made it past Ekutali Village. Hanika would have destroyed us as fast as the light of the sun can touch the earth. You have done more to preserve the lives around you than you give yourself credit for. Stop running away from yourself and do what you already know to do." She stared at him as her lip quivered with the misting of her eyes, and after a moment, she gave him a reluctant nod. She closed her eyes and gathered herself before they reopened, and the force within her erupted like ancient Y'Bayeka. "N'otaba shu M'sahofa ra maunati o," he whispered into her ear, and watched as the power of life exploded out of her as she began to wave her arms through the air with grace unparalleled.

"Y'Go bi sekhel mtanu basiyil," she began, and the pot swirled to life with divine waters freshly manifested...

***

The door to the chohafi opened to the full light of the sun. Shifi was silent, but no longer in the same way as

Hanika's Blood Curse. Overhead, the birds passed by, delighted to greet the fallen city with song once again, and in the distance, J'Kana could hear the bark of an excited Siema. He looked to Nihani and J'Chera, a smile on his face bigger than the hole in the wall in front of them and stretched his newly healed body, but then a moment of realization hit that robbed him of his joy.

"How did she get into the city," he wondered aloud. Before the others could offer a response, he darted along the cobbled paths in search of the ara cub's bark. The others followed after him, each with their guard up, each one poised to speak a command or summon the waters to meet whatever enemy tampered with their vehicle. Another bark emanated from the east, towards the old Seller's Road in the market district. J'Kana led the charge, very much taunted by the ghosts of Shifi's past, by the sights and sounds of that night from ten years ago, but his focus was on Siema. Once she was secure, they would go back and find Chishashi, then make their way out of this place.

They came to the ceremonial square, once alive with noise and celebration, now a heap of rubble emblazoned with a trauma none dared to speak of. The three of them paused, careful to scan their environment for whatever threat still lurked in the darkest corner of the ruins. Nothing, save for three more barks from Siema's tiny throat. J'Kana started to run again, this time towards the edge of town, towards the hutije in the Outer Grasslands that had at one point been just as much his home as the chohafi he dared not seek out. He rounded a corner, Nihani and J'Chera in tow, and what they saw there, staring at the Wehela Stone, none of them could believe.

"I was wondering how long you would have me wait," Chishashi mused, a smile on his face as he stared into the gold and silver paint of the Stone. Siema bounced around him, her mouth wide and tongue out as saliva dripped down her chin. Her forelegs almost lay flat against the ground to sink the front of her body. She wanted to play. She was happy. They all looked at the Asanibo, and it took a moment for them to register the fact that he stood by the fakiye, before a Wehela Stone, in broad daylight.

"What is going on," Nihani asked incredulously. Chishashi looked at his friends, joy deeply rooted behind his eyes as he fought back the urge to cry.

"I don't know," he told them. "Asanibo are supposed to die in the daylight, yet here I am." He chuckled as he ran his hands over his arms and chest as if to prove something to himself. "It doesn't even hurt!" A look of supposition hit him, and his eyes searched between J'Kana, J'Chera, and Nihani. He folded his arms, cupped his chin in a single hand, and asked, "Did one of you have something to do with this?" All three shook their heads.

"We were a little preoccupied trying not to die," J'Chera joked. "Believe it or not, it takes much more focus than the adventurers of any guild would tell you."

"I've never even heard of this," Nihani offered, then adopted a suspicious look of her own. "Are you sure that you're Asanibo? I mean, the Sasabosami can survive the sun—" The shake of Chishashi's head cut her off.

"I am no Sasabosami," he started, the smile still plastered to his face. "It's hard to explain, but when a Sasabosami and Asanibo share a space, we can tell ourselves apart from each other despite the similarities in our appearance. But then…it's more than that. It's almost as if something in our souls is fundamentally different."

"Then this must be some kind of act of Y'Kele," J'Kana supposed. "Either that, or you've somehow managed to break the curse that affects you." Chishashi laughed, which only spurred Siema to greater excitement.

"Considering the fact that nothing else about me has changed, it's very doubtful that I had anything to do with this," Chishashi retorted. He bent down to scoop Siema up and place her back into the fakiye. "In any case, we can explore what's happened more once we find what we're looking for. J'Kana, would you mind telling us what that would be?"

J'Kana stepped forward to survey the Stone, and felt a heat radiate from its top that caused a surge in his ike. It felt familiar, and by itself nearly made him feel like the little kid he had been the last time he walked Shifi's streets. A strange pang hit his heart, but he shook it off as he searched for a way to scan the top of the boulder.

"Yo bushake shu tuketunati," he whispered tenderly, and slowly a platform of earth lifted from its place. In only a moment, J'Kana's eyes met the envelope hidden above their heads, and retrieved it. J'Chera ordered the ground to return to level while J'Kana opened it to read its contents.

"So, what is it," the senior Ijeya inquired. J'Kana looked up briefly and then returned his gaze to the notes written exclusively in J'Karo.

"A list of vocabulary terms and phrase combinations," the Shifi native answered. "There are instructions to train our ike and focus, as well as a method of portal generation, or something like that."

"Let me see that," J'Chera said, and snatched the papers from his friend's hands. He skimmed them for a moment before his eyes went wide. "Well would you look at that…I think your Kanawe might overestimate our abilities just a bit."

"Or he believes we need to be prepared for whatever comes next," J'Kana replied, and felt a shiver fall down his spine. "If he left us a note and isn't here, that tells us that something has happened that he didn't expect. If we are going to find him and survive when we do, then we need to follow his instructions." He began to pace the ground and search for a path forward. They didn't know where Y'Sawe was, nor did they know how to get to him, but those were concerns to be addressed at a later time. For now, they needed to find somewhere safe to refresh themselves, resupply, and train as the Kanawe said.

"So where do we go from here," Chishashi asked, his voice every bit as forceful as it had been in the past. J'Kana brightened with ironic humor as an idea passed his way. He clapped the vampire on the shoulder as his laugh escaped him.

"I know just the place."

***

*Memifi*

Nikeli stood immovable with one foot firmly in a young thief's chest. He squirmed, but he dared not strike at her for fear that the Ayena of Memifi would turn her wrath on him. It was bad enough that he'd been caught. If he showed hostility toward a yifusi, he would be dealt with only in the harshest of ways. What he didn't expect, however, was the sudden warmth behind her eyes.

"Get up," she ordered as she removed her foot and helped him. She motioned for two of her subordinates to come and take the man by the arms. Suspended there, he looked at her with a deep remorse that for some reason tugged at her heart. She groaned loudly, then got in his face. "Go," she ordered. The man looked at her with surprise, then suspicion. "Did I stutter? I said get out of here. And I better not catch you stealing jewels from this stall again!" He ran off without so much as a thank you, which only frustrated Nikeli even more. J'Foja would've at least had the courtesy to crack a joke or flirt or something.

"You look a little out of sorts, Nikeli," came a familiar voice from behind her. She paused to look at one of her soldiers, both of them with the height of incredulity in their eyes, before she turned around and saw him there, dressed in a purple shiki with dark jifona, wrapped in a violet cloak with a blue and white hooded mantle.

"J'Foja," she almost squealed, then remembered that she was on duty and worse, he was once a criminal. He smiled shyly with the mention of that old name, and approached her smoothly while Nihani, Chishashi and J'Chera watched with a mix of emotions. "What brings you back to Memifi? You haven't come back to stir up trouble, na?" J'Kana audibly laughed.

"I'm not the person I was when I left, Nikeli," he told her, his voice only loud enough for the two of them to hear, his eyes full of a kind of mystery that threatened to pull her into stories much deeper than she could fathom.

"So," she said as she cleared her throat, "what *is* your business in Memifi then?" She watched his face darken, heard the change in his breathing.

"Nikeli," he whispered, "we need your help."

***

It took hours to catch her up, though J'Kana figured it would've taken much less time if she didn't stop them to ask questions at every turn. Together they sat in the Hidden Beast at a back table where they would be overlooked. Nikeli's men stood guard outside with Siema, while J'Chera, Nihani and Chishashi joined them at the table.

"So, you're actually an Asanibo," Nikeli started with a degree of pleasure in her voice that J'Kana had never heard before. "I always wondered what would happen if I got to fight one." Chishashi smiled politely as he waved the sentiment away.

"We don't have time for that," he told her bluntly. "Apologies." She huffed in understanding disappointment as she sank back into her well-cushioned seat and took a sip of the sobachi juice she'd ordered with her food.

"Oh well," she shrugged, then turned her focus to Nihani, who was much less taken with Nikeli's person than the boys were. The feeling was apparently mutual. "And what about you? J'Fo—" she caught herself before she could fully default to J'Kana's old moniker. "J'Kana says that you are some kind of…fish woman?"

"I am Jeniju," Nihani almost spat, appalled that Nikeli would even think to speak such a profanity to a mermaid. "We are the healers that bridge the gap between nature and spirit."

"Is that so," Nikeli asked with artificial wonder. Nihani cocked her head to the side in a gesture of aggression that truly had J'Kana worried.

"Both of you cut it out," he fussed. He folded his arms across his chest as he stared down the whole table. "Nikeli, we've told you what's happening in Y'Neshu, so are you going to help us or not?" She rubbed the side of her head as she let loose a deep sigh.

"The best I can tell you is that I will do what I can," she replied. Nihani rolled her eyes. "Y'Rakili as a whole has fallen on hard times since the attack in Y'Baule. Folawan officials tout the story that international terrorists are responsible, and so the trade routes through Y'Baule to the rest of Y'Neshu have all but shut down. Everywhere, food has gotten scarce, profits are down for nearly every business here in the country, and everyday citizens find themselves more desperate than the day before." She turned her focus back to Nihani, and narrowed her eyes in condescension. "You'll forgive me if we have better things to do than procure for you some training ground and act as your personal bodyguards."

J'Chera scratched his chin, then cleared his throat loud enough to get everyone's attention. "What if we helped ease Memifi's pain, then?" Nikeli raised a skeptical eyebrow, but nevertheless leaned forward with her elbows on the table.

"What do you have in mind?" Her tone was as sultry as the dimly lit restaurant, and J'Chera shivered with excitement as he rose from the table.

"Follow me, sweet Nikeli," he told her as he offered his hand. She took it, and Nihani rolled her eyes. "Everyone! Let's take a journey into the Outer Grasslands!"

***

*Loutu Usele*

Footsteps tread the path of darkness once again, and just as before, the flames lit the room. Y'Chifo had become a stiff madness in the time since Y'Sawe first awoke, and between the conditions of their cages and Y'Chifo's screams, it took every ounce of willpower the Ile Kanawe had to retain a grip on his own sanity. He looked out into the immense blackness to find his brother there, a flustered look upon his face that made Y'Sawe's heart soar and ache at the same time.

"What's the matter, ila esho," the Grand Master taunted as he approached the edge of his cage. "You look upset. Did something happen?" Mahute spat out an inhuman roar that roused the other Kanawe from their stupor. Y'Chifo and Y'Jaka cowered against the bars of their cages, and Y'Sawe took pity on them.

"The last thing I need is commentary from you," the Dagger growled. He sliced his palm with a talon that manifested on his hand and chanted, "N'kha we Khafenu a chesiyim o." The darkness behind him began to swirl while Y'Sawe alone watched her appear.

"I live to serve you, my master," Khafenu hissed on bended knee as she pressed her fist into her chest. Without warning, he drove his foot into her face.

"And yet you consistently fail to bring those children to me," Mahute barked, his eyes as merciless as the monster he slowly became. Y'Sawe didn't even recognize him now, couldn't make peace with the idea that this man had ever shared blood with him.

"We are doing the best we can!" The Asanibo cried out in fear, and a pang of sympathy struck Y'Sawe like he never expected. Again Mahute struck her.

"You dare talk back to me?" His voice was even now, filled to the brim with the shade of superiority as he stared down his nose at her. He began to pace, and wiped his hand on his cloak as if to cleanse it of her touch. "Tikhal is dead. Hanika is dead, and now their path has been obscured. So, tell me, Khafenu. What part of this is your best?" He waited for her to respond, but she did no such thing. Y'Sawe breathed a sigh of relief when she didn't, then felt his body tense when Mahute looked dead into his eyes. "Make yourself useful and bring me the shrieker."

"Right away, Master," Khafenu obliged. She bowed her head quickly, and with Mahute's eye still firmly affixed to her, she leaped to Y'Chifo's cage and opened the door.

"No, no, no," he begged. "Please! I will do anything you wish, just let me live!" Y'Sawe looked away when Khafenu slashed her claws over his mouth for the second time, and he heard his rival go limp. She ripped him out of the elevated cell with one arm, and dragged the Kanawe to the center of the large circular platform below. He came alive again, panicked, just as before, but when he tried to get away, Mahute signaled for his servant to pierce their captive's flesh. His screams became louder, more frantic, and suddenly monstrous. Y'Sawe had to look now, had to know what his brother had done this time, but when he peered through the bars at the tablet below, it wasn't Y'Chifo he saw. The monster was massive in form, its eyes as red as blood and its body covered in thick, impenetrable scales that ran from jagged maw to tail. Its arms were thick and long, its legs the same, all four with claws big enough to pierce the metal walls of a Memifian ichera (building). Four dorsal scales crafted like three-pronged forks adorned its back, and in its forehead, nestled between its massive eyes and surrounded by its black scales, was a red jewel that glimmered in the dim light of the Loutu Usele.

"Taba ja khunamo we Ninikinana halayim," Mahute spoke with a twisted euphoria. The Ninikinana, at the mention of its name, roared with a power that shook the foundations of the dark chamber. "Taba we N'ijeya a gbanuyi ku shekhuli we N'kha a chesiyim." The monster roared again, and vanished into the sea of shadows that crept at its feet. Y'Sawe trembled as his brother met his gaze.

"What have you done, Mahute?" The misery in the Ile Kanawe's voice was palpable enough that the Dagger could taste it.

"I have entered the next phase," the commander of vampires laughed. "Three Great Beasts were born to the Batabari, and today you have witnessed the resurrection of the first!"

"Y'Chifo didn't deserve to be—"

"What the screamer did or did not deserve is beyond you to comprehend, Y'Sawe." There was a noticeable bite in the dark one's tone, but then he shrugged. "Besides, I wanted to see what would happen if I offered him whole to bring Ninikinana back. You see, all it takes is a little bit of your friends' blood, and the beasts come back at full power. What I discovered after I ordered Shifi to burn, little brother, is that the more blood you have to use, the less predictable Batabari can become." Y'Sawe struggled to keep his composure through Mahute's words. Every curse he could think of filtered through his mind in J'Karo, Katsedu and Pedestrian, but still he held his tongue. "But I discovered something else as well. Through my servant Bahasu's memory, I watched as the Batabari handed over their culture in a scroll. I beheld Kanawe Y'Leina as he quieted the fears of his people. But do you know what he did when it was all over, ulu esho?" The Grand Master took his seat in his cage, eyes full of rage and disgust with Mahute's collected tone, and refused to answer. Mahute only laughed at the display of insolence. "He gifted the Asanibo a vial of his blood, and offered to return one of their lesser known designs." The Kanawe's eyes widened in horror.

"Why tell me this," Y'Sawe started in cautious measure, his eyes narrowed with focus as his brow furrowed, "why go through the trouble of hunting Y'Leisu and the ijeya ni? Haven't you taken enough? Can you not bend Y'Neshu to your will with only the might of the Three?" The torture in Y'Sawe's expression forced an excited laugh from the Dagger, who spread his arms wide in his bravado.

"Very true, ulu esho," he exclaimed, a sick excitement in his eye that made Y'Sawe slide back from the edge. Mahute turned for the exit as he told his brother, "*I* aim to add to their number…" Y'Sawe watched the Dark One leave, completely unaware of what his brother truly meant.

***

Kamari scratched his head, a puzzled expression written on his face that made J'Kana equally as curious.

"Something the matter," the Kanawe asked. The boy looked at him, then shook his head as he stared at the ornate carpet in the center of their batalu.

"Our family is really messed up," he said with a boyish giggle that warmed J'Kana's heart. The father pulled his son closer as he stared through the window.

"Your grandfather and uncle suffered a lot of trauma, and both of them did the best they could with what they had," J'Kana explained. "The kind of slavery that they talked about, the pain that they were forced to endure, is never something that people can get over quickly. It bears a mark that can last for generations, and the longer the scars go unaddressed, the more chaotic things become."

"I guess with Mahute the Dagger it was too late," Kamari replied, his little eyebrows furrowed in frustration. "Is it wrong that I feel bad for him? He did so many terrible things, but…I don't know how to explain it." The shake in his voice spoke of tears on the horizon, and J'Kana ran his hand up and down the little one's back to comfort him.

"I don't think so," he answered warmly. "Mahute was the product of a broken system, just as his brother was. He was a monster, there is no denying that, but in every such case, we have to look at what created that monster if we want to stop it from happening again. That is why I teach you J'Karo. In order for us to grow as a society, we must look at the mistakes of our past and learn from them, no matter how uncomfortable they make us."

"I understand, Yababa," the child said with a sniffle. "So, where do we begin for today?" J'Kana pulled the leather book from the end table by the couch and flipped to a page without much hesitation.

"Let's look here," he spoke with confidence. "It's guaranteed to make you feel a bit better." The boy nodded, and they began the list together.

| | |
|---|---|
| Fanayu | Music |
| Eluni | Theatre |
| Jajimani | Birthday |
| Nashimari | Wedding |
| Chimukonali | Anniversary |
| Feyemo | Party |
| Isalabila | Concert |
| Ilebila | Event |
| Ise | Song/Sing |

| Feleki | Dance |
|---|---|
| Bibisi | Actor |
| Chesasi | Director |
| Ileashe | Celebration |
| Fanayusi | Composer |
| Ilekakilu | Game |
| Koshichami | Crowd/Audience |
| Shemeni | Ceremony |
| Yebutu | Instrument |

Before long, Kamari’s tears had ceased to fall, and his sole focus rested on the list of words in front of him. He was so innocent, and J’Kana wondered how badly it would hurt him to see the true cruelties of the world…

# 17

# Rise of the Blood Beast

*Memifi*

"Come on, Nikeli," Nihani taunted as she sprinted across the rooftops in the merchant district. "Don't tell me that's all your men can accomplish!" Another yifusi dove for her, but J'Kana spoke a command to make the guards heavier every time they jumped. Diving counted.

"You only get to say that because J'Kana cheated," the Royal Guard Commander shouted back, much to the amusement of the citizens on the streets. J'Kana appeared next to her as suddenly as the blowing out of a candle. She shrieked and lost her footing, but used all the power in her core to prevent a fall.

"You *always* think its cheating when I outsmart you, kenani," J'Kana flirted, then sprinted to another rooftop right as she reached for the hood of his cloak. He made a right while Nihani kept straight, and listened to the panic swell in the yifusi as their paths grew ever distant. Down below, another division of the protectors chased after Chishashi and J'Chera, but they proved just as unsuccessful as the rooftop team. "This is the best training ever," the former thief whispered to himself.

It had been four days since their arrival in Memifi, and more importantly, since J'Chera's brilliant plan to enlist Nikeli's aid. It turned out that the sobachi melon, efisi cobs and ketuketu grain he stole from the farmland in Ekutali wasn't just for his personal consumption, or at least, that was how he phrased it when she was there to listen. The night he pulled their party from the Hidden Beast, the elder ijeya planted a few seeds from each of the crops he'd absconded with. A single command, "Yo relachele," was enough to bring them to life as entire fields of produce. J'Kana would never forget the way Nikeli's jaw hit the dirt at the instant growth.

The best part was that since the issue of food had been addressed, criminal activity fell enough to allow Nikeli some time to help them get their training in, and J'Kana could think of no better way than through his favorite game: Run the City. Nihani and Chishashi started off miserably. Neither had been to Memifi before, so they got too distracted by the glittering flecks of iron sand in the city's metal surfaces. J'Chera, on the other hand, found a way to put those muka beast moves to good use. As the days went by, the Asanibo and Jeniju's skills gradually improved, and by the fourth day—today—they found a way to feel each other's plans and move accordingly.

J'Kana returned his focus to the real world just in time enough to dodge a yifusi's tackle and watch him slip from the rooftop. He winced as the crash of his body echoed through the sky.

"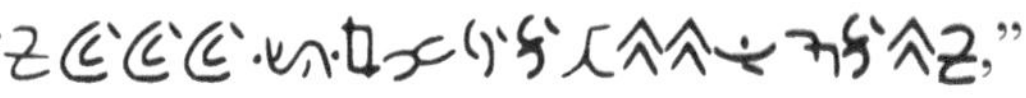," he muttered beneath his breath, embarrassed that he let his earlier command get someone hurt. "Maybe increasing their weight every time they jumped was a bit much…" He ran to the edge to see how badly the soldier had hurt himself, but felt his heart skip when he saw the brute smile up at him. He looked around for an opening to flee, but in every direction his exits were covered by one of Nikeli's guardsmen. He felt his muscles tense, but breathed deeply and spoke under his breath, "

." Each of the yifusi donned an expression of relief if not genuine amusement. Never had they thought that they would spend their day chasing the legendary J'Foja for no crimes committed. For that matter, neither had he.

"You may as well give up," a squad captain called out, a smile on his face beneath the metal helmet that glinted when the sun met the iron sands. "We have you surrounded." J'Kana couldn't stop his smile from spreading across his jaw in the same confident gleam as it had only a few months ago.

"Are you sure about that," he asked, and the captain called for his subordinates to move in. It was too late. "Baa," spoke the former thief, and his body became invisible just in time enough for him to jump down into the alley below. He had to fight to keep his laughter under control. He was already the legendary Great Peasant of Memifi, but he couldn't help but wonder what kind of antics he might have accomplished if he knew enough J'Karo at the time. The thought alone was enough to make him consider a subtle acquisition of goods, but he resisted the urge when the guards cursed him loudly in their pursuit.

He snickered to himself as he weaved through the crowd with all the delicate grace of a summer breeze, and marveled at how much easier it was. It was almost as though the ike that welled up in him could feel that of the people around him. He knew what turns they would make, could feel the heat off their bodies, and could avoid their every move. A dark chill hit him amid the crowd, but unlike the presence of Mahute's servants, the aura of Chishashi's ike was familiar enough to latch onto. They moved north, towards the elite dwellings of the upper district, and J'Kana thought to move that way too—

He jumped between a pair of red- and blue-tinted iron sand walls to climb back up to the rooftops. The pair of jaws that tried to crush him stood frozen for a moment, but trembled with the might of resistance. The people on the street began to run as the great black monster commanded their attention. It let loose a roar that chilled J'Kana's blood as it thrashed its maw free. It stared at him for a while before it sank into the shadows from whence it came. The sky overhead blackened with a rain cloud, and Nikeli's men immediately began to evacuate the merchant district while J'Chera, Chishashi and Nihani sprinted towards J'Kana's location.

By the time they arrived, the monster had vanished. They could feel it. The creature swam in the long shadow cast by the heavens and waited for a moment to strike again, but from where? J'Kana jumped into the air as the creature reemerged from behind him, jaw agape with every intention to taste his blood. The second J'Kana dodged, Nihani pushed her hands into the air as she spoke a line of Y'Maju. The ground in the alley below ruptured to make way for the spring that would guide the monster's mouth towards the sky.

"," J'Chera shouted loud enough for half of Memifi to hear him. He jumped between the rooftops as he spoke the command, and all the metal he passed shattered like glass and reforged into a thousand spears that rocketed into the monster. Nihani released her geyser at the moment that Siema found her way onto the roofs as well. The ara beast inhaled deeply, then released a fiery bark that turned every shard of metal red. They made contact with the underside of the Great Beast, and it retreated to the darkness. "What in Y'Kele's name is that!"

"It's Ninikinana," Chishashi called over the chaos of the city. The glimmer of the metal panels had dulled, and the various shades of red and green, yellow and blue felt an otherworldly gray. It was like the distortion of an Asanibo, but somehow it was worse. "Be on your guard!" Just as the words left the vampire's lips, the beast returned, drawn to his scent like an ara cub to fresh meat. "N'kha a yifuyim," he shouted, and Chishashi was whisked away into a shadow of his own before the Ninikinana could crush his entire body with its massive teeth. It dove from one portal into the next, with the intent to make full use of its powers.

"Y'Go, khemi go mamuke uhujina," Nihani called, and watched as the rain that now scattered about the city became as whips in the sky.

"[illegible]," J'Kana said, and the next exit point of the beast was clear. He jumped from the roof, sprinted through the street and around a corner before he tackled Nikeli and the small child she ran with. The massive head of the beast reappeared right where they had been, and with its prey in sight, it now moved directly for them. "Get out of here, Nikeli!" The little girl cried as the creature closed in on their position, but J'Kana dared to utter another word. "[illegible]

." The monster froze dead in its tracks, eyes locked on Nikeli and the child, and the Commander's legs shook from the potency of her fear. "Go!" She snapped back to reality, nodded to J'Kana, and scared out of her mind, she ran with all the force her legs could generate.

The two ijeya ni, the Jeniju and the Asanibo stood on all sides of the creature, eyes trained on it as even in timelessness it trembled against the order of J'Karo. Each of them braced themselves as little by little the creature regained its faculties.

"It's not going to hold," Nihani called out.

"Chishashi," J'Chera called out. The vampire dug his talons into his palms, and widened his stance to keep his balance when the Ninikinana suddenly thrashed. "Oh, this is helpful," J'Chera shouted.

"Shut up," Chishashi called back, his heartbeat so rapid that it threatened to break his ribs. His eyes flashed deep crimson as he began the Blood Chant, "N'neba lekhan a zotuyim!" The blackness from which the creature emerged began to coil around its body as another dark portal appeared just above it. Chishashi groaned loudly as the strain in his body intensified, but even as the monster thrashed about, the darkness swallowed it whole.

"What did you do," J'Kana asked as the Asanibo fell to a knee. Chishashi gasped for air, pounded the ground with his fist as he visibly fought to regain control of himself.

"I transported it…" he managed as he stood back to his feet. "Outside of Memifi. Have to go *now*." The urgency in his tone was only accentuated by the return of the brilliant violets and reds and golds of the metal fixtures around the city. J'Kana nodded, but pressed against Chishashi's chest to hold him in place. "We don't have time!"

"Nihani," J'Kana beckoned, only to find that the Jeniju had already begun to heal him. Chishashi sighed as his muscles relaxed and his body repaired itself from the overexertion. "We need to go with the day two plan."

"Bah," J'Chera interjected. "That was our worst one! We were too close together, and all of us got captured after only the first hour—"

"That was against Nikeli and the yifusi," J'Kana explained as he silently stretched his ike into the air and felt for any distortions. "We only have one enemy here, so grouping together shouldn't be too much of a problem. It's there, in the Outer Grasslands." He started to move, and his party moved with him despite their reluctance to stick to the plan.

"That one enemy is five times bigger than we are," Chishashi countered as they moved, "not to mention the fact that it can warp between dimensions and strike from our blind spots."

"Not entirely," J'Chera disputed. "It distorts the world around it when it appears, but as soon as it goes away, things start to go back to normal. We just have to watch for when it gets ready to strike."

"And then what do we do there? If it goes for Nihani first—"

"You'll safeguard her, Chishashi. Your Batabari is the most effective thing against that monster," J'Kana was forced to admit. He had always had this perception of J'Karo's limitless power, but the Ninikinana proved that there were some challenges to the notion. He picked up the pace, as did his friends. It wouldn't be too long before they encountered the monster again.

"Did you not see how drained I was," the vampire shot back. "My blood sends the beast into a frenzy. What if it moves while I Chant?" J'Kana rubbed his forehead in frustration, clearly tired of the conversation and frustrated that they couldn't see what he saw.

"Listen," he started in a poor attempt to mask his irritation. "You will safeguard Nihani so that she can heal you and defend you in between your Blood Chants. J'Chera and I will serve as distractions and will restrain the beast as much as we can." The realization hit them all as they approached the gate to the city.

"I see," Chishashi uttered with a tinge of defeat. J'Kana shook his head as he allowed the sight of Memifi to feed his ike to the boiling point.

"There's something else," he told them. "The beast has a jewel in its forehead that I refuse to believe is there purely for decoration. Aim for it at every opportunity. Keep moving. Chishashi and Nihani, move together, J'Chera, you and I will diverge our directions to cause confusion. When you see your opening, strike and strike hard." They all nodded in agreement, and listened as the massive blue metal gate creaked open to the Outer Grasslands. "I hope this works…"

***

*Outer Grasslands—Memifi Outskirts*

J'Kana and J'Chera ran into the field like children on a summer day. Ninikinana raised its voice again, like the scratch of a hammer against a sheet of steel mixed with thunder, as its crimson eyes darted along either of their paths. It turned its massive body to lash out at J'Kana with its armored tail, but the former prince of thieves was too agile for it to work. He jumped over it and launched into a roll along the ground. The monster hissed at him and charged with thunderous fury.

"," J'Chera shouted. He watched as some invisible force pulled at Ninikinana's legs, felt the tremors when it fell to the ground with its head angled towards Chishashi and Nihani, and shouted for his comrades to strike at the jewel when the beast stayed down.

"Bobo ja basi we lekhan a buyi gbayim," Chishashi called as his blood ran down the palms of his hands. The crimson ropes solidified into the same whips he'd used against Tikhal in the Kehemu. He extended an arm toward Ninikinana, watched eagerly as the construct hurdled for the jewel, then felt a knot in his stomach when the creature hissed out a command.

"!"

J'Karo. The monster knew how to speak J'Karo. Chishashi stood stunned as the blood whips exploded into a scarlet mist and Ninikinana regained its footing.

"That was unexpected," J'Kana muttered, then started to run as the jaws of the beast came hot on his heels.

"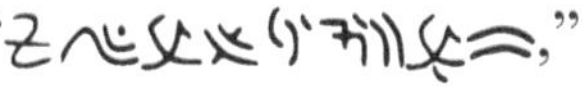," it growled ferociously, and J'Kana felt his body pull in reverse even as his legs sprinted forward. He slipped, and hurdled through the air towards the extended snout and gnashing teeth of the abomination that chased him.

"J'Kana, turn around," J'Chera ordered, and J'Kana did as he was instructed while his senior began to speak. " ." A wall of earth emerged just in front of the monster's maw for J'Kana's feet to slam into. He kicked himself into the air just as Ninikinana crushed the slab in its fangs.

"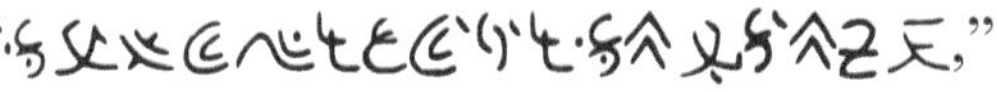," he whispered, and the winds caught him as he flew. He quickly found his footing on the air, and ran towards J'Chera's position. The monster roared again, its eyes contracted as it thought to command the ike once more, but J'Chera beat it to the punch.

" 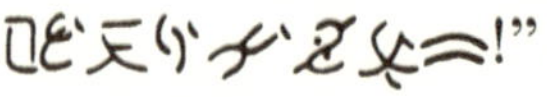!" He barely got the command out before he rolled out of the beast's path. It slid along the ground as it tried to change directions, and in the moment where it paused, the earth split. From it emerged a massive stone hammer that smashed against the lizard's face—and the jewel with it. The crack of the scarlet orb could be heard by them all, and a look of hope emerged between them. "Hey, I got a hit!" The creature lunged for him before he could celebrate, but even as he dodged, his smile stayed in place. The monster chased him now, and again fixed its mouth to rumble a command that was slapped away by one of Nihani's water whips. It turned its head, stared her down, and with neither warning nor hesitation, it blasted a bloody fire throughout the field.

Chishashi jumped into its path without time to think, and shielded Nihani with his own body and blood. She did what she could to heal him, but the beast was too strong, and forced him to overextend just as his body started to function normally again. If something wasn't done soon, both of them would die.

"

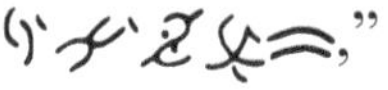," J'Kana ordered from overhead. The sound of his voice was enough of a reason to command the creature's attention, and the wildly evasive ijeya instinctively ran on the wind away from the stream of flames. Smoke rose through the atmosphere as the smell of burning blood permeated the air, but a mighty tempest overtook the heavens, torrential rain fell around the grasslands, and just as J'Kana proclaimed, lightning struck the face of the Great Beast and the gem's crack spidered. The massive reptile thrashed and roared from the pain, the red in its forehead now a distorted black with crimson lining. "It doesn't look like it will take another hit! Finish it, Chishashi!"

Chishashi stood there, his body atremble, as he watched the black scales of the Ninikinana drown themselves in fire. Its eyes secreted a black sludge as the temperature of the plains elevated.

"Y'Go, bi zanuwe basiyil, maju jakha batombe uduo," she pleaded, and as her hands waved through the downpour, Chishashi watched as it lit a tranquil azure. Water seeped into his clothes, his hair, his skin, and through the divine providence of Y'Kele Himself, his injuries healed at a rapid pace. He watched Ninikinana, ablaze in its fiery rage as it bellowed into the darkened sky. He ran towards its left flank, blood ropes extended from his palms yet again, as Nihani moved with him. The frenzied monster ground its foot into the earth as it prepared to charge them. J'Chera shook his head and exhaled in a huff.

"Please, Merciful Y'Kele, don't fail me now," he muttered, then gave himself over to the rise of his silver ike. "!" The rage of the giant lizard turned to J'Chera now, and as it lit a fiery path towards him in the field, the elder apprentice sprinted just out of range enough to issue another command. "!" The rumble of the monster was suddenly drowned out by a rift formed in the ground. Ninikinana, unable to stop itself, fell into it unceremoniously. The sands beneath its feet and body continuously caved under its weight, and the rain only added to the shift. Chishashi used his blood whips to vault into the air, and began to chant as he flipped directly over the beast's head.

"Zabaku ja basi we lekhan a fekhayim," Chishashi called, and the whips reconfigured into the same massive orb of blood that Hanika used in Shifi. It burned bright, and summoned the black liquid from the beast to its core before it dropped. The Asanibo landed on the other side of it, and when the bomb dropped, it exploded with a force that reduced the Ninikinana to ash. The last cry of the creature was a hollow one, but the sound that came with its destruction was one that rattled the foundations of Memifi in all its metallic glory.

Chishashi dropped to his knees the moment it was over, and J'Chera stood with his head tilted back to savor the rain as it fell on his face. Nihani stood at a distance between them and healed them both, while J'Kana cautiously approached the pit. There, at the bottom of the crater, was a charred body wrapped in a pristine orange robe. His jaw dropped, and immediately he muttered a command under his breath.

"Ti nata hafu wu Kanawe harana ra N'hafu shu bibisanati o." A flash of gold took his eyes as the path of the monster became clear. J'Kana felt an icy prick of rage filter into him. He yelled against his firmest desire, but he saw! He witnessed the dark paths of the Hesefa Desert, returned to the eerie shadows of the Kehemu Forest, swam in the murky waters of the western Shukeshu tributaries, but something changed when he saw the Great Kabisu River. A sense of familiarity overtook his senses until there, at the base of the Amejai Mountains, just south of the city of J'Watuna, he found an old fortress built into the rock. Green light surrounded its gates and illuminated the army of elokobi that kept watch over it.

"J'Kana!" J'Chera's voice broke through the stupor caused by the vision. The former Great Peasant found himself in the dirt. He pushed himself up, looked between the faces of his comrades, and gave them a grave look.

"What happened," Nihani asked, and immediately started to heal him. He looked back at the pit, back at the fallen form of the Kanawe, and felt his stomach churn within him.

"I know where we need to go," he told them, and gathered his strength as lightning passed overhead.

***

"Why'd you have to remind me of that," Chishashi groaned as he leaned on the arm of his chair and pressed a hand to his forehead. Kamari giggled.

"That was incredible!" His shout was enough to wake the dead, which instinctively made the Asanibo look out the window. When there was no sign of elokobi, he turned back to the small boy and offered a tired smile.

"Of course *you* would think so," J'Kana chuckled. "You only got to hear about it. *We* were the ones that had to live it."

"And we only barely did that much," Chishashi added as his arms folded across his chest. "You should hope and pray you never have to cross paths with monsters like that." J'Kana waved a hand dismissively.

"It's no use trying to get *him* to be safe," the father explained. "The lele mata longs for an adventure filled with these kinds of battles, ne, Shehefo?" The boy nodded his head so hard, J'Kana thought it might rattle off his shoulders.

"Well, if that's the case, I can see why you teach him J'Karo," the Asanibo admitted. The very word was enough to excite the little one, and J'Kana grabbed the book at his prompting.

"Alright, alright," he said with a hand lifted in calming gesture. "Let's teach you some of the words J'Chera and I used in our battle, ne? Look here…"

| | | |
|---|---|---|
| 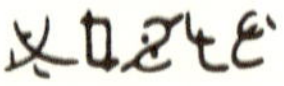 | Bokojiali | Storm |
|  | Behiso | Hammer |
|  | Ilakokoishi | Crater |
| 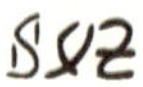 | Tosoti | Focus |
|  | Baesha | Whip/Chain |
|  | Chuti | Metal/Steel |
|  | Baule | Spear |
|  | Kokoishi | Hole |
| 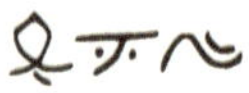 | Biyite | Jaw |
| 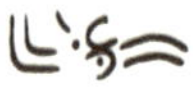 | Chiyosa | Talon |
|  | Saweichera | Trial/Exercise |

# 18

# Ceremony of Heroes

*Memifi*

The streets were alive with cheers and weeping the moment J'Kana and his friends returned through the gates. People ran in all directions out of joy rather than fear, all the leaders of Memifi, from the nobles in the Y'Rakilian Court to the Ubeshu himself, ordered an expedient celebration of their new heroes, and already the citizens who had them gathered their yebame (musical bow), chatochato (tambourine) and batuki (drums), while still others lined the streets, prepared to clap with the songs that would soon lift higher and higher to Y'Kele's ears. Ubeshu

Bamaje and Lord Babanu ushered them through the city as a large crowd gathered around them, dancers, singers, acrobats and the most generous of the merchants, wrapped the ijeya ni, Chishashi and Nihani in fine silks and jewels as they gathered.

"Loutu," cried the Chief, and the crowd responded in kind as the yebame players struck their strings with festive fervor. After the third measure, the chatochato players came in with just as much excitement, and then three more went by to summon the batuki. Those around them clapped and swayed under the infectious rhythm. The clouds began to part, and the warm rays of the Y'Rakilian sun breathed life into the colorful iron sand walls throughout Memifi.

"Loutu nasoinati," sang the first half of the crowd, which began a call and response with the other side while the two ijeya ni, the Asanibo, and the Jeniju walked through them.

"Oye, Y'Kele," answered the others. Fireworks went off in the background to Nihani's surprise. She smiled from ear to ear as the smell of something sweet and fried wafted through the air.

"Bushake tuketuna!" Chishashi was uncomfortable at first, but soon found the joy of the city to be infectious enough to bring a smile to his face. He couldn't remember the last time he allowed himself to have some fun.

"Kanawe, Y'Kele!" J'Chera instantly engulfed himself in the music and festivities. He danced with the crowd and sang along with them with every step, delighted that there was a sound in Y'Neshu that could drown out the volume of their problems, even if it was only for a moment.

"Fajari chiweyubasa!" J'Kana dispensed a sad laugh, his memory flooded with the inconveniences he had caused these people because of how they treated him. It was true, he was a child that deserved better than what they gave, but it was also true that he didn't have to live down to their low expectations of him. He looked at Lord Babanu, who flashed a toothy grin at him, and nearly cried. *I am putting my faith in you*, the ijeya remembered. *Don't make me regret it.* J'Kana could only hope that he had honored that faith.

"N'arila chesina!" The people continued to sing and dance and flip and cry as they came to the center of the upper district. Ubeshu Bamaje and Lord Babanu took their places to the right and left of the district square, while others ran into their chohafi to bring out four ornate chairs, each of a different design, for their heroes. The Chief lifted his hand, and while the instrumentation continued, the voices of Memifi's people fell into silence.

"Who would have thought that J'Foja would go from picking our pockets to saving the whole city, na?" The crowd laughed, some cheered, and others still couldn't let go of the emotions that overwhelmed them. J'Kana thought to stop them, to tell them that such recognition was unnecessary, but the moment he opened his mouth, a sharp glare from Babanu shut it right up again. "In the time that you lived among us, you showed us a lot of what you could do. You were resourceful, witty, determined, and charming enough to get us to fall for your antics over and over." His face sank with a sense of regret that J'Kana never expected, but Lord Babanu stood tall and proud like the spires of the capitol. "In turn, we never treated you with the kindness and community that befits an orphaned child. Instead, we acted as if you were an outsider, because it was easier to ignore a stranger than to be burdened with feeding another mouth." The music stopped. All listened attentively to Bamaje's words. Many averted their eyes now, ashamed of the memories that flooded their minds, ashamed of how they mishandled a little boy. Many more bit back their tears as the sense of gratitude overtook them. "We have been negligent, selfish, and cruel. What you and your friends did for us today, we did not deserve, so as Ubeshu of Memifi, and as Bamaje of the Tilike Tribe, I bow to you and beg your forgiveness."

J'Kana and his allies looked around, and noticed that one by one, every knee in the streets of the City of Celestial Light touched the earth while the jaw of the ijeya threatened to do the same. He stumbled over words to say, but it was clear that the entire city waited to hear what his answer would be. He looked to Babanu, who bowed his head just the same as everyone else. J'Kana took a deep breath. It was hard for him not to think about the cold of the Outer Grasslands in the winter, or the hunger he felt in his belly by the age of ten. He couldn't help but think of the beatings he'd received from shopkeepers who caught him stealing, or the disapproving glares they offered just because he dared to exist. Even the yifusi, the protectors of the Royal House and Lands, faltered in the face of a lonely child with nowhere to go. But still…

"I have been through a lot in this place," J'Kana started, his voice barely above a whisper as he took in the sights. "I have suffered a great deal. I have been lonely.

Hungry. Angry with the people of this city even as I smiled before you all…" He let his voice rumble and trail off as the sadness and anger at the past began to resonate. It was just that, however. The past. He breathed in deeply, then slowly let the air flow out of him. His ike filled him up in its place. "Even after all of that, I couldn't let any of you get hurt." J'Yobena flashed through his mind. He couldn't help but be reminded of her. He insulted her, shamed her, made her angry and doubtful of herself, but she still cared for him enough to nurse him in his most dire moment and watch over Siema in his place. "I once heard the elders say that 'Jeketinawe wu koha ra emi haranachu.' The peaceful road is not far. I have learned that in order to take it, I must forgive, and do away with the path of anger first." The Ubeshu looked at J'Kana, a hopeful glint in his eye as he waited for the young man to say what he meant to say. "We have all made mistakes. All is forgiven."

Throughout the streets of Memifi the people rejoiced, and J'Kana was awestruck by the sudden resurgence of the music and dance. Even the Ubeshu, overjoyed by J'Kana's absolution, danced around the square as if blessed by Y'Kele Himself. The song, "Loutu," continued to ring, and while J'Kana stood in the height of incredulity, Nihani and J'Chera flowed with the rhythm.

Lord Babanu, just as lively as the rest, waved the four heroes over to the line of chairs set up in their honor. Chishashi sat, followed by J'Kana, while J'Chera and Nihani danced for a moment longer. When they finally sat down, Babanu began his portion of the festivities.

"The time has come for us to honor our heroes!" The giant man spoke with such a bravado that matched his golden attire. It was as though he had been born for celebration, and the magnanimity he demonstrated told J'Kana that he was determined to live up to that cosmic expectation. He turned to the four, and with a wink at the former peasant, he asked them, "What are we to call you, e?"

"I am J'Kana of Shifi," said the most familiar of the four, his voice direct and strong. The revelation of his real name was enough to cause a stir, but J'Chera quickly followed his M'ba ijeya.

"J'Chera of the Maanu Tribe in Y'Fuwefo," he almost sang, which appealed to the people either through humor or attraction.

"Nihani, of the Makhewe Tribe in Kahali." Her voice was as melodious as the yebame, and the hearts of every man in the city melted under her gaze. All eyes fell to

Chishashi, who visibly squirmed from the intensity. He took a deep breath as a determination as bold as the acrobats gleamed behind his yellow eyes.

"I am Chishashi," he started, an unfamiliar tremble in his voice, "of the Batabari Clan in Ekutali." The music stopped. Some faces in the crowd darkened with the realization of the Asanibo in their midst while others voiced their curiosity of his ability to survive the sun.

"A little darkness to mix in with the light," Babanu said with a foreboding gravity, then let his brightest smile break through like morning sunlight. "I like it." Lord Babanu turned his focus back to the anxious crowd. "*These* are the four who have risked their lives to save our city! *They* are the ones who have ensured that the sun will shine on our lustrous walls for ages to come! So! As they have honored us with their protection, it is time for us to offer a piece of Memifi for all of Y'Neshu to see!" As Babanu spoke, the cheers began to return. The wariness of Chishashi, at least for the moment, was suspended with the reluctant pianissimo of the music, all ears attentive to the Y'Rakilian noble. His smile broke brighter, his arms spread, and as he scanned the crowd, he asked triumphantly, "What shall we call them na?"

"The Twilight of Memifi," shouted a man from somewhere in the crowd. Babanu mulled it over.

"Not bad," he offered, "but do we have any other suggestions?"

"Heavenly Rain," called a woman, clearly focused on Nihani's proclivity for water magic.

"It should be the Four Heavenly Mountains," cried an elderly man, but the others around him visibly disagreed, even if they audibly could not. Babanu laughed, and J'Kana fidgeted. It was ten minutes of shouting before a name was selected. It was decided that whatever they were called needed to reflect their valor, their determination, and their wisdom all together. It was together that they fought, together that they won, and it was the pool of their insights that had saved Memifi not once, but twice now. They moved and planned like the pack of ara beasts from J'Kana's first mission with Y'Sawe, and it only occurred to him now that it had been somewhere around two months ago.

"Then it has been decided!" Lord Babanu's commanding voice boomed over the noise of the crowd. "Ladies and gentlemen of Memifi, I give you the Y'Rakili wu He Ara Akira! The Four Ara Beasts of Y'Rakili!" The mention of the name made all of Memifi break again into their cheers and songs, and with the ceremony done, Babanu encouraged the merrymaking of his friends and neighbors while he beckoned the Four Ara to follow him to the Hidden Beast. They did so, each of them—save for J'Chera, who longed to be at the center of the party—more anxious than before. "It's good to see that you've made good on my investment of faith, J'Kana." The former thief was surprised that Lord Babanu wanted to begin that conversation, but readily obliged with all the diplomacy he'd picked up from his Master's dealings with others.

"I am pleased to hear you think I have, Lord Babanu," J'Kana replied, and the noble laughed. "It seems like only yesterday that I stole your Bashele."

"With the way the economy has turned out in the last few weeks, it may as well have," Babanu replied more seriously. "With trade disrupted, every leader across Y'Neshu is anxious. As you saw upon your return, it's more than just the money that has been affected. The people of Y'Rakili starve in the streets. It wouldn't be hard to imagine that Y'Fuwefo and Y'Sewana are the same."

"The crops we've planted to the north of the city should last for quite some time," J'Chera offered in a tone more solemn than the occasion would have suggested. His brow furrowed. "Still, it wouldn't be enough to feed the whole country of Y'Rakili." It didn't take them long to enter the Hidden Beast, its gilded walls perfectly accented by the dim candle light in the mounted lamps. The array of pictographs from the Jeniju colony in the Great Kahali Reef made Nihani feel at home, just as it had when they first visited this place together, and the soso wood tables offered Chishashi the same comfort.

"Every seed we could harvest could assist the relief effort," Babanu reassured him. "It will take time, but Y'Rakili is not soon to be defeated by a pack of terrorists to the north." He addressed the barkeep and swiftly made his way to the back of the dining hall, where a special table was reserved for him and him alone. The He Ara followed, and together they sat in the well-cushioned chairs.

"It wasn't terrorists," Chishashi started, which immediately caught the noble's attention. "Mahute the Dagger and his band of Asanibo servants attacked a Summit of the Wayi Kanawe." Babanu's eyes expanded in shock.

"Peace of Y'Kele," he muttered as he massaged his jaw. "How do you know this? What did he want?"

Chishashi exhaled, unable to answer from the limited information that he had received. J'Kana and J'Chera both averted their eyes. To talk about what happened there meant to revisit J'Yobena's death. Even so, if the world around them grew increasingly unstable, withholding information from someone with ties to the Emperor would only help Mahute to redefine all that Y'Neshu was.

"We were there," J'Chera finally said. "Our masters were attacked while they were all together. Two of the Kanawe died right in front of us. One of them, Kanawe Y'Chifo, was somehow turned into that monster we defeated outside." Babanu sat quietly, suddenly unable to believe his ears, and unaware of how much more there was to know.

"All of this he did to end the way of the Kanawe and to rebuild Y'Neshu in his image," J'Kana continued. J'Chera smiled thankfully at him as he wiped away tears filled with more emotions than he could name. "He threatens to release J'Karo and Batabari into the land again, and plunge the Four Empires into the same chaos of the War of the Ancients, only with him at the helm."

"Ebasho," Babanu exclaimed. "What does he stand to gain from this?"

"He claims that when the Languages of Power were sealed, the Kingdoms and their Kanawe stripped the people of their heritage." J'Kana explained. "He wants to return to the people what they lost—"

"And force the Empires to destroy each other in the process," Babanu finished, a pensive pinch between his brows. "That explains why the terrorists' nationalities were never disclosed. To cast doubt in all directions is to cause obstruction to every path…" He trailed off, and the Four Ara of Y'Rakili watched him with the utmost care. He laid his hand down on the table before them, his eyes resolute. "I will take this news before the Emperor in the next two days. We may not be able to easily converse with the other nations at present, but we can at least prepare Y'Rakili for what awaits beyond the horizon. A man like the Dagger cannot be entrusted to educate our people."

"Actually, Lord Babanu," J'Kana started, deep in thought as he went, "I wanted to propose something potentially illegal." The noble raised an eyebrow, and tried his best to suppress an excited smirk.

"What did you have in mind, my young friend?" J'Kana looked at the noble with all the resolve he could muster, while his companions looked on him with concern.

"We must arm our people. I would like to teach the Y'Rakilians J'Karo," he finally answered, and all who heard him fell silent.

***

"What a cool name," Kamari exclaimed, but the excitement didn't last long. "Why didn't you give your tribe during the naming ceremony, Yababa?" J'Kana laughed nervously.

"Well," he started with a shrug, "at the time I didn't know it. Besides, I think it's clear that there were other things on our minds." Kamari smiled brightly.

"Like rescuing my grandfather," he said matter-of-factly, and J'Kana chuckled again with a nod.

"But of course now there was the added pressure of trying to keep the Four Empires from going to war without reason," he explained. Kamari "wowed" under his breath. "I promise to tell you all about it when we get there. For now—"

"Here is the book," the little one interrupted, and handed the leatherbound tome to his father. J'Kana blinked in disbelief.

"When did you…"

"I'm quicker than I look, Yababa," Kamari answered when the Elder trailed off. "You should really keep a better eye on me." J'Kana shot him a wry grin, and after the book was firmly in one hand, he used the other to tickle his son. Kamari squealed as he wrapped his little fingers around his father's hand to stop him, only to find that he did not yet have the strength. "Ah! I give up! I give up!" The Sage relented, and graciously allowed the ulu ijeya the chance to collect himself while he turned the pages of the book.

"Now, let us begin here…"

| | | |
|---|---|---|
| 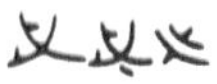 | Hobofu | Should/Must |
|  | Lita | Supply |
|  | Sihu | Sign/Indication |
|  | Sholae | Spring |
|  | Shakutu | Mountain |
|  | Shefeno | Desert |
|  | Kuhaji | Forest |
|  | Eleo | Plains |

| | | |
|---|---|---|
|  | Laelafi | Waterfall |
| 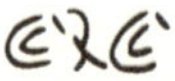 | Laela | River |
| 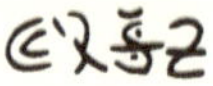 | Laejoti | Tributary |
| 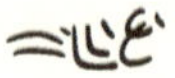 | Shachili | Island |
|  | Ulushaku | Hills |
|  | Tamochu | Delegation |
|  | Uwemi | Legend/Hero |
|  | Wawani | Selection/Choice |
|  | Wajosi | Wash |
|  | Arai | Stick/Staff |
|  | Ofami | Suspicion |
|  | Tunaye | Politics |
| 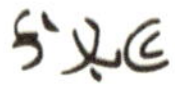 | Lebera | Compromise |
|  | Fetawo | Dimension |

# 19

# Khafenu in the Dark

*Loutu Usele*

The shadows swept over him the moment the words left his mouth, and he found himself trapped, surrounded by darkness in a grim chamber. From behind him came the guttural rumble of an Asanibo. J'Kana turned, only to steep further in the absence of light.

"How can we convince you that we are the hope of Y'Neshu," called the creature from the black. "How can we show you that we act in the best interest of everyone?"

"Maybe start with leaving me alone to enjoy my dinner," he answered, arms folded before him as he impatiently tapped his foot. "Haven't you taken enough from me in the name of your cause?" Footsteps could be heard in the distance, and though his instincts told him to yield to the fear, he remained calm.

"You speak of the past as if all the pain you suffered wasn't directly tied to the Kanawe," she spoke soothingly as again the shadows shifted around the ijeya. "You lost much, but so have we. In that, we share a multitude of similarities."

"I am nothing like you!" J'Kana stepped back as the voice that escaped him echoed through the shadow as a twisted roar. "You are oppressors from time past trying to mount a return—"

"As opposed to the ones who preach egalitarianism but instead maintain social castes based on knowledge?" Her tone was incredulous and accusatory. "For every sin we Batabari committed in the light, your governors and teachers have added to in the shadows. Violence against the common folk. Complicity with slavers. Restriction of education. You maintain the notion that they are somehow better, when all they did at the end of the war was weaken the whole so they could replace one form of oppression with another." The darkness hissed as countless whispers reached J'Kana's ears. The footsteps ran again in a number of directions, and every so often, J'Kana could feel the slightest tap on his shoulders.

"So, they were the ones who destroyed the Yema," the Honored Ijeya shouted over the hushed musings of disembodied voices. The Asanibo laughed in its wake. "They were the ones who gifted the people of Y'Neshu theft and starvation? They killed J'Yobena? They murdered my parents and burned my city to the ground? What is so funny to you about that, na?"

"Do you think that the people you mourn would have died if the Kanawe didn't safeguard the knowledge that would have kept the public safe? Do you think that if all had access to J'Karo or Batabari they would have suffered the way they do now?" She sank into silence, as did the whispering shadows.

"You and your Master still would have found a way to take everything from us," J'Kana shot back. A chill crept across the dark as the light footsteps of a distant figure grew louder with every step. He stood in silence, focused on the connection between all things as he waited to see the face of his enemy. The cold and dark caused his ike to swell just as much as light and warmth would have, but nevertheless, Khafenu stood before him with an arrogant smile.

"If all was as it should be, J'Kana," she purred as she paced the ground before him like a ayena on the hunt, "then Mahute the Dagger would not be my master. The Four Empires of Y'Neshu and the Batabari Clan would have found a compromise that would have allowed everyone to retain their knowledge of self. If peace had truly been sought and worked for instead of a shift in the balance of power, then Mahute and your father never would have been sold by their parents." J'Kana blinked in confusion, felt his eyes warm with the water they produced as his breaths became quicker and staggered.

"What?" The question told Khafenu everything she needed to know. Her eyes narrowed on the apprentice, confident that she would be able to do away with him now.

"Why do you think that Y'Sawe always felt so familiar to you, e? You spent so much time running away from Shifi that you never realized why you were able to bond as quickly as you were. It's why you fight so hard to get back to him now, even though you have no hope of it without my help," she sneered, her fangs bared in the light of her malicious crimson eyes.

"Hafu wu Kanawe ra…yababa haranati e?" The question manifested in J'Karo before it even registered in Pedestrian, wrapped in a shadow of the strong voice J'Kana was known for.

"He's being held here," she whispered into the shadows. They began to swirl and distort, then unraveled into a massive stone chamber illuminated with crimson fire born from golden bowls that protruded from black ornate pillars. Cages lined the ceiling, some of which retained their prisoners, and at its back stood a massive staircase that ascended to an empty throne. A shockwave rippled through J'Kana's body. Something about it felt so inviting that it took all his strength to close his eyes in restraint. "Do you feel it," Khafenu asked as she appeared behind the apprentice and massaged his shoulders. She felt his muscles tremble, his breaths grow tighter as his body adapted to the surge of strength the resurrection chamber gifted him. "This place is alive with the power of Batabari. Only those whose strength is proven can hear the call it makes. The question, ulu ijeya, is what will you do now that you've heard it?" J'Kana slapped her hands away from him, a sharp glare embedded in his face as he whipped around atop the stone tablet at the room's center.

"I will resist," he growled at her, much to her delight. "I have trained to be strong in the ways of J'Karo. I will rescue my Kanawe with the other Ara at my side, and we will be the ones to right the wrongs done in Y'Neshu." She laughed again, and J'Kana felt his anger surge within him. It was all he could do to stand still, to focus on the peace through which his ike thrived.

"How quickly we forget our shortcomings, ulu ijeya," she taunted as she paced the ground again, her jagged talons on full display. "You remember how much more effective your little friend was in fighting Ninikinana, ne? Your J'Karo barely scratched the surface. You had to move a little bit of heaven and earth to stay in the fight. What do you think you can accomplish here, surrounded by the powers of my clan?" J'Kana looked into Khafenu's eyes as the call of the Batabari around him grew louder still. He heard the deep bellows of the Ninikinana emerge again from the darkest corners of the room, listened to its colossal stomps against the ground as an army of elokobi foot soldiers marched on all sides. "Nothing would stand in your way," Khafenu told him with a voice as sweet as a honeycomb, even as more monsters echoed in the dark. "Accept the call. Rule the new Y'Neshu by your uncle's side and all shall be yours without challenge."

J'Kana looked down as his fingertips began to sting and his hands trembled, only to notice that the violet shiki and black jifona had been replaced with his tattered garments from the days before his apprenticeship. *Always the scared little boy,* the shadows spoke to him. *So desperate. So powerless.*

"You are wrong," J'Kana argued as he clenched his fists. He blinked, and found that his body reverted to what it was at seven years old. He blinked again, and regained the last ten years of his life.

*Take our hand. We can give you the power that you desire…* The pain in his chest was undeniable, and was only accented by the sharp resurrection of the bujoki spider's venom. He gripped his arm and fell to his knees as the pain spread slowly throughout his body.

"I…" he tried to speak, but a sudden shot of pain through his shoulder forced him to grind his teeth. "I can't!" He yelled it, then writhed as the accursed agony intensified all throughout him. He wrapped his arms around himself as he shivered in the dim firelight. The voices continued to reach out to him, to taunt him and tempt him toward the cursed power of the vampires of Y'Neshu. His brows pinched together as his mouth spread wide open, but when his eyes opened, he didn't see the foreboding resurrection chamber, nor did he see Khafenu. He saw Nihani's Wekhala, Oleli, tend to his wounds. He witnessed J'Yobena and J'Chera give him what they could from their own training. He observed the back of Chishashi's head as he led their party through the Kehemu Forest. He heard his Master instruct him on Mount Y'Bayeka. He heard his mother's soothing voice as she reminded him of why his name was J'Kana in the first place. His eyes surged with a brilliant gold as he slammed a fist against the stone. "Woata," he shouted with every bit of force he could summon. His gilded ike threatened to wash over the shadows like Nihani's Divine Waters, and suddenly the bravado of Khafenu eked away. "I have heard enough. I will no longer listen as you rationalize derision and genocide! If you truly think your way to be the better one, then here, test it against mine!"

Khafenu bared her fangs as she ran at J'Kana, who simply took a step back and extended his flat palm towards his opponent. She slashed at him with her jagged claws, but the Gilded Ijeya pulled her by the wrist as he sank his body to drive his elbow into her chest. She stumbled back, and he swept her leg as she did so. He stood tall against her, and waited for her to regain her stance before the fight continued. She ripped at his face now, was pushed gently out of the way, then followed up with an attempted cut to his legs. He jumped over it, caught himself on his hands as his body turned over in the air, and with supreme control of his core, brought himself into a crouched position while he watched his opponent whip around.

The vampiress advanced on him, talons raised high above her head and poised to strike, but the wily Shifian swept at her legs with his own. She jumped into a cartwheel and rolled along with his energy. When they stopped, both were supported on all four of their limbs, and she extended a taloned foot towards his groin. His lips spread wide at the close call as he turned back the way he came and kicked like an abata to throw her off balance. The moment her back touched the ground, she rolled in reverse and lunged through the air at the resistor. J'Kana bent backwards just in time to see the hunger in her eyes as she passed over him. He sprung back up to his feet and ran in the opposite direction. Khafenu snickered as she rolled her neck to loosen it.

"N'kha ja lekhan ja wuli we fajari a gbayim," she called, and just a few feet from J'Kana erupted a wall of fire. The apprentice was unfazed, and thought it time to use a command of his own.

"Ti kifiti N'tebi koha wu nunu shu kelenati," he responded as he abruptly changed directions. Khafenu watched as the path he tread grew higher and higher as a road of ice sprouted from the stone beneath. She opened her palms and laughed as the fires she brought forth drifted to either hand. She extended them forward with delight as the flames jutted towards her prey. He barely dodged them with a slide along the ice, only to be kicked in the sternum by the Asanibo.

"You didn't think you would be able to escape me, did you," she asked playfully as his breath left him. She jumped into the air and bore down on him again, this time with enough force to break through the ice road he had engineered. He hit the ground, bounced, and was met with Khafenu's fist to his stomach. He felt his ribs crack under the pressure, and knew that it was only by Y'Kele's grace and the power of the jilaba wu ajiwele that he didn't die on the impact. Khafenu licked her lips. "If only you had taken the offer." She shrugged, but when his lips started to move, she couldn't help but lean in closer so that she could catch what he said. "So, the begging has started alrea—"

"Yo otaba wu fahila shu kofajabasa o," he interrupted with a slick smile as her hair burst into flames. She shot up in an instant as she sought something—anything—with which to put out her hair, and as her screams filled the chamber, J'Kana slowly staggered back to his feet. He watched her carefully as she dropped to the ground, rolled along it, and again he doused her in flames, this time in the ones she had summoned from before. Within moments, her body was reduced to ash. J'Kana stumbled back and sat on the floor of the great stone stage with a satisfied smile as he tried to catch his breath.

"What are you smiling at," came the aggravated grumble of the vampire in his ear. Her mouth widened to take a bite out of him, her arms already wrapped around his shoulders to keep him bound to this position. He slid down to the uneven rock and rolled away from her just before her fangs bore into his neck. She pierced her palms with her claws as she started another command. "Bobo ja basi we lekhan a buyi gbayim o!" J'Kana knew what it meant as soon as she dared speak it, and watched the two streams of blood arrange themselves into thick whips that yearned to rend his flesh.

She shouted as she deployed the first one, then the second when the apprentice managed to dodge. Again and again, she slashed through the air with the manifestations of her will, and over and over J'Kana pulled out a narrow evasion. He couldn't take the time to breathe a command so long as he was in range, and so with all the strength left in his body, he jumped across the stone. Khafenu was content to let him, and paced the ground again with the firm belief that the upper hand was hers.

"This would be so much easier with the others here," J'Kana couldn't help but joke. Khafenu rolled her eyes, then ran at him with astounding speed. "Ti muata wu baesha shu N'nunu molekenati o!" The command came just at the moment that her Blood Whip lurched to lick his flesh again, and to her great alarm, both of them crystalized from the cold. She struggled to move them, but only for a moment. The shadows swallowed her again, and J'Kana was left to try and figure out where she would emerge from next.

"Ha!" J'Kana whipped his head straight up, and rolled out of the way as the Asanibo descended. He looked back at his prior position, only to realize that there was no collision. She was gone, and just as fast as he had turned to look, she reappeared and drove her nails into his back. He rolled across the stone tablet, but was stopped by a sharp kick to the spine. Another sent him along the ground again. "The shadows are my ally," she told him as she advanced on him methodically, careful to savor every distortion of his agonized face.

"Ti N'loutu ra chiweyu shu molekenati o," J'Kana whispered. *Set explosions in the shadows.* "Yibe bewana shu reshilina, chiweyubasa." *When she enters, detonate.* Against his body's wishes, he pushed himself off the ground and stared the vampire in the eyes. He smiled at her, then ran as fast as his aching bones would carry him. His speed was at least impressive enough to make her drop her smirk and open a rift into the darkness. She tried to enter, but both of them were blown back by the force of the explosion. Only one of them smiled. J'Kana knew he was in a state, but even so, he shifted the ike again and let it surge through him. If he was going to die, there was no way he would allow Khafenu to leave this place and torment Y'Neshu further. He listened for a moment while she shrieked in the background and he regained his bearings. His body refused to move, but he could still speak. For the moment, that was all that mattered. "Ti yibe bewana ra N'hafu shu tekufona, ilelawo Khafenu shu natiebasa." His tone was even, his eyes determined, and his breath sharp. He was hopeful that that was close enough to the command that Y'Sawe had used way back when all this began, albeit with a more permanent twist.

Khafenu stalked the ground, her eyes bright red and hungry for the blood of one so gifted and strong. Her saliva dripped along her chin as she flexed her talons wide. J'Kana could feel his heart pulse from the activation of his ike. Surely Y'Kele would protect him in this. Just in case, though, he prayed that the command would take effect in an instant, and that he would escape with his life.

"Do you have any last words before I turn you into an elokobi," she asked in a tone that was strangely seductive.

"Just that your mother was a fruit bat," he told her defiantly. "Hurry up. We don't have all day." She snarled at him, then raised her arm high in the air and brought it down right on his chest. J'Kana closed his eyes and screamed in short, loud bursts until he realized that the claw had never gone through. Khafenu stood petrified, angled toward him with a horrid look about her, almost as if she were a stone statue meant to keep evil away. *Ironic,* thought the ijeya. He stood up, which tipped the frozen vampiress over to the side, her face still stuck mid-growl. He couldn't help but smile in amusement as he gazed upon her form. "What's the matter? Bat got your tongue?" He laughed uproariously at the stupidity of his own joke, then when the laughter subsided, he sobered as the command exited his mouth: "Ti fajari ra N'Khafenu wu josu shu nanibenati." All around her body, fire split the rock until Khafenu was completely consumed.

***

*Memifi*

J'Kana was instantly returned to his seat at the Hidden Beast, his body still torn to rags and his eyes burdened with the gleam of candlelight against the golden walls.

"J'Kana!" It was Lord Babanu, surprisingly, who called his name. Nihani immediately started to tend to his wounds, and already he felt better.

"Where did you go," Chishashi asked more forcefully than intended. J'Kana met his gaze, and saw that he was far more concerned than he ever showed himself to be. It was hard for the ijeya to keep his composure now, and simply tilted his head back to keep the tears from falling.

"And what happened while you were there, because you look rough and you smell like the backside of a chitana beast after dinner," J'Chera offered. The others around the table looked at him with mouths agape and heads cocked. "What?" J'Chera's dismissive attitude was enough to bring the shadow of a smile to the corner of J'Kana's mouth, but he dared not humor it. A thousand thoughts swirled in his mind, but he knew that his friends deserved an explanation. He breathed, and tried to focus on the soothing waters that mended his body. He opened his eyes and faced the others.

"I fought her," J'Kana started bluntly. "Khafenu. I fought her." Chishashi's brow furrowed in a look of sheer astonishment.

"Come again," J'Chera demanded. "You disappeared in a cloud of shadow to go fight an Asanibo over dinnertime?" Chishashi slapped him in the back of his head.

"It clearly wasn't by choice, J'Chera," he said. "Khafenu was known for a kind of Blood Chant called the Blood Shadow. While the other Asanibo have learned her technique, none could perform it with her level of proficiency." J'Kana's mind went back to her abuse of the darkness to get inside his head, and her instantaneous transportation in the midst of battle. He needed no reminder of what she could do with it.

"Sounds creepy o. So, I take it you won," the elder ijeya asked J'Kana, who nodded solemnly.

"I also discovered the exact location of my ya…my Kanawe in the process." He couldn't bring himself to say the word. Not yet. While the question was on everyone's mind, none dared to ask it when J'Kana cried. Nihani took his head in her arms and pressed him against her in a tender hug. There, he sobbed until he could do so no longer, even as his mind swirled with thoughts of what the world could be now that he knew his father was still alive.

***

"Breathe, Kamari," J'Kana told him. Kamari sat on a dirt patch surrounded by the hutije of the Outer Grasslands. He smelled the sulfuric aroma of Mount Y'Bayeka not terribly far away, heard the cacophony of life within Kilana at his back, and felt the earth beneath his body. "Feel every change to your surroundings." J'Kana couldn't help but think back to when Y'Sawe had given him the same instruction. He continued with a wistful smile. "Every rule and wonder of this world is by Y'Kele's design. We are a part of it, and it is a part of us. Feel the connection." Kamari smiled as his every sense was engulfed in the majesty of the Grasslands and the comfort of knowing his father trained him to properly harness his ike. Then he started to wonder what it would be like to have an encounter with Y'Kele. What was the Creator God like? What did He will for His creation? "Focus, Kamari," J'Kana told him, as though he could see into his young mind.

The boy sank deeper into his ike, and even with his eyes closed could see the turquoise light drift around him. It was starting to get easier for him to hold it. The first time they'd done this training, Kamari could only sink into the ike for a few seconds before he was out of breath and sore all over, but now it bordered on a full minute. He thought about the vocabulary from a new list in the book. His Yababa had already given it to him a day ago in preparation. Now he was determined to see how much he could remember, and how it would help him build his ike.

| | | |
|---|---|---|
|  | Moleke | Set/Settle/Sit |
|  | Woata | Enough |

| | | |
|---|---|---|
|  | Tamili | Vengeance |
|  | Mechukoko | Disk/Tablet |
| 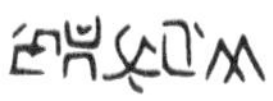 | Memibachani | Literacy |
|  | Shebili | Literature |
|  | Sikikana | Guide |
|  | Ilafikiri | Salvation/Saving |
|  | Kunono | Demon |
| 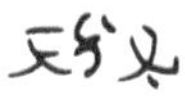 | Olebe | Temple/Church |
|  | Hera | Prayer |
| 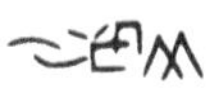 | Shemeni | Ceremony/Ritual |
|  | Samahe | Holiness/Sacredness |
|  | Samaju | Sacrament |
|  | Jebasi | Sin |
| 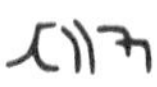 | Isike | Vessel |
|  | Juane | Nature/Natural |
|  | Ilejuane | Supernatural |
|  | Samawu | Reverence |

# 20

# Strategy and Infiltration

*Memifi—Babanu Estate*

The moment Chafi saw J'Kana again, the air in the room tensed like the muscles in a strained body. The giant of a man, clad in ornate red clothes with gold trim to match the signature of his master, had been instructed to serve them with the same fervor that nobility was due. The night they arrived, J'Kana barely spoke a word, and two days later, he was still reluctant to actively engage with Lord Babanu's right hand. It was after Chafi had brought the echa (tea) and leyeki (cakes) into the room that J'Chera thought to question it.

"So was the breakup that bad," he asked, a smile strewn across his jaw.

"Shut up, o," J'Kana uttered with an unwilling chuckle. "Our history is nothing like that."

"Besides," Chishashi said with the full effect of a pseudo-parental glare, "we need to get back on track." Nihani snickered in the background, delighted to see the two ijeya refocus from the reprimand. They cut their eyes at her, and she cleared her throat in self-correction.

"We know that Mahute has come to occupy an abandoned Batabari fortress in the Amejai Mountains to the south of J'Watuna," she recapitulated.

"We also know that if Ninikinana has returned, then the Dagger has found and made use of its resurrection chamber," Chishashi added, his voice as grave as the scowl on his face. He explained to them the implications of an active chamber, and how they were used to replenish the number of Batabari soldiers during the height of the war. They overflowed with the darkest taint of blood magic in all Y'Neshu, and if they were to be successful in stopping Mahute, they would have to destroy it before the other two Beasts could be brought back.

"There is still the matter of finding the chamber," J'Kana interjected, and took a sip of his tea. "All Khafenu showed me was a glimpse, and judging by the swarms of elokobi that roam the halls of the fortress, it doesn't sound as though we would be able to take our time and explore."

"Ehh," J'Chera groaned, just as disinterested in the strategy session as always, "I can't stand those things…"

"With any luck, we can get in undetected," Nihani suspected. Everyone around the table stared at her with a mix of concern and expectation. She looked back at them as though they should've already figured it out. She sighed, mildly exasperated as she explained. "The mountain south of J'Watuna is Berenika Mountain. You know, the home to the legendary Berenika Falls?" Chishashi and J'Kana hardly knew what that meant, but J'Chera, a native of Y'Fuwefo lit with a childish glee.

"Oh!" His sudden shout came as a surprise to his friends, as did the bump of his knee against the table. "I have always wanted to go there!" He paused for a moment as he suddenly understood what the mermaid spoke of. "Wait, does this mean that we get to ride the ubuji fish?" J'Chera looked around the table like a small child, back and forth between his comrades with his hands balled into fists that he excitedly shook up and down as he bounced in his chair.

"Only if the Laelafi-Yifusi grant us the privilege," Nihani told them. She saw that J'Kana and Chishashi still hardly understood, so she delved yet deeper in her suggestion. "Ubuji fish are known for their ability to travel between dimensions. Mostly, they exist in Berenika Falls, but they are known to travel to the North Amuneti or South Sobosa Oceans to visit with my people. If we were to enlist the help of the Guardians of the Falls who train them, then it would be theoretically possible to travel between dimensions and enter the halls of the fortress before the elokobi have the chance to notice us. Do you understand now?" The two sheltered individuals at the table nodded, Chishashi at least embarrassed that it took him so long to get it.

"And what are these fish like," J'Kana asked with an air of suspicion.

"Usually they are very sweet," Nihani answered with a smile.

"What do you mean, 'usually,' Nihani?" Chishashi's darkened turn of voice produced a nervousness in her that made the two ijeya ni stare daggers into her.

"What aren't you telling us," J'Kana prodded, but J'Chera raised his hand to stop her from saying whatever it was she was about to.

"No, no, no, no, no, no, no," he interrupted. "Whatever it is you're about to say is likely going to be the death of my childhood dreams. I will not stand for this!"

"The ubuji have been known to rip a person to shreds when they feel threatened…" she told them all slowly and let her voice trail off.

"I just told you not to tell me, o," J'Chera whined, and Nihani rolled her eyes.

"Oh, get over it already," she scolded. "The entire fate of Y'Neshu hangs in the balance and here you go, whining over your hurt feelings."

"If we could get back on subject," Chishashi redirected for the second time this afternoon. "It should be good enough to sneak in, but there is still the problem of navigating the fortress once inside."

"We should divide our number," J'Kana suggested with a thoughtful look in his eye. He took another sip of his tea, then continued. "If we stick together, it will be hard to move if we get pinned down." J'Chera shook his head, then bit into one of the tea cakes as he began to speak.

"We only have the one healer," he reasoned behind the spew of crumbs. He swallowed, wiped his mouth, then continued. "What if we get hurt but we're too far away from the other team?" His point was well understood, and the room grew quiet as all thought of another way.

"If we were to be honest with ourselves," Chishashi began slowly, and the silence around them shattered into the gentle auburn color of the bakirati wood floors, "it would be a miracle if we came out of this battle intact. Our best course of action is to do as J'Kana says. We will simply have to be more careful." J'Chera opened his mouth to argue, but the shake of Nihani's head closed it once more.

"Then what will our formation look like since we'll operate in two person teams," he asked. It was a valid question that J'Kana had already considered.

"I will go with Chishashi to confront Mahute," he answered, "while you and Nihani find a way to rescue the other Kanawe. Our goal is the resurrection chamber, but by no means should we enter it all at the same time."

"We'll go first, then," Chishashi announced, and was met with a nod of confirmation from J'Kana. "Our presence should be enough to call Mahute from his throne. While he has his hands full with us, you two slip into the room from another entrance. Open the cages, get the Kanawe to safety, and heal them. Nihani and I will be at full power inside the fortress, so you magicians need to tread with caution."

"All of this sounds good," J'Chera said with the kind of upward inflection that hinted at a "but," "but how are we going to get to J'Watuna in the first place?" J'Kana pulled the envelope from his pocket that contained the written instructions of his Yababa. His gaze lingered on it for a little while longer now that he knew what he did. The others watched him in silence, unsure what went through the gilded one's mind. J'Kana cleared his throat as he opened the folded paper to retrieve Y'Sawe's note.

"Do you remember the second day of our training in the merchant district," he asked them with his head back, eyes focused on the white floral patterns that decorated the amethyst walls.

"That was when we figured out how to move as a unit, but did so against the wrong kind of opponent,"

J'Chera reminded everyone. J'Kana tilted his head over and looked at his friend.

"And when that was over, we both got so frustrated that we—" he continued to explain, but then J'Chera understood and snapped his fingers so loudly that Chafi peeked into the room.

"Oh! You mean when we worked on our transportation command! With so much happening, I almost forgot that we had that in our arsenal." The Mermaid and Asanibo sat in silent intrigue.

"So, your Master taught you how to transport yourselves, but how far will it carry us," Chishashi asked, full of skepticism. J'Kana smirked, then shrugged.

"We don't know, but even if it won't carry us all the way there, we'll still figure something out."

"Wonderful," Chishashi said with an unenthusiastic clap. "When should we begin to put this plan into motion?"

"We'll take the week to gather supplies and practice the transportation. We should also speak with Lord Babanu about Y'Rakili's preparations for the future," the younger apprentice thought aloud. He looked around at his comrades with radiant determination. "After our affairs are settled in Memifi, we should head to Y'Fuwefo with haste."

***

*Loutu Usele*

Y'Sawe no longer had the ability to tell how much time had passed since he was captured, and wasn't sure he wanted to know either way. Y'Chifo was gone, and now the Wayi Kanawe had dwindled down to three: Y'Leisu, Y'Jaka, and himself. Even now, while he hugged the bottom of his suspended cage in the dark of the resurrection chamber, he grimaced at how unbalanced Y'Neshu had become. In the cell not far from his, Y'Jaka, the ever-resolute and unyieldingly lawful Kanawe, wept quietly with the same revelation.

***

*Memifi*

In the two days that passed since the strategy meeting, the He Ara Akira were careful to savor the extravagancies of Lord Babanu's residence. They ate from the finely polished golden trays and elegantly designed plates and bowls that Chafi chose to serve them with. They admired the library, adorned with texts from all over the continent, accented by a large map of Y'Neshu with notches that told of where the noble had traveled. Siema rolled around in the backyard, content to chase whatever sira cats that poked their heads up from belowground. J'Kana watched her as a bittersweet rumble seized his heart. He would have to leave her here while they fought. He gave her a regretful look, and decided to stroll through the streets of the city when the front door slammed loudly.

"Ebasho," exclaimed the furious voice of Lord Babanu as his footsteps thundered throughout the chohafi. J'Kana was the only one who cared to go and meet him. He found the noble in the batalu with a glass in one hand and an ornate bottle in the other.

"I take it that the conversation with Katani Ukubesi didn't go as planned?" Babanu grunted without looking up. The liquor poured into the glass with a relaxing ripple, but his anger would not be so easily assuaged.

"Ukubesi is a fool," he spat. In the next instant, the drink was flushed down Babanu's throat and then replenished by the bottle before he could feel the burn. "I gave him every reason to release J'Karo back into the hands of the public, but according to him, that kind of suggestion is a threat to Y'Rakili's security."

"Does he not understand that the Great Beasts are on the verge of returning?" J'Kana's tone was urgent as he paced the floor. He had half a mind to ask the noble for a glass of whatever cocktail he mixed next. "Our people are already in danger!"

"I know that," Babanu said coldly, his eyes firmly affixed to the glass that he rotated back and forth. "S'Katani reasons that our military is enough to handle a Beast or two, but he didn't see what they are capable of. He reasoned that if every commoner had access to the Languages of Power, then it would only stir up conflict across Y'Neshu, just as in the days of old."

"J'Karo will come back, regardless of the desires of the Katani," J'Kana protested, his arms folded across his chest. Babanu leaned against the cabinet of alcohol as he looked the boy up and down. He sipped calmly as the gears in his mind turned tirelessly. "What are you planning, Lord Babanu?"

"Well, it's just that—" he interrupted himself to take another sip of his drink. He waved his free hand about before his lips were ready to form words. "Trying to control the He wu Kiraji wu Kana will either create resistance, or give opportunity for the wrong voice to educate the people.

The balance of power right now will ultimately shift in favor of the one who controls education, and that will be determined by who takes the opportunity to reintroduce J'Karo first. If we cannot receive the support of the Katani and the Royal Court of Y'Rakili, then we should enlist the aid of those who safeguard the information…" He looked at J'Kana over his glass as he sipped again for a bit longer than before.

"Then we need to move fast," J'Kana said with a hope in his voice that pricked Babanu's ears. The nobleman moved past him, and clapped the ijeya on the shoulder with a force that nearly drove him to his knees. J'Kana smiled at him, and whispered prayers to Y'Kele through his ike alone as he wondered which was more important: the mission of the Kanawe, or the restoration of a culture.

***

Kamari sat on the floor now, his eyes closed under the dim light of the luseme. He was curious before the story began about whether or not he would be able to shift his ike as he listened. J'Kana was kind enough to let him explore. Now that his father had finished, Kamari smiled as he opened his little eyes to reveal a bright turquoise that threatened to singe the Kanawe's eyebrows. Even so, J'Kana raised one.

"So hafu wu shehefo, how do you feel?" Kamari's ike had grown strong in the last few days, but even as it did, J'Kana noticed that the lele ili made a similar mistake to the one he had long ago. Only today, it seemed as though the mistake was on the verge of correction. The little one rolled his shoulders back to loosen them.

"Hafu ra jatonawe chuwehunati, Yababa," he responded. He felt strong, and this admission brought a stare of neutrality.

"Kamari," the elder began slowly, "what is your ike?"

"It's my soul," he answered with surety. Nothing else was offered in the way of explanation, and so J'Kana continued.

"And what is your soul?" The father watched as his son opened his mouth with the full intent to answer, but found none. J'Kana smiled. "It is okay for you not to know everything. You are still very young, and there is no need to rush through the discoveries of life."

"Do you know, Yababa?" The child's question was innocent enough to bring warmth to J'Kana's aging bones. He waved the boy over to the couch and placed him on his lap.

"I do," the Kanawe enlightened. "Our ike, our soul, is more than just a source of strength in battle, just as it is more than just our life force. The ike is our very essence, the thing that makes us who we are. It allows us to connect with the world around us and the Creator of that world through a kind of touch that goes beyond words and feelings."

"But then, what is J'Karo," Kamari asked with a scratch of his head.

"By itself?" J'Kana chuckled. "It is merely a collection of words and rules. What makes J'Karo so powerful is its connection to Y'Kele and His creation. For the people of Y'Neshu, our people, language is made powerful because it carries the essence of all while maintaining an essence of its own. It is not enough for you to see things as being from a position of power or not. You have to learn to see them for what they are, and that includes yourself. No matter how long a log sits in the water, it will never be a kokojile beast." Kamari was silent for a while, and his Yababa with him. He grabbed the leather book and turned to a fresh page while the yilele looked on. "I will show you some new vocabulary. Don't just read the words this time. Stretch out your ike and ask Y'Kele what our ancestors meant when the words were forged. Let's start here…"

| | | |
|---|---|---|
|  | Katani | Emperor/King |
|  | Majene | Empress/Queen |
|  | Jolala | Prince |
|  | Betere | Princess |
|  | Walafi | Soldier |
|  | Kujeke | Rival |
| 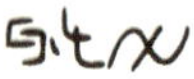 | Muata | Enemy |
|  | Bekeniya | Civilian/Commoner |
|  | Tokafi | Governor |
|  | Jelolo | Beautiful |
| 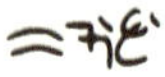 | Sacheli | Scum |
|  | Jurasha | Lieutenant |
|  | Ojichu | Addition |
|  | Fojara | Peasant |

| | | |
|---|---|---|
|  | Yujuba | Banker |
|  | Jusha | Scholar |
| 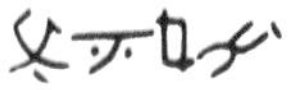 | Bayikolo | Diplomat |
|  | Yechu | Doctor |
| 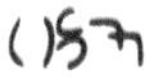 | Rureke | Farmer/Agriculturalist |
| 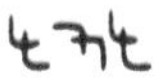 | Akea | Priest |
|  | Benari | Open |
|  | Yinari | Close |
|  | Leyeki | Cake |
| 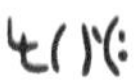 | Aluwu | Breath |
| 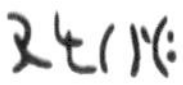 | Ealuwu | Breathe |

Little by little, Kamari's eyes were opened to the plethora of emotions that surrounded each term. He felt their meanings, who they described, who described them, and how they all came together to shape a future that still lingered beyond the horizon. J'Kana watched with pride as tears of understanding streamed from the little one's eyes.

# 21

# Falls

*Memifi*

Each day that passed felt like a millennium. J'Kana split his time between his training with J'Chera and strategizing with Lord Babanu about their silent endeavor. Nihani scoured the merchant district for medical supplies to enhance her maju takhani while Chishashi searched for bread, sausages and cheeses to take along with them. Siema, who understood that she would not be going along for the ride this time, peed on Babanu's wood floors, and while J'Kana expressed a deep remorse, the noble burst out in a hearty laugh.

"Omo it will take more than that to breach the bakirati wood of this place," he exclaimed with confidence. "And besides, I like a girl with fire and spirit!" As if on command, the little ara beast puffed out a small spark that lit her wet spot aflame. Babanu yipped in surprise, and J'Kana struggled to hold back his laughter as he scooped her up from the floor and glared into her eyes. She stared back defiantly for a moment, then her ears slumped and she averted her gaze. "Chafi!"

"I am already on it," the servant called back as he banked around the corner faster than one of the Katani's chariots.

"Yo fajari ra N'nera belenati," J'Kana commanded, and the fire went out as quickly as it started. For the first time, Chafi looked almost grateful to have the ijeya around, though it was still abundantly clear that he hadn't forgotten the trouble J'Kana had caused in the days of J'Foja. The door opened just as J'Chera emerged from one of the back rooms, curious as to why he suddenly smelled burning urine.

"We are home," Nihani called out as they walked into the shaded hall of the chohafi, then quickly grabbed her nose. "Ugh, what is that smell?"

"Your friend Siema is acting out because she has to stay here," J'Kana said with emphasis, and watched the ara cub turn her head away.

"We have the supplies," Chishashi informed as he moved into the dining room and set a few bags down on the table. J'Kana sighed, then set Siema down on the floor.

"Then we should take a few moments to pack our things," J'Kana said, much to the chagrin of J'Chera, who had already gotten used to living the high life. He muttered something under his breath as he returned to the back to get his bag.

***

An hour later, the He Ara Akira stood on the porch of Lord Babanu's estate, well supplied and as ready as they could be for what would soon transpire. Even Chishashi was nervous, and though he probably resisted, it hardly proved enough to hide it. Babanu appeared in the doorway, a now silent Siema rested in his massive hands, and smiled upon the four heroes.

"You have grown mightily," he commended J'Kana, and reached with his free hand for a handshake. "Keep going, and never let anyone tell you who you are." The

Gilded Ijeya couldn't help but smile warmly and fix his face when emotion threatened to overtake it. The noble looked to them all, and with a proud smile and a fist over his heart, he said, "Do what you must to come back to us safe. I doubt that Siema will be too pleased if she gets stuck with us…" He cut his eyes at the ara cub, but smiled playfully when she ignored him.

"Don't worry," Nihani told him, "I'll make sure they can't do anything too reckless." She gave him a wink, and then a hug as the others turned around. Siema barked out her goodbye, and together they started to walk down the street. With every step, they could feel the eyes of the people on them, each one hopeful that they would return, each one sure of their heroes' place in Memifi.

"It's strange," Chishashi said to break the tension of the moment. J'Kana looked at him, noted that the Asanibo stared straight ahead and gave no attention to the denizens of the upper district. He still furrowed his brow with a kind of confusion that was alien to his face.

"What is," J'Chera asked as they moved together. He nodded at J'Kana, and together they began to stretch out their ike. They felt the calm wash over them as their eyes registered the brilliant colors of the metal walls. Their senses heightened with the cool brush of the wind, the sounds of life in Memifi, as well as the tufts of white amid the great azure expanse of the sky. In only a few seconds, they felt connected to all creation, and as their ike started to resonate, they prepared to speak the command that would take them to Y'Fuwefo.

"No matter where you go in Y'Neshu, the Asanibo are feared. We are the monsters heard of in bedtime stories, the ones thought to lurk behind every dark door. Even the Sasabosami refuse to interact with us for fear that we will bring them ruin, yet here," he paused, unable to reconcile the thought with his tongue at first. "Here, I am celebrated, treated as a hero—"

"Because you are," J'Kana cut him off. "You have done a lot to prove yourself more than what others expect. I don't see why you should continue to put stock in the prejudice of those around you." The vampire smiled, and the four of them walked a bit further to the northern edge of the city. "Everyone ready?" The other three nodded in silence, and J'Kana took a deep breath.

"Remember," J'Chera said, "we need to walk as we give the command. At least, that was what my Kanawe always said." Wordlessly, J'Kana nodded, and together they gave themselves over to the flow of their ike. Gold intermingled with Silver, the temperature rose as if a second sun had appeared in the sky, and Chishashi and Nihani flinched back from its sting. The ike resonance reached its peak, and together the ijeya ni walked, their eyes overshadowed by the hues of their souls, while their companions followed as closely as they could. As one, the four of them focused on their destination.

"," they whispered.

Nihani watched in awe as the space around them warped under the colors of their ike. The two apprentices continued their onward march as though in a trance, focus their dominant emotion as the distortion stabilized. Within the portal they could hear an amalgamation of all the sounds of Y'Neshu, from the lowing and snorts of the chitana beasts to the laughter of the ayena. Growls of the ara beasts in the plains of Y'Rakili intertwined with the screeches of the muka in the Kehemu Forests, the hisses of filafue snakes mingled with the chirps of beetles and the snarls of the kokojile beasts that drifted as logs in the three great rivers. Brays of the abata sounded majestically through the cacophony, but were drowned out by the mighty roar of the rayemo beast. Then silence. The calls of Y'Neshuan fauna subsided with the coming of the towers of Y'Fuwefo.

They had arrived. Just beyond the alabaster gate stood the City of Spires, whose plaster and wood buildings spiraled high into the gold and silver tips that touched the clouds. Each one was adorned with patterns of plants and animals, of mystic symbols, all in a multitude of colors. The portal closed behind them, Memifi left in the distance while the He Ara Akira stared from the Outer Grasslands into the city, and J'Chera broke down in tears.

***

*J'Watuna*

All of them felt it, the pangs of grief and guilt that came with the disembodied roars of rayemo beasts. It came to them enveloped in the visions of J'Yobena's form as it ripped apart before their eyes. All of them felt helpless, and little by little the sense of power granted by the shift of their ike faded into the gloomy skies of J'Watuna.

"She should be here," J'Chera finally spoke, nostrils aflare as his eyes watered. "She should be here to let loose her anger on the monster who killed her master."

"I know," Nihani spoke with a soothing lilt. It was at times like this where she wished her voice could be anything other than the melody natural to her kind. "But if we stop here, if we allow ourselves to be controlled by our anger or grief, then it only increases the chance that Mahute gets away with it." J'Chera wiped his face.

"I know you're right," he sniffled. "I know that J'Yobena would be hitting me if she could see me like this. But I can't help how I feel."

"Nobody is asking that of you, o," J'Kana assured him. The junior ijeya approached his senior, and lay a hand of comfort upon his shoulder. "Use it. Every rotten thing that has happened to you since the day you were born. Our battle with the Dagger cannot afford to spare the truth of our existence, and it is through that truth that we will ultimately prove to every force in the world that J'Yobena existed too." The elder student lifted his head to the gray skies and inhaled deeply. His body shook for a moment as the storm of emotions raged for a minute more, but when it subsided, he was full of a kind of fury and flame that bore resemblance to his lost friend.

"Let's go," he finally said. "And J'Kana? Thank you."

"Don't mention it. For now, let us reach Berenika Falls."

"So that was your plan," the voice of Y'Leisu chimed from behind them. All four whipped around to stare into the deep green eyes lightly covered by the white mane that adorned her head. "Use the ubuji fish to get inside, and then what? Rescue Y'Sawe and the others from Mahute?" Something about the way she spoke alerted the He Ara to the danger they were in. Even so, J'Chera was happy to see her. It was only when he witnessed her eyes wash black that his denial fell to pieces.

"Kanawe, chilu otaba ra bibisanati e," J'Chera asked. *What are you saying, Master?* Y'Leisu only laughed as she stared them down, a fanged suchara serpent in human form. He dared ask nothing else when she refused to answer, but instead whispered to his comrades, "Something feels off." J'Kana already knew, but didn't have the heart to tell his friend of his suspicions, that something had been off with her since their encounter in the Kehemu. Together they watched as she moved closer, a sinister quality to her otherwise angelic appearance.

"You know," she started as she pointed to J'Kana, "when I helped you in the forest, I simply wanted to see how far you could make it before Mahute and his Generals captured you. I didn't think you would make it far, but I thought that the maa bacha would even the playing field enough to give the old Dagger a challenge. But, you see, the Generals are off the board, one of the Great Beasts has been destroyed, and I have grown tired of playing this game with you."

"Master, is he controlling you," J'Chera demanded with more authority than he should ever be allowed to take with a Kanawe. She grinned with all the wicked intent of the Asanibo that attacked Shifi.

"It would be more accurate to say that *I* am controlling *him*," she corrected, and J'Chera's eyes widened with sorrow before they narrowed in abject disgust. "Who do you think helped him track down Y'Sawe? Or helped to keep his escape from Febetu a secret long enough for the brothers to meet in Memifi? Who do you think tipped off the guards in Ekutali, or oversaw the Dagger's little experiment in Shifi that night a decade ago?" The four were dumbstruck. Every moment where it seemed their luck had been horrid, for all the times it seemed that Y'Kele Himself caused them to stumble, it was one of their own.

"Why," J'Chera asked softly. He quaked with rage, and a malevolent force welled up deep within him.

Y'Leisu, wrapped in her white jilaba wu ajiwele, crossed her arms before her chest, and lifted her hand to rest in front of her mouth as she laughed.

"What does it matter," she asked in return. Darkness swirled high above their heads, and with a thunderclap, rain descended upon them. "Do you want to hear that it was some kind of survival tactic? That I turned over my fellow Kanawe to ensure I would remain? Or perhaps you want me to admit that I acted in the interest of protecting you." The more she spoke, the harder J'Chera breathed.

"J'Yobena died because of you!" His voice boomed with the thunder, and Y'Leisu narrowed her eyes in preparation. "And you looked us in the face not two days after, acting as though you were our saviors!"

"I would remind you to watch your tone with me, you sacheli wu kashinawe sekiti." The bite to her tone was like an arrow to J'Chera's heart. His face darkened and his eyes went cold. "You were nothing more to me than some means of passing the time, and before you even had the chance to bore me, I found other ways of keeping myself entertained. Mahute intrigues me, and at least for the time being, he doesn't show any signs of growing tiresome."

"So that's all this is to you," J'Chera growled, "the fruit of your childish pursuit of amusement." He breathed out sharply, the tremble in his body subsided, and he basked in an ethereal calm that only made his comrades more nervous. Y'Leisu's eyebrows raised as the scowl on her face was overshadowed by an intrigued smirk.

"Eke, J'Chera," the darkbright Kanawe almost sang as her twisted delight rippled through the air. "It almost sounds as though you wish to challenge me."

"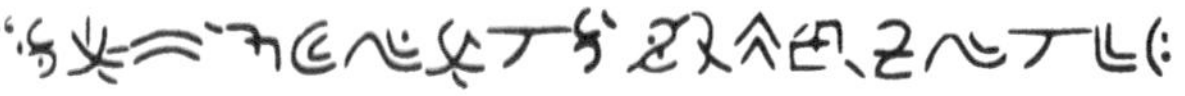

." The elder apprentice spoke commands at a rapid pace, and the traitor Y'Leisu was nearly caught off guard. She cackled as the wall of fire enclosed her like a wild beast.

"To kham basi ye tuzo," the Teacher spoke in aggressive Batabari. She gasped as her palms split open from the utterance of the phrase, and through the flames they could see her smile. "Kha ja lekhan ja fajari a gbakuyim o!" The fire dissipated, doused by the power of Batabari blood magic, and the moment the flames faded, the angelic demon had to roll along the ground to evade the spears of earth that waited for her.

Ten spears lunged one after the other, and with each new projectile, the Kanawe had to alter her direction. Before she could clear the last of the stone weapons, J'Chera started up again. "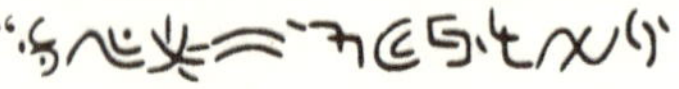 ," he spoke with great speed. The ground beneath her softened enough to sink her weight within it, but with sinister confidence, the turncoat spoke a reply.

"Bushake we fiyim ku bobo ja basi we a gbayim." Her tone was as cold as the black of her eyes. The ground that surrounded her fractured like ice under a hammer, and whips of blood carried her out of the crater. "N'lekhan a gbatabayim."

"," J'Chera commanded. He walked forward, even as the blood whips on which his Master walked lashed out at him with a violence that exceeded anything Chishashi could manage. She laughed at him, but he let himself be taken over by his ike as J'Kana's words swirled within his mind. *Use it. Every rotten thing that has happened to you since the day you were born.* He started to whisper again, this time something similar to what had brought them to Y'Fuwefo.

"."

Behind Y'Leisu, all reality seemed to distort in a silver light. When she noticed it, she slashed at the openings with all the fury she could channel into the blood whips, but it was far too late for that. She turned back to J'Chera, a grave look on her face.

"When did you learn how to tear a rift? Such a thing should be beyond someone like you," she growled, then pushed off the ground with the full force of the whips and lunged for her former apprentice. One of the strands pierced through his protective airfield, and forced him to roll along the ground.

"," he said as he eyed the portal. The ground produced a dome inside of a dome inside of another dome to protect him from the fierce lashes of the whips. J'Chera began to sweat beneath the fall of the rain, but all that happened beyond his field of vision proved mere background noise to him. There, from deep within the portal came the same cacophony of sounds that they'd heard upon their arrival. This time, he gave himself over to the echoes of Y'Kele's creation, and as the brilliant silver in his eyes gleamed brighter still, the fierce roar of the rayemo beast sounded once again.

Y'Leisu heard the sound herself and watched as four of the majestic felines emerged from the rip in space. They were bigger than those they'd encountered in the Kehemu, their coats lush and golden brown, their black manes alive with an air current that disrupted the atmosphere of the battlefield. A roar from the largest one signaled the others to begin their assault on the traitor. All the lashing of her chains meant nothing to the rayemo, who ran along the air currents and roared the blood away. It was all that Y'Leisu could do to protect herself, and just as she dodged the hand-sized teeth of a passing beast, the shrieks of the muka could be heard in the distance.

Ten of them burst through the portal and ran straight for the stone spears that lay strewn around the plain. As they lunged forward, J'Chera jumped back to establish distance and give himself the opportunity to speak again. He opened his mouth, but was blindsided by the crack of a blood whip across his face. He spiraled through the hutije grass, but before he could stop, another strike launched him airborne. A rayemo caught him before he could fall and allowed him to take his place on the beast's back. He noticed that spheres of blood circled the battlefield, and through them the whips traveled to their intended targets. He grimaced, just as another whip struck his back.

"J'Chera!" J'Kana's voice rose through the chaos. He ran onto the battlefield, dodged through the forest of violent blood and beasts, and started to chant as the sky lit with lightning overhead. "[illegible]!" The younger ijeya reached for the clouds and lightning struck at his palm. He dodged the swing of a muka beast's spear as he clasped his hands together and pulled them apart to reveal a chain made of the very lightning he summoned. He let his ike swell, focused it within him and pictured the person he wanted to see the future of the most. His eyes lit with the might of maa bacha, and when Y'Leisu came into view, so too did the bloody constructs she controlled.

J'Chera watched as his friend ran through the battlefield, careful never to let the electrical chains touch the ground. Y'Leisu's attacks came, but for every one, J'Kana met it with one of his own. The blood that formed them liquified and spattered the greens and blues of hutije grass and tukali grain with red. A pair of rayemo and half of the muka beasts followed the path that he created, and J’Chera steered his mount to the opposite flank.

“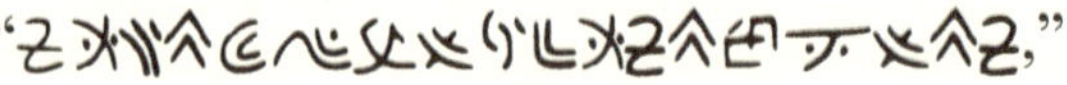,” he commanded with thunder in his tone. The sky burst with streams of lightning that surrounded the airstream of the rayemo beast. The remaining muka, stone spears in hand, followed behind them as they ripped through the white-clad Kanawe’s constructs with rage and force.

“Interesting,” she muttered as a bead of sweat slid down her face. She scanned the battlefield for anything she could use to quell the pressure these na ijeya ni applied, and smiled when she saw the gathering of people by the gates of the town. For a moment, it struck her as strange that she would dare strike at those she once swore to protect, but it was either them or her, and nothing in the world would make her forsake herself again… She revolved one hand around the other, and the blood that covered the Outer Grasslands formed spears that gathered line after line above her head. She gave a sinister chuckle as she extended her arm towards the gate.

The bystanders gasped, thunder roared, and with an urgent command the two ijeya raised a layered wall of earth to shield the people of J’Watuna. Shadows wrapped around

Y'Leisu as the two apprentices watched, and with the cracking of the thunder, she was gone.

***

*J'Watuna—Y'Maya Inn*

Rain poured over the city, and forced the Four Ara into the lobby of the local inn to stay dry. It, like nearly every other building in J'Watuna, was a mountainous spire that twisted high above the earth, and within were various paintings and sculptures that betrayed the artisanal flair of Y'Fuwefo's capital. Chishashi and Nihani approached the front desk and paid for their rooms while J'Kana sat with J'Chera near the window. For a while, neither of them said anything. Nihani and Chishashi came to let them know the rooms were ready, and opted to take a short reprieve. Neither of the ijeya moved. J'Kana couldn't help but stay by his friend's side, even if J'Chera had nothing to say. It was when the rumble of rain and thunder reached its peak that he decided the contrary.

"She was like a mother to me," he started quietly. He didn't want anyone to hear the heartbreak in his voice. "The Maanu Tribe are of the lowest class of people here in Y'Fuwefo. By all rights, I shouldn't even be able to tread the ground of J'Watuna because of the caste my people were born into. We were fit to be slaves and little else, until one day Y'Leisu heard me speak a smattering of Y'Maju to a passing Mamiwatu. She asked if I knew anything else, and when she heard me speak a bit of Katsedu, she…" he paused, his eyes narrowed on the space between the droplets of rain. "She told me I was just interesting enough to become her apprentice." There was a shudder to his voice as the words crossed his lips. "Even now, this jilaba wu ajiwele is the only reason I am allowed through the city gates."

"You are allowed here," J'Kana spoke evenly, "because of the good you provide to your people. Regardless of how they have treated you, you still protect them, and you make them laugh uncontrollably as well."

"My Master called me 'scum of low class,' J'Kana," he said with a deep pain barely hidden behind his reddened eyes. His lip quivered, and he knew that if another word was spoken on the subject, he wouldn't be able to control his tears anymore.

"A traitor underestimated your value," J'Kana corrected. "If all she saw when she looked at you was a construct of Y'Fuwefo, then she never saw you at all. My Kanawe once said something when he was trying to teach me to shift my ike better. He told me that people become what they want to become. You wanted to be more than a slave, and so here you are. You are a commander of J'Karo, one of the Four Ara Beasts of Y'Rakili, our friend, and even more than that." J'Chera chuckled as the tears finally fell.

"Where do you come up with this stuff," the senior student asked, then wiped his face. J'Kana shrugged.

"I have no idea, I grew up on the streets," he told him with a smile. "The best I can tell you is that I have seen a lot in you, M'ba Ijeya. I only want you to see what I do." The rain continued to pour as if Y'Kele wished to replace the land with sea. J'Kana slapped his knee as he stood from the table. "I am going to rest a while; give the sky a chance to stop crying so we can finish all this."

"You go ahead," J'Chera told him warmly. He turned to face the window again and let the patter of droplets against the spire replenish his ike. "I think I'll sit for a while longer."

***

*J'Watuna—Y'Maya Inn*

Some time after the Four had fallen asleep, so too did the rain. Nihani was the first one awake, alerted by the decrease of moisture in the air as the sun rose to take its place in the heavens. She hummed as she dressed herself, then left her room to find Chishashi and J'Kana already in the hall. She raised an eyebrow.

"Where is J'Chera," she asked, her voice an anxious melody in their ears. Chishashi and J'Kana looked at each other, shrugged, wordlessly, then looked back at the empty space that once held Nihani's form. She had already started down the corridor towards the room of the Y'Fuwefo native. She knocked on the door, but when she received no answer, her sense of alarm escalated so that she knocked once more. When J'Chera failed to respond for the second time, she opened his door and found him sprawled upon the bed with his mouth open wide enough to catch a whole muka beast. She stood in the doorway for only a second before she spoke to the Divine Waters and summoned a water whip to lash at his ankles.

"Ahh! I'm up, I'm up!" She giggled at his alarm.

"Don't you know how rude it is to make people wait," she asked. He rubbed his eyes and yawned as he stretched, then quickly hopped out of bed and scoured the room for his jifona and shiki.

"I didn't know we were all in such a rush to stare death in the face again," he quipped as he started to dress. Nihani shrugged and placed her hand on the doorknob.

"You would think you would be used to it by now," she replied, which made him smile. She closed the door behind her and headed back to the others. They raised their brows as they awaited her report. She flashed a quick grin as she headed for the steps. "He's on his way."

***

*J'Watuna—Berenika Falls*

The march south only took about an hour, and for the first time in a long while, J'Kana had no sense of dread about his life. No Asanibo threatened to distort his senses, no elokobi emerged from the grass around him, and at the present moment, nothing but the future threatened his life. He and the others merely walked the path that led to the mountain, and it felt…weird. It shouldn't have, as it was such an ordinary thing to do, but the last two months had been such a strange experience for him that the ordinary didn't seem to have a place in his life anymore.

They came to the base of the Berenika Mountain, the last in the Amejai Mountain Range and one of the highlights of northern Y'Neshu altogether. Even though the Falls were much higher up, they could hear the crash of water from the ground. There was a sense of mystique that surrounded the path as they began their incline, and the further they traveled, the more they felt as though this place was one to be revered. J'Chera's excitement restored itself little by little, but Chishashi remained uneasy.

"We are being watched," he whispered to his comrades, to which Nihani only smiled.

"The Laelafi-Yifusi are known to do that," she explained. "They are guardians of the sacred waters of the falls and administer healing to those in need so long as they prove themselves worthy." J'Chera glanced behind him and raised an eyebrow at her.

"How do you know so much about them, Nihani?" She shrugged in answer.

"When a Jeniju is chosen by their Wekhala, one of the first things we are shown is the shrine at Berenika Falls. Long ago, before the Thousand-Year War when all mermaids were unified as Makhewe, there was a man from the Watuna Village who was rich and powerful. The man believed his wealth to be the source of all that was good in his life, from the food that he ate to the comfort his family enjoyed. It is said that the caste system of Y'Fuwefo started with his greed and overindulgence. One day, the man's only son, heir to all that he had, fell ill with an incurable disease as punishment for his father's actions. The man spent all he had to cure his son of the illness, but it was only after he lost everything that he realized there was no cure that money could buy. Despondent, the man climbed to the heights of the Berenika Mountain, where he discovered three maidens, beautiful in form, sun-kissed like his people, but with moonlike eyes encircled by ocean blue."

"He found mermaids in the mountains," J'Chera asked incredulously, but then realized where they were when Nihani started this story. "Never mind." She gave a light chuckle as they marched on.

"He watched them as they knelt before the Falls, their heads lifted to Y'Khali and voices lent to the maju takhani, the healing melody. The man, overcome with the gentle harmony of the mermaids' song and a desperation to save his only son, revealed himself to them with his head bowed low to the ground. 'Have mercy,' he begged, 'I do not know what to do.' Yemoja, the Queen of the Makhewe, picked his head up from the stone and stared into his eyes. She could see all that he had done, all the waste that he had created and the example that it set for the people of Y'Fuwefo. But she could also see how deeply he longed to protect his child. He had learned the value of life and the nature of Y'Khali's design all through his efforts to save his little boy, and so he proved himself worthy of the healing. Yemoja took a small pot and transferred some of the waters of the mountain into it. 'Have him drink this,' she told the man, 'and all will be well.' He blessed her as he took it, then began the journey back to the village of Watuna where his son lay sick and waiting. The moment the boy drank the water, his body was healed. Right then, the father fell down and blessed Y'Khali, and he swore that he would never forget the kindness shown to him that day." They neared the top of the mountain, and the crash of the waterfall grew in its strength.

There in the path stood a lone warrior, clad in a blue robe adorned with silver constellations. His head was devoid of hair, and his deep green eyes spoke of a devotion to this place that should never be called into question, as did the silver spear he held in his hand. Nihani stepped forward, and so did three other warriors hidden in the brush and rock of the mountain. The air intensified, and as the ubuji fish, adorned in teal and green scales with eyes that resembled a starry night appeared before them, J'Kana, J'Chera and Chishashi stood resolved to face whatever came next.

"Are they worthy to tread these sacred grounds," the leader asked the Jeniju. His brow furrowed and nostrils flared at the sight of the Asanibo among them. "You dare bring *his* kind here?" Nihani raised a hand with a calming elegance that proved more authoritative than any would have thought. It was all she needed to calm him.

"These are the ones who will protect all Y'Neshu," she answered, a strange magnanimity in her voice. "They have lost much, but never has their focus waned." The leader looked back over them, a skepticism in his eyes that could not be overstated.

"Jekoro shu malanati," he commanded, and his warriors took their places before the ijeya ni and Asanibo. J'Kana watched the young man before him place his free hand on his shoulder, and motioned for the ijeya to reciprocate. He reached out with apprehension, but the moment he made contact with his reviewer, he felt a kind of vulnerability that he couldn't describe, as though the warrior had opened the door to his deepest thoughts and insecurities. Then, in an instant, it was done.

"What just happened," J'Kana asked with labored breath as sweat dripped from his brow down the tip of his nose. He looked to the other two, who were just as easily exhausted as he was.

"They are worthy," the three defenders shouted in militant fashion, and their leader returned his focus to Nihani. He bowed to her, his spear gripped in both hands and pointed to the sky before him. The other Laelafi-Yifusi followed suit, and formed a circle of reverence around the mermaid.

"Forgive me," he spoke, the sincerity in his voice of the highest degree as his eyes bore into the ground. "After everything that's happened, we can't afford to be careless."

"It is no trouble at all," Nihani spoke with the regality of a queen. She bade them stand, and they snapped to attention in an instant. "Now that that's settled, though," the mermaid continued with a begrudged smile that somehow still conveyed her determination, "we have a favor to ask."

***

"Yababa?" Kamari's voice broke through the story, his tone quizzical as he looked up at his father. "The J'Karo in this part was too fast. There was so much to think about and so little time to do it!"

"I will admit, that can happen," J'Kana said with a squeeze of the shoulders. "But there is a trick to that, shehefo."

"There is? Tell me! Tell me!" Kamari beamed with anticipation. J'Kana retrieved the leather book of J'Karo and turned back to the list of particles.

"Look here," he started, and pointed to the familiar symbols. "You remember these, ne?"

"Of course," the little one said with bursting confidence. "Each particle tells of a different part of speech. They help us make sense of what is said." J'Kana nodded, pleased that his son proved to be such a bright child.

"But did you know they have another function?" The question caused Kamari to look up to him with curiosity all about his face. "Take the subject particle, ne? Think about what the subject is."

"The subject is what we are talking about right now," Kamari answered with intense focus. J'Kana chuckled at his seriousness. He wondered if all this study was taking away his ability to be a child.

"That is correct, shehefo. But as you understand it, the subject is usually something concrete, like a person or place or thing. What if I told you that you've already seen it applied more to abstract concepts like feelings or positions or thoughts?"

"Like when you overloaded me with the Kanawe Summit," Kamari guessed, which brought a full laugh from his father's belly.

"Exactly," he affirmed, "or when I wanted to be shown my Master's location. I said, 'Ti nata hafu wu Kanawe harana ra N'hafu shu bibisanati,' but you notice, I only apply the subject marker after the first verb. 'Ti nata hafu wu Kanawe harana,' means 'Where is my Teacher,' or 'Where my Teacher is,' if we were to translate into Pedestrian directly. Why would that be marked with subject 'Ra?'"

"Because that is what you were talking about," Kamari realized. "You weren't speaking only of your teacher, but of Kanawe Y'Sawe's location." J'Kana nodded in approval.

"And it was after I established the subject that I gave the object, me, and finished the command with a verb to act on that object, 'bibisanati.' Do you see what is happening?"

"I do," Kamari said, "but I don't know how to explain it." J'Kana chuckled.

"That's okay, I can do that part for you. The particles you see all throughout the sentences of J'Karo create little pieces of the idea you want to communicate. When you can identify the pieces as they are intended, it becomes easier to understand the whole idea. Baunanati e?" The little one nodded.

"So then I have to practice spotting the different places where the particles shift," the boy said with a seriousness that made his father worry a little.

"Yes, but for the time being, let us focus on building your vocabulary a little bit more. The next part of our story is a long one, with a bit more J'Karo but used in interesting ways. I hope you are excited ulu Kamari. You never quite know what to expect in Y'Neshu."

| | | |
|---|---|---|
| 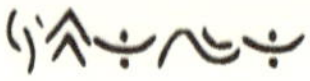 | Shunawatewa | Snare/Trap |
|  | Watewa | Net |
|  | Yisu | White |
|  | Naba | Black |
|  | Ebu | Blue |
|  | Rohi | Red |
|  | Fefo | Green |
|  | Mije | Purple |
|  | Leshi | Yellow |
|  | Rele | Gold |
|  | Boshu | Gray |
|  | Nuwe | Brown |
|  | Mushe | Orange |
|  | Jafu | Silver |
|  | Nile | Pink |
|  | Wawe | City |
|  | Chewe | Village |
|  | Chuku | Tribe/Community |
|  | Tua | Clan |

| | | |
|---|---|---|
| | Lifike | Country |
| | Ushe | Region/District |
| | Bashani | Continent |

# 22

# Realm of Darkness

*Berenika Mountain—Berenika Fortress*

The ubuji fish rippled into the shadows of the fortress as though they splashed into a fresh pond, and immediately J'Kana and J'Chera felt their power wane. Chishashi breathed out a partial roar, and a dark aura shaded his features as his power spilled out of him.

"Well, I'm glad *he* can feel something," J'Chera joked. The fish swam about the air for a moment before, one by one, they splashed away, back to the Falls from whence they traveled. He looked around at the great stone walls, the Batabari text etched into every brick, the high arches and the various walkways that loomed overhead. He looked back at J'Kana then again at their dark surroundings. "You fought *here*?"

"Now is not the time for that," Nihani interrupted as she moved through their formation and looked around at the five open paths that stretched out from their position. "Chishashi, where would the chamber be?" The Asanibo hesitated to answer. His eyes flickered between yellow and red, and the muscles of his body pulsed with the power that flowed through them. "Chishashi?" The second mention of his name pricked his ears and brought him back to the moment. He groaned as the talons on his hands flexed open and closed.

"I'm sorry," he strained. The vampire took a moment to regain his sensibilities, then answered with the same calm hardness that he always displayed. "From what I know, the resurrection chamber should be several floors below us."

"Fantastic," J'Kana groaned. "Any idea what kind of welcoming committee we should expect?" Chishashi inhaled deeply, then exhaled. His eyes narrowed as his shoulders trembled with fear.

"There are thousands of them," he shuddered. "Elokobi are everywhere. It will be impossible to sneak around them." J'Kana flashed a cunning smile.

"Do you think that I had the opportunity to sneak around every time I stole something," he asked them with a bit more pride than intended. They all turned to look at him. "More often than not I was discovered with my hand in the leyeki pan, so I learned to improvise. If we cannot go around, then we go through, and I have just the idea to pull it off." His smile grew wider with a kind of deviousness that felt more like the J'Foja in the stories they'd heard, rather than the J'Kana they all had come to know.

"Does anyone else feel uncomfortable," J'Chera asked, but the others were far too stunned to answer. "Just me? Okay…" J'Kana let the excitement overtake him and feed into his diminished ike. He once again drew on the chill afforded by the shadows, the stillness of the citadel, the barely perceptible breaths of his friends. When his ike swelled up within him, he smiled as he focused on their party. In his mind, he saw Chishashi's intensity, felt J'Chera's powerful clap to his back, and heard the otherworldly melody that was Nihani's voice.

"Yibe elokobi ni ra N'hafu ni shu malana, chiweyu wu baeshanawe baeri kelenati."

"What did you just do," Nihani asked from the depth of her discomfort. J'Kana said nothing, but in the case of J'Chera, nothing needed to be said. The elder ijeya had to hold his mouth to keep the eruption of laughter in check.

"Oh, Sekejayishu Y'Kele," he exclaimed, far louder than a member of a stealth team should, "that's great! You, hafu wu M'ba ijeya, have come a long way since the Summit."

"Can you keep your voice down," Chishashi asked with great irritation. He started to move towards the second to last pathway on the left as he shook his head in exasperation. "J'Kana, let's go ahead and move out. That way, if the elokobi swarm this location, J'Chera can deal with them himself." J'Kana laughed, almost in an attempt to bring them here so he could see the results of his command.

"Unbelievable," Nihani muttered. They heard a dragging sound against the stone floor somewhere in the darkness around them. Quickly, she took hold of J'Chera's arm and pulled him down the rightmost pathway to begin their search.

***

*Berenika Fortress—Eastern Path*

Not even ten minutes down the path, J'Kana and Chishashi found themselves faced with a wall of elokobi, wrapped in the vines and foliage that now protruded from their flesh. Their eyes were white, and their arms outstretched as they shambled to and fro down the length of the corridor. Before they could be seen, the Asanibo and the ijeya hid behind one of the pillars that lined the hall. Chishashi allowed the yellows of his eyes to turn red as the power of his blood magic seeped into him to greater measure, but when he stepped forward to attack, J'Kana held up his hand.

"What are you doing," growled the vampire. "I can take them down myself!" J'Kana shot him a look, and Chishashi was yet unamused.

"As if I would let *you* start the fun on *my* command," he told him, and without another word, emerged from his hiding place with a loud shout that, in any other case, would have been comical. The elokobi hissed, growled, roared as they tracked the direction of the sound, and then, without warning, the first to see him exploded, and then the three who saw the explosion followed suit. J'Kana laughed hysterically as he walked the hall and watched his enemies break apart from his presence.

From behind, Chishashi heard another shift of dragging feet. He prepared himself for the fight, waited for them to come into view, but was caught by surprise when they began to detonate without cause. Every time they exploded, the sound resonated through the darkness to the depths of the fort, and all the vampire could do now was stare at J'Kana. He ran after him, caught up, and from the height of incredulity, asked the wily apprentice, "*This* is what you chose to do? Wouldn't it have been more discreet to try and take them out from the shadows?" J'Kana shrugged dismissively with the biggest smile on his face. It was clear now that he was playing.

"It would've been tiresome to try and fight our way through with so many enemies to speak of," J'Kana reasoned lightheartedly. "This way, they take care of themselves while the four of us are free to look for the resurrection chamber." Chishashi jumped at the sudden bursting of an elokobi that lurked around the corner, but calmed as the others around it exploded all the same. "Normally I would say that we should run with this many enemies after us, but honestly it's kind of fun watching them pop, don't you think?" The vampire was speechless. He didn't know whether to address J'Kana's intelligence, or the darkness that this place seemed to bring out of him. All he knew for sure was that the quicker they found Y'Sawe and the other Kanawe, the quicker they could leave for somewhere safe.

***

*Berenika Fortress—Western Path*

Nihani ran as the grunts and screeches of the elokobi drew nearer, and J'Chera, swept up in her fear, ran alongside her. She smacked him on the arm as they turned a corner.

"What was that for," the ijeya gasped with a smile plastered to his face. She cut her eyes at him and hit him again for playing dumb.

"You know what you did," she all but snarled between breaths. "If you had just kept your mouth shut, we wouldn't be in this mess!"

"Oh, come now," J'Chera said in his best attempt to soothe her. "You should've heard what J'Kana's command wa—" He cut himself off as the realization came to him. He stopped running, much to the alarm of his Jeniju companion, and simply stood in the path with his eyes on to the shadows.

"What are you doing, you idiot?" J'Chera said nothing in response to Nihani's panic, but stood with the biggest smile on his face. The elokobi dragged themselves forward from the dark, the vines that grew from their skin alive and in search of living flesh to devour.

"Oye!" The heads of the monsters all snapped up in search of the source of the sound, and when they saw J'Chera and Nihani, they exploded like overripened fruit in summertime. J'Chera stumbled with his laughter and lazily flailed his hands before his chest while Nihani blinked in confused astonishment. "I knew I liked that J'Kana!"

"Whatever," the mermaid said, and took hold of her comrade's arm again. "We have a job to do, you know." J'Chera rolled his eyes as he allowed himself to be dragged along.

"Whatever you say, Waleya," he mocked, but smiled even bigger when another wave of enemies came and went.

***

*Loutu Usele—Resurrection Chamber*

Mahute the Dagger sat on the throne in the chamber and rested his head against his palm as he looked out over the stone and flame and shadow. His Three Generals had been defeated, and Ninikinana returned to oblivion, but even as his palace began to quake with the commotion beyond this room, Mahute was more amused than he was worried.

"They did it," Y'Sawe exclaimed from his suspended cage. He moved to the edge and sat near the bars. "My apprentice and his friends have arrived!" Mahute laughed darkly.

"You say that as though it gives you hope, ulu esho," he said dismissively. His eyes narrowed on the golden double doors shrouded in the shadows beyond the pillars and flame. From his sleeve, the Dark One retrieved a vial filled with a blackened crust. He waved a hand and watched eagerly as it returned to the fluid blood it had once been. He pulled the cork, and after he had taken the blood into his body, chuckled as he told his brother, "I look forward to crushing it in front of you."

***

*Berenika Fortress—Grand Hall*

"The way down should be over here," Chishashi called to J'Kana as they ran through the remnants of an old dining hall. Chishashi could hear the triumphant calls of countless Batabari, all faded into the backdrop of Y'Neshuan history. He bit his lip hard enough to break the skin, and forced his reddened eyes to revert to their yellow state. Behind them, the floor began to collapse as more elokobi met their explosive end and the force of their swift detonation overpowered the stability of the architecture.

"Safe to say that I did *not* think this one through," J'Kana thought aloud. Chishashi held his tongue. It was hard enough to keep himself under control as they moved deeper within the castle. His head throbbed, his teeth ground, and his senses heightened. He could feel it. Something within the chamber called to him…

"Oye!" It was J'Chera who called to them, Nihani in tow as they strove to outrun the collapse of the floor. "You didn't really think this one through, did you?"

"We've already established that," Chishashi growled as they all banked towards the door at the righthand side of the room. He knocked through it on the strength of his shoulder, and took to the spiral staircase with feeling. The others followed, just as the floor behind them broke completely. A cloud of dust erupted through the doorway and coated the He Ara with enough force to nearly knock them over. When it subsided, everyone took turns slapping J'Kana on the arm.

"Okay, I get it," he said as Nihani struck him last. "How was I supposed to know that was going to happen?" J'Chera pressed a palm against his temple.

"Didn't your Kanawe ever teach you about the dangers of a poorly spoken word," he asked. J'Kana folded his arms across his chest and glared at his friend. He couldn't help but take it personally, given everything he had learned about Ile Kanawe Y'Sawe over the last few days.

"Not in any depth, what with him being kidnapped shortly after taking me in, o." The retort sobered everyone instantly. J'Kana gave them all a look as he pushed past them. He looked down the spiral into the darkness below. From the pouches in his cloth belt, he pulled a single Bashele coin and let it fall. They waited in silence for a few moments, but when they heard it ring against the stone floor at the bottom, he began to walk. "We should move. We can't be far from the chamber now."

Even with the threat of an unstable floor gone, the He Ara moved with haste as they repeatedly rounded the staircase. Every step took them closer to a place where monsters were made and darkness beckoned. Every step raised the speed and power of their heartbeats, and as the air grew colder and light faded from their sight, each of them could feel how easy it would be to go the way of Mahute.

"Get ready," Chishashi told them as they reached the bottom of the stairs. Before them stood monumental double doors, gold in color and surrounded by the black stone walls of a mountain cave. On them were engraved images of men and women of Batabari glory, garbed in ornate armor with swords in hand as they liberated their enemies of various body parts. While J'Kana, J'Chera and Nihani stared at the carvings, Chishashi approached a bowl to the left side of the door. "J'Kana," he summoned as he rolled up the sleeve of his left arm, "help me with this." He started toward the door, but then turned back to look at J'Chera and Nihani.

"You two find a separate entrance," he told them seriously. "Stay out of sight until you hear the battle start. Help the Kanawe and then get them out."

"Be careful," Nihani told J'Kana with a hug that raised his temperature a few degrees. She let him go, and noted his sad smile.

"You, too." J'Chera and Nihani walked into the darkness to tend to their mission while J'Kana took his place on the right side of the door. "So, what do we do?" Chishashi cut his palm without a word while the Gilded Ijeya looked on. He shrugged. "Alright, then." He mimicked the gesture, and together they held their open hands above the bowls before them. Slowly the wounds dripped, but as the blood fell, the space within the bowls warped and skewed. The door glowed faintly as the air around them swirled then stilled. J'Kana blinked, and with firmness of mind he commanded in J'Karo, "Reshinati."

***

*Loutu Usele—Resurrection Chamber*

The many black columns of the room lit with their red flames caused the two to marvel. All around them stood the statues of Batabari warriors long past, steeped in darkness now just as they had been in life. The room was circular, with an array of the black pillars every few feet. The great stone tablet pulsed with their arrival, and every step they took toward the center of the room filled them with a higher sense of dread. All around them they could hear the screams of those sacrificed for profane ritual. Flashes of the damned appeared and then vanished in the dark between the flames. There, upon the throne that overlooked it all, rested the Dagger that worked to rend the heart of all Y'Neshu had ever known. He spread his hands wide in welcome.

"To think that I would be visited by my nephew of his own free will," the commander of vampires said with a smile. He rested his back against the throne and looked down on J'Kana just as Chishashi stared at him. "I will admit, I never imagined a mere boy to be able to overcome my Generals, much less Ninikinana. It is almost enough to impress me."

"And why would I care anything about that," J'Kana replied as he moved to the edge of the stone tablet. He stared down at it for a moment, surprised that he looked for any trace of Khafenu's body, but when he saw that there was nothing left of her, he decided to stand triumphantly on the slab. "You have tried to kill me several times over, and now you act as if your opinion has sway with me?" Mahute gave a half-hearted chuckle.

"So defiant," he spoke calmly, and rose from his exalted seat to descend the stairs before him. "But then, you who are strong enough to stand before me have earned the right to speak your mind."

"That right is not yours to give," J'Kana retorted, and Mahute narrowed his brows in scrutiny.

"Isn't it, though, siwebawu?" He stepped onto the platform opposite the ijeya and his khimbenzi friend. This close, J'Kana could see the red hue of Mahute's iris. He drew power from this place just as Chishashi did. "Look at what I have done for Y'Neshu. I have destabilized the governments that would oppress our people and removed the 'Teachers' who would rob them of education and heritage."

"You have destroyed countless lives, created monsters, and betrayed your family," J'Kana fired back. Mahute's dark eyes affixed to the boy, and the unpredictable criminal began a methodical pace about the tablet.

"It is because I did those things that the root of my plan has taken hold," he answered coldly. "The entire continent is in chaos. Kanawe turn on each other. 'Terrorist attacks' threaten the peace and prosperity of the Four Empires for the first time since the end of the war. Even as I labor, government leaders actively seek more power to meet me, unaware that I possess it all!"

"You are mad," Chishashi growled. Mahute stalled his pace to glare at him.

"I am a *visionary*," he barked, and pointed to himself. "All of Y'Neshu answers to *me*, and on *my* order will restore to the people their birthright! The Batabari will come out of hiding to lend their aid to the strongest nations! Even the lowest of us will be afforded the chance stand tall in my new Y'Neshu!"

"At what cost?" J'Kana thought about J'Yobena, about the people who nearly died at Y'Leisu's hand, about the destruction of the Yema in Folawu, and about his zombified Waleya in the streets of Shifi. His nostrils flared with a rage as fierce as the sunlight in the Hesefa Desert, and with no fear to speak of, he stared into the eyes of his corrupted uncle. "You stir contention between allied nations! You speak of the evils of the Kanawe and the Empires and all the while excuse your own! You sacrifice the inconvenient, not for the education of our people, and not for the restoration of our culture, but so that you can call yourself king of all." The disgust in his voice rippled through the air as his eyes radiated gold. "You, who had been a victim of Y'Rakili's worst and Y'Sewana's greatest atrocities, have come to deem yourself the only person worthy to pass judgment, all in an attempt to tip the balance in your own favor." Mahute laughed uproariously as he shook his head.

"I suppose my aspirations are far too great for a mere *child* to understand," the Dagger insulted with a dismissive wave of his hand.

"Or perhaps *you* are too blinded by your own hypocrisy to realize the horror on the horizon," J'Kana snapped in return. Mahute snarled, and in that instant his teeth became fangs, his ears pointed, and the nails of his hands grew into the same talons of the Asanibo. J'Kana cut his eyes, unbothered by the display. "Oh no, you mean to tell me that you were a monster all along? I *never* would have guessed." Mahute lunged for him, his claws opened wide to catch his nephew by the throat, but J'Kana was wise enough to roll out of the way. Chishashi leaped through the air and met the Dagger with a swift kick to the jaw, but Mahute barely moved.

"To kham basi ye tuzo," chanted the criminal, and as his blood dripped from his palms, the room drained of all color and sound. He slapped the Asanibo's leg away and struck him in the hip with his jagged nails. Chishashi grunted with pain, but elbowed at the bridge of the Dagger's nose. He stumbled back a step, but then used his freshly widened stance to deliver a stiff kick to the khimbenzi's legs. As Chishashi fell sideways, he was met with the clubbing force of Mahute's elbow. He crashed down into the tablet, and the Dark One promptly stepped over him.

"," J'Kana spoke, and the void created by the Dagger was promptly upended. The Gilded Ijeya sweat, but not nearly as much as he had against Khafenu. The chamber had the power to weaken him, but the longer he stood here, the more he grew used to it. "[illegible] [illegible]." Lightning struck the boy even as his enemy advanced, and his hands and feet became engulfed with flame. As thunder ripped through the air, so did the Dagger as he clawed at his nephew. J'Kana stood there, his eyes overlaid with the golden hue of his ike as the elements that touched him fed into it.

"You are mine," the monster hissed, but before he could take his first swing, Chishashi wrapped an arm around his neck and stabbed into his side three times before he was thrown by his target towards the ijeya. Mahute blinked, but the second he reopened his eyes, he saw that J'Kana had vanished and struck like thunder from behind. Fire touched the blood from his side and seared the wound with exceptional pain. The Dagger turned with a slash of his claws, but just as before, there was nothing to receive it. Again he was struck, this time with a kick to the back that made him roll across the floor. "Kha ja basi we N'lekhan a febetoyim!" The order burst from the Dagger's throat as he forced his talons into the ground. The blood from his hand, what spilled out of his hip from Chishashi's attack, slithered across the black stone and shot through the air.

J'Kana, enshrouded in lightning as gold as his eyes, dodged the blood-fashioned needles that sought his flesh, but realized fairly quickly that they would not be so easily outrun. He jumped into the air, landed on a pillar, angled for the ground and rolled as the bloody wires spidered from all directions. The Golden Apprentice thought to speak, thought to command the blood directly, but every moment where he thought he could catch his breath was ripped from him by their relentless assault.

"N'kha a deluyim," Chishashi shouted, his arm outstretched towards their enemy. The blood under the Dagger's command twisted and morphed into a ball that came to rest in the Asanibo's hand.

"Fekhayim," the dark orchestrator demanded, and the orb of blood exploded with enough force to send Chishashi across the room and into a far-off pillar. J'Kana thought to call out to his friend, but there was no time for that. Mahute returned his focus to the student before him. "Jiharo N'kha a deluyi ku bele a nobuyim o!" He stood again, crimson eyes tied to J'Kana's brilliant golden orbs, and stomped one foot against the stone platform. Three immense fragments of the rocky roof broke from their suspended angle to surround the Dagger as a protective shield. He smiled and licked his lips as he pushed his arms forward. Two of the massive shards split the air as they rushed for the apprentice, who disappeared in a flash of light.

J'Kana emerged behind his uncle, an infernal fist poised to strike, but a shift of Mahute's foot whipped the third stone around and into the boy's arm. J'Kana felt his body turn against his will, followed by a hard elbow to the back of the head that brought him to his knees. He rolled out of the way, just in time enough to dodge another, and flinched when the stone intended for him broke a piece of the slab upon which they fought. Another came with twice the force, but the Ara of Y'Rakili dodged again and bounded back to his feet.

"Has anyone ever told you that you have some serious issues you need to work out," J'Kana teased. Mahute roared, and that provided him with the opening he needed. "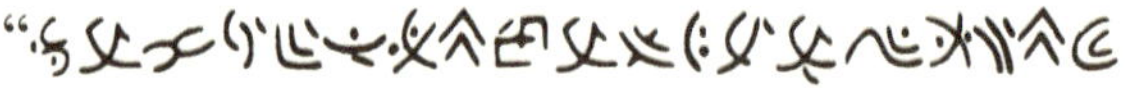

." The Dagger charged his nephew, unaware that the color of his stones had shifted from black to a dull red. He punched, and the force of his own fist triggered a triple explosion that caused him to stumble back, and summoned J'Kana to the space just before him.

The former thief drove his electrified palm into his uncle's sternum and unleashed a shockwave strong enough to kill a man. Mahute screamed as it ripped through him. His body refused his control, and he sank to the ground in a heap of smoldering flesh.

J'Kana disengaged, took a moment to watch the Dark One carefully, and stiffened when he only laughed. His dark skin became the color of shadow, his locked hair grew in length, and a pair of immense bat wings sprouted from his back.

"You have managed to amuse me for longer than I anticipated," the killer called. J'Kana glanced back at where Chishashi had landed, but when he saw that the Asanibo was out cold, he returned his focus to his enemy. "But the time has come to end this little game." J'Kana watched as the monster returned to his now clawed feet. He stepped forward, and J'Kana caught sight of an unusual movement at the upper level behind him. When he realized what it was, he smirked.

"Bold of you to assume that you have any say on when *I* am finished playing," J'Kana said as playfully as ever. Mahute smiled at his insolence, and for a moment mourned the fact that Khafenu failed to turn him when she had the chance. At the same time, he recognized this boy for the threat he had become, and realized his potential should he be allowed to live. Mahute flexed his hand, and decided that he would never allow the boy to see it for himself.

***

J'Chera couldn't believe where he was. He looked out over the dark room, felt the chill in the air despite the fire on all sides, and he hated himself for his position.

"How could I let this happen to myself," he muttered as he slid along the upper ledge around the cages. His back was to the wall so he could lean comfortably away from the floor below, but there was no comfort in the view he beheld. Nihani followed his lead, but with half the reservation of her companion.

"Just keep going," she told him. "We are almost there. I swear, you can be such a child sometimes, J'Chera."

"I'll have you know that I take that with great honor," he quipped. Together they scanned the seven cages suspended above the chamber. Four looked as though they had never been used, which proved a comfort to them both.

Nihani gasped as she quickly covered her mouth with her hands. J'Chera almost asked what startled her when he saw the pool of blood for himself. They exchanged a look, then with increased urgency they slid along the wall towards the west. It wasn't long before they realized that all of the cages were empty now. All of them but one.

***

J'Kana exclaimed as Mahute's kick met with his crossed arms. They stung, even with the stone wrapped around him for his own protection. He ground his teeth in frustration. Mahute was too strong to engage directly with his fists, but the way he flew around the stone tablet left J'Kana with little room to speak commands. Still, he had to find a way to buy the other team the time they needed to rescue Y'Sawe. Mahute swooped down from above, his legs extended again, this time with their pointed talons spread with intent to grab.

The Gilded Ijeya rolled off to the side and finally, finally found the opening he needed to speak. " 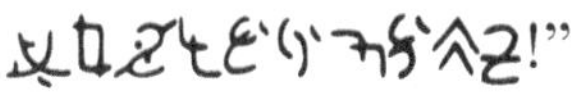!" Thunder ripped through the atmosphere as storm clouds formed over Mahute's head. Winds blew with enough force to topple the spires of

J'Watuna, and rain fell from the makeshift heavens upon the slab. Mahute didn't care. He shifted directions on a pin and flew with added aggression towards his adversary. J'Kana disappeared again, but when he reemerged, he found that his target had vanished as well. He glanced up to the cages, hopeful that J'Chera and Nihani had found a way out by now, but the darkness and the storm obscured his vision. Carefully he paced the floor, watchful of all directions. He remembered that Khafenu could move through the shadows, and deduced that Mahute now did the same. Another sinister laugh erupted from behind him. He turned frantically, but there was nothing there.

Lightning flashed the moment he whipped his head, and under the light of the storm the Dagger was revealed. He smiled at the boy, and as another burst of electricity ripped its way through the clouds, he was gone, shrouded again by the darkness.

"You could join me," the monster called. "I can feel your fascination with this place, your thirst for power. Why not give into it and rule by my side?"

"Not interested," J'Kana shot back, his eyes ever watchful of the shade. Claws ran across his stone-armored back. The sting of ripped flesh followed suit. He fell to one knee, his vision blurred all of a sudden, and then he realized with horror that he'd been poisoned. Mahute stepped out of the shadows, his demeanor as calm as the day of the Summit.

"Then I have no further use for you."

***

"Nihani, help me with this!" J'Chera said as he struggled to pry the lock from the cage. The Jeniju returned to the present and shoved J'Chera aside.

"Y'Go, khemi go mamuke N'vina," she whispered, and the rain that fell across the resurrection chamber concentrated at her fingertip in a whip-like shape. She slashed it through the air with blinding speed and watched as the lock fell apart before their eyes. Y'Sawe, far thinner than what J'Chera recalled, stirred from his groggy stupor and lifted his eyes to look upon his rescuers. "It's alright. We're going to get you out of here." Y'Sawe opened his mouth, but there was no sound. Tears slid down his cheeks as gratitude swelled in his heart, and instinctively Nihani knew what it meant to him. J'Chera faced the chamber as he walked backwards into the cell. He smiled. Mahute wouldn't be able to see him here.

"Great," J'Chera said almost happily as he turned to face the wall. "Now let's go before he notices us."

***

J'Kana lost the strength he needed to support himself and fell to the ground at the Dark One's feet. The Dagger gazed upon him with twisted delight, then took a moment to admire the power of his own two hands.

"You should feel honored," the monster rumbled as it sauntered around the fallen ijeya. "In all Y'Neshu, you are the first to behold my new form, the culmination of our culture and power!" His laugh rivaled the roar of the thunder, his excitement almost infectious as the poison spread through J'Kana's body. Then, the sound of metal against metal echoed over the storm. The prostrate apprentice tried to force himself back to his feet, but he could barely lift his head from the floor. Mahute turned in the direction of the sound as a snarl escaped his maw. He saw the intruders, and now their escape was in jeopardy.

***

J'Chera fixed his mouth to speak the command, took a deep breath and let the feeling of relief replenish his ike. His eyes lit silver, and he began to say with urgency, "Ti N'J'Watuna ra nerati shu—"

"Are you leaving already," Mahute whispered from the edge of the cage. Y'Sawe, Nihani's arms wrapped around him like a shield, looked up at his brother with defiant fire in his eyes while the apprentice stepped back in fear. The Jeniju buried her face into the Grand Master's neck, not out of fear, but out of deceptive intent. She prayed to Y'Kele that what she intended to do would work, and then followed the scent of the sickness with her mind.

"Y'Go, bi zanuwe basiyil, maju jakha batombe uduo," she whispered. Three times she issued the chant, and the rain around them grew three times brighter.

***

J'Kana tried again, only to slip on the wet stone and fall with his chest to the ground. He slammed his fist, angry with himself that he could do nothing while that monstrosity terrorized J'Chera and Nihani.

"I can't—" he started to speak, but noted the sharp pain in his tongue with every flex of his mouth. Even so, he had to try. He closed his eyes, let the wetness of his clothes seep into his soul and he began to speak, not to the things around him or even the monster he hoped to stop. He stretched his ike with everything in him and spoke to the Great God, Y’Kele. “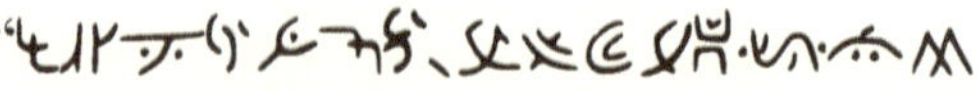  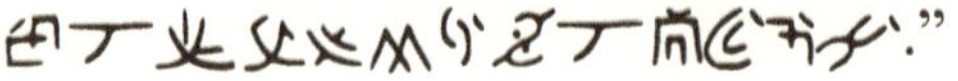.” *Wise Y’Kele, I thank you for my friends. You have been with us and watched over us from the beginning.* With every word, he felt his strength return little by little, and little by little he grew louder in his prayer to his Creator. “ !” *Still you guide my spirit and restore my strength.* The rain turned a radiant blue now, and as it struck him, J’Kana found the power to stand.

“I thought I put you in the dirt,” Mahute roared as he flew back across the resurrection chamber, his crimson eyes aglow in the dark, his claws spread to either side, occasionally covered by the beat of his giant wings.

“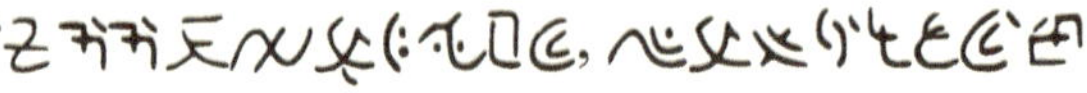 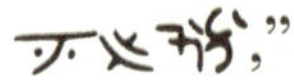,” J’Kana shouted, his eyes open now, alight with golden rays as intense as sunlight. He felt his ike rage as the air swirled around him with such a speed that it formed a barrier. Mahute struck it from the outside, frantic now as victory slipped between his jagged claws. "  !" J'Kana's voice deafened Mahute and the others to the storm as the air repulsed the monster and encircled the apprentice's body. J'Kana began to walk, and every step caused the great stone slab to shatter until its fragments flowed through the air current. Lightning fell from the clouds that danced above to the ground beneath him. As fire emerged through the cracks in the stone, lightning struck again, this time into forge a spear by the Ara's side. He took it, and as Mahute watched the boy spin the weapon above his head and drive its shaft into the rock, he roared with all the power of a demon from another age.

The Dagger plunged forward, only to find that J'Kana appeared in the air before him. Mahute pulled back in time enough to evade a kick, but the flames that jutted out from J'Kana's leg blasted him in the face. By the time the Dagger regained his bearings, the apprentice was already behind him. Jagged stones punctured the demon's back, and when he slashed back where the boy should have been, the rainwater solidified into chains around his arms and legs. Mahute resisted, but the might of the descendant liquid was too great for even his wings to overcome. He was driven into the remnants of the slab, and when his body bounced from the impact, flames erupted from the cracks in between.

J’Kana appeared above his uncle’s inhuman form, the lightning spear in hand, and drove his knee into the creature’s sternum to force him to ground again. He took a moment and peered upon the beast with his sunlight eyes, and with fury written on his face, he stabbed through the shoulder to the other side of the wing. A monstrous screech echoed through the hall as the Dark One writhed from his injury.

“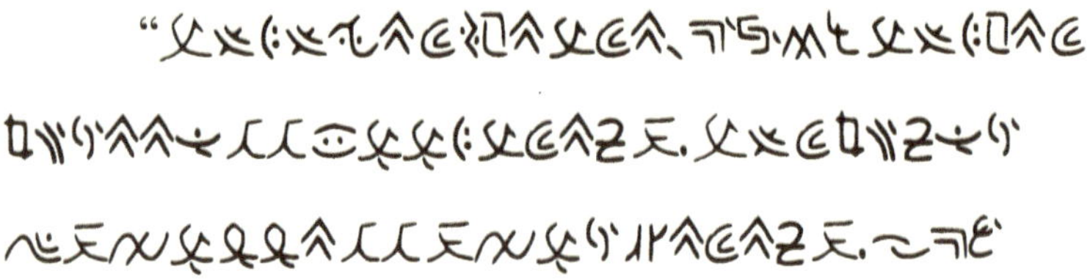

,” the apprentice demanded with such authority that the demon felt a chill run the length of his spine. Mahute breathed in short bursts and growled at his nephew.

“I will remember this,” threatened the enemy. “N’kha we Kehemu a deluyim.” The shadows overtook him, and as he drifted away, the ground began to shake. J’Kana fell upon his hands and knees as the ceiling gave way around him. A large piece of spiked rock fell overhead, and before he knew what happened, a pair of hands pulled him through a rift. The sounds of Y'Neshu filled his ears, but as the power of his hato with Y'Kele waned, J'Kana found himself unable to process much. He came to rest in a thicket of hutije in the Outer Grasslands, and as the sun warmed his skin through the dampness of his clothes, he allowed his consciousness to fade.

***

"Kamari?" J'Kana said as he looked at his son. The boy was, again, in shock, his back pressed against the couch and his body seemingly unable to move. "Are you alright, Kamari?"

"It's so much," he murmured after a small gulp. "The Y'Maju. The Batabari. The J'Karo! Yababa, I know you didn't think I would be able to follow that!" Suddenly the little one abounded with energy, but J'Kana's raised eyebrow made him shrink back.

"Eeh, do I look like one of your little friends that you can get loud with me," he asked. Kamari rapidly shook his head "no." "In any case, Shehefo, you are at the point where you know to study."

"I did," the young ijeya answered with a disheartened shrug. "I just didn't expect that much to come at me at once. What did you say to Mahute at the end?" J'Kana smiled in triumph at the memory.

"I told him the reason my name is J'Kana. That I showed him more mercy than he deserved, and that he shouldn't waste it," the Kanawe explained. Kamari looked at him with wonder in his eyes.

"So, did he? Waste it, I mean," the ulu ili asked. J'Kana shrugged, much to the boy's chagrin.

"Another story for another time, my son," he answered with a wry smile. "For now, let's work on the words you didn't know and get you proficient at those, ne?" Kamari sighed and lifted his hands in defeated measure as his father found the page in the small leather book.

"Fine, Yababa, let's get started."

| | | |
|---|---|---|
| | Siwebawu | Nephew |
| | Aloye | Wrap/Roll |
| | Bema | Guidance/Leadership |
| | Jaka | Edict |

| | | |
|---|---|---|
|  | Fonara | Deserving/Expectation |
|  | Sekuli | Waste |
|  | Yaheta | Neice |
|  | Kana | Flow |

# 23

# Calm Before the Storm

*J'Watuna—Y'Maya Inn*

A week had passed since the confrontation with Mahute, and the He Ara Akira licked their wounds at the inn in J'Watuna. Nihani went from room to room to perform her healing on her allies. J'Chera, who carried them one by one through the rift, had been unconscious in bed for three days. Nihani couldn't help but wonder how much worse it would have been if she was not there to heal him. Chishashi, on the other hand, was the first awake, though he was far from in the best mood. He sat locked in his room, thinking of ways to get stronger so that what he experienced would never happen again.

Kanawe Y'Sawe, who was ever grateful for the mermaid's help, recovered in a couple of days after a little rest and food to recover his strength. Even when he was barely conscious, he couldn't help but sample the Y'Fuwefoan delicacies of Joba stew and sweet toho bulb pie. And then there was J'Kana. What he did against the Dagger was reckless and could've gotten him killed. Just the thought of it made her ball her fists at her side. Even so, she walked to his room apprehensively. His was the most critical condition, as he had been asleep for the entire week, with no signs of regaining consciousness.

She stood outside the door for a moment, and wrestled with her worry that he might never rise again. She wiped away her tears as she shook the idea out of her head. She didn't want to think of what life would be like if she never again had the chance to hear him laugh at his own jokes. She pushed open the door, and when she saw him so still in a room dressed in a lively sky blue, she had to fight the urge to cry all over again. She moved to the curtain to give herself some time, and slowly opened it for the radiant rays of the sun. Nihani took a deep breath, not quite ready to turn around, when she heard her name croaked out from behind her. Immediately she spun to see J'Kana's eyes open, a wounded smile on his face.

"Why do you look like that," he groaned out with a wry look about him. "I wasn't dead, you know." She clasped her hands over her mouth as the tears started to fall. J'Kana strained to sit up, and reached out his hand to offer her comfort, only for her to run right out of the room. He stared at the doorway as his brow wrinkled in confusion. "Okay…"

When she reentered, it was with a man on her arm that the ijeya immediately recognized to be his Kanawe. His *yababa*. Joy and relief overtook him, and now his eyes leaked upon the bed. Y'Sawe bore a stern look as always, and for a while, neither of them spoke. It was when Nihani sat in the chair beside the bed that the Ile Kanawe approached his apprentice. The mermaid handed J'Kana a cup of water, and as he drank slowly, his eyes on his father, he felt the tension in his throat ease with the passing of the stream.

"I am glad to see you are doing better," Y'Sawe spoke, his voice much more tired than it had been in the past. J'Kana noted the look in his eye, the sadness that he tried so hard to suppress. He wanted to respect it, wanted so badly to focus on the issues of the present day, but like so many times before, he was drawn to the fires of Shifi.

"Did you ever look for me," he asked through the sobs that burst through the dam of his conscious mind. He folded his arms, a hug unto himself. Y'Sawe wiped the moisture from his own cheek as he nodded furiously.

"Every day," he told him slowly, with emphasis, determined not to choke on his own words. "Even as you traveled by my side, I never gave up hope. Even when my mind told me that you might be dead, my heart would not accept that reality." J'Kana could hold nothing back. For so long he had been alone, forced to wander the streets of Memifi and beg from a people who only recently saw his worth; forced to steal whatever he could just to stay alive on the hope that one day his yababa would rescue him from the cold isolation. Before he could steep in his thoughts any further, Y'Sawe placed a hand on the boy's shoulder and told him in a voice filled with more love than what he had heard in years, "I am so proud of you, hafu wu ulu ara."

"I'm sorry," Nihani interrupted, and both Kanawe and Ijeya looked at her with humor in their eyes. "It's just so beautiful! Go on, go on, pretend I'm not here." With the mood broken, both father and son wiped their faces and once again tended to matters of the present.

"So, what happens now," J'Kana asked. "Mahute is still out there, now stronger than ever. The Kanawe have been…defeated. The balance of power has been disrupted all over the continent, and the Dagger has the means to steer it all in his favor." Y'Sawe raised an eyebrow at his apprentice as a half smirk rested on his jaw.

"Who are you and what have you done to the disinterested street urchin I picked up in Memifi?" His heart leaped at the sight of his son's smile. He felt as if a piece of him, long thought dead, had suddenly returned to life. He sighed as he considered the weight of the boy's words. "For now, we must address one problem at a time. The Saweshe are *not* defeated. *I* am still alive, and determined to return to Mahute everything he gave to me tenfold. As for our number, we will fill the ranks again over time. I believe that starts with you, and the other ijeya that lurks outside the room even now."

"How did you know I was here," J'Chera asked as he opened the door and entered. Nihani shot him a look.

"Because you are too loud to be stealthy," she answered with an eye roll. "Have you really learned nothing from the last few days?"

"In any case," Y'Sawe said, his serious demeanor restored as before, "Y'Leisu's betrayal stings, and the death of my peers hurts beyond anything you can fathom. I have no doubt that were the traitor and my brother to have their way, I would have joined them. The only reason I didn't is that you four figured out how to save me. You rose beyond a thousand challenges that no teacher could have prepared you for, and it has made you stronger than the rank you currently possess." The two ijeya ni exchanged a look of confusion, and Y'Sawe smiled. "It is because of this, J'Kana and J'Chera, that I grant you the rank of Lele Kanawe, Young Teacher." They looked at the Ile Kanawe, who now enjoyed the sight of a beautiful day through the window, then at each other as childish grins decorated their countenances. Nihani gripped their shoulders, and shook her head even as she smiled from the pride she felt.

"Great, something new to worry about," she said, and the Kanawe laughed.

"Now," Y'Sawe started up again, his steely dark brown eyes trained firmly on his apprentice, "tell me about this plan to spread J'Karo through Y'Rakili…"

***

*Y'Sewana—Febetu*

Another explosion shook the foundations of the great desert fortress. The guards trembled in fear while the inmates around them cheered, even as the sound distorted and color vanished from their vision. A shade speared through the winding corridors and when it did, all that could be seen of it were the pools of blood left behind in its wake. Block by block, the cells of the legendary prison opened, and the inmates made a break for whatever exit they could find. Guards stood in their path in one moment, only to be reduced to a pile of bloody limbs without color in the next.

Before long, the guards threw down their weapons and ran with the prisoners, only to be picked off one by one, mercilessly slaughtered by the beast that lurked in the shadows. Whatever it was, the convicts that now ran into the desert heralded the monster as their savior. They turned back to face the fallen prison, and finally, their senses restored, they saw what—or rather, *who*—it was. There on the roof, with wings spread out in the darkness, stood Mahute the Dagger, Killer of Yifusi and Enemy of Kanawe.

"For too long," he started, his voice the only thing heard now, "we have been left to rot in this place, handed down judgments by those who refuse to be judged. For too long our worth has been disregarded, our crimes deemed a flaw in our judgment alone when we are merely the products of a system designed to fail us. Our leaders have sold us into a slavery of our own trauma, our teachers have censored the very power that could have unlocked our cages. No longer." As he spoke, the crowd began to cheer him, and the Dagger felt a rise to his own power. "No longer will we be regarded as criminals for having the grit and determination to fight against the sins committed against us! No longer will we accept the cloud of ignorance cast around Y'Neshu by the ones tasked with educating it. Together, we will forge a new path on the blood of our enemies, and on the pride of our heritage."

"Mahute," one of the inmates cheered, her fist raised to the night sky, "Mahute!" Others joined in now, filled with hope on the Dagger's promises, and as they chanted his name, the Dark King chanted loudly over their roars.

"Febetu a gbatabayim o!" The blood of the guards wrapped around the prison from all over, and in the blink of an eye, reduced it to ruins…

***

Kamari threw his hands up in the air as he looked at J'Kana. The father smiled warmly, but the son would not have it.

"Why did you stop," the little one asked, certainly more careful of his tone this time, even as the emotions from Y'Sawe and J'Kana's reunion spilled over into him. J'Kana simply grabbed his head with one hand and shook him playfully.

"Because old people get tired after a certain point, shehefo," he lied. "You have heard enough of the story for now, and besides, I had something special planned for you after your lesson today." The ulu ijeya looked at his father from the height of skepticism.

"What could you possibly have planned that is better than this story?" J'Kana smiled brighter as he retrieved the leather book.

"Your mother and I had planned to take you to Memifi for a visit with J'Chera and Lord Babanu," said the

Kanawe with a shrug. He cut his eyes at his son, the smile still firmly in place. The boy lit up like the morning sun, and hundreds of possibilities entered into his mind. "However, if you would rather stay here and listen to me talk even more, we can—"

"On second thought, Yababa," Kamari interrupted in a tone far more magnanimous than what a child of five should be able to make, "I wouldn't want you to tire yourself out. Let's get to our lesson so we can just as quickly take a break."

"Hmm, only if you think it's the right thing to do," J'Kana agreed with exaggeration. He flipped open the leather book, found the page, and pulled his shehefo close to him. "Now, look here," he said, and rested his head against that of his son, overcome by the peace of the moment.

| Kulani | Ability/Talent |
|---|---|
| Niwema | Achievement/Accomplishment |
| Nejosi | Account |
| Liwewe | Activity |
| Nishala | Adventure |

| | | |
|---|---|---|
| 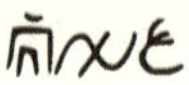 | Matari | Bear/Hold |
| 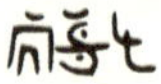 | Majoa | Story |
| 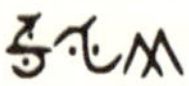 | Jojani | Book |

# About the Author

Jordan Hampton is an award-winning author, founder and CEO of Kabulu Global Press, LLC, minister, martial artist, and educator based in Goodyear, Arizona. After graduating from Grand Canyon University with a BA in English for Secondary Education and MA in English for Education, Hampton spent hours in independent research into Pan-Africanism, African languages, mythologies, cultures, and religions to retrace his ancestral steps and engage with a part of him that was lost long before he was born. When he's not writing, he can be found inhaling stories in all mediums from anime and manga to movies and TV shows, with a particularly vested interest in helping others tell their stories the way they need to.

# Author's Note

Since I was a kid, I've always been in love with language, so much so that I majored in English twice and began a Master of Divinity degree just to add Hebrew and Greek to my linguistic repertoire. It was in the midst of my studies that it occurred to me how easy it was for me to engage with the languages of people from all over the world (I've learned a good amount of Japanese and a fair amount of Brazilian Portuguese from practicing kenjutsu and Capoeira respectively). Then it occurred to me that I had trouble connecting with the languages used by my ancestors, what with a fair amount of African cultures being forced from us when the slave ships forced us onto American soil.

It should come as no surprise, then, that J'Karo, Katsedu, Batabari and Y'Maju are all amalgamations of linguistic quirks from across the African continent, carefully studied and recombined to create expressions of culture meant to feel familiar to our spirit yet fresh in our minds. I wanted to build a bridge between the distant past of Black people within the diaspora and the present, where we yearn to express our culture in ways that augment who we really are. In J'Karo alone, there are elements of Swahili, Xhosa, Mandinka, Fulbe, Yoruba, Igbo, and Zulu, spoken with the rhythm of Brazilian Portuguese and organized in a syllabary style akin to Japanese. In reading this book and the ones to follow, my hope is that all of us, however far this goes, will be able to indulge in a new language that was made with us in mind, and use it to explore the history and future that we share in a heightened sense of unity. I pray that J'Kana and his friends highlight the beauty of Black and African cultures in as many different aspects as I can address, and that this book proves to be a sufficient introduction.

# Acknowledgements

First, I want to give honor to God, hafu wu koshi jiunawe katani, for everything that He has done to guide me to this point of self-discovery and exploration. Every hurdle that I have experienced personally, professionally and otherwise has been overcome by His eternal grace and mercy, and every person that I've had the pleasure to work with has been a gift.

To my mother and father, thank you so much for the gift of your guidance, as much as your balance of collected and crazy. You have made it so that nothing can surprise me and even less can shake me from the path I'm determined to go down. I'm strongest for having you as a part of my past, present and future.

To Betty Jean and Marie, the two greatest and most supportive grandmothers in the world, your years of support are only outmatched by the wisdom and love you've showered me with from the time I was a half-pint correcting everyone's English and refusing to take naps until now. Love you more!

To my beautiful wife, Nicole, I know you don't like being put on the spot, and I know you know that I love to do it. You have been the greatest sounding board for my ideas before they even reach the page, and I'm so fortunate to be building a life and a family with someone who can put up with the gears in my mind turning endlessly. You're single-handedly the most loving, sensible, compassionate, and good-natured person I've ever met, and it was an honor writing you into this story as the Jeniju, Nihani. I'll always take the time to show the world how I see you, hafu wu laela wu siema. Thank you for all that you do for me.

To Azulao, you are the inspiration for Y'Sawe. Your strength and wisdom permeate everything that you do, and it astounds me how much you seek to indulge in history and culture of all kinds. You've always shown to your students that there is no such thing as limitation, and that in every way we should strive to learn as much as we can and improve ourselves daily. Thank you for taking me on as your student, and being a second father to me. Ti otaba ra sawekinawe Ile Kanawe harana me somi uhuna shu N'hafu bibisana ke, hafu ra otaba shu koshi arani jotinati o.

To Darian, Q, and Kaleb, you three are weird. You three were the kids who adopted me, and it has been my absolute pleasure to help you grow, to provide you with a nurturing environment, and to have a front-row seat to your inevitable successes. Koshi kenaninati, hafu wu shehefo ni, and I am so immensely proud of you for who you are and where you're headed in your respective futures. Thank you all for being the inspiration of so many characters across multiple books and universes, and for always inspiring me to be a better man.

To Lolo, you know who you are and you know why you're in here. If you want more detail, check the note at the front written in J'Karo. That's just for you.

To Roz, my GCU mom, thank you for looking out for me for all these years and helping me through a list of problems that probably runs thicker than this book! You've been a truly instrumental part of my life from my grief period to my greatest triumphs and I pray that I continue to give you a reason to stick around.

To Kenne, Luke, Tiara, James, Jay (no relation to my apprentice), and Caleb, thank you all for the work you've done over the years reading and editing and designing covers for my books. A big part of my evolution as a writer has to do with you and your investment into me. Thank you for loving my stories as much as I do and helping me take them as far as they'll go. You all are the best.

To my wonderful co-teacher, Jenny, my co-conspirator, Chevlin, and my awesome business partner Sholanda, not only were you there for the creation of this project, but I've had the pleasure of your feedback every step of the way. Thank you for putting up with me and my linguistic weirdness, my out of the box personality, and my tendency to do too much. You have been the ones to help me hold it together for a few years now and I know at least Chevlin would want that in writing, so here you go!

To Damien, a godsend of a roommate and best friend, thank you for being someone I can rely on, bounce ideas off of, and wind down with through a children's card game. You are amazing, and honestly you could stand to hear it more.

To Jay, hafu wu ijeya, I am extraordinarily proud of you for all that you do. You, in many ways, keep me grounded because I know that you're watching my example. I look forward to the day where you wow the rest of the world with the stories that you have to tell. You are gifted beyond your years, and I'm honored that you've chosen me to be a mentor to you.

To Kiraji, Kekoa, and Shukara, my three apprentices in swordsmanship who have gone on this journey together with me, I don't even know where to begin. You have grown so much in your confidence, in your strength, in your expectations for the future, and you have all given me the freedom to evolve in as many ways as you've come at me in sparring matches. Thank you all for your dedication to creativity and art, martial and literary. I want you to know that I've been more than just a little inspired by you three and I hope that you can say the same of me.

To my students, both in academics and swordsmanship, you have taught me more than I could've ever imagined. You've grown my patience, my kindness, my compassion, and my willingness to fight. I've learned more about my strengths and weaknesses from working with all of you, and above all, I got to see how much this story already means to so many of you. I hope that you can look on this book and where it came from not just as a story, but as a tribute to the time I spent working with each and every one of you. Remember that you never have to settle for anything. Always continue to strive for what you want, even if that changes. Be as kind as you've taught me to be, but maintain your standard like I've taught you to do. Remember, we are excellent, and we will not be shamed by the mediocrity of others. I'm rooting for you all!

To my wonderful colleagues at Superteam 8, y'all are still getting to know me but that hasn't hindered your willingness to help me in everything. I can truly say that I've learned so much from all of you and I'm proud to be a member of the team.

To the friends and family who have talked me up, supported me, advertised for me, and contributed in one way or another to my publishing company, you all have been so good to me and my only regret is that there are too many of you to name. Thank you a thousand times over, and I pray this book is able to convey something of what you mean to me.

To Kabulu Global Press, my new publishing home, I want to thank everyone on my team who signed on because they believe in the dream of creating a platform for multicultural creators to share their voice. You are saints, and I value all of you so much. The work you do is phenomenal from the cover design to just keeping me consistent in my part in all this. I know that we're going to do a lot of good for a lot of people, so thank you for being on this journey with me.

Finally, to my readers, thank you all for stepping out of your comfort zones to experience the emerging cultures of Y'Neshu. I truly hope that this was enough to make you want to explore more of the Four Empires, the tribes and clans, the languages and the mysteries that are yet to be revealed in this first continent on our planet, Kabulu. I look forward to showing you more of who I am, and supplying you with a story not quite like what you're used to.

Now, onto the next…

www.ingramcontent.com/pod-product-compliance
Lightning Source LLC
Chambersburg PA
CBHW030543310726
48979CB00010B/2003/J

* 9 7 9 8 9 8 5 8 3 4 6 6 6 *